G. F. Newman is the author of several novels dealing with social issues, including *The Guvnor, Sir, You Bastard* and *The Obsession.* Of his highly controversial BBC television series *Law and Order*, the *Daily Express* said: 'Author G. F. Newman secured himself a place in television history with this powerful quartet of plays . . . a brutal assault on the police and the manner in which some of th

By the same author

Sir, You Bastard
Billy
You Nice Bastard
The Player and the Guest
Three Professional Ladies
You Flash Bastard
The Guvnor
Law and Order
The Obsession
Charlie and Joanna
Operation Bad Apple (stage play)

G. F. NEWMAN

The Nation's Health

GRANADA
London Toronto Sydney New York

Published in paperback by Granada Publishing Limited in 1983

ISBN 0 586 05230 5

First published in Great Britain by
Granada Publishing 1983

Granada Publishing Limited
Frogmore, St Albans, Herts AL2 2NF
and
36 Golden Square, London W1R 4AH
515 Madison Avenue, New York, NY 10022, USA
117 York Street, Sydney, NSW 2000, Australia
60 International Blvd, Rexdale, Ontario, R9W 6J2, Canada
61 Beach Road, Auckland, New Zealand

Printed in Great Britain by
Richard Clay (The Chaucer Press) Ltd, Bungay, Suffolk
Set in Times

Book I

Objectivity and humanity cannot coexist
more than a little.

1

The marble floor was polished like glass and Jessie Marvill almost lost her balance as she hurried along the corridor, the old walls of which carried a network of pipes and conduits and were painted pale green; tests conducted long ago had determined green to be the most relaxing colour. She was late; the traffic had been heavy, parking difficult; slipping over on the floor would put her in a wonderful frame of mind to make a favourable impression with the appointments board. Getting a surgical job was difficult enough at the best of times. She stopped herself thinking about the problems of being a woman in a male dominated specialty. Perhaps she was being over-sensitive, just as her boyfriend sometimes suggested she was; he was male, white, well-qualified, and out of work. He was also passive.

Checking the name plaques as she passed administration doors, Jessie Marvill went right by the hospital administrator's office, then stopped and turned back, taking a moment to collect herself. Like her mother who was also a doctor, Jessie was invariably late; her father dismissed them both as being pathologically unpunctual, but it was more a case that both tried to do too much.

There were ten other candidates waiting, one of them Asian, which looked like tokenism in a roomful of white males. Jessie Marvill wondered fleetingly if her presence wasn't tokenism also.

'Am I late?' she said to one of the two secretaries in this central office, which held more filing cabinets and chairs than was ever intended. 'Jessie Marvill.'

'Have a seat, doctor.' The secretary ticked her name on

the list before her. 'They're running a bit late.'

'A difficult choice,' the elder of the white applicants said dismissively for anyone to hear as Jessie took the seat next to him.

Jessie Marvill wasn't sure of his meaning, but instinctively felt embarrassed. Shortly she was to realize that his attitude reflected that which existed for third-world doctors generally, but especially in the surgical specialties.

'There are quite a lot here.'

'A sign of the times. There were twenty-five short-listed for the last post I applied for. One's in there now.' He gave a clear shake of the head.

Jessie Marvill looked away, not wanting to be associated with this man.

The door to the administrator's office opened and a Nigerian was shown out by the medical staffing officer.

'Thank you, Dr Chikezie,' she said. 'We'll let you know after we've finished interviewing.' The woman, who was in her late twenties, glanced at her sheet. 'Dr Marvill?'

As she rose, the applicant next to her smiled, suggesting that she, too, was wasting her time. He was tanned and self-assured, and at that moment Jessie Marvill was inclined to believe him.

'Come in, Dr Marvill.' The administrator half rose from behind his desk. 'Have a seat. I believe you've already made contact with Mr Thompson. This is Mr Smith-Sampson,' he said, nodding towards the second consultant surgeon who was seated by the desk. His informal manner was intended to put the applicant at ease, but a briskness indicated that they had a lot of interviews to get through.

The two consultants glanced over copies of the written application, waiting for Jessie Marvill to settle. Neither showed any emotion, not even a suggestion of empathy for once having been in her position.

'You qualified at Oxford,' the administrator, who was called Roy Needham, continued, reading from her application, 'and got your MRCP Part 1 earlier this year. You've had two appointments since your house jobs at West Middlesex. Senior house officer in A and E at Hammersmith; and as medical SHO at King's.' He turned to the consultants. They had most say in this appointment, as they would be most affected by it. In deference to his seniority he addressed Mr Smith-Sampson, 'Ronald?'

'Yes,' the older surgeon began, glancing at the application balanced on his knees. 'You seem more suited for a medical post than SHO in general surgery. Why did you sit the MRCP instead of the Fellowship?' he wanted to know.

'Well.' She hesitated, feeling that he was telling her she was wrong-footed. 'As I stated on my application,' – the wrong tack with this man. 'Originally I considered doing general practice. But I'm no longer sure about that. I always had an aptitude for surgery. I thought it would be sensible to explore that avenue.'

'That might be rather costly, if at the end of the day you find yourself not suited to the job,' Smith-Sampson said. He was in his mid-sixties, stamped from the traditional medical die, one that showed no sign of breaking. His three-piece pin-striped suit was in need of brushing around the collar, but there was no other indication of degeneration; he had a grey, clipped moustache, and an aloof peremptory manner.

'I didn't think time spent in general surgery would be entirely wasted,' Dr Marvill said, rather too frankly. She assumed by this time that she wouldn't be appointed, and refused to call either consultant 'sir' as a lot of her contemporaries would.

Mr Marcus Thompson smiled at her response. It got them over an awkward moment. 'How long would you need to make up your mind?' he asked. He was twenty years younger than his colleague, and brighter; his clothes were less traditional, the pale grey suit he was wearing had a distinctively expensive cut; baldness accentuated his round face. The relaxed professional manner he had derived from his never having been seen to be unsure in his entire working life. Thompson liked the look of this doctor more than any of the other candidates, despite some of their excellent qualifications, and liked what was on her application; he could live with the fact that she wasn't entirely sure of her chosen specialty. As the contract was only for six months he didn't see that it mattered greatly.

'I would hope to know during this appointment,' she said.

'If you're successful,' Mr Smith-Sampson put in. He thought her arrogant.

'What if you decide after all that you want to go into general practice?' Thompson asked. 'I don't object to employing an SHO who subsequently leaves the specialty. But I would prefer one who's going to specialize.'

'I don't know. I suppose I would look for a vocational training scheme, or put my own together.'

'There is never any shortage of doctors wanting to become surgeons,' Thompson told her. That was a fact borne out by the applicants who had been short-listed today. He couldn't remember when the candidates had been so well qualified before. He knew why it was.

'That's what my father says. There's a family tradition,' she explained, feeling a slight cheat for doing so, but justified herself on account of being unfairly treated as a woman doctor. 'The women become GPs; the men go for one of the surgical specialties.'

This impressed both surgeons more than anything else she had said. She didn't add that part of her reason for choosing surgery was to break that awful tradition, and show her father that he wasn't king. She had been brought up with the expectation of entering the medical profession, and although she offered no resistance, she wanted to do her own kind of medicine.

'That tradition is very sensible,' Smith-Sampson told her.

'The stamina needed for an eight-hour session in theatre is often peculiarly masculine.'

Jessie Marvill didn't respond.

There was a pause.

With little else they needed to know and no further questions, Roy Needham said, 'Good', bringing this interview to a close, and turning to the medical staffing officer. 'Pam?'

'The rota's one in four,' she said, 'with nine A-UMTs. So the salary is £8,800, with up to four weeks study leave per year. We don't have married accommodation available . . .'

'I don't need married accommodation,' Jessie Marvill said as if that might be in her favour. The information that she was single was in her application. Her thoughts moved on; she would no longer be living with anyone if she got this job. She would use it as the jumping out point in a relationship that was no longer working for either of them. She would move into the room the hospital provided for when she was on call, depressing as that sort of accommodation mostly was.

'The appointment would be to Mr Thompson's firm. The post becomes vacant on the 19th,' the medical staffing officer went on. 'Would you be free then?'

'I finish my present job on the 11th.' That information was in her application also.

'Well, if you wait outside, doctor,' Pam Loade said. 'We'll let you know shortly.'

Dr Marvill rose and went out.

The patronizing smile of the doctor she had sat next to earlier deterred her from waiting in the outer office as was the custom. Instead she went for a walk around the hospital.

Both Roy Needham and the medical staffing officer took their cues from the consultants when considering the candidates for the post of senior house officer, neither favouring nor arguing against any particular doctor.

'I think I'll put my money on Marvill,' Thompson said. He preferred to take on a female as they tended to work that much harder in order to prove themselves.

'I thought there were any number of them more inspiring,' Smith-Sampson said. 'The job advertisement's got a good response.'

'Fantastic, especially as it was advertised at short notice,' the medical staffing officer told him. It might have been a personal achievement rather than due to circumstances.

'It's bloody depressing, Marcus, I know that,' Roy Needham said.

'We had 160 applicants for this job. It's all due to cut-backs.'

'It might improve standards in the long run, Roy.'

'I'd like to believe it.' He didn't see how out-of-work doctors could generally raise standards but didn't put the argument.

Thompson said, 'She's a good-looking woman,' coming back to his choice of applicant, as if looks were a valid consideration, which curiously they were. It wasn't a matter of chance that most doctors were at least regular featured.

'I thought Miller was a good candidate,' Needham said, indicating the safe alternative. He knew there would be no point in suggesting the African doctor, even though he was well qualified.

'Yes,' Smith-Sampson agreed. 'He's had some good cutting experience. But there is the question of his reference.'

'His last consultant didn't reply to the letter I sent,' Pam Loade said. 'I couldn't get him on the phone this morning. He was scrubbed.' That was ominous. Most consultants would come to the phone to give a reference, even when in theatre, knowing how important it was to a doctor.

'I liked his self-confidence,' Smith-Sampson said. 'I found Marvill a little arrogant.'

'Interview nerves, I think,' Roy Needham put in.

'We could almost let them draw straws,' Mr Thompson said, which made Dr Marvill all the more suitable to him.

'Would you like Miller in again?' Needham asked.

'Not without seeing a reference,' Thompson said. His mind was made up.

Seeing no point in arguing with his colleague, Smith-Sampson said, 'Marvill has a sound background.'

'We'll settle for the little lady,' Mr Thompson declared, as if the decision might affect any of the others present.

'Dr Marvill?' Roy Needham hesitated, offering one last change of mind. There was none. 'Ask her to come in, Pam. Thank the others. Make sure they get expenses claims forms.'

The selection was a brisk process, one that indicated self-assurance on the part of the surgeons, confidence in their ability to make swift, accurate decisions, rather than a willingness to live with possible mistakes.

On being told she had got the job, Jessie Marvill felt surprise, delight and relief; then anxiety and apprehension followed. The last feelings were to do both with her doubt over whether this was the right job for her, and the earlier decision she had made about ending her relationship with Roger Trentham. Even at this stage she could always change her mind about that, and not take the job, as applying for it had been mostly to do with her need for a new direction in her life. She would take the job now she had been offered it, and she wouldn't let the relationship drift on as it had for a long while through apathy, emotional laziness, or lack of energy. In some ways she had felt herself too assertive, and Roger had allowed her to ride roughshod over him, and she had disliked herself for doing it. It might have been easier had she been leaving him for someone else. Easier for her, as there would be times when she would need someone intimate and supportive, something more than the friendly social club crowd that was to be found at most hospitals. She would tell Roger today, and that would give them both the best part of a month to get used to the idea. The last feeling that washed up through Jessie Marvill was guilt, when logically she knew she shouldn't feel guilty. It wasn't only to do with her getting this job which she wasn't entirely sure she wanted, but also that there were others there who didn't get it, along with all those who didn't even get on to the short-list. She avoided looking at the unsuccessful applicants, but couldn't be unaware of them. The black doctor seemed more resigned than most; Dr Miller, who had spoken to her on her arrival, was becoming increasingly angry. Others collected their expenses claims forms and went, only one of them congratulated her. At that point Jessie Marvill knew she had no choice other than to take up the surgical post.

2

The rigid order that surrounded Ray Taylor's existence in his post-war, semi-detached house reflected none of the inner chaos felt at that moment. He was sitting on the edge of the nylon quilt-covered bed staring at the grey light beyond the bleached net curtains. His wife imposed this spotless, ordered régime, and although he had always enjoyed it, it gave him no sort of comfort just then. Chaos had begun to descend three weeks ago after receiving the hospital letter, instructing him to come in today. His wife interpreting the delay as his problem not being urgent hadn't reassured him. His complaint being non-urgent was what he chose to believe more than twelve months ago when he had gone to his GP, only to be told it was a sore throat that had hung around due to him being run down. He had wanted to believe that, hadn't wanted to challenge the doctor, not even after he had developed a persistently runny right nostril. Had it been anything more serious than the specialist who had seen him last month had suggested, Ray Taylor would have preferred not to know. Having been told there was possibly an abscess at the back of his throat, he had to some extent been reassured, reasoning that the specialist knew what he was talking about. But as the day for going into hospital for his tests approached so fear seeped deeper.

Ray Taylor wasn't very skilful at disguising fear from his wife, and although Brenda Taylor was infected with it, she did manage to block against any possibility of her husband's problem being more serious. She usually worried about her own health, suffering as a consequence from hypertension, but over these past few weeks the worry of what might have ailed her had taken second place.

Despite hoping that this day would never come, Ray Taylor lay awake most of the night watching for it. The hospital had told him to telephone in the morning to confirm coming in, but he resisted, thinking instead that he might get there only to be told there wasn't a bed available.

There was a haunted look about Ray Taylor, and neither his newest shirt nor smartest suit, which he had on, did anything to dispel it. He had lost so much weight that both looked as though they had been made for someone else.

He stirred immediately his wife came in, bringing a pair of newly pressed pyjamas. There was an air of lassitude about him.

'I'd best be off,' he said, collecting his grip. It was a defensive action.

'These tissues, Raymond,' she said sharply, snatching up two used Kleenex that he had left on the bed. Brenda Taylor couldn't disguise her edginess, which was made worse at the uncertainty of the situation.

Ray Taylor didn't respond. At one time he would have snapped back, but there was no fight in him.

'It's too early to go yet.'

'I'll walk to the bus. Might make me feel better.'

'Jack's coming round,' she reminded him. 'I can run you up in the car.'

'I'll be all right.'

'I can bring your clothes back. They said there wasn't room for them on the ward.'

'Hardly worth it for two or three days.'

The pause that followed made the statement seem like a lie, and increased their awkwardness.

'You've got everything?' Brenda Taylor straightened the bedcover. It matched the curtains. The room reflected their comfortable lower-middle-class existence. But money being available to buy bedroom units didn't mean they were able to make the right choices.

'I've probably forgotten something,' he said.

'I'll bring it in this evening, if you have. You won't be in there any time, Raymond.' She frequently called him Raymond rather than Ray when in company or unsure of the situation.

'I've put up with this on and off for twelve months,' he said, wiping his nose. 'I wonder why I'm bothering.' He had some notion that he could go on living with this problem.

'There's something not quite right,' she said. 'They'll get it sorted out with those tests. Mr Thompson's a top specialist. It'll be as well to get it out of the way in time for Spain.'

That was only three weeks away.

Jack Taylor was as fat as his elder brother was thin, and unselfconsciously ate all the cake his sister-in-law put out for them on the kitchen table. Family tended to be entertained in the kitchen.

'It's wonderful what they can do in hospital nowadays,' he said. 'They'll probably give you a bigger handkerchief.' His voluble frame rippled with laughter. 'My supervisor had a prostate done the other week. Straightforward enough.'

'Is he all right?' Ray Taylor asked, as though the outcome of any operation had some bearing on his.

'Oh, fine. He sings in the church choir now.'

Brenda Taylor stopped clearing the cups away and looked puzzled. 'What does that mean?'

'The scalpel slipped,' Jack Taylor said and roared with laughter.

Ray Taylor gave a chuckle, trying to disguise his tension. Just then he appreciated his brother's humour little more than his wife's increasing anxiety, and was determined neither of them should go with him when it was time to leave.

3

Roger Trentham didn't look up from the *Guardian*, which he read with little concentration at the messy kitchen table. He was refusing to respond to Jessie Marvill whom he could hear in the doorway behind him. He wanted her to stay, but wasn't going to ask again, knowing he pleased her least of all when he was self-pitying.

Jessie waited a moment, then put the large case down and came into the kitchen. She placed her two keys on the table, as if trying not to disturb him.

'Why don't you keep them, Jess?' he suggested, more hopefully than realistically.

'I'll use my room at the hospital,' she said as if it were an acceptable alternative. He had used similar rooms and knew what they were like.

'What about the rest of your stuff?' he asked.

'I'll put it at my mother's,' she told him.

There was an awkward silence.

'Good luck with the new job,' he said.

'I'll probably need it.'

'No, you'll be fine.'

'I hope you get something you want soon,' she said.

'You know me,' he said.

Silence fell between them again.

'It is tidier this way.' Her tone more than what she said brought to a conclusion their discussions over the past fortnight.

She thought about the word tidier, and didn't like herself for using it, only couldn't unsay it. The attitude which that word seemed to reflect made her uneasy. She had been in this relationship for two years and was now talking in terms of ending it tidily, and Roger accepted it submissively. He had suggested that she keep the flat keys so that she could make a decision to return rather than him making a decision about her staying.

After a moment Jessie turned and collected her suitcase. She banged the door after her, expressing some of the anger she felt. Over the past few months she had been a bit unfair to him, making him the object of the frustration which their mutual profession caused her as a woman. Her behaviour was about as illogical as the behaviour she sometimes had to cope with from male doctors.

St Clair's was a 500-bedded general hospital, one of the units in an inner city teaching district of which Queen's Hospital and Coldbrook mental hospital were a part. Having gone through many management rethinks, policy changes and changes in economic climate, St Clair's had become polygenous, with many and varied annexes grafted on to the original workhouse it once was. Single-storeyed prefabrications stood on whatever ground had become available within the seven-acre complex. In headier days a new block of wards and theatres was built, but the follow-up plans to pull down the rest and rebuild in the same style had to be shelved, leaving the whole with an uneasy duality of ancient and modern. All that could be afforded now were occasional ward upgradings, these being made possible by capital grants from the Regional Health Authority. Any scheme costed at £75,000 and over could be proposed by management for a capital grant, although it by no means followed that it would be given; maintenance such as painting and small building works had to be paid for out of revenue income, supplied by the District Health Authority. Other than essential maintenance was constantly being left undone or carried over into next year's budget as money supply got tighter. As a result the place took on a shoddy appearance.

A painting contractor's flatbedded truck pulled through

the gates of St Clair's past the porter's lodge, which owing to trimmed budgets had been left unmanned for two years. The truck travelled faster than the five mph limit, passing the new A and E department, which stood with the outpatients clinic in sensible relation to the gate, but a long way from operating theatres in another new block, and even further from those in the old block. As the truck turned right towards the loading bay area of the kitchens in the old section, Jessie Marvill who was following it in her green Citroën Dyane 6 turned left and stopped in a parking space reserved for medical staff.

'You can't park there, love.' A man in his fifties with a white moustache was waiting when she lifted out her suitcase. He was Dave Shaw, the head porter.

'Why not?' Dr Marvill asked.

''S for medical staff.'

'I've joined the staff,' she informed him. 'I'm Dr Marvill.'

Her appearance wasn't entirely convincing, but his manner changed. 'Oh, I see. Well, leave it there for now, I'll see if I can't find you a little space.' He looked her up and down, noting the blue jeans she was wearing. 'D'you want a porter to help with your case?'

'I can manage, thanks,' she said, lifting the case.

'D'you know where to go?'

'The medical staffing officer.' She knew where to go.

'She's next door to the administrator,' Dave Shaw said. 'Through them doors there, the second corridor on the left. That brings you right on to the admin's corridor.'

As she went along the first corridor with her bag, the smell of institution food reached her nostrils. That smell was the same at every hospital, regardless of what was cooked, and almost made Jessie regret her decision to move into her room here as she would have to rely almost entirely on this sort of food. Roger had been an excellent cook; that was partly the problem, he liked home life, taking care of her; she didn't.

Painters were moving equipment into the kitchens, which were active with lunch preparations. As Jessie passed, one of them said, 'You wanna hump with your bag, darling?'

Ignoring the inane sexual connotation behind the remark she gave him a polite smile. She steadfastly refused to think of herself as a sex object, even though she was attractive to men. But it was difficult to avoid thinking that way or using sexual attraction in the present climate.

The medical staffing officer had her small office in the administrator's suite, where the two secretaries were getting started when Dr Marvill arrived. Mrs Val Kay, the deputy administrator, arrived at the same time and was glancing through her post.

'Is the medical staffing officer around?' Jessie asked. 'I wanted the key to the room I'm using.'

'She's not in yet,' a secretary said, and went back to her conversation about last night's TV viewing.

'I don't think it's there,' Val Kay told her. 'Didn't your predecessor give it you?' She went into the office next to her own. Jessie Marvill followed. 'The MSO needs to know which medical defence organization you belong to. Did she get the details from you?'

'The Medical Defence Union.' She retrieved a copy of the policy from her bag and handed it over. Mrs Kay glanced over the information.

'Is your subscription up to date?'

'I would say so,' Dr Marvill said.

When the MSO arrived she informed Dr Marvill that the domestic supervisor had the key. 'Hopefully the room's been cleaned,' Pam Loade said. 'You'll get your bleep at the switchboard.'

'The domestic supervisor's four doors along,' Val Kay told her.

'Mrs Kay!' A secretary extended a phone. 'It's the catering manager. 'S trouble in the kitchens.'

'If you have any problems, doctor,' Pam Loade said as

Jessie Marvill left the office, 'just give a shout.'

The problem was the accommodation in which she was expected to live for the six months of her contract, and she knew that no amount of complaining would improve the stark box with its narrow bed, cupboard, small table, bookcase, desk lamp and telephone. The green floral wallpaper was old, dozens of numbers had been scribbled near the phone; the curtains at the window were ill-matched and overlaundered. By tradition junior doctors tended generally to be uncomplaining. One simple fact of life understood by all was that complaints weren't good for career prospects.

Jessie Marvill set her case on the bed, along with the white coats she had been supplied with; a badge proclaimed: Dr J. Marvill, SHO Surgery. She refused to dwell upon the level of existence this room offered, but instead opened the case and hung up some of her clothes. She removed books she had brought, a notepad, pencils, stethoscope. One of the books was *Practical Surgical Management.* This she put in her pocket along with the bleep.

She checked her watch: 9.15 A.M. It was time to get started.

4

The doctors' dining-room at St Clair's was a large, light room with cloth-covered tubular tables and a long serving hatch from which meals were collected. Consultants had two tables set aside for them at which a waitress served. It was part of the Medical Centre, which housed the doctors' sitting-room, a badminton court, snooker room, TV room, library and mail deposits for medical staff. This centre had been a battlefield in recent years, seeing numerous skirmishes before the current uneasy compromise was arrived at. The protagonists were a handful of junior doctors who had taken up the fight on principle, but the price they paid was a setback in their careers; once a doctor had been identified as a troublemaker, rightly or wrongly, it was almost impossible to lose the tag. The battles were with management, which had steadfastly resisted a separate centre for junior doctors, having decided they were being unreasonably élitist; it maintained that all staff should be able to eat in the canteen, if not use the other facilities. The few doctors who spoke for the many resisted; the compromise was that nursing officers and senior management were allowed to use the canteen along with the consultants if they wished, but that separate facilities should be provided also. The argument put forward by junior doctors was that the hospital was their home, very long hours in providing medical cover often meant their staying on duty for days at a time, the medical centre provided some seclusion, a place of escape when pressure built up. No other group of hospital workers were resident as part of their contract, no other group suffered the same pressures. Junior doctors felt this entitled them to special consideration, to some exclusive space for their own peer group. However, it was a view not universally shared, even among their own profession. The war was by no means over, and the peace was fragile.

Entering the mess, Jessie Marvill's eyes swept over the dozen or so doctors in the room, and she identified Mr David Passmore, the senior registrar of the firm she was joining.

If not overtly, there was clearly a separation of both black and Asian doctors here, each sitting in their own group. The practice was fairly consistent, as it had been at her previous hospital. There were neither black nor Asian doctors on Mr Marcus Thompson's firm, nor were there likely to be, she would later discover.

'Ah, you found us,' David Passmore said as Jessie Marvill approached him. He was thirty-six, speedy, often brusque; an FRCS who had some expectation of getting his own consultant post. 'Have you had some coffee?'

'I'm okay, thanks.'

'Good. You've met Frank Willoughby, our houseman?' Passmore indicated the young house officer sitting with him.

'Yes. How are you?'

'Nice to see you again,' Willoughby said, and pulled a schoolboyish face. At twenty-four he was actually younger then Jessie Marvill, and much less mature. He was junior to her, this being his first job since qualifying. A registrar was senior to her and would make medical decisions she was incapable of making. Next in line to the consultant was the senior registrar, but few firms carried both registrar and senior, though a number carried more than one SHO.

'Settled in, have you?' Passmore asked.

'Trying not to touch the sides.'

'That's the idea.' Passmore swirled the last of the coffee in his cup to mix the sugar, then swallowed it, ready to move. 'I ought to stop drinking this filthy stuff up – 's worse than cigarettes.'

'Have you given those up?'

His look suggested that her question rather than his observation was pointless. 'The old man's on the Golden Mile today. I'm doing the ward round.' Although in almost all other respects, save experience, a senior registrar was equal to a consultant, lack of a consultant post effectively debarred him from Harley Street.

'Have you had an opportunity to see any of the patients?' David Passmore said.

'I came in last Friday.' Jessie Marvill smiled at Dr Willoughby who had showed her around.

'There is just one thing, Jessie,' Passmore said as he went through the door, leaving it for Dr Willoughby to hold. 'The old man won't enjoy seeing you in jeans on the wards. Just thought I'd mention it.' He smiled apologetically and went down the steps.

'He's a leg man,' Dr Willoughby whispered.

His irreverence immediately made her feel better. That attitude of Mr Passmore and indeed Mr Thompson was something she would often meet; but wasn't likely ever to comply with.

The ward round conducted at Mr Passmore's pace helped Jessie Marvill not at all to get further acquainted with patients she would be responsible for. She would come round afterwards on her own, take time to read the notes and talk to the patients.

Joined by Ann Morrison, a medical social worker, they then went swiftly through the surgical ward on the new block.

An endless corridor connected the new block to the old Nightingale Block where there was a men's surgical ward. Sikh cleaners pushed large polishing dusters wrapped around brooms over the worn lino squares in an unhurried manner that was made noticeable by the surgical firm's walking race. Islands of broken furniture were parked along the walls, the floor being polished around them.

'There's talk of closing this block down,' Ann Morrison explained to Dr Marwill. 'But I don't know if it'll ever happen.'

'Not in your lifetime, or mine,' Mr Passmore threw over his shoulder as he crashed through the rubber doors on to the stairwell of Nightingale Block.

'Hello sister,' Mr Passmore said to the Singhalese ward sister who emerged from the office as the firm arrived on the twenty bedded men's surgical ward, S1. 'This is Dr Marvill. She's joined us.'

'Hello.' The sister gave her a warm smile.

'Any beds spare, sister?' Mr Passmore asked as they started along the old ward, which was sectioned off into flimsily partitioned bays of four beds, each open the length.

'No one died, Mr Passmore,' Sister Mehta said, following him. A nurse pushed the grey records trolley rather like a pram. 'You have two of Mr Smith-Sampson's beds still.'

'Well, we'd better turn some patients out.'

They stopped at the bed of a middle-aged man who had had a partial gastrectomy for a duodenal ulcer. Sister Mehta produced the appropriate blue folder.

'How are we this morning, Mr Wright?' Mr Passmore said expansively as he opened the file. 'Still feeling a bit sore, are we?' He had the habit of dropping into the first person plural, which the nursing staff used also.

'A bit, doctor,' the man replied.

'But the pain from the ulcer's gone?'

Pain was something patients had before surgical intervention, after it they had soreness. Only the medically qualified made this distinction.

'Yes, doctor. 'S little easier.'

'Sleeping?' Instead of waiting for a response he turned to Sister Mehta, believing the opinions of the nursing staff to be more reliable than the patients'. 'Any problems, sister?'

'Some restlessness. Unable to get back to sleep,' the sister said. 'I think Mr Wright is letting the problems at home worry him again.'

'Yes, Mr Wright does let the problems at home get on top of him,' Ann Morrison said. The social worker's presence was a gesture to convention. Sometimes they supplied useful background information, but surgical firms generally had less interest in social aftercare than the less acute specialties.

'He's on Mogadon,' he observed, unable to avoid the habit of trade prescribing despite the present trend in hospitals away from this. 'Try some Valium for his anxiety. 5 mg three times a day.' He glanced at Frank Willoughby, who wrote it up on his medication chart.

'Is that in addition to Mogadon?' the sister inquired.

'Yes. Any problem with the waterworks?'

'Some difficulty passing urine.'

'We'll keep an eye on that.'

He returned the file to the sister. 'You're making fine progress, Mr Wright. We'll be up and home very soon.'

This was success. Surgery had been performed, the patient recovered. He could now go home to resume the worrying that had led to the problem.

They moved on out of the bay. The other three beds were Mr Smith-Sampson's.

In the next bay they stopped at the bed of a large seventy-three-year-old, Thomas Simpson, for whom no one was claiming much success.

'How are we today?' Mr Passmore mistakenly believed the patient to be deaf.

'I know you're all doing your best,' the fat man responded. He was feeling uncomfortable but wasn't particularly complaining, being of the generation that was grateful to the 1948 NHS Act for bringing limitless medical treatment to everyone.

'There's a problem with Mr Simpson's diet,' Sister Mehta said in a low voice, not intended for the patient. 'The fistula is continually leaking. Whenever he eats solids they pour out.'

'Let's have look.'

This brought a flurry of activity. Curtains were drawn, enclosing both bed and doctors.

'We've had a difficulty here,' the surgeon explained to Dr Marvill. 'This patient had carcinoma of the sigmoid. We've done two sigmoid resections, each time the anastomosis has broken down.' He didn't lower his voice, relying instead on technical description to exclude the patient.

The doctors edged in at the bed when the sister and a nurse peeled back the man's dressing. The wound was raw and ulcerated, the smell it gave off was sulphurous. This was one of the more unpleasant nursing tasks.

'Liquid diets haven't been entirely successful. Leakage of the faecal fluid from the colon has been making this area raw.' He indicated the open fistula.

'It's unpleasant for both the patient and the staff,' Sister Mehta said. 'We have to change him hourly.' The flexible bag that usually created a messless seal around the opening would no longer adhere to the skin.

'I'm not sure what more can be done,' the surgeon said, now making sure the patient didn't hear. 'How are the pressure sores?'

'They're quite bad on his heels and buttocks,' Dr Willoughby said. 'They're being treated with benzoin cream.' As yet he was uncertain of his own opinions.

'There's nothing more to be done here,' the surgeon said, writing this patient off. 'I'll speak to Mr Thompson.' That was necessary as he was the consultant, but he was unlikely to reverse his decision, after all the senior registrar ran the firm. 'Pop him on five per cent dextrose, just to stop him dehydrating.'

Mr Passmore closed the file and handed it to the sister upon whom fell the burden of nursing this patient to the end. She didn't say anything. It wasn't her place.

Nor did Dr Marvill, but the decision didn't glide off her easily, even though she had had no involvement with this case. Without reading the notes she wouldn't know what had been tried, but even when she had all the facts, where the only practical course was to let the patient die, she found such decisions difficult to live with.

As the firm moved through the curtains, Mr Simpson asked in a confused voice, 'Have I got to have another operation?'

'I don't think so, love,' an agency nurse, who was dressed in a brown uniform, said cheerfully. 'They're going to change your diet.'

Close to the end of this ward round, Dr Adrian Crawley, a medical research registrar approached them outside the office. His excited manner heightened his school-boyishness. 'My God!' he said. 'Guess what's happened. Smith-Sampson's just popped out the wrong lung of a woman with CA. The old bugger's gone and removed a perfectly sound lung.'

'Oh really, Adrian?' Mr Passmore said, passing a chart to sister. 'Sounds like a leg-pull to me. Have you met Jessie Marvill, our new SHO?'

'Nice to meet you.' He was momentarily distracted, not immediately disguising his obvious interest in her.

'Adrian's doing medical research,' Mr Passmore explained. 'He's not usually as excitable.'

'Popping off the wrong toe's commonplace,' Dr Crawley said. 'But a lung's a bit over the top.'

'I'm sure it's grossly exaggerated,' Passmore said with a smile, leaving himself uncommitted.

'Weren't there tomograms? A biopsy report?' Dr Marvill asked, uncertain whether she was dismayed or being drawn into a game.

'Cut first, is his motto.'

Both nursing and ancillary staff were showing open interest Mr Passmore noticed, and knew this could become a preoccupation for the rest of his ward round. Whether fact or fiction, Mr Smith-Sampson making such an error was nothing to do with him, but Passmore knew that his own consultant post depended to some extent on the approval of that surgeon, and so didn't want to be involved in gossip.

'I've got some students to see at 11.30,' he said, glancing at his watch. 'Are you joining my ward round?'

'No, I'm looking at a Mr Streeton.' He was one of Mr Smith-Sampson's patients.

'I see.' Mr Passmore started out. The other three exchanged looks.

'Perhaps I'll see you in the mess at lunchtime,' Dr Crawley said as they went out.

Jessie Marvill assumed he was addressing her, but didn't respond.

5

The subconscious expectations Raymond Taylor had this morning of not arriving at the hospital if he travelled by bus rather than car weren't fulfilled. The bus seemed to get him there faster than any car could, he mused, as he stared from the window. Seeing ordinary people in the street doing ordinary things, he wondered, why me? Why did it have to be him going to hospital for tests? Possibly to have an operation. Why couldn't he be going to work, or walking a dog? He felt a sense of injustice, but not enough to cry out in protest, or make him get off the bus. He knew he couldn't do that. Instead he stayed seated all the way to the hospital.

When he was at school, Ray Taylor remembered, he sometimes tried to avoid the inevitable by doing silly things – half paces or walking between cracks on the floor along the school corridor when sent to the headmaster. They could never stop what was coming, but if he delayed, he always thought that then some other disaster might overtake him. Earthquakes or wars starting were what he had hoped for on those short walks.

Today as he crossed the hospital forecourt, he realized his thoughts were travelling along similar lines, unconsciously seeking something that would prevent him arriving here. Even the ambulance that swung on to the forecourt failed to run him down; he stepped out of the way. At the desk in the reception area a receptionist was dealing with an ambulance driver and an old woman. Ray Taylor waited, he was in no hurry.

'Are you taking her?' the receptionist was asking.

'Well, I don't know. I'm s'posed to collect someone for

Coldbrook. I'm not taking one of them loony buggers down on my own,' the driver protested. 'Not after what happened last time.'

'The thing is I can't get her lunch now.' The receptionist chose to make this an insurmountable problem.

'Could you tell me where I go?' Ray Taylor asked the other receptionist, when she put the phone down. He showed her his admission letter.

'Have admissions moved yet, Dor'?' she asked her colleague.

''S tomorrow, I think. I think they're moving tomorrow.'

'Well you can see,' the woman told Ray Taylor. 'Go through those doors, down the corridor to the end. Turn left out the door. Along the walkway to the next block. The third door on the right. Now have you got that?' Before Ray Taylor could respond she added, 'If they're not there, there'll be a notice on the door. Or come back here and we'll tell you where to go.' Turning to the ambulance driver, she said, 'Can you take Mrs Phillips home from G2?'

'I don't know as I can take anyone now.'

'Can you just have a seat a mo', love,' the receptionist said to the elderly lady, who was confused.

'I'd better call in and see,' the ambulance man announced, adding to the confusion.

'Well, I can't get any of these lunch now. You have to order it before 10.30.'

Ray Taylor saw hope in the situation. If it was this chaotic, he might accidentally slip through the net of medical process.

The admissions office hadn't moved, but hopes of escape were renewed when he reached the large, tall room which had cardboard boxes of files standing in every available space. The impression was one of utter confusion, as if some crazy scheme had been embarked upon to empty all the filing cabinets, then inexplicably cancelled. There were five desks, but only one admissions officer present, the others were either at lunch or involved in the move.

'Did we send you a registration form?' the woman asked as she riffled through a bunch of files.

'Yes. I posted it back to you,' Ray Taylor said.

'I can't seem to find your record.' She went to search on her colleague's desk. 'Everything's going on to the computer. We're moving to new offices. You wouldn't believe the confusion it's causing. It's more trouble than it's worth.' She sighed and went on searching. 'You saw the consultant here, did you?'

'Yes, I did. Three weeks ago,' Taylor said.

'You're not going private, are you, dear?' she inquired.

'No. He asked if I wanted to as there might be a delay.' The reason he decided against private treatment wasn't the cost, but rather because of it hastening something he preferred putting off.

'I'm not certain you can come in today. We're having trouble finding enough beds.'

'Oh, I see,' Taylor said, but not really understanding. 'I was sent a letter about coming in today.'

'I know, Mr Taylor. The bed situation changes daily. You were advised to telephone before setting out.'

'Well, I don't want to be a nuisance. I've lived with this for long enough now,' Ray Taylor said, feeling relieved. Yet curiously depression followed at the thought of further delay.

'Here it is!' she said triumphantly. 'We'd better try and fit you in now you're here. Maybe someone's going home.' She gave him a reassuring smile and picked up the phone.

'Are you taking any tablets from your own doctor, Mr Taylor?' Sister Mehta asked when she sat him by the desk in the office on S1. She wrote his personal details in his folder.

Despite the admissions officer's efforts no suitable bed was available for Ray Taylor, only the promise of one provided a patient could be sent home.

'Only these, he gave me for my throat.' Ray Taylor produced a bottle of white tablets. 'And some distalgesic for headaches.'

'I'll take those. I'll ask doctor if you should continue with them. Any pain now?'

'A bit uncomfortable around here.' He indicated the sinuses, which he could scarcely bear having touched. He didn't tell her that.

'Well, doctor will be in to see you as soon as we find you a bed. Meanwhile you can sit in the day-room. Perhaps we can get you some lunch.'

She rose from the desk. Ray Taylor got up too, and reached for his bag.

'You can leave that here,' she offered. 'Nurse Kenny!' she said as a nurse went past. 'Would you take Mr Taylor to the day-room, find him a chair.'

As Ray Taylor went away Dr Marvill came on to the ward. She was his single hope of getting a bed today. The sister waited to greet her, sensing in this doctor a concern that she all too often found absent in others. It was just a feeling she had, but no one trusted such feelings around here, and she found herself suggesting it was the doctor's 'new post interest'.

'You've a Mr Burton going home, sister,' Dr Marvill said, unfamiliar with the patients.

'We will push him out if you say so, doctor.' The sister smiled, as she collected the patient's file off the desk. 'Are you clerking Mr Taylor now?'

'Is he here?'

'Waiting for Mr Burton's bed.'

'I'll come back and see him after lunch,' Dr Marvill said, and started along the ward. One more unwitting link in the conspiracy to get Ray Taylor treated.

All patients were interviewed and examined by one of the doctors on the firm when admitted; the whole procedure was described by this curious historical phrase, coined in more brutal times and never let go. Somehow Mr Taylor was aware that the attitudes and consequent actions of those frock-coated doctors still lingered – this was the cause of his anxiety if only he realized it.

6

Confusion in its purest state gave the impression of running amok in the large, somewhat antiquated kitchen at St Clair's. At the best of times it wasn't slow to raise its head, but with the arrival of painters, who were trying to wash down, prepare and repaint all surfaces while meals for both patients and staff were being prepared, it descended with a vengeance.

The kitchen was laid out around two centre blocks of ovens and boilers, with more ovens, grills, preparation benches, sinks, mixers, mashers and sundry equipment ranging around the outside, along with the special diet and salad kitchen.

On the walkways between the equipment painters had set up trestles with staging boards crossing the four bubbling cauldrons, all but one of which were open as if in expectation of something falling into them. The painters were presently at a standstill awaiting the outcome of the discussion between Val Kay, Felix Greene, the fifty-year-old Jewish catering manager, Peter Clearless, the thirty-three-year-old, slightly nervous catering supervisor, Frank Badham, the black works manager, and the painter foreman.

The kitchen staff, comprising five Spanish and one English chef, various porters, mostly Spanish, and black and white catering assistants, worked on as best they could. This was the build-up period to lunch, which was the biggest meal of the day, and brought a fury of activity in a carefully worked out routine that everyone could cope with, provided there were no interruptions. The painting gang caused endless interruptions.

'You can appreciate our difficulty, Mrs Kay,' Peter Clearless was saying, indicating the activity going on. He was a worrier and made his comment sound like an apology for causing difficulties. That was the last thing he wished to do, as one day he hoped to be catering manager, even District catering officer. 'There's nowhere the painters can be without working above at least one of the kitchen staff.'

'We knew it wasn't going to be easy,' Val Kay said, as if believing that was all he wanted to hear.

'What about if they work one side of the kitchen, Peter?' Felix Greene suggested, stabbing the hot, dry air with a pudgy finger. 'They work here, while you use those boilers.' He was a compromiser, a placator.

The catering supervisor wasn't unhappy with this, though it was far from ideal. He had been seen to support staff complaints about the painters working while food was being prepared, but he didn't want to make too much of it.

Val Kay referred the suggestion to Frank Badham, who in turn looked to the painter foreman.

'Oh, we'll work round you the best we can, 's no problem,' he said accommodatingly. 'So long as it don't hold us up. Know what I mean.'

'Can we leave it like that?' Val Kay said, anxious to extricate herself from this situation to which there was no economically acceptable solution.

'Yes, I think we can manage all right, Val,' Felix Greene said.

There was general agreement among them. Unconsulted and far from happy, was Mike Boyle, the only English chef, who was on late turn and responsible for getting the suppers ready. He was a big, redfaced, hypertensive ex-alcoholic, with a habit of hiding his knives, rather than keeping them in the drawer each chef was provided with. Boyle's favourite hiding place was the rim of the canopy over the boilers. From the way the meeting broke up he guessed the outcome. They would have to put up with the painters. He shook his head in disagreement, then angrily resumed boning a small side of bacon. He wouldn't put up with it, he told himself, even if those blacks and dagos working with him were too scared for their jobs to complain. He wouldn't hesitate to take the matter to the union if the painters came near him.

At around 11.40 every morning the tall, stainless steel dinner trolleys started going out from the kitchen to the wards with theoretically hot and wholesome meals for the patients. As they were loaded the trolleys were unplugged and wheeled away by a motley collection of porters in an assortment of uniforms. One was Del Brewer, a young half-caste, who wore the bottom half of a blue boiler suit and a white jacket. Like most he wasn't issued with a proper uniform; in order to protect her budget, the linen supervisor waited to see if a porter was staying before issuing one, by which time it didn't matter too much about a blue serge suit. The long service porters had them, but Del Brewer had only been doing the job two years. Returning to the kitchen from a delivery the next trolley wasn't ready, and there was another porter still waiting. Brewer joined him.

'D'you hear what happened in the theatre this morning?' he said, pushing his glasses back up his nose.

'D'woman losing d'wrong lung?' the black proter said.

'They'll be some stick over that, Sam', you see.' He threw his head back in disgust, as his colleague swung the trolley away, yanking out the plug from the wall by the flex.

Del Brewer brought the next trolley across. That wasn't his job but he didn't mind helping out as the kitchen staff were getting behind.

Most of the lunch staff were working on the conveyor belt at the top end of the kitchen. The chef at the front end dealt with patients' menu cards, laying each on a tray which the porter opposite set on the conveyor with a base and plate. The chef called 'Roast Pork'; the choice having been made from the menu the previous day, included two veg and gravy, as no single items could be substituted or omitted. Consequently if patients didn't want something they left it, wasted food being cheaper than wasted labour. The meat chef ladled on a slice of pork from the trays before him, catching the juice drips; the catering assistant splodging on the two vegetables, the conveyor not stopping if she missed and food dropped on to the side of the plate. She didn't often miss. Another catering assistant dealt with other veg, another with soup. A chef brought bread-and-butter pudding for dessert from the warmer; the porter at the far end finally put the cover on, then placed the tray in the trolley. The system rarely broke down, and only occasionally did the operators crack up during the hour or so it took them to get out five hundred lunches.

Despite the painters there had been neither mechanical nor emotional breakdowns this morning, and most patients wouldn't notice their lunch being five minutes late.

Further along in the kitchen, above where chef Mike Boyle was preparing bacon and cream macaroni, a painter working on a trestle was cleaning off the ceiling. This didn't please Boyle when he stood a huge colander over the metal drain in the floor in front of an open boiler. For the past half hour he had watched with growing impatience as the man worked towards him, and Boyle blamed his minor accidents, a cut and a burn, on the distraction he caused. And blamed him when, on tilting the boiler to strain the macaroni in the colander, a splash of scalding water hit his arm. He glared at the painter, not disguising his displeasure as he went to the next boiler. The colander was left standing over the drain.

''S bit fucking warm,' the painter said, climbing off the trestle. 'I dunno how you stand this heat.'

''S worse before they put them fans in,' Mike Boyle said, despite himself. He reached over the lip of the canopy for his large kitchen knife.

''S ridiculous working like this.' The painter took out his

tobacco tin. 'We should be in here at night. S'pose they're too tight for a ghoster.'

'I'll tell you something,' Mike Boyle informed him, 'I'm not putting up with much more of it. Working like this. I'll have the union on to it.'

'I wouldn't stand for it m'self.' He lit a handrolled cigarette.

'You ready for colour up there, Terry?' the foreman asked as he approached.

'Jus' that last bit to clean off. That old plaster's none too clever. 'Sall crumbling.'

'Try and get out with a bit of filler. If it's too bad, they'll just have to have a new ceiling.' He glanced around. 'Slip into the bog and have your snout, 'case the catering manager sees you. I'll get your filler.'

The painter followed Mike Boyle through the kitchen, going to the toilets beyond the walk-in fridge.

The huge coldstore was divided into two rooms, one of which was intended for meats alone, but various foodstuffs such as butter, lard, cheese, and even desserts and puddings, unfinished from other meals and destined for the next day's menus, had found their way on to the open shelves above the greasy floor; raw meat stood next to cooked meat, ready to re-contaminate it.

Reaching down the bacon he had earlier cooked, Boyle paused to question what he was putting up with. It was ridiculous, he told himself, the union should do something about these conditions of work. He threw the cooked bacon back on the shelf next to a raw piece and went out.

'You busy, Chris?' Mike Boyle said, as he came into the locker room, where he had tracked down the NUPE branch secretary. The restroom was small and lined with narrow grey steel lockers, some with broken door hinges and locks. The place was in poor repair, it hadn't been touched in years, but no one seemed to mind. That might have been a mark of respect for the fading, curled-at-the-edges nudes taped to the walls. No one knew who had put them up and no one wanted to disturb them.

Chris Hogan was big and overweight and forty years old, with a querulous nature which was reflected both in his life and his job; the prime reason he was the hospital branch secretary was that no one else wanted the job as it meant a lot of work, in addition to his duties as a porter. The evening involvement away from his family had suited him fine.

He turned his attention from the newspaper covered table, where he was playing cards with two of the maintenance staff.

'Well, I ain't had an 'and yet,' he said. 'Nor a foot come to that.' He threw a card away and picked up another. 'What you got in mind, Mike?'

'It's them bloody painters. 'S bloody murder with them working in the kitchens. You don't know whether you'll get paint or shit or anything down your neck. I mean, it's not right is it, working like that.'

'What's Mr Greene say?'

'Says it's gotta be done,' Boyle replied. 'It should be done at night. That's when.'

'I'd better look into it, Mike. I've got a meeting with management this after'. I'll see if I can get it on then.' He picked up another card and threw one clear. 'That's it!' he said, showing his hand. 'Leave it with me, Mike. I'll see what can be done.'

7

The bed that Ray Taylor was eventually put in had been made available by discharging another patient, if not recklessly, certainly earlier than was comfortable. Taylor was now inexorably caught up in the system, to be done with as the medical profession decided. In theory he, like any other patient, had the final word on what treatment he received, but in practice, like the vast majority, he wouldn't exercise that right, preferring to give himself on trust to those who, he thought, knew better. Regardless of how decisive people were in life, on becoming ill most preferred deferring to specialist knowledge, no matter how vast or scant, whether belonging to a practitioner who was the major influence in a particular specialty or a receptionist in a GP centre.

Neither his fear nor his earlier resistance to finding out what was wrong halted Ray Taylor in this process now. He went without protest.

In the bathroom on S1, bone-thin and lost inside pyjamas, he slipped off his plaid dressing gown and stepped on to the scales. An Asian male nurse adjusted them.

'53.46 kilos,' he announced.

'What do you normally weigh, Mr Taylor?' a 2nd-year student nurse asked, noting down the weight.

'Oh, I'm not sure,' he said, not wanting to admit to an enormous weight loss.

'Have you lost weight lately?'

'A bit, I think.'

'172 cm,' the male nurse said, measuring his height.

His colleague wrote that down. Then she said, 'Could you let us have some wee?' Treating the patient a bit like a child was her way of dealing with the embarrassment she had first felt on making this sort of request. Now it was a habit. 'The doctor'll take some blood from you back at the bed.'

'Would you press on that?' Dr Marvill indicated the cottonwool over the puncture where she had pulled the needle from his vein. 'It'll stop you bruising.'

She emptied the syringe into the sample bottle, which a nurse labelled for the haematology lab, and popped in the rack on the trolley.

'That's fine.' She smiled, sensing his anxiety. 'You've lost weight,' she commented, glancing over the notes.

'Just a bit, I think,' Taylor said, more self-deluding than evasive.

Her look suggested it was more than that. 'Over what period? Do you know?'

'I can't really say I've noticed, doctor.'

'How do you feel in yourself?'

'Well enough, a bit tired at times. Apart from this soreness in my mouth and throat. Doesn't seem to go away.'

'Is breathing still difficult?' she asked, picking up on the notes her boss had made from the response to a similar tack in his outpatients clinic.

'Only at times,' he said.

'A bit anxious about that, are you?' Her manner was friendly and reassuring, being aware how stressful these times were for patients. Her father, who was an orthopaedic surgeon, had a brusque bedside manner; her mother, who was a GP in Sussex, was kindness itself and never lost sight of the fact that patients were people too. Her father rarely remembered that people were people. Occasionally she wondered if that wasn't the reason she had chosen a surgical specialty. 'Tender anywhere?' she asked, palpating the lymph nodes in his neck and shoulder with her fingers. There was swelling here.

'Not really.' His neck had been tender at one time but no longer was.

'How long have you had this swelling, Mr Taylor?' Dr Marvill explored further with her fingers.

He thought it came and went; he wanted to believe that.

With a wooden spatula and a torch she looked into his throat. There was a small ulcerated mass on the naso-pharynx, she observed. Although Taylor said this caused him no pain, other than general soreness, and none radiating through the side of his face, she didn't know how honest he was being. On examining his mouth she found thickened patches of white plaque along the right hand side of the tongue and extending back towards the throat.

'Am I still in there?' Ray Taylor asked when the doctor removed the spatula. This wasn't bold enough.

'I'm sorry?' she responded, not having heard him.

He shook his head, but when she waited, said, 'Just asking if I was all right.'

'Do you worry about your health, Mr Taylor?'

'No,' he said without thinking. 'Well not much. A bit lately, I suppose. This throat business seems to have been going on a long time now. I keep fairly busy, so I just put it down to a sore throat.'

'Any bleeding in your mouth or in the nasal discharge?' Dr Marvill asked as she pulled open the lids of his eyes to check for anaemia. The colour was fine.

'No, I don't think so.' He knew differently, but was avoiding the reality.

'We need a couple of swabs. Did Mr Thompson tell you what the plan was when you saw him in outpatients?' she asked, taking the nasal swabs, which she popped into a glass swab tube, before taking one of the plaque in his mouth.

'About coming in for some tests, that was all,' Taylor replied. 'He said he'd probably remove a little abscess in my throat,' he added as if remembering an incidental piece of information.

Dr Marvill considered him a moment, then nodded, as if confirming that was all they would do. She was later to discover that both her senior colleagues avoided confronting patients with their problems for fear of emotional involvement on any level. 'We'll get some more X-rays done, then have a closer look at your throat under a general anaesthetic. See if we can pin down the exact cause of your problem. Can I get you to sign the consent form?'

She had concluded her examination.

In the doctors' sitting-room, which was directly adjacent to the dining-room, there were five junior doctors dotted around in armchairs, either reading a text book or newspaper, or giving that appearance; in fact three of them were asleep. Mr Passmore did nothing to disturb them when he came in carrying a cup of coffee. Dr Marvill followed him, also bringing coffee, plus a number of folders.

'It's less than realistic for us to be considering anything other than carcinoma at this stage,' Passmore said casually. Jessie Marvill had been discussing her findings on Ray Taylor. 'It's a question of finding out what the extent of it is and what we do about it. What was his bloodcount?'

'I don't know. The report isn't back from the lab. His colour's good, he isn't clinically anaemic.'

He settled his muscular frame in an armchair. 'I didn't bring any sugar. You don't have any?'

'I don't take it,' Jessie said.

Passmore looked around for spare sugar that might have littered a nearby table. At that moment this was as important to him. 'I think the bone erosion and soft tissue swelling shown on the X-rays, together with lymph node enlargement and loss of weight, clearly suggest what's in prospect. Does he have any idea as to the extent of the problem?'

Having formed an accurate opinion of Ray Taylor, Jessie Marvill said, 'He's choosing to believe it's an abscess in his throat.'

'The old man probably left him with that impression intentionally,' Passmore confided. 'Taylor's a candidate for a block dissection.'

'How did he end up with this firm,' she asked, 'rather than with ENT firm or oral maxilla?'

'Not by accident, Jessie, I assure you. Marcus enjoys heroic surgery. He's gaining a solid reputation for hacking out major malignancies. He's published several papers, which I recommend you read. Is that the rest of the list tomorrow?' He reached for the next folder. 'The old man'll do the adrenalectomy.' Watching her closely to observe how well she might fit in with the specialty, he saw her doubts. 'Not particularly heroic, but he's welcome to that.' He sipped some coffee.

The plan for tomorrow's theatre was for the consultant to remove from a middle-aged man, an adrenal gland with a tumour sited on it. Mr Passmore would take the rest of the list, including Ray Taylor; then supervise both Dr Marvill and the house officer in some minor procedures. There were often a number of cancers on a general theatre list, but nothing of particular interest to Marcus Thompson, which was why Mr Passmore was doing most of his list.

'Are you on call tonight?'

'No. The SHO from Mr Smith-Sampson's firm wanted to swap with me.'

'Dr Arif,' he said flatly. 'You said yes?' There was a cautioning note in his voice but he didn't expand on it. 'What else do you have there?'

They would go through the rest of tomorrow's list, familiarize themselves with the complaints, discuss what would be done. Quite soon she would be given her own list of minor operations, such as appendicectomies, circumcisions. At first she would be nervous, and even make mistakes, but her confidence would grow, so that the staff in the theatre wouldn't notice the knife shake in her hand.

8

Meetings between hospital management and unions were held on a regular basis now that unions had established themselves as a force to be reckoned with in the health service. At one time the old style management in the form of a hospital secretary, who was answerable to a board of governors, wouldn't have given them office space.

At St Clair's they were held fortnightly, chaired by the administrator. Only one union was represented, NUPE, this being the strongest in the hospital. Although a recommendation had been made by the DHSS on joint union negotiations, the unions refused to conjoin in any area.

Roy Needham who was tall, slightly stooped and a careful conservative dresser, was behind his desk, trying to keep his patience as he listened to the one-note-argument. He wanted to be shot of this problem, and knew the answer, only couldn't afford it. These sort of arguments struck him as futile; Chris Hogan wasn't unintelligent, he realized they wouldn't paint the kitchen during the working day if a night rate could have been afforded.

Despite tactical opposition from the administrator, Chris Hogan had managed to get the matter of painters in the kitchen on to the agenda this afternoon, so at short notice Felix Greene, Frank Badham, the recently promoted works manager, and Chef Boyle had been brought in for the relevant discussion. All other matters had been dealt with or left pending. It was at these meetings that most local difficulties were resolved. If any party felt aggrieved or couldn't get satisfaction from this level of management within three days the complaint could be taken via the union to the next tier of management, through District, and Region right up to the Secretary of State if necessary. In practice there was little that Roy Needham couldn't deal with, unless it resulted directly from District policy, such as cutting porters' regular overtime. That item was raised every fortnight by Chris Hogan, who would go on doing so until they achieved satisfaction; namely the guaranteed overtime restored in order to make their wages liveable.

'I know painting's necessary, I know all about that,' Chris Hogan was saying. He made a habit of suit and tie for these meetings. 'But it's still a bloody scandal. My members shouldn't have to work in these conditions with dirt and paint falling everywhere. 'S ridiculous.'

'Chris, I know there are difficulties,' Needham said evenly, 'but it's in everyone's interest, improving working conditions.'

'Don't give me that, Mr Needham. You wouldn't have had them painters in if it weren't for the Health and Safety Executive. If you're concerned to improve our members' conditions, what about the restrooms,' Hogan said, feeling sure he had a valid point. 'Health and Safety don't visit those.'

'They would if your safety officers asked them, Chris,' Needham responded, not letting his exasperation show. Being a pre-1948 entrant to health care he was unqualified but was practically skilled in man-management, having worked his way to his present position. He could have risen higher, but preferred this level where he could deal with most aspects of health care and be on first name terms with everyone.

'What about reopening the old kitchen on Nightingale Block?' Val Kay put forward, having discussed the idea earlier with Needham. He didn't feel threatened by her ideas. 'Close the main kitchen for a few days.'

'It would take a while to get that kitchen operational,' Badham said.

'Even if that's possible,' Greene argued, 'I doubt it would have the capacity.'

'That'd mean a lot of extra portering,' Hogan pointed out. 'It's not on, unless you restore the porters' thirty hours a week regular overtime.'

'Well, nothing's changed since we discussed that half an hour ago, Chris,' Needham said drily. 'Cutting it was District's decision.'

'It means losing forty pounds or more a week,' Hogan said, not missing the opportunity to repeat his members' grievance. 'That's half of some of my members' wages. You try a cut in salary by a half, Mr Needham.'

Needham nodded sympathetically. 'District are sick of hearing me put your case.'

'I think you're gonna have to do this painting at night,' Hogan declared. 'Like it should've been done in the first place.'

'It'll double the cost,' the works manager observed, his inexperience resulting in this indiscretion.

'We can't afford to,' Needham saw no point in disguising the fact now.

'What about cold meals for a couple of days?' suggested Brian Rickard, the senior nursing officer. He regularly attended these meetings.

'Even they have to be prepared,' Felix Greene said.

'We'll have to try and arrange for one of our neighbours to help us out. Will you look into that, Felix? Try Branston and St Luke's.'

Val Kay's bleep interrupted the meeting. When she rang the switchboard she was told to phone admissions. This seemed to Needham a natural point at which to close.

'Leave this one with me, Chris. I accept you have a valid grievance. I'll do my best to resolve it.' He looked over his papers. Then at his watch. 'I'll report back to you about the ward closures.'

'Something needs to be done,' Hogan concluded, rising

with his two shop stewards who had remained silent throughout. 'And quickly.'

'Leave it with me. Thank you.'

Neither Needham nor anyone else at the meeting had considered the patients in all this.

The union branch secretary, the two shop stewards, and the chef filed out without a good day. In the brief silence that followed they all became aware of Val Kay's conversation.

'Isn't there an extra bed on the surgical or medical wards?' she was saying into the phone.

'We haven't had any luck anywhere,' the admissions officer at the other end of the line told her.

'Well as it's an EBS admission we'll have to take her. I'll call gynae,' Val Kay said. When beds were blocked in the general hospitals in any one area resulting in a GP not being able to find a patient an emergency bed, the doctor could call the Emergency Bed Service and hand them the problem. When the EBS contacted the hospital a bed had to be found, even if the hospital had previously been closed to admissions.

'They told me they don't have anything,' the admissions officer said, as if believing she was being criticized for not doing her job properly.

'Tell Dr Lambolle to admit her. I'll sort something out,' Mrs Kay said. It was hope and prayer; beds were desperately short.

'How soon could the painters finish in the kitchens, Frank?' Needham asked. 'The very earliest.'

'They only just started,' Badham said. 'They reckon five or six days. That without running into overtime.'

'Well, let them press on for now.'

'What about the unions?'

'We're talking about Chris Hogan and maybe two chefs at most?' He looked to Felix Greene, for confirmation. 'He'll be back tomorrow. By the next day he'll insist on taking his grievance to District. But that's three days. We might have to finish it off at night rate.' He turned to the catering manager. 'Try St Luke's first, Felix. They probably have spare catering capacity with half their wards closed.'

'Do you need me any more, Roy?' Val Kay said. 'I have to find a bed from somewhere.'

'I don't want casualty shut,' Needham told her.

'If the bed situation doesn't improve dramatically,' Brian Rickard said, 'I think we might have to shut the hospital for a while.'

'Juggle the beds as best you can. Let the Chairman of the medical committee deal with it for now,' Needham said.

Shutting the hospital, which in fact in these terms meant closing the casualty department to admissions by ambulance, was the last resort, no matter how short the supply of vacant beds. To do so amounted to failure on the part of hospital management. The fact that they were able to keep this channel of admissions open, despite all odds, vindicated District management's decision to cut beds; patients weren't being turned away to die in the street! Once the patient was through the portals he or she was a medical problem, one the doctors had to sort out, even if it meant putting a post-heart attack patient on a geriatric ward, where the nursing levels weren't sufficient.

Doctors sometimes unreasonably called for their hospitals to be closed temporarily, while management were equally unreasonable in their determination to keep them open, and while the overall trend of taking beds out of service continued the problem would increase.

Roy Needham would win this round, he wouldn't shut his hospital; nor would he shut the kitchens. They'd get painted; everyone would get through the day somehow.

The kitchens were quieter with lunch finished and the trolleys returned with the plates and cutlery washed. Patients' suppers were still being prepared, but the frenzy had abated, and there was more room for the painters to work.

At his bench Chef Boyle, less than satisfied after his meeting with management, was slicing tomatoes for grilling for breakfast tomorrow. He slowly counted individual slices on the tray instead of counting the tomatoes and multiplying by five, which was the number of slices he got per tomato. Movement from a painter working above him distracted him and he lost count.

No sooner had he started again when a piece of plaster fell and shattered on the bench.

''Ere, can't you stop for two fucking minutes?' Boyle waved his knife at the painter.

'Language, Mike,' Peter Clearless said, stepping from his office. 'Ladies. Can you stop for five minutes?' Clearless asked the painter. 'Till we get the supper away.'

Mike Boyle was churning inside. He wiped the plaster away and picked off the flecks, trying to salvage what he could of the tomatoes.

At the top end of the kitchen the last of the patients' suppers made its way along the conveyor belt server. The kitchen porter switched off and put the tray in the trolley. He then pushed it over to the wall with the rest which were queuing up. The porters and the catering assistant started to clear away.

'Why are the trolleys taking so long to go up?' Felix Greene asked as he came into the collection area.

''S nothing to do with me, Mr Greene,' Chris Hogan said. He was working the supper trolleys. 'They go as fast as we can. 'S only two of us on.'

'We go to so much trouble to provide hot, nutritious meals, they stand there getting cold.' He strode away in disgust.

''S all right them saving a few quid on our overtime. Just means the work don't get done, Kev,' Hogan winked at the scruffy young porter in a soiled short white coat and leather tie.

They started out, each with a trolley.

''S your turn to go sick tomorrow, Kev,' Hogan reminded him.

'I wanted to try and pull that new bird in X-Ray,' Kevin said. 'How long am I s'pose to be off?'

'They're insisting on certificates even if you take a day off. 'S on the noticeboard,' Hogan warned him. 'So you'd better see your doctor, get a certificate for a full week, hadn't you.'

They were hoping to beat management unofficially through attrition and so have overtime restored. Ordinarily public sector employees were permitted up to three days off without a certificate, but having recognized the ploy, after due warning, Roy Needham had enacted this one-day certificate rule. Keeping the portering understaffed by constant sick leave, in addition to the overtime ban made endless difficulties. It wasn't bloodymindedness, but a move that Chris Hogan believed was in patients' long-term interests, as well as his members'.

9

On account of seniority and status both registrars and senior registrars on most firms attempted to imitate the hours kept by consultants, leaving all night cover to the SHOs, being called only to give an opinion when the SHO was reluctant or uncertain about doing so. The practice on surgical firms was no different, except when patients were going to theatre the next day, then the registrar would see them the previous night. Mr Passmore was no exception; a few words to the patient about the procedure was, he believed, reassuring, and sometimes spared sleeplessness.

Such visits even suggested that they truly cared about the people they cut open.

However, Ray Taylor wasn't reassured when Mr Passmore put in an appearance with Dr Marvill; he shared a common hope with most patients awaiting surgery, which their presence denied, the possibility of being overlooked, slipping out of the system, his problem miraculously resolved for having been there, and his being allowed home.

'You didn't get any supper tonight, Mr Taylor,' Passmore commiserated.

'I wasn't hungry anyway,' Ray Taylor said. Increasingly food held no attraction.

'You didn't miss anything.' He smiled at Dr Marvill as if sharing a private joke, but one she wasn't aware of. Perhaps he was apologizing for the fact that she would eat most of her meals there. Although the food wasn't good she had known hospitals where it was worse.

'We expect to pop you in to theatre about 9.30 tomorrow. You're second on my list. There aren't any particular problems. You're a bit anaemic, but not enough to cause concern. We'll give you a general anaesthetic and take a little piece from your nose, and a tiny piece of the bone from your upper jaw to complete our tests. Quite straightforward, there'll be minor discomfort. I'll probably pop that growth off at the same time.'

'Will that be the end of my trouble?' It was the first substantive question Ray Taylor had asked.

'It will remove the obstruction that's causing your breathing difficulty,' the surgeon replied with skilled evasion. He was equally skilful at evading emotional involvement with patients struggling for some sort of understanding as to why such a thing should befall them. He paused and considered the patient. 'Anything troubling you? Anything you want to ask about?'

With an uneasy, slightly embarrassed look, Ray Taylor glanced at Dr Marvill, as if suggesting a response might be possible without her present.

Being more sensitive than most to patients' feelings, she excused herself and went to talk to the staffnurse, who with a student nurse was settling into the routine of the evening.

An awkward silence followed. Ray Taylor found it no easier to talk about what was troubling him to one male doctor. The questions themselves were a problem, without the answers he might get. Simply to frame them was to acknowledge what he had been denying so far.

'Was there something, Mr Taylor?'

His thoughts jumped tracks as he deflected his fears. 'Well, I was wondering if this business would affect my sexlife, doctor. It's just that I haven't felt like doing anything . . .'

'I see.' He seemed almost disappointed. That wasn't a tack he had anticipated. 'It's likely that worry and general debility might affect that area, Mr Taylor.' He hesitated. 'I should have a chat with your GP.' He wasn't able to deal with this sort of question without it drawing him into a relationship with the patient other than the one he chose.

'I'm not worried myself, doctor. My wife's still a young woman.'

'Well, talk it over with your GP,' Passmore advised. 'Get a good night's rest. I'll see you tomorrow.'

Mr Passmore moved away to see another patient.

'You'll be all right,' the man in the next bed told Ray Taylor. 'That one knows what he's doing, not like some of them foreigners. 'S them you've gotta watch. Half of them can't speak English.'

Ray Taylor wasn't listening. Anxiety was swamping his thoughts.

When David Passmore and Jessie Marvill left S1 and called for the lift they met a colleague, who was climbing the stairs around the lift cage. He was Roger Crick, whose thirty-year-old homogenized good looks were only slightly marred by the moles on his face.

'Heavy day tomorrow, David?' He was commenting on him being on the ward at night.

'Are you in training?' Passmore countered over him using the stairs. 'This is Jessie Marvill. Did you meet?'

Crick displayed his even, white teeth. 'I'd've said Smith-Sampson was more in need of some extra help. You heard what happened?'

'Is there going to be an inquiry?' Passmore asked.

'Why would there be?' the physician said sarcastically. 'After all he only did a resection on a reasonably sound lung. He really has gone over the top this time.'

'Does seem a bit extreme,' Mr Passmore said cautiously. It hadn't been established that the consultant had removed the wrong lung, but already the stories were entering hospital mythology.

'The patient shouldn't have had surgery in the first place,' Dr Crick said. He was a registrar on a medical firm. 'I did the lung function studies and in my opinion she couldn't manage on the remaining lung, that was diseased as well. Even if they had got it right she would have been a respiratory cripple. Vernon's set on complaining to the Three Wise Men.'

'But Smith-Sampson is one of them,' Passmore pointed out, pressing for the lift again. 'I doubt if he'll make much headway.' He resisted smiling at the irony of that: Vernon Davis, Mr Smith-Sampson's registrar, complaining to the Three Wise Men committee, which comprised the most senior consultants in the hospital, one of whom was Mr Smith-Sampson himself.

'I admire his nerve, even though he's bonkers,' Crick said. 'Complaints about his consultant won't help his own career one bit.' He looked at Jessie Marvill as the lift arrived. 'Do you have a full list tomorrow?'

'Fairly,' Passmore guessed the purpose of the inquiry.

'Could you pop me in for ten minutes' worth on these?' Crick indicated a clutch of flat, brown hairless moles on his face.

Passmore examined them, then said, 'They're rather becoming, Roger.'

'They look suspicious to me.' Unlike a lot of doctors who subscribed to the complaint-of-the-month-syndrome, Crick consistently worried about his moles, which he believed might be melanomas. Already having had several removed, he wouldn't be satisfied until every last blemish had been erased from his skin, turning his regular features into perfect homogeneity.

'Possibly I could fit you in around lunchtime.'

'Excellent. I'll clerk myself,' Crick offered.

He nodded to Jessie Marvill, then continued on up the stairs. Passmore joined his colleague in the lift.

'Would you like to pop those off for him?'

'I wouldn't mind having a go,' Jessie Marvill said.

'There may not be time, of course. I expect he's asked Vernon Davis as well.'

'Is his boss really so bad?' Dr Marvill asked.

'Smith-Sampson? He's a senior consultant,' he said noncommittally. 'Rare as they are, mistakes do happen. Unfortunately one can't correct that sort of mistake.'

Despite indications to the contrary, he wasn't actually admitting that such a mistake had happened. Even when the evidence was incontrovertible, professional courtesy caused other doctors to demur from such admissions.

As the night crept on the thought of his operation was making Mr Taylor increasingly anxious, and the possibility of sleep was becoming more remote. He was sweating, and had made both his pyjamas and the bed damp and uncomfortable. He wanted the nurse to come, to make contact with him and offer him reassurance, but didn't like to call her, knowing that if he did he would then be obliged to make some declaration. Instead he used his restlessness to attract attention, turning first one way, then another, boosting himself up only to settle down lower in the bed right away.

The 2nd-year student nurse, on her own just then, glanced up and again noticed Mr Taylor's restlessness. Finally she put her book down and rose out of the easy chair.

'Are you all right?' she whispered, coming to his side.

Ray Taylor nodded, but realized his mistake. Her smile meant she would return to her chair. He wanted to delay her, have her sit with him but couldn't bring himself to ask.

There was a groan from a patient on the other side of the bay.

'Nurse,' Ray Taylor said, as her attention turned. 'What's the time?' That was all he could think to ask.

'Ten past one,' she told him. 'Can't you sleep?'

He shook his head.

'You worried about going to theatre?' she said. When he didn't respond she took his hand. 'It'll be all right. It's only a minor operation. Try not to worry.' The stock clichés that were now a habit were sincerely meant. 'I'll see about getting you a sleeping pill when staffnurse comes back from her break.'

The man across the bay moaned again, and the nurse went to him.

This patient was haemorrhaging from an operation he had had that morning. He was hot and restless and unconscious.

'Mr Shannawaz,' she said, but got no response from the dark-skinned patient. She reached into the bed for his wrist, his pulse was rapid and feeble. His blood pressure was low at 70/40, and she decided to call Staffnurse Harris back from her break. Something might need to be done in a hurry.

Ray Taylor was still as restless when the staffnurse returned. He watched her go through the same routine as the other nurse, checking the patient. He suspected something was going wrong with the man's operation as the staffnurse went briskly away into the office. That only increased his anxiety.

'Dr Arif,' the staffnurse said, when she was eventually connected with the SHO on call, 'this is Staff Harris. I was wondering if you could pop over and look at Mr Shannawaz.'

'He's the colostomy Mr Smith-Sampson did yesterday?' Dr Arif said sleepily, from his bed.

'I think there might be internal bleeding,' Staffnurse Harris ventured. 'His blood pressure is 70/40. His pulse is very feeble.'

'I cannot come. Keep him on half-hourly observations. Call me if there's any change,' he said.

He put the phone down, leaving the problem with the nurse.

It wasn't simply a case of laziness on Dr Arif's part, but the general air of lassitude and apathy that pervaded Mr Smith-Sampson's firm. No one would particularly appreciate his efforts; if the patient's condition became any worse he would simply call Dr Davis.

Ray Taylor didn't hear any of that. From his observations he assumed everything would be fine once the problem was seen by the nurse and brought to the attention of the doctor.

10

Most consultants, particularly in the acute specialties, worked only part-time for the NHS; their contracts were devised to enable them to pursue their careers elsewhere and so attract an incremental return in accordance with their status. Mr Marcus Thompson held what was termed a maxi-part-time contract, which meant he did eleven sessions a week for the NHS, dividing his time between St Clair's and Queen's Hospital. In theory a session was four hours, while in practice it was whatever the consultant decided it should be. None of them punched a clock. Aside from his NHS work Marcus Thompson had rooms in Harley Street where he saw referrals once a week; he also held a consultant post at a BUPA clinic, and had private patients at St Clair's. To fit all this in he kept his NHS sessions short; he was fortunate in being able to rely entirely on his senior registrar to run his firm at St Clair's, simply holding himself available to be consulted at any time – that rarely happened. Marcus Thompson knew precisely what he was doing with his career, and unlike a lot of general surgeons he didn't cut a swathe through huge lists from 8.30 A.M. to 4.30 P.M., but chose his patients judiciously. He took perhaps only one or two, those who were likely to enhance his reputation, certainly all the major malignancies. Being part of a teaching district he had some commitment to students, but in a world of increasing specialization he saw it as no bad thing that they saw with him mostly surgery for major cancer.

The middle-aged patient on the table this morning with his back opened to expose the adrenal glands seated at the top of the kidneys, wasn't a gross malignancy, but was major surgery. Having exposed both glands, Mr Thompson could find nothing of the small tumour that would suggest Cushing's syndrome. This was a combination of symptoms resulting from hypersecretions of the adrenal cortex in which there was excessive production of glucocorticoids. The syndrome wasn't always due to the presence of a tumour, but one had been diagnosed.

'I see nothing wrong with either of these glands,' Thompson said, leaning away and pressing his spectacles against a piece of equipment to push them back up his nose.

From behind the mask his words were difficult to hear. As a newcomer to this theatre, Jessie Marvill, who was retracting, had difficulty identifying who was speaking. It would be overcome within two or three sessions by which time she would be used to the surgeons' speech patterns. Often there wasn't a great deal said in theatres, certainly not about the patient.

'We have got the right patient, I suppose?'

'I hope so,' Passmore said from the opposite side of the table, but glanced over at the list board where the operations were chalked up. 'Frederick Winner, 47. Cushing's syndrome.'

'What did the arteriogram show?' Mr Thompson asked. He pushed his glasses back and glanced at the X-rays on the viewer. 'Well that clearly suggests a tumour on the right gland and something on the left.'

'Cushing's syndrome resulting from a tumour of the adrenal gland was Dr Mathias's conclusion when he referred him,' Mr Passmore said. 'His blood pressure was very high. There's a loss of protein, general fatigue, adiposity; osteoporosis – he's had a series of fractures from very minor knocks over the past year.'

'How elevated is the cortical?' Mr Thompson asked, still exploring the glands with his fingers, feeling for the pea-sized tumour.

'Really very high.'

'Well I'm beginning to suspect we do have the wrong patient here. Unless he's had a miracle cure. Isn't there an SHO who dabbles in healing on Dr Mathias's firm?' he added drily. 'Phone Dr Mathias, he'd better take a look. Ask him if he could come directly,' he told the theatre runner. 'I don't want to close here and send him back.' That was a possible option, but not one he was considering at this stage.

He glanced at the clock on the wall: 9.27 A.M. He was getting behind.

'I have a meeting at eleven. These look clear to me,' Mr Thompson said again. 'But an adrenalectomy would solve a lot of his problems.'

'Wouldn't he need to be on drugs for the rest of his life?' Dr Willoughby asked.

'The alternative is for him to be on drugs to keep down the blood pressure. There won't be markedly more side effects with cortisone acetate,' Mr Thompson explained. He saw little in the choice, but favoured his way. 'Is it study leave you're going on,' he asked David Passmore, as they waited, 'or holiday?'

'A bit of both, I hope,' Passmore said. 'It's a micro-surgical course in Miami.'

'Is management paying for you?' Thompson asked, a note of surprise in his voice. Doctors in training posts, which was what all levels under consultant were, supposedly got study leave, but it was discretionary and often a battle to secure let alone have a course paid for. Although he never got such study leave himself, Marcus Thompson only slightly resented the fact that his senior registrar had somehow managed it.

'The air fare and hotel are paid.'

'What luxury!' was Thompson's response. 'Have to buy your own hamburgers. A decent hotel I hope?'

'The Hilton, I think.'

'Oh, that's acceptable. Food's relatively cheap in America.

You won't go broke eating out,' Thompson told him. 'I haven't been found a locum registrar yet, David.'

'I thought there was someone,' Passmore said, knowing a locum registrar had been put forward. 'A Nigerian.'

'He's not acceptable.' Thompson's tone invited no argument. 'I daresay we can keep the list manageable while you're away. But I think we're on-take two days that week, and the weekend.'

'I'm afraid I couldn't get any of the other firms to cover for us,' Passmore told him. 'I did try.'

'I'm sure. It's not your problem, David. The alternative is simple. They'll have to close casualty for our on-take, unless I'm found a suitable locum.'

There the matter was left. They went on to discuss the merits of the micro-surgery course; the weather in Miami; places to visit. This was a conversation that neither Jessie Marvill, the house officer nor any of the three students present took part in. Junior staff rarely conversed with the consultant in theatre, speaking mostly in response to questions or to ask questions.

'Dr Mathias isn't in the hospital today,' the runner said, when she returned from the office, which was adjacent to the theatre. 'Nor is his registrar available.'

'I see,' Mr Thompson said. 'Well his blood chemistry certainly suggests an adrenal tumour. So too do the arteriograms. I doubt that his problem has got up and walked away. I'll remove the right gland completely and part of the left. That'll cover all contingencies.'

He glanced at the clock then reached out to the scrub nurse, who placed artery forceps in his hand.

Lying on the trolley in the sterile pre-op area of the theatre, Ray Taylor was aware of his surroundings, of people moving around, their voices, but everything seemed one removed from him; he could reach out but not touch, hear but not understand, move his lips but not communicate.

Had he been able to he might have said how he didn't wish to go through with this after all. He had wanted to tell the staffnurse that when she had given him his pre-med injection, but the fear of being thought silly or unreasonable had prevented him. Being unable to articulate the instinct that told him to say no to all this, he simply kept quiet when the staffnurse on the ward had asked him if he was all right. He imagined he made some response when the sister here leaned over him from time to time. 'I'm fine, how are you?' he believed he said, but the words felt thick and he wasn't sure if they emerged.

Trevor Holland, a young theatre porter who had brought Ray Taylor off the ward an hour ago, sent two more patients on trolleys across the supposedly sterile transfer zone between the theatre complex and the connecting corridor.

'For goodness sake!' the sister said on seeing the congestion with four patients now waiting. 'Don't bring any more up. They'll be out in the corridor soon.'

'I have to bring them now, sister, if you want them ready. They need us to do the dinner trolleys today,' the porter said. 'They're short-staffed. 'S nearly eleven.'

'Well don't bring any more. I'll telephone through when we're ready for the next patient.'

Dr Crick put his head around the door frame, and seeing how stacked up they were his expectation of getting on the list faded.

'How's it going?' he asked.

'They're getting a mite behind, doctor.' The sister gave him a coping smile. 'I'm not sure we'll get through the whole list.'

'I'll look in later.' He left.

A nurse came out and said they were nearly ready for Mr Taylor. She told the patient too and the sister wheeled him into the anaesthetic room.

Mr Thompson had almost completed the adrenalectomy.

Mr Passmore would close for him; Jessie Marvill would be allowed to suture the skin over the wound, she would be criticized for taking more care than was necessary to close on the back of a middle-aged man. Dr Willoughby had gone into the surgeons' room to put the kettle on for coffee.

'Hello, Tom,' Dr Willoughby said, glancing up at a doctor who entered the surgeons' room, which was adjacent to the theatre.

Dr Tom Bielicki had come in by the door that led directly on to the corridor. This enabled surgeons and staff who were unsterile to come and go. The office was overcrowded and untidy; clothes belonging to the consultants were hung here; there were odds and ends of theatre garments and rubber boots belonging to consultants, which if left elsewhere would be worn by junior doctors. There were records of operation procedures and operating lists. On a side table was a kettle, a tube of plastic cups, sugar, milk, jar of instant coffee and biscuits.

'Looking for bits and pieces?' Dr Willoughby asked, as he waited for the kettle to boil. He had removed his operating gown but not his greens.

'You had an adrenalectomy. The gland would be useful for my research project.' Dr Tom Bielicki was an American bio-chemist doing research on cancer.

'I don't suppose anyone'll mind you having part of it,' he said, 'as it's in a good cause. I'll get it from the scrub room.'

'A gang of us going to Chelsea on Saturday,' Bielicki said.

'Chelsea! What for, mass leucotomy? It's all that will save them from relegation.' Willoughby laughed. 'Pop the water into those when the kettle boils,' he said, indicating the line of styrofoam cups as he went back into the theatre.

Glands such as those adrenals suspected of harbouring tumours were supposed not to be diverted to research but go to histology, there to be frozen and sliced wafer-thin on a bacon slicer and microscopically examined. In fact surgeons obliged researchers quite often as tissue and organs that had been hashed over and discarded elsewhere weren't of prime use.

Leaning over Ray Taylor in the anaesthetics room, where there were cupboards of drugs, dressings, hypodermics, rows of bottled gases, Dr Nick Alderton, the anaesthetics registrar said, 'Hello, Mr Taylor. How are you? Nice and drowsy?' He proffered a well-practised smile. 'That's the ticket. No problems here. Just a little prick to put you under. You'll wake up back on the ward most likely. What are the nurses like there? Pretty dishy?' Using an old-fashioned term. 'Just count to ten. Count to ten. That's the ticket. Well done . . .' He managed to get the needle into the right vein with ease.

Ray Taylor only counted to three in his slurred fashion. The anaesthetist, a man used to having one-sided conversations, went on talking for a while. He often didn't listen even when the patient was reasonably coherent. This made for some difficulties in his existence outside the theatre where people often had some expectation of being listened to.

Without finishing her coffee Dr Marvill went back into the theatre as Ray Taylor was brought in, though there was nothing for her to do. The staffnurse, who was alternating as scrubnurse with the theatre sister, was supervising getting him on to the table and in position. Jessie hadn't enjoyed either the coffee or the conversation that went with it in the surgeons' room, but that wasn't entirely her reason for coming back to theatre. She knew not why, but felt compassion for Mr Taylor, only tried shutting it out believing, as indeed they were taught as students, that emotions involving patients as people interfered with clinical judgement. Jessie Marvill wasn't sure about that, having met both extremes in her parents, but hadn't resisted the notion. She paused to explore the reason for this current feeling, which hadn't been entirely absent in dealings with other patients. Perhaps it was Ray Taylor's fear, or the medical deception; his sense of helplessness, or maybe the fact that he was her first identifiable patient in this post. Without pursuing that line of thought further, she returned to the surgeons' room.

Coffee was available here for doctors only. Nurses had their own restroom. In her previous hospital the arrangement had been less formal. Then that hadn't been a teaching District.

'Joan, could you ring the committee and tell them I'm on my way?' Mr Thompson was saying into the phone. 'Oh, about ten minutes. Is there any progress with my locum registrar? . . . I see. No, I told them the black isn't acceptable. I'll call administration myself. Thanks.' He put the phone down. He was dresssed now. His theatre greens were left on the floor. 'The rest of the list is yours, David. I'll see you before you depart for America.'

'I'll be here till Friday,' Passmore said.

'My secretary knows where to get me.' He swallowed the last of his coffee. 'I suppose those adrenals had better go to histology. They might give us the answer.'

'I think they've gone.' That was what Dr Marvill believed had happened.

Dr Willoughby stared into his coffee cup.

'Perhaps you could try one of the other firms again, David,' Thompson said as a last ditch thought. 'See if they could provide surgical cover while you're away.'

'I'll try, if a suitable locum isn't found by Friday,' Passmore replied.

'The alternative is to stop surgical admissions,' he said. 'Yes, it's a simple matter.' He put on his jacket and departed.

'How's he looking, Nick?' Mr Passmore asked the anaesthetist, who was attending the patient in theatre.

There appeared to be more activity around the operating

table than there in fact was. Ray Taylor's position was being corrected. The scrub nurse was still laying out sterile instruments. Those from the previous op were now being washed and sterilized. The three students were standing around chatting, disinterested.

'Are any of you scrubbing?' Passmore said as he pulled on his gown, which he removed from a sterile pack. The theatre runner followed him to the table, doing up the strings behind him.

One of the students responded and went to scrub up.

'His blood pressure's up a bit high,' the anaesthetist told him.

'Yes, he was somewhat anxious, this one, wasn't he Jessie.'

Dr Marvill went to the table, fully scrubbed. She didn't respond, as if to do so might somehow commit her further.

Mr Passmore inserted his right hand into a rubber glove, hooked the rim of the opening over his thumb, tightened the cuff of his gown then pulled the glove over it. Then he did the same with the left.

'The torch,' he said, and was given the small torch by the scrub nurse. 'Let's see just what we have here now.'

He shone the light down the patient's throat and pushed in a spatula to look around while Dr Marvill held his tongue clear. It had been enwrapped with gauze to enable her to grip it.

'Oh dear,' Passmore said. 'No wonder the poor chap had difficulty breathing. I can see the problem clearly. It looks like invasive carcinoma.' He decided his course of action directly. 'I'll see what I can do about that. I'll need to do some biopsies. I'll want about half an hour, Nick,' he told the anaesthetist.

This surgeon could usually estimate how long he would need for a given procedure. If both he and the anaesthetist got it right the patient would start to come round in the recovery room only minutes after the operation.

'Would you like to look,' Mr Passmore said to Dr Marvill.

She experienced a sinking feeling as she looked into Taylor's throat and saw how advanced the carcinoma was. Jessie Marvill remembered the reassurances she had given this patient when getting him to sign the consent form. Even though she pointed out that his signature effectively gave them the right to tackle anything related to the operation which they believed to be in his best interest, that possibility hadn't been the impression he had been left with. In an instant she saw what she knew to be this patient's prognosis, and suddenly had serious doubts about the course they were now embarking upon.

11

Three days had passed without the problem of the painters in the kitchen being resolved, and it didn't look like it would be other than by them finishing the job. Chris Hogan, the union branch secretary, had no faith in management's expressed intention of finding a solution, and was growing more angry with each new complaint he received from the kitchen staff.

When he arrived at the general administrator's office Hogan was ready for a row.

''S he in, is he?' he said to one of the secretaries.

The woman immediately got into a flap. She had been stalling Mr Hogan, but could no longer keep him away from her boss. She looked round at Roy Needham's door, expecting him to appear at any moment. 'Well he's on his way to a meeting . . .' she said as the door opened and Needham emerged.

'Can you spare a minute, Mr Needham?' Hogan said. 'You know what it's about.'

'Yes, I know the difficulties . . .' he began flabbily.

'You'll have us on a promise till we all retire.'

'I'm not ignoring the problems in the kitchen.'

'The working conditions there are even worse now them ceilings have to come down,' Hogan argued.

Needham nodded, realizing his stonewalling was no longer working and that he would have to change tack. 'I know it's unsatisfactory . . . Is it a question of money?' he said, cutting through the verbal shadow boxing.

That stopped Hogan momentarily. 'Some kind of bonus for kitchen staff would help.' He never passed up any opportunity of more money for the membership.

'I'll be frank, Chris, we can't afford a ghoster. Especially not now they've got to put in a new ceiling.'

The maintenance budget which was managed by the District works manager and not handled at St Clair's, was already over its projected estimate as a result of the Health and Safety Executive insisting that all asbestos lagging be removed from hot water pipes in the underground passageways. That job wasn't yet halfway completed.

'Excuse me, Mr Needham,' Val Kay said, looking into the room. 'Were you coming to the site meeting on Valentine Ward?'

'I'm not keen. I just wanted to find out what Mr Montagu was up to,' Needham said. He was puzzled by the consultant gynaecologist's interest in the closed wards. But one thing was certain there would be a purpose behind his interest. 'Christ knows why he wants to attend. Unless he's hoping to get those upgraded wards for gynaecology. Ring him, Val. Remind him about the meeting.'

'What about them closed wards on Nightingale block?' Hogan said after Val Kay departed. 'When they coming back into service?'

'I wish I could say. Unless we're able to recruit more nursing staff we won't be able to maintain the present service.' That was a matter of deep concern to Roy Needham. As an administrator his function was to keep the hospital both operational and efficient, so it went against the grain when he had to close one service in order to maintain another which the District Management Team determined more important. He regretted that money was taken out of the health service, which he believed was under-financed in the first place, but that didn't prevent him doing the job he had to do as well as he could, even when it meant closing wards. He knew that if he didn't do it, then the District Administrator would, and Needham believed he could achieve those measures more tactfully.

'We keep hearing rumours about Nightingale closing

altogether,' Hogan said.

'I don't think the DMT would be pursuing an upgrading policy if that was so,' Needham said as if the practice must inevitably follow the logic of that statement. Nothing was further from the truth, but Hogan conceded the point nonetheless. It was what he wanted to believe.

'If the CHC agrees, hopefully three of the wards will become a psycho-geriatric unit. But it's early days.'

The Community Health Council, whose purpose was to act as a watchdog over local health care, was always consulted by the District Management Team before major changes in the service or building use were implemented. Sometimes it failed to act on the recommendations of the CHC, but never ignored it.

'Well we won't stand by and let the block close.'

'If you've any suggestions about how to get money for more nursing and ancillary staff, we'd like to hear them. Meanwhile we're living with the cuts.'

'That still leaves this problem of the kitchens. I mean, you've had long enough to sort it. I'll have to take the grievance to Mr Morwell at District.'

'We will sort something out, Chris. Even if it's only a bonus for kitchen staff, we'll find it somehow. Please leave it with me a while longer.'

Chris Hogan considered the man, whom he had known fourteen years, ever since starting at St Clair's as a porter. He trusted him more than most, but not entirely, on account of his being management, whose aims didn't always accord with the interests of his members. One area where he didn't entirely trust Roy Needham was over the question of Nightingale Block, partly because that wasn't something he had within his control. He would have to keep a close watch for developments, and be ready to take action, in case temporary closure of some wards slid casually into the permanent closure of the entire block, which could put some of his members out of work.

Valentine Ward on Nightingale Block was one of the Florence Nightingale type wards, open-plan with twenty beds, most of which had the old iron frames. This was M2, a women's medical ward where the average age was seventy-two. A lot of these women should have been in acute geriatric beds, the reason they weren't was due partly to the fact that some physicians, being no less possessive about patients than other consultants, resisted going outside their own specialty and calling in the geriatricians; however, a large part of the problem was the shortage of acute geriatric beds, which was compounded by the reluctance of some geriatricians to take on potentially long-stay, bed-blocking patients. So here a lot of them stayed, often resented by frustrated staff who could do little for them.

Sitting on the bed of one such patient was Dr Laurence James, a thirty-nine-year-old medical SHO, doing GP vocational training. He was a late starter, having trained as a physiologist initially rather than a doctor, only to find that in order to function effectively in his chosen field of alternative medicine, he needed the MRCP credentials. He was Welsh, and a bit unkempt; one consultant described his manner as unprofessional, but what he meant was that the doctor wasn't as distanced from his patients as most felt comfortable with. No one said anything to Dr James about his conduct, which might otherwise generally be disapproved of, mainly because he took time and trouble with patients most had given up on; but that in itself sometimes caused problems, making colleagues feel guilty.

'I haven't been taking my tablets, doctor,' the woman confided as if in the confessional. 'Not for three days now, I haven't.'

'Was your pain any worse?' he asked, holding her swollen hands. He had told her she could stop taking the drugs that had been prescribed for maturity onset diabetes, and those to counteract renal impairment and adrenocortical dysfunction which had resulted from the treatment for rheumatoid arthritis.

'It's still there. But it's not worse.'

He nodded. 'Take the painkillers if you need to, lovely. What do you feel now?'

A smile settled over her wrinkled face. 'There's a warm, tingly sensation going up my arms.'

'Why do you think that is, Mrs Draper?'

'Well now, that's the secret, doctor, isn't it,' she whispered. 'That's the secret.'

His smile was warm and engaging, his vivid brown eyes once encountered weren't easily avoided. 'You've started caring about yourself. You've decided you want to be well.'

His attention stayed entirely with his patient, and he was unaware of the site meeting that was taking place on the ward.

'These wards ought to be put into single-bedded units when they're upgraded,' Mr Philip Montagu, the gynaecologist, said as he came along the ward with Val Kay.

With them was Frank Badham, Sandra Flockhart who was the Medical Unit Nursing Officer, the Regional architect, and the District works manager.

'It makes no sense putting them back into this arrangement. It's time we treated patients in the NHS in the same way we treat private patients,' Montagu continued with no sense of irony. Although only in his mid-forties he was one of the most senior consultants at St Clair's, which said a lot about his ambition. He was immaculately attired, making people seem garish or tawdry by comparison.

'I'm not sure Region would agree to that,' Val Kay said, trying to establish her authority in chairing this meeting.

'Would single units be cost-prohibitive?' Montagu asked the Regional architect.

'They would certainly cost more than the £270,000 provisionally allocated,' the architect said. 'It might not be impossibly expensive, depending on the units envisaged.

But more important it would reduce bed density.'

'You might need to increase the nursing staff,' the nursing officer said quietly, in deference to the consultant.

'With fewer beds,' Mr Montagu argued, 'it'll even itself out.'

'Single units make nursing more difficult.'

Montagu was undeterred. 'We should plan for the future, not constantly take palliative measures.'

'There has been some discussion with Region about a Capital Scheme to build on bathroom annexes,' Val Kay said.

'Which would mean wards closing again,' the consultant said, allowing a note of intolerance into his voice. 'What's required is pressure on Region by the consultants.'

None of the others could comment about that, for in such matters consultants were supreme. They would decide unilaterally on policy within the Medical Committee then doggedly pursue it. That would be the next move in his tactical game for control of this block. Montagu had no doubts as to the outcome.

'Thank you for your time,' he said abruptly ending his involvement in the meeting. He wheeled away and out.

Confident in his ability to get on with everyone from the most influential consultant to the lowest grade health service employee, Roy Needham recognized that most of his man-management difficulties came from consultants. Usually centring around ambitions to carve personal empires from limited resources.

Today the problem brought him by the medical staffing officer arose out of Mr Marcus Thompson's overt racism. Needham wasn't about to point this out when he called to see the surgeon in his office to argue for the only locum registrar who was available.

'There's no fucking way I'm accepting a spear-throwing-wallah as a locum registrar,' Mr Thompson said angrily at the suggestion that he'd have to take the Nigerian. 'If you can't get one of the other fucking firms to cover surgical on-take, close the fucking hospital.'

'I've no cause, Marcus,' Needham stated. 'Mr Chanaga's a fully-qualified surgical registrar, and he's available. I know he was trained in Russia, that's unusual, but he does have the FRCS, after all. What's more he's prepared to do the job.'

'It's out of the fucking question, him coming on to my firm, even for a week.'

'But why?' the administrator wanted to know.

Marcus Thompson considered this then thought better of saying what was on his mind. 'He's unacceptable.'

Exasperated, but keeping his temper, Needham said, 'I'll have to refer it to District.'

This wasn't a matter that could be delayed on, hoping it would resolve itself. Contractually the hospital had to supply the consultant with a suitable registrar; if they didn't and something went wrong while the firm was carrying out its normal function then the hospital would be liable.

'Did he actually call him a spear-carrying-wallah?' Stephen Morwell, the District administrator sounded surprised when Needham rang him in his comfortable office.

'Those were his words,' Needham confirmed. 'Mind you, Marcus thinks anyone who's a darker shade than pink is a spear-carrying-wallah.'

'That might prove embarrassing. Won't one of the other firms cover for him?' Morwell inquired.

'Absolute refusal from all three consultants. They'll only cover if he's suspended. For the life of me I can't say why they're taking this line. Maybe they object to his white supremacy line.'

'Their firms aren't exactly crammed with third-world doctors,' Morwell observed. 'I'd better try reasoning with him. If he won't budge the Chairman will have to wave the big stick.'

Mr Marcus Thompson continued to resist the Nigerian registrar, making it necessary for Dr Clarence Vine, the Chairman of the District Health Authority, to get involved. Mr Marcus Thompson denied that his refusing Chanaga as his locum registrar was based on racial prejudice.

'However you look at it, Marcus, it's going to be interpreted as racism,' Dr Vine said.

'I can't help that. The man hasn't sufficient experience for my firm,' Mr Thompson said.

'He seems well enough qualified.'

'Qualifications mean little compared with experience.'

Unsure of his next step, never having matched brinkmanship with a consultant in quite the same circumstances, Vine said, 'The position is this, Marcus, unless you accept him as your locum registrar, I'll have to suspend you in order to provide cover for St Clair's.'

'I might welcome suspension, Clarence. It would give me an opportunity to get on with my book,' Thompson said. He had been contracted to deliver a book on surgical resection for major malignancies, and was behind schedule with it, partly because he hadn't got enough material; but a week's solid work on it would take it forward considerably. However he knew suspension might damage his reputation, so decided to compromise. 'If there really is no one else available for the whole period, I'll accept Chanaga for weekend cover. But for the rest of the week I want another locum registrar. Or five if necessary.'

'I think something along those lines might be organized, Marcus,' Dr Clarence Vine said, feeling himself set free.

He had won a minor battle; the war, as he saw it, was looming on the horizon in the shape of the policy being formulated at District as a means of saving money. The plan was to stop employing locums to replace junior doctors who were away. They expected a lot of objections from the junior doctors' committee, but if the general medical committee, comprising all the consultants, supported the junior doctors that might be the end of it. The District Chairman was glad this matter was resolved, and without Marcus Thompson losing face, as they were going to need all the consultant support they could get.

12

Jessie Marvill was startled awake by her bleep, which she instinctively reached out and touched. She was not only surprised at finding herself asleep, but especially for the fact that Roger Trentham was curled on the narrow bed next to her. It took her a few seconds to realize where she was and what was happening. She remembered that Roger had called round at the hospital to see her to talk about a job he had been offered in Australia – he wouldn't take it and wanted her to confirm that he shouldn't. They had had an indifferent meal in the doctors' social club. Although they had been separated just over a week Jessie Marvill had found herself offering little resistance to his suggestion that he went to her room with her. That pattern would be repeated for a long while, even though she told herself that she didn't want this relationship to continue, and would eventually lead her to psycho-therapy to try and sort through the emotional chaos in her life.

'It's all right,' she said to Roger as he stirred at the second signal from her bleep, 'it's for me.'

She dialled the night operator and was asked to phone S1. There the charge nurse wanted her to look at a patient who was vomiting.

After washing and dressing Jessie Marvill didn't kiss her ex-boyfriend goodbye nor did she say anything but she was aware of him watching her leave. She simply regretted her weakness.

'How long has he been like this?' Dr Marvill asked at the bed of the patient on the men's surgical ward.

'He started vomiting an hour ago.' The male staffnurse was large and black and soft-spoken, and articulated precisely.

'Nurse,' came a moan from another patient.

'Has there been any diarrhoea?' Dr Marvill said.

'Yes, there has.'

'He's very hot. What's he having done?' she asked, glancing over the chart. He was Mr Smith-Sampson's patient.

'He has a gangrenous toe.' He eased the bedclothes off the frame to reveal the blackened toe and foot, which was wet and smelly.

'That doesn't look very good,' Dr Marvill observed.

'It was dry when he came in a week ago,' he said, 'so Mr Smith-Sampson decided to wait for it to drop off. It's spreading. Is that the problem, doctor?'

'I wouldn't have thought so,' she said. This wouldn't have been her way of treating a gangrenous toe, but she had to assume Mr Smith-Sampson knew what he was doing. 'I'll give him something for the vomiting. Someone can see him in the morning.' She removed the thermometer from his mouth. It read a hundred and one. 'He'd better have something for that as well.'

In the bed opposite Ray Taylor's recovery was slow after the biopsies and the removal of what proved to be a malignancy from the back of his throat. It was almost as if his body could no longer deny the presence of disease following the operation.

Jessie Marvill stopped at the side of the sleeping Mr Taylor's bed, and watched the shallow movement of his chest. Neither that, nor the nasogastric tube up his left nostril indicated the extent of his problem. Both his condition, resulting from the local spread of the carcinoma and the course he was now embarked upon increased the dilemma she felt more and more over the high level of paternalism in medicine. She favoured a more open approach, one where patients were told their problem, with a suggestion of how it might be put right; if it couldn't be put right, told that also. The process of involving patients in their illness needn't have been brutal, and wasn't necessarily harmful to them, or their families, some of whom became patients themselves as a result of the initial illness.

The sort of medicine where doctors pretended that everything was all right, that patients shouldn't worry about things they didn't wish them to understand, that left to the clinicians would be resolved, was dishonest Jessie Marvill felt, but nevertheless found herself practising it. Both the consultant and senior registrar knew what was wrong with Mr Taylor, but neither had discussed it with him or allowed him to get involved in the limited choices. Nor would she now.

'How has he been?' she asked the student nurse who was at the next bed.

'He was conscious when his wife came in earlier this evening,' the student nurse said, as if finding it necessary to evade the issue.

Dr Marvill didn't comment, but moved on to the office. She wrote up the drugs for the patient she had been called to, an anti-emetic, antidiarrhoeals, and antibiotic, but felt slight unease. Although his symptoms suggested food poisoning, there was a chance the condition was due to that gangrenous foot. She wondered about calling Dr Davis, the registrar, but didn't know him or know whether he would object to being called out at night.

'There's another patient started now,' the staffnurse said, returning to the office.

Dr Marvill looked relieved. It was D and V after all and nothing more serious to contend with, such as post-operative shock. 'I'll have a look at him in a minute. I think you'd better ring the duty nursing officer, you're going to need help,' she said, and went to see the second vomiting patient, while the staffnurse went to get the drugs.

The morning brought a number of D and V cases,

including some staff members. Food poisoning was suspected.

This caused problems for Brian Rickard and his nursing officers as they had to cope both with the extra nursing this involved and the shortage of staff alongside existing understaffing.

The medical unit nursing officer, Sandra Flockhart, moved briskly along the corridor and turned into Brian Rickard's office, rapping the door as she entered.

Brian Rickard, who was a big, energetic man in his forties, was under pressure now. 'Give me the bad news, Sandra,' he said, flapping his hands nervously.

'Four of the eleven suspected cases are confirmed,' she informed him. 'Jackson, Robertson and Chandak have been taken ill on the wards this morning. Plus four of the learners: Cray, Donaldson, Vaughan and Wung.' She always used the nurses' surnames.

'This is terrible,' Rickard said. 'If we lose any more we'll have to shut another ward.'

'We might well have to stop admissions.'

'I'll see if I can scrounge a few agency nurses, Sandra,' he said. Then anticipating her disapproval, added, 'We'll be lucky to get anyone at such short notice. Have they identified the source?'

'The lab's taking swabs now,' Flockhart said.

'We could all go down with it,' he said with alarm.

'I'd better see the secretary.' He meant the administrator, but was brought up with the old style management and refused to make those mental changes. He didn't mind at all when he was called matron, as he sometimes was.

The kitchen was the obvious source for any outbreak of food poisoning, and the kitchen at St Clair's was even more suspect for recently having had painters in.

But both the painters and plasterers, who had remade the ceiling, were now gone, leaving the place looking very smart; the equipment looked good too, and the floor.

Amidst the bustle of lunch preparation a pathology lab technician was taking swabs with cotton buds, which he popped into test tubes held in a rack. Because of the effort that had gone into cleaning the kitchen with the decorators' departure, he had to search the cracks and corners of work surfaces, and crevices of the floor. The chefs and staff purposely took no notice, and dismissed the idea of their kitchen being contaminated. As if to prove this they picked at the food they were preparing; some made themselves bacon rolls. Most of them ate their meals this way, and each of them had two pounds fifty a week deducted from their wages for the privilege.

Roy Needham came in with Brian Rickard and the catering manager, and wandered through, admiring the spotlessness, as if their comments would impress the lab technician.

'Any sign of the cause, Terry?' Needham asked. He made a point of knowing first names.

'At a guess,' Terry Guildman, the lab technician, said, 'the painters were a likely source.'

'The utmost care was taken when they were here,' Felix Greene assured him pointlessly.

'It's not certain all my nurses stricken with the bug ate food from this kitchen,' Rickard said.

'Have you checked that, Brian?'

'Sandra Flockhart is doing so now.'

'It could have been that chicken on the menu yesterday,' Guildman suggested without smiling. 'It looked a bit ropey.'

'That chicken was perfect,' the catering supervisor said defensively. Peter Clearless took this personally.

'It had probably been dead three weeks, Peter,' Guildman joked. 'We'll know better when we've identified the bacteria.'

'Well, let's have your findings as soon as you can,' Needham said. His visit was showing the flag. 'Do you want anything shut down?'

'I'll get these swabs tested first,' Guildman said not wishing to disrupt anything more than necessary. As a result of identifying meat-bound bacteria in his job he had become a vegetarian, and at times like these he was glad.

Meanwhile Roy Needham had to contend with another problem looming large; one to be avoided at all costs, except when there was a danger to patients' lives – closing the hospital. But it looked as though he couldn't avoid it this time.

13

An ambulance, with light flashing and klaxon wailing, swung through the open gates of St Clair's, the driver braking and throwing the switches to cut both light and bell as the vehicle glided across the forecourt to the casualty department. The urgency the ambulance attendants showed in bringing the patient in suddenly disappeared as it sometimes did when the patient died on them. This one hadn't died. The reason for their response was that no assistance was forthcoming from the A and E department.

'A bit of help would be handy, Staff,' the driver said when he found the staffnurse on her own in the deserted department. 'We got a CVA here.'

'Casualty's closed,' she informed him.

'It's an emergency admission, Staff,' the ambulance driver said, not listening to her problem, but returning to help his colleague with the stretcher trolley.

The staffnurse came out to them.

'We're not taking admissions,' she said. 'He'll have to go to the Branston.'

'No one's bloody well told us. That's typical!' The driver felt outraged, a sense of impotence, knowing that if this patient wasn't treated soon it would be too late. There was no time to take him to another hospital.

'We've an outbreak of food poisoning,' the staffnurse said.

'He'll have to come here,' the ambulance attendant said, jiggling the trolley past the staffnurse into the department, as if that were the answer. 'You can't leave the poor sod to die.'

The staffnurse checked the blue-looking stroke patient,

who seemed to be having heart and respiratory difficulty too. She hurried into the office, suddenly caught up in the emergency.

'Could you find the casualty officer,' the staffnurse said when she dialled the switchboard operator. Casualty officers rarely carried bleeps. 'Inform the medical nursing officer that we've had a CVA sent here.' She didn't want to ring the woman herself, but replaced the phone and went quickly along to the treatment room.

'You on your own?' the driver asked as he helped lift the patient on to the couch.

The staffnurse brought in the oxygen trolley and placed the mask over the patient's face. 'I'm not sure he's getting this,' she said after a moment.

'This is no way to run a bloody hospital.' The ambulance driver's sense of frustration was increasing.

The staffnurse searched for the patient's pulse. 'I am trying,' she snapped, feeling pressured now that the patient was her responsibility. Pulling his eyelids back, she checked for pupillary response with a torch. 'I think he's arrested. Get the boards under him.'

The patient was a large man, and it took a lot of effort to lift him and slide boards under his back for support when giving cardiac massage.

Staffnurse Wildwood hurried from the treatment room to the nearest telephone and dialled treble-2, the crash-call number, which took priority on the switchboard. 'Cardiac arrest!' she said, and stated where; then on a calmer note, having found the means of sharing her burden, 'Thank you.'

Two men in overalls wandered in off the street, one with a roughly bandaged hand. Even though the decision had been made to close the A and E department – the ambulance having arrived due to a breakdown in communications – it remained open to walking casualties.

'Nurse,' one of the men said. 'He's had an accident.'

'I'm sorry, I can't attend to you now. Have a seat.'

'He's done his finger – he's cut it off.' He proffered the severed digit wrapped in a handkerchief.

Seeing at once that it was more of an emergency than she could deal with, she said, 'Try the Branston.'

'Cor, fucking nice in' it. That's fucking nice, 's what we pay our fucking taxes for,' he protested on behalf of his injured workmate.

'I'm sorry,' Staffnurse Wildwood apologized, backing away.

'That's t'rific. Get a seat, John, they gotta see you.'

A Singapore doctor came through the department, he was Dr Sim Kum, the casualty officer. He carried his white coat and stethoscope, as if not expecting to work.

'I thought we not taking admissions,' he said, seeing the ambulance outside.

'He's done his finger,' the workman informed him.

'We've a CVA who's arrested.' The staffnurse competed for his attention.

'Yes.' Dr Kum was confused. 'You call the arrest team? I be with you in minute,' he told the workmen and followed the staffnurse. She went for the arrest trolley, while he went into the treatment room.

A cardiac arrest was dealt with by the cardiac arrest team who through practice got to be very adept at their job. Unless they were all under the mistaken impression that one of the others would respond and so didn't themselves, they would arrive shortly, but meanwhile Dr Kum felt obliged to examine the patient and see what might be done.

Mr Marcus Thompson's small office at St Clair's, with furnishings that didn't extend beyond the utilitarian, reflected his attitude: a man's worth being in his ability, his reputation based on that skill, not the possessions he surrounded himself with. This office might have been anyone's rather than his exclusively. Other consultants along the block filled theirs with personal mementoes to complement the permanence of tenure that they had. Here there was a grey-painted steel bookcase half full of books; a white coat hanging on the desk, a diary, nothing more.

He rarely saw patients in this office, sometimes he saw relatives of patients here when having something unpleasant to tell them, like Mrs Taylor, who waited tensely on the edge of the chair while the surgeon spoke on the telephone. More often Mr Thompson saw relatives after his outpatients clinic.

'. . . I can't speak for other consultants,' Marcus Thompson was saying, 'but I can tell you the position with my surgical beds. There isn't anything spare.'

'Couldn't you discharge someone?' Val Kay almost pleaded down the phone. She was trying to find space for the stroke patient who had inadvertently been admitted, and had already been told the position by the senior registrar.

'You may as well put the CVA back on the street. Who am I to make value judgements?' he said ironically. 'If I had a space, my dear, you'd be welcome to it. I suggest you badger the medical firms. It is a medical problem after all.' That was his final word. He could possibly have created space, but wasn't about to help in this way while management were closing beds. He put the phone down, and turned to the woman opposite the desk. 'Sorry about that, Mrs Taylor.'

There was a rap at the door and his secretary brought in coffee. Although he didn't wish to extend this meeting longer than necessary, coffee was a diversion.

'Thank you, Joan. Could you not put any more calls through.'

'Sorry about that,' the secretary said. 'Mrs Kay was most insistent.'

Mr Thompson rose as his secretary went out. 'You take sugar or milk, Mrs . . . ?'

'Yes, thank you . . . Thank you,' she said when he passed her the coffee.

Mr Thompson sat again and waited for her to feel her way through the initial onslaught of the information he had given about her husband. She had no notion of what the problem had been. That was frequently the case, and even after having the information spelled out some patients and their relatives still managed to block it from consciousness. Generally he favoured not telling patients everything but in some cases it was necessary to do so if he was to proceed with such radical treatment as he believed was needed to save Taylor's life. He felt this woman would be able to cope with what he was telling her, women usually did better than men.

'It's strange,' she said into her coffee cup, 'you never suspect anything like this will happen to you. He never dreamed it might be that other business,' – avoiding the word cancer. 'Least he never said. He was fine before he came in, didn't seem very much wrong with him.' She was confused and looking for a harbour of hurt to anchor herself in, but the substance of her belief was that. 'He had that trouble with his throat, and had lost weight, but nothing serious. He always got enough exercise. I mean, he gardens, goes to football. I suppose that's not exercise really, is it? He'd only asked for a week off work for this. We didn't suspect anything, I mean you don't, do you?' She was having a struggle to keep the tears back as she started considering the alternatives. 'It seems like he could've gone on, not letting it bother him. Look if he hadn't had this operation he might never have known. He wasn't even sure about coming to see you in the first place. I said he should, I persuaded him it was best . . .'

'I know this is difficult to come to terms with, Mrs Taylor,' Thompson said. 'But the growth was there. It could only get worse.'

'Oh, if only he'd come here twelve months ago, instead of waiting all this time. I begged him to ask his doctor about seeing a specialist,' she said, feeling angry, mostly with herself, and therefore a need to justify her position.

'It's a great pity we didn't see him sooner,' the surgeon conceded. Surgical procedures for carcinoma of the head and neck could be effective if caught early, and the patient was able to live with the result. However by their nature detection usually didn't occur until quite late on.

'I begged, I begged him to come in for a check-up,' Mrs Taylor said, then fell silent for a moment. 'Will he get better, doctor?'

'That depends what you call better, Mrs Taylor. There's a reasonable chance he will recover from the growth Mr Passmore removed,' Mr Thompson informed her, not untruthfully. 'But we're awaiting the result of the biopsies to see if further surgery is advised. I think I should warn you that it is likely that local spread will almost certainly have occurred in the jaw and tongue by this stage.'

'I still can't take it in. When I came in the other day and saw how ill he looked after the operation, I knew something was seriously wrong. I still didn't suspect what it was. You don't, do you?' she said. 'We were going to Majorca for a holiday next week.'

'That'll do you both good. It means putting it back a little while,' he said cheerfully, as though that could still be a prospect for the immediate future.

'I'm not sure they'll give us a refund,' she said almost to herself, turning inward with her distress. 'I suppose we have insurance cover for that sort of thing . . .'

She was avoiding the truth. She didn't want to know any more, and Mr Thompson didn't press the matter. Curiously he felt some sense of relief that the patient's wife was dealing with the problem in this way.

The other general surgical firm wasn't without its problems. These were mostly a result of the poor relationship between Mr Ronald Smith-Sampson and his registrar, Dr Vernon Davis. Their relationship had rapidly deteriorated when

Davis discovered how incompetent his boss was. That was soon after joining the firm, when he found he was spending as much time putting right the consultant's mistakes as he was operating on his own list. But the situation reached its lowest ebb the previous week when against all advice Smith-Sampson had performed a pneumonectomy on a patient with carcinoma of the right lung. Not surprisingly the woman had died, as had been indicated by her lung function tests. The two surgeons had rowed openly. The animosity between them was common knowledge, yet curiously neither could do without the other. Mr Smith-Sampson, although he would never admit it, needed Vernon Davis to go on tidying up for him, often after simple procedures like the circumcision he had done two days ago on a seven-year-old. Vernon Davis had had to re-do it the next day because the lad had been sewn up too tightly. For his part Davis couldn't leave the consultant not only because he couldn't readily get another job if he broke his contract – he certainly wouldn't without a reference – and Smith-Sampson had more than once threatened him over that. But the situation was deteriorating so much that Davis was considering life without either a reference or a job, as the alternative seemed certain to be a nervous breakdown. He was convinced that that was what Smith-Sampson hoped would happen, while his hope was that he might just outlast his boss, who had about a year before retirement at sixty-five. The prospect that this surgeon could continue making the sort of mistakes he was making for another year troubled Vernon Davis, and despite the advice of colleagues not to make a complaint against his boss, that was what he was wrestling with. Their advice was well-intentioned, but he knew it mostly related to the requirements of the career structure, whereas he was being moved out of concern for his patients.

It was almost a calculated insult, Vernon Davis thought, that his boss should have a teaching ward round one afternoon a week. As Mr Smith-Sampson moved out of a female bay on the modern surgical ward and on to a male bay next door six students from the undergraduate medical school at Queen's Hospital followed him. Also on the ward round was their SHO, Dr Arif, the ward sister, a nurse and a social worker. A dozen people was a formidable crowd to arrive at a patient's bed, and no less daunting for the student who had to step forward and present the patient.

Stopping at a bed where a man in his fifties was propped on pillows and looking quite ill, Mr Smith-Sampson asked, 'Which of you clerked this case?'

A space was made for a student, who came forward clearing his throat. He seemed about thirteen and, like each of his equally young-looking fellow students, he had been given a patient to present.

'Well, tell me about this patient,' Smith-Sampson said, not unkindly.

'This is Mr Jasewicz, sir,' the student began. 'He's a Polish Jew. He lives in the highrise block half a mile from this hospital. He lost his wife two years ago. She had breast cancer. They were very close . . .'

At this point Mr Smith-Sampson signalled irritably for the student to stop, and rounded on Dr Davis. 'Why on earth don't you teach these students to present a patient properly? It's both pointless and time wasting when they come out with this woolly nonsense.'

Vernon Davis froze, and briefly considered defending such information as being relevant and relating to what he taught students about the patient-doctor relationship. He always told students never to treat patients as anything less than human, and to find out as much about them as possible. In practice he knew that would be lost, but it was a good principle.

'Dr Arif?' Mr Smith-Sampson said, turning to the SHO, when it became obvious Dr Davis wasn't going to give an argument.

The student shuffled back in shame as the house officer said, 'This patient had a carcinoma of the colon, operated on five days ago. We have the barium enema pictures here.' He reached round as the sister extended the X-rays.

Dr Davis caught the student's eye, but didn't smile.

Although not arising directly out of this incident, but partly because of it, he knew what action he had to take regardless of consequences. Probably his career wouldn't progress far anyway on account of his activities on the junior doctors' medical committee.

Crossing the area of balding grass with Dr Arif, the following morning, on their way to the medical centre, Vernon Davis, who was thin, and intense-looking, saw the newish Renault 20 driven by Dr Ralph Mathias pass them. He was a physician, and the most senior consultant in the hospital. He was therefore one of the Three Wise Men.

As the car slid into its reserved parking space and Mathias got out, Vernon Davis answered the impulse he felt, and leaving his colleague, lengthened his stride to catch Dr Mathias. It was better that he spoke to him casually rather than formally requesting a meeting.

'Dr Mathias! Could you spare a moment?'

'Morning, Davis,' the consultant said, looking him over. He knew his reputation and didn't like it much, believing that junior doctors should keep to medicine and avoid politics. 'Is it important?'

Davis twitched with indecision, now on the point of this drastic action, and then plunged in. He said, 'I wish to make a complaint about a consultant, sir.'

'Which consultant?'

'Mr Smith-Sampson,' Davis said.

'I see. Have you approached him yourself? I always think it best if one can avoid this sort of unpleasantness.'

'I've tried. He dismisses me out of hand.'

He felt anxious and found his mouth dry, he was unable to moisten it as the consultant considered him.

‘What is the complaint?’ Dr Mathias wanted to know.

‘I’m questioning some of his procedures which I don’t think are in the patients’ best interest.’ Davis found that difficult.

‘You believe he’s incompetent? Have you thought this through carefully? Considered the consequences?’ It was a veiled threat, but Mathias knew what it could mean to Davis’s career, and if for no other reason knew the surgeon would have thought it through. On seeing that Davis wasn’t about to withdraw Dr Mathias had no option but to accept the complaint, unpleasant as he found hearing anything against colleagues. He looked at his watch. This was something best not put off. ‘You’d better come to my office.’

Mathias moved off, expecting Vernon Davis to follow. The registrar hesitated, wondering if this was the right move. He wasn’t sure, but knew there was no going back.

14

The lunch period, which stretched from 11.45 to 2.15, was the busiest period in the medical centre at St Clair's. Doctors came to lunch and left. Some came and read, others caught up with sleep. None stayed for the full lunch period, that was a luxury only afforded consultants, but few indulged it.

There were about two dozen junior doctors in the sitting room, most of them straight from the wards. The decibel level of the animated conversation, all of it about medicine or medical politics, was high, and although at least two-thirds of the doctors present were Asian or African no language other than the medically recognized English was used. It was as if to do so meant loss of status.

There was an uneasy atmosphere surrounding Vernon Davis's group, Jessie Marvill noticed as she joined it from the dining-room, bringing with her a Picnic bar and a cup of tea. She knew at once that it was because of the complaint Dr Davis had made, although no one was talking about it. There was a rumour that the Three Wise Men were sitting today. Perhaps it might have been better if they did discuss the matter, or perhaps they already had and the unease was the result.

'Ah, Picnic,' Bill Durn, an obstetrician, said with some expectation.

'Would you like a piece?' Jessie extended the half eaten chocolate bar. He wasn't enamoured of the offer.

'Oh germs!' Jessie Marvill said without embarrassment, and offered the other end, which he bit. She then popped the rest of it into her mouth, undeterred by his germs.

The conversation between Dr Davis, Dr James and Dr

Sally Hite, an Australian gynae SHO, paused briefly.

'We were discussing the move that's afoot to end locum replacement of junior doctors, Jessie,' Laurence James explained when she sat next to him.

'. . . It was quite bad enough that the decision was accepted not to employ locums when consultants were on leave,' Dr Davis said. He had made this a critical issue in committee, and was becoming especially unpopular with management.

'That fact gives some indication of who does the work around here,' Dr Durn put in between chews.

'It confirms that consultants don't take on complaining juniors,' Dr Hite said. She was as committed to the rights of junior doctors as any of them, despite the possible consequences.

'They know they don't dare,' Dr James put in.

'Come on, there are honourable exceptions,' Bill Durn said. 'Take Ollie Caldecott. You won't find a more up-front consultant.'

'There are ten who won't back their junior staff for every one who will.'

'If management try making custom and practice of not employing locums while we're on leave,' Vernon Davis argued, 'I think we should withdraw our services altogether.' He was prepared to do that.

No one suggested that soon he might be in no position to withdraw his services.

'It'll mean some specialties doing a one in one rota,' Sally Hite pointed out, 'if locums aren't used.'

'Of course. It contravenes the Terms and Conditions of Service,' Vernon Davis told them. He was considerably more informed than most about their rights and duties, and didn't mind taking issue over them. But what he found hurtful was suddenly being left on his own to carry on the fight, his colleagues running scared of their career prospects. It wasn't that he was afraid of being identified as a troublemaker, rather that he knew he couldn't win the battle on his own. 'Can we draft you as a delegate for our protest to District, Jessie?'

'I'm not sure,' Jessie Marvill said. But then realized this was to be a joint effort. 'Oh, if it helps. How many have we got?'

'Five, maybe ten – if we're lucky.'

That surprised her. There must have been nearly a hundred junior doctors at St Clair's, and more like four hundred in the District.

'Is the BMA taking this up?' Dr James asked.

'The industrial relations officer is involved. But he'll only advise on possible action if such a situation actually occurs . . .' Davis said. He had little expectation of real support there. The BMA was the doctors' union but loathed the connotations, and didn't actively enforce the terms and conditions of service doctors entered into.

An orthopaedic registrar called Alan Sainsbury approached the group, but not to join any protest; he was pursuing Sally Hite, professionally.

'Sally, would you be available for a spot of cutting in Belgium over the weekend?' he asked, coming straight to the point. He had a lucrative business of agenting for clinics in Belgium, finding British qualified doctors who could go over to assist with operations on Saturday and Sunday and return to their own jobs by Monday. Even after paying doctors all their expenses this was profitable for the clinics, but also there was a shortage of qualified doctors in Belgium.

'In Belgium?' She was surprised at being asked, and wondered why she was suddenly approved.

'Pop over Friday evening, back Sunday evening. They're one short on a gynae team. You were the first person I thought of,' he lied.

'I'm on call,' she told him.

'Can't you change it?' He saw the interest her cohorts

were taking. He had once made the mistake of asking Vernon Davis to go, and they had rowed about the fee-for-service ethic. He believed Davis was mad, and wouldn't have approached Dr Hite in his company had he not been under pressure, having been let down at the last moment. 'Look, think about it. See if you can fix up someone to cover for you.' With a fleeting glance at Vernon Davis, he strode away.

After a moment Bill Durn said, 'The only thing about that, Sal, is make sure you get your money up front.'

No one else said anything.

'I'll see you later.'

Jessie Marvill went across the room to David Passmore, who was sitting with an unctuous-looking man in a cheap, fashionable business suit.

David Passmore was still quite tanned from his jaunt to Miami, where he had spent as much time on the beach as in the lecture theatre.

'Jessie,' he said as she joined them. 'David Soper, Dr Marvill, our SHO. Mr Soper reps for Cavandish. He's just been showing a bactericidal spray to prevent wound infection.'

'One sprays the cavity before suturing,' Soper explained. He was on the point of leaving. He would go on to bigger things in this field, and recognized immediately that Jessie Marvill was in no position of influence so was not about to waste time.

'I'm sure it'll get a lot of use,' Passmore told him.

'Thank you for your time, sir. Doctor,' he said to Jessie Marvill.

They watched him approach another doctor and introduce himself. Drug companies' reps weren't welcomed in the medical centre, unless by appointment to see a specific doctor. Once there they often found ways of seeing other medical staff.

'Can you take some more blood from Mr Taylor, on S1,'

he said as if she might have forgotten who he was. 'Both his bone and tissue biopsy showed tumour. He seems to have no end of problems.'

'Yes,' Jessie Marvill said. 'He's certainly not a well man.'

'He's going for an EMI-scan at two. We'd better find out if there are any other sites before we consider tackling this problem. He has an appointment with the radiotherapist afterwards.' He paused, and his glance strayed to Vernon Davis and his thoughts jumped track. 'That little enclave will do nothing for your career prospects, Jessie.' He said this like a pompous elder brother who had decided he should look after his sister's moral welfare.

Jessie wasn't deterred. 'It's a bit unfair,' she said, looking across at the group, which Dr Roger Crick had joined looking, she suspected, for someone to remove his moles. His hypochondria was a longstanding joke she had discovered. 'The plan is not to employ agency locums.'

'Medicine is a way of life, Jessie,' he announced. 'You don't do the job for the conditions of service, at least that's not been my experience. The hours are sometimes unbearable, but somehow we manage. The strain this puts on our profession, particularly women members, seems out of all proportion to the reward. Especially when one considers that doctors and their wives have a much higher incidence of divorce, suicide, depressive illness, alcoholism. Doctors tend to have families late, and that can bring difficulties. As a result a lot give up medicine. Because postgraduate training's compulsory in all fields now, the minimum age you get to be a registrar is twenty-six, but more realistically it's twenty-nine or thirty. It's difficult to stop much before that point with a view to having a family, then resuming one's career.'

When her colleague finally stopped Jessie Marvill wondered what the purpose of all that was, whether he thought she was leaving medicine, or was he apologizing in advance in case she didn't; whether he didn't like women doctors or didn't think junior doctors should defend themselves. Jessie didn't debate the matter.

'I'd better go and take that blood,' she said and rose out of the chair.

Notwithstanding the rivalry that existed between consultants of different specialties, and bearing in mind the reason they were meeting, Dr Ralph Mathias and Mr Ronald Smith-Sampson were behaving amicably towards each other. They were in the boardroom at the hospital where Dr Mathias had convened the Three Wise Men committee. This committee was the only body to have any effect on a consultant's contract, but had no power to suspend or dismiss him; it could only listen to the complaint, then make a recommendation. Consultants were rarely suspended, and almost never dismissed, unless after being struck off the register following a GMC professional conduct committee hearing.

Lately the surgical and medical specialties, like many others, had united on a common front, to complain about the shortage of beds, and especially about the likelihood of more bed closures on Nightingale Block.

'I can't say that I'd be pleased to lose beds on Nightingale, even temporarily,' Smith-Sampson was saying while waiting for the third member of the committee, Mr Philip Montagu, to arrive.

A black kitchen maid brought in a lunch trolley, one of the smaller, older type.

'There's many a slip betwixt cup and lip. The promise of an upgraded ward and its actually happening.'

'There are supposed to be alternative beds provided,' Mathias said.

'I'd like to know where before I agree to letting go my beds,' Smith-Sampson said.

'Sorry,' Mr Philip Montagu said as he arrived briskly. 'The subcommittee ran over. Have I held things up?'

'No,' Mathias told him. 'I ordered you some lunch.' 'Thank you,' he said to the maid, who had opened the trolley up and set the plates out. Dr Mathias locked the door after her so that they wouldn't be interrupted.

They helped themselves to the food, which they took to the table in the centre of this old-fashioned room.

'You don't have a bed to spare on gynae,' Philip?' Smith-Sampson asked. 'I'm trying to get two booked admissions in tomorrow. I have nowhere to put them.'

'Regrettably not. Dorothy has one or two who could go out if only she'd look for turnover. She's got three sterilizations that'll be blocking beds for days on end.' Philip Montagu was irritated by Miss Dorothy Caine, the other consultant gynaecologist, for doing salpingectomy sterilizations, which was the surgical removal of the fallopian tubes, rather than the simpler, quicker method of sealing them with a diathermery through a small incision in the stomach wall under local anaesthetic. But it wasn't for him to tell another consultant how to treat patients. 'Is that roast pork?' he said, and forked some of the slices on to his plate. Although his antecedents were Jewish – he was a Sephardic Jew whose family went back centuries – he would eat pork just to show he was not influenced by such orthodoxy.

'We'll soon get a situation where we're asking patients to share beds,' Smith-Sampson suggested.

'I think it's time we started flexing our muscles,' Montagu said.

'The only problem, Philip, is that we could end up with egg on our faces if our wishes weren't acceded to,' Mathias pointed out. 'In some areas they simply aren't able to provide more beds. How is the new unit in Nightingale progressing?'

'It'll be an age before those beds are back on stream.'

'I heard that one wing was to be a psycho-geriatric unit,' Smith-Sampson said.

'That might relieve pressure on medical beds,' Mathias said as he ate.

'I'd oppose such a move,' Montagu said. 'In fact I'm raising the matter at the Medical Committee meeting this afternoon. So perhaps we could press on.'

They ate in awkward silence, avoiding one another's eyes, variously cutting fat off their meat, putting pepper on vegetables, prodding food with their forks, each knowing they eventually had to get to the purpose of their meeting.

'This is rather embarrassing, Ronald,' the most senior consultant began, 'the substance of the complaint being against yourself.'

'I appreciate your position,' Smith-Sampson said as if the matter was of no consequence. 'If you wish I'll withdraw.'

'I don't think that's necessary.' In fact all three knew it was impractical. 'Philip?'

'Who's the complainant?' Montagu asked. He had been told, but other matters dominated his thinking space.

'Vernon Davis,' Dr Mathias said.

'I'm surprised he had time, with all his politicking. In fact I'm surprised he has time for medicine at all,' Montagu said with some hostility. He wouldn't tolerate junior doctors' opinions unless they accorded with his own.

'His complaint is that you're no longer conducting yourself in the best interests of patients, Ronald,' Mathias said with a smile.

'I doubt any of us could measure up to Davis's expectations,' Smith-Sampson said adding sarcastically, 'Perhaps we should be grateful to him.'

'I doubt if he undertook this lightly.' Although Dr Mathias didn't believe there was substance to Dr Davis's complaint, and believed he was suffering as a result of overwork, he did want to be seen to be fair.

'Possibly that's his problem,' Smith-Sampson explained. 'If I thought him cavalier he wouldn't have lasted on my firm.'

'Is he diligent?' Montagu asked.

'I've had better registrars in my twenty-nine years here. But I've certainly had worse. That black chap I had before Davis. He was hopeless.'

The other two consultants nodded, remembering some of the stories they had heard about that doctor.

'How competent is he, Ronald?' Montagu asked, continuing his tack.

'I can't fault his technique; his attitude's another matter. Arrogance tends to cloud his judgement. He seems obsessed about management and consultants conspiring against junior doctors. I wish he would concern himself more with patients' and less with colleagues' welfare. I've no evidence that patients suffer as a result,' he added craftily, being seen not to be too unkind.

Each of these consultants seemed completely unaware of the irony creeping in here; in spite of the complaint being against Mr Smith-Sampson, Dr Davis was being examined and found wanting.

'Just what did happen with the pneumonectomy?' Mathias asked. 'I seem to have heard all sorts of wild rumours.'

'It appears there was a mix-up with the lung function reports from the medical firm,' Smith-Sampson explained. 'On the evidence my opinion was that she was a reasonable prospect for a right lung resection. As it transpired she got into difficulty soon after surgery, and had to remain on a ventilator.'

'Davis maintains that he told you she was unsuitable for pneumonectomy,' Mathias said.

'That's understandable in the circumstances,' Mr Smith-Sampson allowed.

'What's the prognosis?' Montagu asked, looking at his watch, and thinking about his afternoon schedule.

'The patient died three days after surgery,' Smith-

Sampson said. 'It's tragic but difficult I think to readily ascribe blame.'

'Do procedures need reviewing, both for the transmission of reports and in theatre? With closer attention on getting the right patients to the right surgeon, with the right information.'

'We have triple checks, Ralph,' Montagu said. Physicians rarely appreciated how carefully theatre procedures were followed.

'Yet tragedies happen.'

'On those rare occasions when they do occur they tend to be very dramatic,' Montagu said, 'and seen out of all proportion.'

'It might be profitable to review our procedures,' Smith-Sampson said. 'One practice I'd like to see outlawed is taking patients out of order on the lists. That can lead to confusion.'

There was general agreement.

'I think the matter worth raising at the medical committee,' Montagu said. 'Something positive might come out of this.' It was almost self-congratulatory.

No blame was attached for what had happened to the patient who had died as a result of the lung resection; the only person on whom the complaint reflected badly was Vernon Davis. No official action would be taken against him, but each of the three consultants would doubtless remember him for his complaint, and doubtless talk to other consultants. None of this would affect Vernon Davis for the duration of his current contract. Difficulty would arise when he came to apply for another job.

15

Ordinarily the patient on the side ward of S1 shouldn't have been there, not being a surgical case, having suffered a coronary with a CVA. However, there were no medical beds available, and even less space in the intensive care unit where he should have been. Under protest from the surgical firms, and especially the nursing staff, who had to cope with this extra burden, Jack Preston was put on S1 where even his vast bulk was almost lost among the elaborate equipment that had been brought there; the person had subjugated his identity to the symptoms. He was being ventilated through the mouth, drip-fed through the nose; he had an intravenous infusion through the arm for drug intake; an ECG recorded the electrical activity of his heart, while a catheter running from his bladder disposed of his urine.

Sheila Preston, who was sitting by the bed, knew that for her husband the catheter would have been the final ignominy piled upon the many indignities he would have refused to suffer had he been conscious. She was normally an energetic woman, in her mid-fifties, but was stunned and subdued by all that was being done to maintain life at this abysmal level. Her husband had long ago come to terms with the prospect of dying. He wouldn't want to be maintained as a vegetable. Having made a rational decision about that, he had joined Exit, the euthanasia organization; he had written letters setting out his wishes in the event of having a stroke or becoming brain-damaged. Yet despite hammering on the hospital administrator's door, and badgering both the medical and ITU consultants, Sheila Preston hadn't come close to having the life support system switched off so that her husband could die as he would have wished.

She watched a staff nurse change his drip, taking down the collapsed plastic bag and linking up another, while Dr Batacharya, an Indian SHO on Dr Sharwood's firm, placed his stethoscope on the patient's chest and listened to his lungs. Afterwards he connected a syringe to the top of the venous catheter in Preston's arm and pushed some antibiotics in.

Dr Batacharya glanced at Mrs Preston, feeling uneasy. Like most of his colleagues, he had been asked by her to turn off the life support. He pretended not to hear what she said now. 'Sorry?'

'What's the point of this?' she repeated.

'His lungs start to congest, Mrs Preston.' He ignored the real meaning of her question. 'We give him more antibiotics. Prevent pneumonia.'

He went out, refusing to be drawn into a discussion about death.

Mrs Preston watched him go, and in the corridor saw him speak to Dr Marvill, whom she had spoken to a couple of times, before realizing she had no responsibility for her husband. She couldn't hear what the two doctors were saying, but guessed the subject. She turned back to consider her husband and the support system that separated this pointless existence from his wishes. It would have been a simple physical matter to disconnect the power supply by the plug in the wall, if not as easy an emotional task. She wouldn't do this, despite her belief that he would never recover to be recognizably the man she had lived with for thirty-five years.

A similar thought ran through Dr Marvill's mind as she went along the ward to take blood from Ray Taylor. Even though their complaints were very different, if either recovered it wasn't likely that they would be restored to anything resembling their former selves. At times she questioned the point of the intense effort that went into such patients, while knowing part of her professional ethic was not to pose such questions.

Ray Taylor was conscious but grey-looking as Dr Marvill took the blood from his arm. He didn't respond at all when she examined his eyelids for anaemia and felt his neck.

'How am I doing, doctor?' he said finally in a tired, hoarse whisper that was barely audible. It was as if he didn't want the question heard, rather than because talking was difficult.

'How do you feel, Mr Taylor,' she asked him, side-stepping the problem, but feeling uncomfortable.

She waited for him, sensing for the first time that he wanted to go further.

'It wasn't an abscess, was it?' His words came out with even more difficulty.

She hesitated, and considered lying to him. Doctors who lied easily, did so, she suspected, as a way of dealing with their own problems of confronting death.

'I'm afraid it wasn't,' she said, and saw the patient avert his eyes, clearly indicating now that he wished her to say no more. 'Mr Passmore will be in to see you tomorrow to explain just what's happening. You should try to rest your throat and not talk.'

She gave him a smile, but he turned away.

'You're going down to X-ray soon. We'll see what the radiotherapist says about the possibility of treatment.'

Such statements were often a device used for breaking to a patient the presence of malignancy rather than saying it directly, the belief being that everyone knew what radio-therapy meant.

Dr Marvill considered the man in the bed, knowing he hadn't chosen to make the connection.

At the bottom of the ward the crash-call team was rushing into action for Mr Preston. Dr Crick, Dr David Wilkes, a Trinidadian, two porters trundling in the defibrillator trolley, a staffnurse with the ward crash-call trolley. Although not part of the team, Dr Marvill went to see if she was needed.

All that could be done for Mr Preston was being done, so she kept to one side. Jack Preston interested her, and without being sure why she admired him. He was a GP, one who had, it seemed, come to terms with death. So few people did, especially not in the medical profession, but any expectation of more understanding of death there was an illogical concept, as the entire profession was in itself a denial of that process. Possibly that was why many doctors were arrogant behind their veils of concern, believing themselves god-like and capable of interceding to halt the inevitable. Here was one doctor who had found the answer, and she would very much like to have talked with him to discover whether his answers came from philosophy, religion or pragmatism.

'How long was his heart stopped?' Dr Crick asked, as he pushed isoprenaline into his arm via the butterfly-like venous canula. Dr Wilkes applied external heart massage, which together with the adrenalin was having the desired effect.

'I noticed it about ten past two,' the staffnurse said.

'What's that, four minutes? Four and a half? I think he probably had another infarct,' Crick observed. 'I won't need that, George,' he said to the porter, who had plugged in the defibrillator.

The electrocardiograph was registering a heartbeat. The ventilator was working, pushing air into Preston's lungs, sustaining life.

Dr Marvill didn't know whether to feel relieved or disappointed, and glanced across at Mrs Preston, who slipped from the room, her presence forgotten. The notion crossed her mind that maybe she had caused this crisis by momentarily switching off the life support. She was brave if she had, Dr Marvill thought, for no one else had the courage to. Ironically, only medical staff had the right to decide when a patient was to be let die, not the patient. This patient was qualified to make such a decision. Jessie Marvill thought he would know what state he would be left in after a massive stroke, and whether he would want to go on living like that.

Although hearing Mrs Preston's words from where he sat opposite his desk, Roy Needham had closed his mind to her arguments, and she could return to his office every day, as he began to suspect she would, until her husband died and he wouldn't change his position. He had felt sorry for her initially, but now sympathy was giving way to impatience, and if she returned tomorrow, he wouldn't see her, he decided.

'I'm sorry, Mrs Preston,' he said when she stopped talking. 'I'm only the hospital administrator. The decision to take your husband off the life support machine isn't within my power. As I've already told you, it's a medical decision.'

'The doctors won't even consider it,' she responded. 'My husband's written letters expressing his wishes.' These were spread on the table before them. 'He knew this might happen; he doesn't want to vegetate. That's what his future is, if he can survive at all without a ventilator. That's why he joined Exit.'

'I can only refer you back to the medical team,' he said wearily.

'Everyone refers me somewhere else. No one wants to take responsibility. I can't get through to them that they don't have to. Jack's already made his decision.'

'I'm sorry. You'll have to talk to Dr Sharwood.'

'I've talked to her. And members of her firm,' she said. 'They're not very helpful.'

'I'm sorry, Mrs Preston. I can't help.' He closed the meeting by rising from his chair.

Mrs Preston collected her husband's letters and rose.

After she had gone Roy Needham telephoned Dr

Sharwood, who told him that Preston's position hadn't changed. Confronted with the possibility of Mrs Preston, far from giving up, taking direct action, the consultant suggested that it was a nursing problem.

'Either he'll have to be transferred to the ITU,' Dr Sharwood informed him, 'or have a nurse with him the whole time.'

When the administrator referred this to the senior nursing officer, Brian Rickard almost hit the roof.

'The nursing staff on S1 are already under strain with the extra work involved in having him there,' he said.

'Perhaps if another nurse was found from somewhere?'

That brought laughter from the SNO.

What happened in fact was the staff on S1 were stretched a little further, with someone sitting in with Preston whenever his wife was around.

This made life especially difficult for the night staff, as Mrs Preston turned up just after the evening visitors had left, which meant only one nurse being on the main ward. But they couldn't tell Sheila Preston not to visit her husband.

'Are you on your own?' Dr Marvill asked the staffnurse when she came to see Mr Taylor after her evening meal.

'Sort of,' the staffnurse said. 'Sorry to have called you up like this.'

Dr Marvill knew that when the nursing staff were stretched it was often necessary for them to share the burden with medical staff. She took Ray Taylor's file and opened it.

'Mr Taylor's not feeling very good,' the staffnurse said at the patient's bed. 'He feels he's going downhill.'

'What makes you think so, Mr Taylor?' Dr Marvill asked. Ray Taylor didn't respond or so much as look at her. He was grey and drawn and appeared to have shrunk during the afternoon.

'I think he's been having a lot of pain,' the staffnurse said.

'I'll give him something for that,' Dr Marvill said. 'Feeling a bit low, Mr Taylor? It's not unusual after surgery.' She tried sounding cheerful. 'Mr Thompson is very optimistic about the next course of action. So try not to worry too much. We're having a meeting in the morning to plan your treatment.' She smiled, but disliked herself for it, knowing she was avoiding the issue here. 'Hasn't the pain eased at all?'

He shook his head, on the point of breaking down.

She scribbled a note in his file about his emotional state in case anyone was interested. That wasn't usually included in patient notes. 'Did he have some Acupan this evening?'

'About two hours ago,' the staffnurse told her.

'Try him on DF118, 25 mg, intramuscular. See how he gets on. Call me if it doesn't help.' She wrote up the drug. 'Mr Passmore will be along to see you tomorrow after the meeting, he'll explain what's happening. I'm giving you something stronger for the pain. It should ease it so you sleep. You'll feel a little better in the morning.'

She started to smile, but stopped herself, and instead took his hand in hers. Jessie Marvill wanted to give this poor man something other than false, if well-intentioned, reassurance. She wanted to give him some spiritual support. It was a feeling she had experienced on more than one occasion, and then, as now, she was unable to express it. Primarily this was because of the conditioning that came with medical training, it made no allowance for the spiritual needs either of patient or doctor.

'You'll start to feel better quite soon now,' she said, letting go his hand.

That well-tried smile started to appear again. She checked it and went out.

Coming along the corridor past the side ward, Dr Marvill stopped. Mrs Preston, who was sitting by the bed reading, looked up, so Dr Marvill greeted her and went into the room.

'How is he?' she asked.

'He hasn't picked up his bed and walked,' Mrs Preston said sharply. 'This is the best any of you can offer.'

Dr Marvill said nothing.

'Am I being watched in case I do anything silly?'

Jessie Marvill knew Sheila Preston was referring to the nurse's presence. She was slightly manic through stress, and Dr Marvill wondered how much of the book she had managed to read.

'Your husband was a doctor,' she said uneasily. It wasn't a Freudian slip, her meaning was that he was unlikely to practise again.

'He's still alive, so they tell me.' Mrs Preston turned and looked at the patient in the bed, committed to the belief that this wasn't life worth preserving. 'He never tried to persuade patients to hang on, not like this, not when life was so abysmal.'

Jessie Marvill waited, though she had a lot she wanted to ask about this patient.

'Jack never had any fear of dying. This is what he always feared.' She paused again.

'Was he a religious man?' Jessie Marvill asked.

The woman hesitated. 'He had no conventional belief in God the Father. He believed there was a purpose to life, he thought it was to seek as much knowledge as possible. Jack could never tolerate the stupid or the mentally lazy. He always said how the quality of a person's life determined how much time and effort was put into them. He would find this situation ludicrous.'

Jessie Marvill thought the person Mrs Preston was talking about was a medical pragmatist rather than spiritually enlightened. There was a part of her that agreed with the philosophy, yet a part that was disappointed.

'Could you disconnect this machine for me?' she asked.

Dr Marvill hesitated. 'I think quite soon he'll be taken off the ventilator to see whether he can survive,' she said, avoiding the appeal.

Mrs Preston looked at her, not wanting this answer.

Dr Marvill shook her head. 'I would if it were my decision.' But of course it wasn't, so the patient had to struggle on.

16

The weekly meetings Mr Marcus Thompson held with his firm to discuss patients' prognosis, progress and prospects were informal, which was as much to do with the hour as anything. They always took place late afternoon, prior to his ward round the following morning, and in the small reception area to the consultants' offices. The whole firm was present, the air was blue with cigarette smoke. In addition to the clinicians, a hospital social worker called Amanda de Courcy sat in, and the consultant's secretary, and occasionally a radiotherapist.

Marcus Thompson was relaxed at this meeting, and here, unlike on the wards, he allowed people to air their views; but that didn't mean he heeded them.

'Judging by the extent of spread,' Thompson was saying from an easy chair, with Ray Taylor's file open on his knees, 'further surgery is the only option. Dr Cloutman doesn't consider the tumours suitable for radiotherapy.'

The gravity of his tone was generally noted. Jessie Marvill thought about Jack Preston, juxtaposing his prognosis with Mr Taylor's. She couldn't avoid Mrs Preston's statement about the quality of life being what made it worth living.

'We're talking about something quite radical. Does he know the position?'

'I've explained to him just what we've done so far,' Mr Passmore said. 'But I fancy he doesn't want to consider the notion of there being spread to the tongue and mandible.'

Jessie Marvill said, 'I think he does realize the biopsy wasn't the end of the matter. But I'm not sure he wants to think beyond that.'

'Has anyone spoken to his wife? Does she know what's in store?'

'She knows there are further sites, and was warned additional surgery might be necessary.'

'She doesn't know how much will be involved?'

'When I saw her we hadn't had an opinion from Dr Cloutman. There was still the possibility he'd be going for radiotherapy,' Passmore said, justifying himself.

'It's pretty heroic,' Thompson said. 'Maxilla, mandible, half his tongue; the deep cervical lymph nodes. He'll probably lose his right eye. I think perhaps you'd better arrange some cancer counselling for both of them,' he told the social worker. 'Are you familiar with the commando procedure?'

'Well in textbooks. It's only been textbook stuff until now,' Dr Marvill said. Ordinarily she wouldn't have expected to see such a procedure on a general surgery firm. The commando operation, as head and neck resections were called, usually fell to ENT or maxilla-facial surgeons, with the help of a chest surgeon if the problem went into the oesophagus. The tendency in surgery nowadays was increasingly for sub-specialties. This was how Marcus Thompson came to be undertaking such an operation, having made a sub-specialty out of major malignancies, regardless of where they were, outside of the brain and vagina.

'I published two papers on the procedure last year,' Thompson told her. 'You might like to read them.' He expected her to make a point of reading them. 'This might make a companion paper. As gross as the procedure sounds, it will in fact save his life.'

'We'll literally be removing half his face and neck,' Jessie Marvill observed.

'We'll rebuild it with skin flaps from his chest and forehead,' the consultant said, as if it were an easy matter with satisfactory results. 'He could have two or three useful years.'

'Is there perhaps not an argument here for just leaving the carcinoma to take its course?' Jessie Marvill said impulsively, and soon wished she hadn't.

'Why?' Marcus Thompson wanted to know.

'Well,' she began hesitantly, 'basically because this will diminish the quality of the patient's life so much. I wonder if he'd really want it in extra quantity?'

'You know him that well?' Mr Thompson inquired, seeing a potential threat to his paper.

Dr Marvill felt foolish. She couldn't argue that she was basing her opinion on another patient's wishes, one who wasn't being treated by this firm.

'Er, no, I don't,' she said.

Both Mr Passmore and Dr Willoughby were smiling. They knew the consultant better than to raise such an objection.

'And if you're wrong?' Thompson wasn't satisfied with merely having his way. 'What if the patient wants to live? People often do prefer to live, whatever the quality of life. He's a relatively young man. He presents well. I doubt if his family would thank you for writing him off.' He gave her a tight, condescending smile. 'We mustn't be tempted to play God,' – as though unaware of the irony. 'We must get on with the job.' He turned to David Passmore. 'Would you care to have a word with Mrs Taylor? It might be an idea if she's there when I tell the patient what we propose.'

Mr Marcus Thompson was like a man who had won a lottery prize, Jessie Marvill decided. When she had first met him she had thought him fairly decent, less arrogant, less chauvinistic than most cutters. But seeing him go for a procedure he obviously wanted to do, possibly for his own reasons, caused her to wonder if she had chosen the right specialty after all. Her concern was that if she ever made it into a consultant post she might have a similar attitude. Her boss was a man who was convinced that he had never been wrong about a medical decision, and Jessie Marvill knew that no one could be that good.

On S1 Jenny Mackaness, a 1st-year student nurse, was angry and confused when she came from the side ward, where she had been replacing Preston's drip bag. She went into the kitchen, where a 2nd-year student nurse was making hot drinks, while a young black auxiliary, who was washing up, was saying, 'My mum loves Stergene.'

Hearing that stopped Nurse Mackaness. What was going on in here seemed as unreal as what was happening in the side ward.

'Jen? What's the matter?' Chrissy Gooch said.

'Why on earth don't they let that poor man die? It's cruel him dragging on like that,' Nurse Mackaness said. She was close to tears.

'It doesn't make sense, does it? On the geri' wards they sometimes put patients in side wards with the windows open so they get pneumonia and die.'

'His wife's ever so upset,' Nurse Mackaness said. 'She asked me if I could switch the ventilator off. You don't know what to say, do you?'

'They're testing out some new treatment on him,' Nurse Gooch informed her.

'That's terrible.' Jenny Mackaness was shocked.

'Do you know that for a fact, Nurse Gooch?' Staffnurse Rita Hobson asked, coming into the kitchen.

'When I was on the cardi' unit at Queen's that's what happened,' Nurse Gooch said. ''S true, staff,' – seeing her doubts.

'I've never heard such nonsense.' Staffnurse Hobson chose this line as a matter of course. 'Have you done the temperatures?' she inquired of Nurse Mackaness, abruptly changing the subject.

'I've been seeing to Mr Preston.' Oddly no one called him Dr Preston.

'The temperatures should have been done – I'll let you off this time.' Staffnurse Hobson was wrong-footed, but refused to backtrack.

'There's nothing to let me off,' Jenny Mackaness insisted. 'Sister told me to do that.'

'Sister's off – I'm in charge now.' The staffnurse turned and went out.

Nurse Mackaness clamped her hand over her mouth in an expression of frustration, making her colleague laugh. 'Roll on five o'clock,' she said, looking at her watch.

'You'll be lucky to get off at five. She'll keep us behind doing all sorts of stupid things.'

Despite the upsets the nursing staff suffered they tended to show a reasonably friendly face to the patients, certainly to those they liked. Although fairly inexperienced Nurse Mackaness was no exception.

Going along the ward, taking temperatures, pulses and blood pressures, she came to Mr Reed, their most unpopular patient. He had had a second operation for an anal fissure, which had resulted from the passage of hard stools, and wouldn't heal because each defecation reopened the crack in the mucous membrane of the rectum. Unfortunately Mr Reed's first operation wasn't a success, the sphincter hadn't dilated sufficiently for the tissue to heal, and he felt he had cause to complain.

'Have you had your bowels open today, Mr Reed?' she asked as she took his temperature. She wasn't so inexperienced to know when to ride a patient.

'No,' he said. 'There's nothing in there. Nor will there be until the food improves.' He was on a special low residue diet instead of a high roughage one.

'Oh I thought it had after your complaints.' Nurse Mackaness hid her smile.

'I don't think you're passing them on.'

'Why not tell the nursing officer when she comes round?' she suggested.

'I plan to,' he said. 'And that's not all. I'm going to tell her about the nurse smoking at that bed with the curtains closed.' He indicated his neighbour. 'I saw the smoke. I know what she was doing.'

'I expect it was steam from his bed bath.' She marked his chart and started away.

'I need the mobile telephone,' he said.

With her back to Mr Reed as she crossed the bay to the next patient, Nurse Mackaness pulled an exasperated face at the auxiliary who appeared. Carmen Kandal made no bones about what she said to patients like Mr Reed.

'What you want?' she said, going to Mr Reed's bed. 'You always make d'fuss, man.'

'I don't think some of you realize how much pain I'm in.'

'I'll get you d'phone honey,' the auxiliary said. 'You call your MP.'

Nurse Mackaness put the thermometer into Mr Taylor's mouth. He didn't respond to her smile, but she didn't hold that against him. She met Mr Reed's look from across the bay and turned back to Mr Taylor, wishing Mr Reed knew a little of his suffering.

The surgical nursing officer, Mrs Janice Woodrow, came on to the ward, putting her head into various offices as she did.

Staffnurse Hobson hurried to meet her as she reached the sluice. 'Commode!' she hissed at Nurse Gooch and started signalling behind her back for a nurse to remove the commode seat from sight. Nurse Gooch ignored her, and continued getting the patient who had used it settled again. She wasn't in a flap over the nursing officer's visit, it rarely affected the nursing staff nowadays, except some of the sisters who remembered the old-style matrons, and staffnurses like Rita Hobson. Most nursing officers weren't concerned if the ward régime wasn't absolutely tight.

'Good afternoon, Staff,' Mrs Woodrow said cheerfully. She looked into the sluice room, which was a bit untidy and smelly, with laundry left about. None of it affected the nursing officer's bland expression.

'It's a bit untidy,' she said.

'I've been getting on to the nurses since lunch to tidy it up,' the staffnurse apologized.

'It's a bit smelly too. I know there's an extra problem here with Mr Preston.'

It was a reasonable observation, but left Staffnurse Hobson looking stricken.

'Can you do something about the sluice as I asked you,' she said sharply to Nurse Gooch who came off the ward with the pressed paper bedpan.

'They've certainly got a wonderful shine to this floor,' Mrs Woodrow said. 'Is all the equipment working properly now?'

'Yes, I think so.'

'Hello, Mr Taylor,' Mrs Woodrow said with a smile. 'How are you feeling today? A little better? You're looking better.'

Ray Taylor stared vacantly. He looked worse than he did yesterday, which was worse than the day before. When he didn't respond, she glanced at the staffnurse.

'Yes, Mr Taylor is feeling better today,' she said.

'Good.' She moved on, sweeping the rest of the bay with a smile. 'When's he going to theatre again?'

'It hasn't been decided.'

They moved on, the nursing officer satisfied that everything was as it should be, the patients' needs attended. This was the purpose of her visits, and despite being less formal than the old style matron, the senior nursing staff were no more in touch. For the record everything was functioning normally.

However, if things appeared as they should on the nursing side, that wasn't the case with administration. Their problems were almost entirely governed by factors beyond their control – money. The Treasury determined how much was available to the DHSS who, based on estimated requirements for the year, in turn doled it out to the fourteen Regions. They funded the District Health Authorities who distributed the dole to the management teams in the front line, which was where the thinness of spread began to show up.

A problem frustrating the administrator of St Clair's, and one, like most of them, directly related to the shortage of money, was the telephone system, which needed replacing. They had a scheme for a new system with direct dialling on both internal and external calls, with automatic paging, but it had been put back often, only to suffer a cost increase each time it was brought out for reinstatement.

Roy Needham was trying to get through to the District Administrator, but couldn't. Each time he dialled he got a long, sharp, farting sound on the telephone. He dropped it back on the rest, rose and went to the door.

'Carol. What's wrong with these bloody phones today? See if you can get the District Administrator.'

Val Kay, who was in the outer office searching through a filing cabinet, turned and said, 'It's British Telecom. They refuse to go into the tunnels because of the asbestos lagging on the pipes.'

'What? I don't believe it,' Roy Needham said in dismay.

'I went down there with their foreman. He almost ran out when he saw it,' Val Kay said.

'Silly bugger. They've been encountering it for donkeys years. Especially in hospitals.'

'Ah, but there's a scare on, Roy,' she reminded him.

'Does that mean the phones will be out until the asbestos is removed – you'd better get me some transport, Carol. I'll go over and see Stephen Morwell.'

'I've a site meeting with the engineer in the morning,' Val Kay said, as though hopeful of a solution then.

'We'd better have some cleft sticks in here for now.'

The District Administrator was a tall, intense man in his late thirties. Unlike Roy Needham he was a university graduate who had chosen Public Service for a career, feeling unable to compete on equal terms in the Civil Service. He prided himself on his physical fitness, and played squash aggressively two nights a week, and enjoyed winning, which he did often. In his enjoyment he rarely smiled, but instead he would arch his dark eyebrows towards his close-cropped hair and blink rapidly.

Despite being well-disposed to Roy Needham he stared at him from across his large desk with an expressionless face.

'You came close to an epidemic, Roy,' Stephen Morwell said, his tone disguising his concern at the size of the problem that might have resulted from the food-poisoning.

'I suppose we should be grateful not too many people fancied the bacon pasta,' Needham said.

'Is anyone going to sue?' That was a serious worry as there was no special fund for when patients brought a legal action against a hospital.

'I doubt it. But we must make sure it doesn't happen again.'

'There's no doubt about the source? It wasn't the painters?'

'There's the possibility it was the faecal-oral route,' Roy Needham said. 'Felix Greene's posted new notices about washing hands after using the lavatory. Pathology was convinced this lot resulted from standing the colanders on the floor by the boilers. There's a lot of traffic along that section. It gets washed, but how well? The only solution is to put in a rack to keep things off the floor.'

'What's it going to cost?' Morwell asked.

'The best we can get it done for is a little over eight thousand pounds,' he said, passing him a copy of the estimate. 'The trouble is, when we put the rack in we have to raise the boilers, or they'll be too low.'

'Couldn't the chefs hold the colanders?'

'We'd be talking about ten or fifteen kilos. I'm not sure Health and Safety would allow it. They might object to this scheme, as it'll mean reaching over the racks to get at the boilers.'

'They're not likely to be unreasonable,' Morwell commented. The Health and Safety Executive was a statutory body which tended to pick fights it could win. It didn't prosecute other public bodies like hospitals.

'It would make life difficult if they slapped a prohibition order on the boilers.'

'Presumably you haven't got this sort of money lying around?' He knew the answer as well as Roy Needham, seeing everything that concerned finance within his District.

'Every spare penny's going on asbestos removal,' Needham said. 'But I do think this has become a priority.'

'Unless of course it was one of the chefs who didn't wash after using the lavatory,' Morwell suggested.

Needham didn't reply.

'They couldn't do without those colanders, Roy?'

'I suggested that.' Needham shook his head.

'Then you'll have to decide what other scheme you can drop to finance this work.'

'I was hoping District might stump up,' Needham said.

'Well unless your needs are greater than anybody else's, Roy,' Morwell commiserated. 'At the moment we're on target for a deficit bigger than we can carry forward into next year's budget. Region's asking for five per cent cuts across the board.'

'Five per cent? Our schemes are picked to the bone,' he protested, as though it would make some difference. Roy Needham waited for a suggestion but knew from experience that if he didn't make a cut so as to pay for getting the colanders off the floor the District Administrator would. 'The only thing we might put off is the new community room for the geriatric wards. I'll have the Community

Health Council on at me if that's delayed again. I won't be able to look them in the face soon.'

'Well we're trying to conclude this agreement with junior doctors about not using agency locums. Potentially there's a £186,000 gross saving on last year's figures for St Clair's alone. Of course, the junior doctors' committee is resisting. Davis is getting them stirred up.'

'It's understandable,' Needham said. He sympathized with the junior medical staff to a point, knowing how over-stretched they were, often dangerously so. A likely outcome of such an agreement was that mistakes might start to become commonplace. Working from the District administration building which had been converted from a terrace of Georgian houses, Stephen Morwell wasn't involved emotionally with the hospitals within his District and so wasn't fully cognizant of the problem. 'I'm not sure how reliable they would become, especially not some of those on a one in two.'

'The solution might be in closing another ward, Roy.' That notion Morwell came to reluctantly; he was an administrator who saw his authority diminished by bed closures so fought to keep them open. However he saw no viable alternative.

'I expected that,' Needham said.

'We've been looking at the feasibility of closing a surgical ward. It's either that or another geriatric ward, but I don't see why they should bear the brunt the whole time.'

'I'm not sure the nursing and support staff will agree either,' Roy Needham said. The wishes of both those groups weren't something to be lightly ignored. The surgeons wouldn't resist provided they were given beds elsewhere; the geriatricians would resist, knowing that beds they were promised elsewhere wouldn't materialize.

'If the ward was closed for upgrading, that should forestall serious protest. Region has some money to spare for capital schemes. I think another ward upgrading is the answer.' He arched his eyebrows and blinked with satisfaction. Once they were allocated the money they might be able to divert it into Health and Safety schemes or elsewhere, but Region had threatened them before for doing just that.

Going through such bureaucratic hoops seemed to present neither of these men with problems; both being helpless to initiate any constructive alternative. There were rules governing the allocation and expenditure of money within the health service, and these weren't broken lightly. The money available at Region for what was termed a capital scheme, that was any alteration or building programme costing over seventy-five thousand pounds, could only be used for such schemes. It couldn't be diverted to maintenance or raising the colanders off the floor, nor removing asbestos lagging and replacing it with fibreglass; it couldn't be used for extra nursing or medical staff to keep open a ward. Some administrators considered it better to submit capital schemes that weren't essential, rather than risk the allocation being withdrawn, and there was always a chance that they could divert some of the money elsewhere, even at risk of Region's ire. Both Stephen Morwell and, to a lesser extent, Roy Needham had learned to live with such facts of life, knowing that they had to deny the needs of one section in order to keep another functioning, and so on no matter how desperate the situation, no longer arguing on principle that money should go to need rather than category. The fact that the £270,000 needed to convert an old ward was more than the proposed saving through not employing locums to cover for absent junior doctors hadn't escaped their notice. Nor the probability that the newly upgraded ward wouldn't open. They went through the hoops just the same.

Chris Hogan, the NUPE branch secretary, didn't allow himself to be restrained by the niceties of protocol. He believed that the way the health service was run was a scandal, especially as his members suffered in just about every area as the result of cuts. When there was money available he wanted it to be used where it was most effective, at the sharp end, on the patients. Whenever he put this point to management they informed him that he didn't see the overall picture; maybe that was true, but he saw enough to know that the service wasn't being run as it should.

Chris Hogan was bringing a supper trolley out of the lifts in the modern part of the hospital when a theatre porter, Trevor Holland, came along the corridor, just having returned a patient to a ward.

'Chris,' he said. 'What's this I hear about them shutting men's surgical on Nightingale Block?'

'I ain't heard nothing more, Trev',' Hogan said. In fact he had heard the rumours. There wasn't a single rumour in that hospital which didn't reach him. The line he took was to do with the membership crisis. Although he wasn't losing members, they tended not to be active until there was a problem that affected them personally. He wanted them active the whole time.

'They keep this up, they might as well shut the whole fucking hospital. Know what I mean?'

''S no way we'd stand for that,' Hogan told him.

'Soon we'll all be out of work. Know what I mean?'

'Well why don't you come to the branch meetings, you got something to say?' he said slyly. 'You blokes make me die, you join the union, you think all you gotta do is pay your subs.'

'I'll have plenty to say if they try closing any more wards.'

'They will, 'we let them get away with it, Trev'. I'll see what silly ballocks has to say.' He started away with the food. 'Oi, come to the meeting next week.'

'You're on,' Holland called back.

Chris Hogan smiled. At the rate he was going he'd have the entire membership banging on the administrator's door. If he had his way there wouldn't be a single bed shut anywhere in the service. That was what he was fighting for.

17

Morning in the doctors' sitting-room at St Clair's, as with most hospitals where there was a decent sitting-room, was something like a gathering of the clans. Doctors from various firms started in here with coffee and newspapers, or case notes, depending how their day was made up, a lot of them having breakfasted in the adjacent dining-room.

Jessie Marvill was there feeling tired and miserable and over-stretched. She needed someone to talk to, preferably someone outside the hospital, who was no part of medicine, someone who had a clearer perspective on life than she had at that moment in time. Working, eating, sleeping, living at the hospital tended to distort one's point of view she found. Despite all the things that had been wrong with her relationship with Roger Trentham, he had been good to talk to at times, and she had thought about telephoning him. But she hadn't done that, knowing that he still wanted them to get back together. The fact that she would sleep with him strengthened her resolve not to get in touch with him again, not even on just a friendly dinner basis. She looked around the sitting-room hoping to see Laurence James, who she felt she could talk to, or even Vernon Davis, but barely knew any of the doctors there. She smiled, noticing one with odd socks on; another close by was sleeping, nose against her paper. Just the thought of sleep made Jessie Marvill feel more tired herself.

David Passmore came into the sitting-room, saw Jessie Marvill, and came across bringing his coffee.

'God, you look terrible,' he said, with no consideration for her feelings. 'Were you called out last night?'

'What?' she responded flatly, coming out of her reverie.

'Yes, a couple of times.'

'You're lucky it's only a one in four rota here, Jessie,' he said with a forced smile. 'I did one in two jobs for two years.' Although technically he was still a junior doctor himself, he believed, like most consultants, that it was good for junior doctors to be stretched . But he knew he couldn't get away with saying that, particularly not to her this morning. She might break down, and he detested emotional scenes.

'Mr Preston died in the night,' she said vacantly. 'Odd how people mostly seem to die at night.' She looked over at him.

Mr Passmore looked blank. He didn't know who she was talking about, they had no patient called Preston.

'The CVA from medical,' she explained. 'He was a doctor,' she added somewhat irrelevantly.

'I see.' He obviously wasn't interested and couldn't understand why Dr Marvill was concerned about someone else's patient. 'Was that one of our beds? The old man has a private patient coming in.'

'I was called to Mr Ellicott – the ruptured kidney on S3. He's doing very badly. There's continuous haematuria.'

'Once he's done his ward round, you could slope off,' he told her, suspecting he had underestimated how fragile this doctor was today.

Jessie Marvill sipped her coffee. She was reluctant to talk about what was troubling her, but felt she had to.

'What about Mr Taylor, David?' she said. 'Can he survive such heroic surgery?' she used the word mockingly. Heroic in surgical terminology meant radical, on a large scale, bold, and requiring courage from both the surgeon and patient. Jessie Marvill wondered if the surgeon in this instance wasn't embarking on this procedure for the wrong reasons, and if the patient had any real notion of just how devastating the operation would prove for him.

'Some do survive the commando operation, and lead

fairly useful lives,' he said, sounding remarkably like Marcus Thompson. 'Statistically the prospects aren't encouraging. But then statistics tend not to mean much. Going on Taylor's physical and psychological state, there's a chance he will survive. But of course, if he does, there is the possibility that he'll be so emotionally disturbed it'll seriously change his personality. It's worse for women, having that much of their face chopped off and rebuilt,' he added.

'Will Mr Thompson tell him that?' she wanted to know.

'I wouldn't think so,' he said. 'Patients are better off with simple options, Jessie. Things they can just about understand.'

He saw her doubtful look and hesitated.

'The truth is, Jessie, we can offer him nothing else. All the alternatives have been looked at. Although there's that SHO on Simon Neave's firm.' He gave an embarrassed chuckle. 'He's been looking at all sorts of alternatives, from B17 to faith healing. He's a bit of a nutter.'

'Do you mean Laurence James?' Dr Marvill asked. She knew precisely who he meant.

'The old man wouldn't let him near his patients. I can't say I would either.'

'What does his own consultant think?' She hadn't discussed alternatives to orthodox treatment with Laurence James but thought perhaps she should.

'We couldn't possibly have anything to talk about.' He laughed again, more embarrassed now. 'They tend to be in the hope and prayer business, Jessie. Often patients are so far gone they won't even bother referring them here. I don't suppose much harm's done letting healers loose on them.' He looked at his watch. 'Our master beckons.'

He finished his coffee and rose.

Fleetingly she wondered what would happen if she refused to be party to what was being planned for Mr Taylor. Nothing that would alter the course of his life; she would be reprimanded, which in turn might affect her reference. She suddenly felt guilty for thinking that. Maybe the course of action Mr Thompson planned for Ray Taylor was right and she wasn't taking an objective view. But she wasn't convinced. As she rose to follow the senior registrar, Jessie Marvill decided she should talk to Laurence James about possible alternatives.

Marcus Thompson started the ward round from his office. The pace he set out at was brisk, as it was on the wards themselves. Mr Passmore kept up; Drs Willoughby and Marvill were two steps behind.

'Is Mrs Taylor coming in this morning, David?' the consultant asked. The head and neck resection was of major interest.

'She said she would.'

'It would perhaps be as well if she was present when I talk to her husband. I could manage him on Thursday. Is that possible?'

'You won't get much else on,' he observed pointlessly.

'I'd like to start early, and be finished by lunchtime, hopefully,' Mr Thompson said. Then, as if to counter any possible arguments, 'He'd have a few miserable months at best.'

'Will you write a paper?' Passmore asked.

'It might make a paragraph or two for my book – when I get down to it.'

They crashed through the doors of the ward block.

About three minutes was the average time the consultant spent at a patient's bedside. Some were dealt with a lot quicker. Bernard Reed was one such patient. He looked as miserable now as he did before having his operation for an anal fissure.

'. . . We cut the sphincter muscle in your rectum,' the consultant explained brusquely and, he assumed, fully. 'So you shouldn't be troubled further. There'll be some leakage of gas and fluid stools, but you can wear the pads you'll be provided with.'

'That'll stop, doctor, will it?' the patient asked anxiously. 'That'll stop?'

'In due course, Mr Reed,' he said, suggesting that it would. 'We'll see you in outpatients in a month.'

The surgeon started away, leaving Mr Reed unsure that they had got it right this time. But like most patients Mr Reed was intimidated by doctors.

'Well, I hope it does,' he said quietly. 'I mean, I don't want to go out too early.'

The firm had moved on to Mr Taylor's bed. Mrs Taylor, who was sitting there, started to rise.

'Don't get up, Mrs Taylor. How are you today?' Thompson asked cheerfully, but didn't await a reply. 'Morning, Mr Taylor, how are you? You're looking stronger.' He reached round for the file, which the black sister handed him. 'D'you think he's looking better, Mrs Taylor?'

'Well, he's looking a little better,' she said more encouragingly than truthfully.

'Excellent. You're sleeping better since we changed your medication,' he observed, glancing over the notes.

Mr Taylor mouthed that he was. He was poked so full of drugs at night that it was almost impossible for him not to lose consciousness. But sometimes he didn't and lay in a numbed, sleepless state.

'He's still in a lot of pain,' Mrs Taylor said.

'Of course,' he said sympathetically. 'We're going to do something about that.' He reached for a chair and sat close to Mrs Taylor.

The rest of the firm stayed beyond the end of the bed, and talked among themselves in whispers, their eyes, like their thoughts, occasionally flicking across to the consultant or patient.

'The news isn't all good, Mr Taylor,' Thompson said gently. 'The growth wasn't confined to the nasopharynx,

I'm afraid.' He paused for a moment. A lot of CA patients were ahead of him by this stage, but not this one. It was as though Mr Passmore hadn't previously talked to him. 'It may have spread a little further. Now this isn't as terrible as I know you're thinking. I am confident that we can eradicate these sites completely. The spread is local, this means we can take direct action without the likelihood of secondary growths popping up in other sites.'

'Oh dear, oh dear God,' Mrs Taylor quietly wailed.

The surgeon's words reached into Ray Taylor and he closed his eyes, as if against the possibility, but couldn't prevent tears tipping over his eyelids. Mrs Taylor gripped her husband's hand. She also understood what was being said and was crying. She had feared the worst for days now but had been trying not to acknowledge it.

'At this stage I think the best and most successful course of treatment is another operation.' He paused, to give them a moment with this information. 'We have to cut out the growth, cut back to clean bone and tissue.'

'What does that entail, Mr Thompson?' Mrs Taylor managed to ask finally.

'The growth has spread through the jaw, and into the neck,' he explained, indicating the right side of the patient's face. 'To be sure of taking it all out, we'd have to remove part of your upper and lower jaws,' – he didn't say about half – 'some of the tongue and throat, and the glands in the neck as well.'

A hiss of despair escaped from Mr Taylor.

From Mrs Taylor too. 'Oh God!' She couldn't articulate her fear and horror beyond that.

Jessie Marvill who was watching the man in bed saw the last ghost of hope leave him and couldn't even begin to understand how he felt. She knew how she felt, and was no longer hearing what Mr Passmore was saying about a paper he had recently written on oesophago-gastric reconstruction.

'I do understand how you feel, Mr Taylor, believe me,' Thompson went on, although he couldn't possibly have any near notion of this. 'You feel shocked and terrified. It's the sort of tragedy that makes one think life isn't worth living, that one may as well be dead. I've encountered that reaction hundreds of times from patients, but let me tell you most of them have lived to change their minds. If I don't operate, I'm afraid the only alternative isn't very good at all. We can of course do something about the pain but it won't be very pleasant. I want you to think carefully about this operation, Mr Taylor,' he said with an earnest note in his voice, as if giving the patient a real option, 'bearing in mind I've pointed out the very worst aspects of this, as I don't believe in being anything less than absolutely frank. However, on the credit side, this operation will save your life. We can achieve quite splendid results in reconstructing the face out of skinflaps drawn up from the chest.'

Ray Taylor remained a total blank, while his wife groped for some understanding. 'You mean some sort of skin-grafting?' she asked.

'Exactly that, Mrs Taylor.' Marcus Thompson felt he was gaining ground. 'I don't say the result won't be noticeable, but it will be acceptable.' He paused. 'Right now you feel desperate and despairing at the shock. But after the operation, living for a little while with the result, you'll feel very different. I promise you will feel very different indeed in a few months from now.'

There was a long pause.

Ray Taylor was in shock, he was blinking his eyes to try and push back the tears, not daring to meet anyone's look for fear of breaking down. His wife tried to stop her tears, knowing they wouldn't help him.

'You have a wife and family,' Thompson said directly to Ray Taylor. 'You might consider how they would feel if you were to give up. Perhaps you'd like time to think about all this.'

'When would you have to do it, d'you think, Mr Thompson?' Mrs Taylor managed to ask.

'The position is this, the longer we delay the less chance there is of success, Mrs Taylor. I've rearranged my schedule to operate the day after tomorrow. I have an excellent team assisting me, and we've every reason to believe we'll be entirely successful.'

There was an awkward silence, during which the focus of attention found Mr Taylor. No one noticed that this radical operation had shifted from a possible alternative to being slotted in on a theatre schedule.

Ray Taylor tried to speak, and had he been able to he would have said he was sure the doctors knew what was best. Finally he hissed a barely audible yes.

'That's the spirit. The only way we can beat this is to fight it,' Mr Thompson said, half-rising, ready to move on. He had spent a lot of time with this patient and so would shorten his bedside visits elsewhere.

Self-pity swamped Ray Taylor now that he knew the worst, or believed he did, even though he couldn't fully realize the extent of what would be done. The barriers he had erected earlier were swept away, leaving him naked and vulnerable. He was going to die, he told himself, holding no other belief as firmly as that. Yet in his most lucid moments throughout the day, moments when drugs were wearing off and pain was at its height, he welcomed death as a release from his misery. Then when a nurse gave him an injection and the pain eased, before drifting into unconsciousness he reviewed all the things he hadn't done and wanted to do; those missed opportunities in his life; the regrets he had about being too harsh with people, especially his children, whether they would forgive him, how he would no longer be able to make it up to them. He had worked hard for his family and life was comfortable at last, he didn't want not to be able to enjoy it. The conclusion he arrived at was that what was happening to him wasn't fair.

'Why me?' he managed to ask his wife in a lucid moment.

She had stayed with him throughout the day despite his being unconscious a lot of the time. And when he was conscious she might have not been there for she couldn't help him. There was a distance between them, the result of psychological uncoupling that had taken place over the years. Now even in adversity they were embarrassed about showing their feelings to each other, or touching each other in public. Brenda Taylor had mostly kept her hands tensely clenched on the edge of the bed.

'What have I done to deserve this?'

His wife hadn't any answers, and when she thought about the questions all she could do was cry.

His daughters visited during the evening. He was alert enough to recognize them at one point. The extent of what he had wrong with him and was going to be done to him wasn't talked about. His wife thought it best that they shouldn't dwell upon it. They all stayed until he was given his evening injection, 50 mg of DF118, when he drifted off for a night free of pain. So they believed.

Ray Taylor woke on the darkened ward with searing pain and his thoughts filled with dying. He immediately looked for his wife and got frightened when he couldn't find her. He didn't want to die like this on his own.

The student nurse on night duty came to Mr Taylor's bed when he first cried out. She had no real experience of coping with such suffering, despite having been on another ward with cancer patients, and all she could do was offer platitudes and drugs, the first being worthless, the second increasingly so. She squeezed his cold thin hand, as if to make him less restless. 'Is your pain worse?' she asked quietly. 'Are you worrying about your operation? You shouldn't worry. You're in the best possible hands. Mr Thompson is the best surgeon there is for this sort of thing, I promise you. Everything will be fine.'

Finding the atmosphere at the bed oppressive and not

being able to hide her feelings, she started to leave, but he gripped her hand. Even having a stranger present was better than dying alone, Ray Taylor thought, and started to cry.

'I'll get Staff, see if she can give you something for your pain.' She felt a sense of panic, a need to get away.

50 mg of the synthetic narcotic pain reliever prescribed to Ray Taylor was not enough, so Dr Marvill increased the dose to 75 mg. Afterwards she sat on the patient's bed and tried to talk to him about his proposed treatment, but found she couldn't easily break through the fear and anxiety he was experiencing; these states she thought were being heightened by the drugs.

'Would you like to talk, Mr Taylor?' she asked in a low voice so as not to disturb the rest of the bay. Two of the patients were sleeping, one was listening to the radio. 'About what's troubling you.'

'I don't want to die, doctor,' he managed hoarsely.

That was all he would say.

It occurred to Jessie Marvill at that point how little people learned in their lifetime. Here was a man who in forty-five years of life came no closer to understanding about dying than at the start of it, if anything he was probably further from understanding. To a large extent she, along with the entire medical establishment, was responsible for that, she realized. Medical propaganda had promised cures for almost everything that ailed a body, and that was the nation's expectation. The operation Ray Taylor was soon to undergo was part of that propaganda, and wasn't necessarily being done because it was the best course of action, rather because they were capable of performing it; not to do it might diminish the status the surgeons had achieved.

Jessie Marvill's thoughts shocked her, and for the first time she questioned not just whether she had chosen the right specialty, but if she was in the right profession.

In the medical staff social club, she found Laurence James, who was also on call and bought him a drink. Instead of a barman there was a bar book in which everyone wrote up their drinks to be paid for at the end of the month.

Laurence James was on his own, and she was glad for she needed to talk to someone, and might have sought him out.

He smiled sympathetically as he listened to her doubts. When she had finished speaking he said, 'That's not a problem that can't be overcome, Jess. You simply change your job. Talk to Vernon, he has those sort of doubts all the time, poor fool. Of course surgeons perform the operations they're good at, stands to reason. I daresay old Cutter Thompson will do a smashing commando operation. Whether your Mr Taylor should be put through it is another question.'

She hesitated. 'Any chance you might talk to him?'

'It's a bit late for alternatives.' He saw her look. 'Oh I don't mean because the CA is too advanced he's a no-hoper. That's how a lot of patients are when healers get to see them. Mr Taylor's treatment seems mapped out. Healing concerns itself with the whole person on all levels, without necessarily curing the disease.' He saw her doubts, knew it was partly the fault of the channel that materialistic medicine drove its practitioners through. 'We only see sickness from our own subjective perspective. Disease really results out of conflict between soul and mind. You can be sick in body, but well in spirit and mentally alert. Changing the patient in mind and spirit was sometimes enough, Jessie. Most people expect to be cured when they go into hospital; healing is something people come to when they're ready; enlightened, if you like. Some never are; with others, well, it's a last ditch, try anything, won't they? Perhaps your Mr Taylor doesn't want to be helped. Some people cling to illness.'

She found that proposition difficult to go with. 'I'm not

sure about that. Isn't consulting a doctor and going into hospital a conscious act of wanting to be well?'

'Going into hospital has become an inevitable process which most of us don't question,' Dr James said. 'Often it reinforces the need to be ill. On this conscious level I dare say he wants to be well. I wouldn't have thought cancer develops on a conscious level. Take someone like Mr Taylor. At that age the body's immune system has to deal with probably 100,000 cancer cells per hour. That's over two million a day. This is going on the whole time – what we must ask is why some people aren't able to resist the disease. The answer can't be that some people are in contact with known carcinogens. Because everyone who smokes doesn't get lung cancer, all red meat eaters don't get cancer of the colon. So we have to look to the unconscious process. Because of his emotional psychological state the patient creates the right environment for his illness.'

Although she tried to keep an open mind all her medical conditioning veered her away from that argument. 'I've seen no evidence to support that – certainly not between meat-eating and cancer.'

'No real studies have been made – there's a vested interest similar to that which resisted the connection being made between smoking and lung cancer. Thirty years ago you'd have said the same about that. Medicine's getting a bit bogged down in empirical explanation. The fact is, Jess, most of the medicine we practise works as a result of the ritual of laying on of hands or writing a prescription.'

'There are no papers published establishing cause and effect.' She was beginning to feel uneasy.

'No,' he said quietly. 'Most gungho researchers want to be in with the hardware, impressing the medical establishment. They don't want to go off on some insane project and risk the scorn of their peers. How do you think the Cancer Research Institute would react if I took along such a thesis? But if I had a scheme to get a thousand beagles to smoke a million fags in ten minutes, with some spurious end result, they'd pour money into it.' He was angry, but instead of becoming demonstrative he got quieter. 'We're led to misunderstand the real nature of disease, concentrating it, as we have, on material factors. What we've done is increased its power by localizing it in the body. We've raised a huge disease complex of fear by our attitudes. If cancer reflected a material, social, economic, or even a political bias then the disease would have been eradicated. But here we are, still trying to help people in isolation, instead of coming to terms with the real problem.'

He paused and drank some of his beer. 'A lot of doctors have lost their gift of healing, Jessie,' he said. 'Or don't consider it. If they did, I think it would probably embarrass them. I embarrass some of my colleagues. They rely instead on technology and pharmacology. I suspect they don't really care too much about people.' That caused him serious concern. Even in his relatively short career, since he first came into contact with the medical profession as a physiologist he had seen the attitude in medicine change from one of a caring position to a largely technical, impersonal, goal-orientated approach, like the one taking Ray Taylor on his present course.

'I don't think that's true,' Jessie Marvill said defensively out of a sense of loyalty to her profession. 'Some get very real satisfaction from helping people.'

'Yes, I know,' he said. 'I'm sure you do, Jess.'

Jessie Marvill pulled a face, experiencing the embarrassment he spoke of earlier.

'I do think you're in the wrong specialty, Jessie. You should be doing medicine not surgery. General practice for preference.'

She shrugged. 'Oh dear. I do hope I've got it right. My father said I wouldn't hold up.'

'I bet your boss isn't considering the alternatives for Mr Taylor.'

'He probably did,' Jessie Marvill said, without knowing what Marcus Thompson's inner thoughts were.

Dr James nodded reflectively, holding her look.

'Do you think there might be some realistic alternative for Mr Taylor?' she asked. 'It doesn't seem fair, having brought him this far just to throw him back on himself.'

'If you mean a cure, Jess, I don't know. Getting him to look at why he developed cancer would be a start, rather than no study of his oncological history.' His bleep went off. Both doctors felt their bleeps to quieten them; it was an obsessive habit.

'That might defy analysis,' Dr Marvill suggested.

'That's what we're led to expect.' He finished his beer in a brief pause that followed. 'It's like starting therapy – you do it to know what's good about you rather than what's wrong with you.'

Jessie Marvill thought about the analogy.

It would be that positive concept rather than simply the pressure she felt under that would bring her to therapy.

'We'd have to find out whether Mr Taylor wants to get rid of the cancer. It's wrong to assume he does. I'm sure he does on a conscious level. Some alternative treatment could be worked out. I'd willingly find him a healer. But only if he wants one.'

'I do sense he's embarking on something that is very wrong for him, going to theatre.'

Dr James smiled. 'I'd better see why I'm wanted,' he said, reluctant to leave this conversation and her company.

'I'll have a word with Mrs Taylor. She'll be easier to talk to.' She finished her drink.

He hesitated, and held her look a moment. There was a feeling beyond professional understanding between them and he wanted to pursue it.

18

Dr Marvill was on S1 in Nightingale Block several times during the morning and afternoon, and on each occasion saw Mrs Taylor at her husband's bedside. When she spoke to her it wasn't to raise the question of healing for her husband as an alternative to the radical surgery. Even though her boss would take exception and complain to Dr James's consultant if he found out about it, Laurence James was still willing to see the patient; he was that sort of man. She was, however, even more convinced that Ray Taylor was taking the wrong course, though had no proven medical basis for recommending that he changed.

Finally she approached Brenda Taylor after her husband had drifted off to sleep and invited her to the ward office for some tea.

'He seems to sleep so badly. He's in such pain most of the time,' Mrs Taylor said. 'I can't bear seeing him like this.' She drank some of her tea, holding back her tears.

Dr Marvill said nothing, sensing it was better to let her talk, that she would reach a point where she could raise the question of alternatives. A general problem with medicine, she found, especially the kind practised in hospitals, was that there was never enough time to counsel either the patients or their families. Going to hospital or to one's doctor could be very stressful, and often wasn't helped by the attitude of doctors themselves.

'Will he be all right, doctor, if he has it?' Mrs Taylor asked, overcoming her fears sufficiently. 'I mean, it seems so drastic. I mean, I don't see how it can be the same person left. He can't be the same. It'll change him so much, won't it? He couldn't be the same. He won't be so recognizable.'

She started to cry.

Dr Marvill waited.

'I'm sorry, behaving like this. But it's so awful. I haven't slept for thinking about it. I try not to think about it. I don't know what to think for the best, doctor. It's so awful. It just seems so unfair that he should get something like this. I've always been the one to worry about my health. I always seem to have something wrong. If it's not one thing it's another. I have high blood pressure. Raymond's never ill. I'm on tablets from the doctor. He never complained.' Mrs Taylor broke off from her outpouring and looked at Dr Marvill. 'What do you think will happen, doctor? Will it all be all right?'

Dr Marvill hesitated. 'I can't say, Mrs Taylor. I wish I could tell you otherwise. Your husband's very ill. The operation will be very disfiguring. There is a good chance it will save his life, but you might find the result difficult to live with. He might find it especially difficult.'

'It sounds awful, I can't quite grasp how awful it will be. I don't think he does at all,' she said in a barely audible voice. 'Do you think he shouldn't have it, this operation?'

She hesitated again. 'Mr Thompson is a first-rate surgeon. If your husband goes through with it he will be in very good hands.' She paused, knowing that wasn't the answer, but not knowing where to go directly. She wondered briefly how she had started on this, and didn't know if she wasn't just adding confusion to this woman's already confused and wretched state. 'Do you have any particular faith, or religious belief?'

Brenda Taylor was embarrassed. Being asked that was like being asked about one's sexlife. 'We used to go to church. I mean, mostly for the children's sake. When they got older and pleased themselves, well, we got out of the habit. I've said my prayers these last few weeks, I've said them over and over again.'

Jessie Marvill nodded. That answer meant no, which

didn't help her much. 'Have you talked to a counsellor at all?'

'The social worker? I can't remember her name . . . I can't remember anything lately. She brought someone to talk to us. They mean well, I suppose. But it's not them who are going through it, is it? I mean, it's not like their family.'

'This might seem strange to you, Mrs Taylor, and perhaps I shouldn't be suggesting it . . .' she hesitated. 'But would your husband agree to seeing a healer, do you think? Would he agree to that?'

'I don't know. He'd probably try anything.' She seemed puzzled. 'A faith healer, you mean?'

'We call them faith healers for convenience, but they have various methods. Consulting a doctor is an act of faith,' Dr Marvill told her.

'I once saw a programme on the television about a woman who was cured of breast cancer by a faith healer,' Mrs Taylor said. 'I didn't think hospitals allowed that sort of thing.'

'We're not exactly opening the wards,' Dr Marvill said. 'But more doctors are taking an interest.' She didn't know many, but Dr James had told her there was increasing interest, there was even a consultant physician who allowed healers on to his wards – not at St Clair's. Some members of the medical profession would resist heterodox medicine forever.

'I doubt if Ray believes in it,' Mrs Taylor said. 'I'm not sure if I do.'

'Did you believe what happened to the woman in the television programme when she had a spontaneous remission of breast cancer?' She waited, but Mrs Taylor didn't respond. 'I'm not altogether certain one has to believe in it. One doesn't have to believe in penicillin for that to be effective. I think what a strong belief gives is comfort and reassurance. I'm not suggesting healing will necessarily cure your husband, but it might give him comfort. There is little else we can offer, apart from the operation.'

Those words reverberated around inside Jessie Marvill's skull. She realized she had not only gone against most of what her training had led her to believe, but she had also admitted it to a patient's wife. That was something a doctor did at risk of destroying the myth which the profession had worked so skilfully to create. Thinking about the poor prospects for Mr Taylor, and the limits to surgery, made her depressed about her chosen specialty, but she didn't know how much Laurence James alone was influencing her.

Ordinarily Brenda Taylor would have felt silly talking to her husband about faith healing and especially as he was going to have such a major operation in the morning; she thought this situation unreal in many ways, yet with the parts of her mind that understood what was happening, she was prepared to try anything.

Propped up in bed, staring fixedly into the middle-distance, Ray Taylor wasn't aware of much going on around him, only his wife who in odd moments broke through the cloud of pain.

She reached out and took his bony hand and squeezed it, to reassure him that she was still there.

After a long while he whispered hoarsely, 'I keep asking, why me? It doesn't make sense. Not to me it doesn't.'

The situation made no more sense to Brenda Taylor. She broke down again and wept, but her husband could do nothing to comfort her.

'The girls will be in later. About seven, they said,' she told him with difficulty. 'Will you see this other doctor? Dr James?'

He didn't respond to the question. 'I saw Mr Passmore earlier. He explained it all again. He's a decent sort, seems to know what he's doing. The consultant's a top man in this field. He specializes in this sort of thing.'

'He's not a faith healer,' his wife said, following her own line of thought. 'He's properly qualified.'

'I'm scared, Bren'. Something's got to happen.'

He screwed up his eyes as pain tore through the righthand side of his face. The pain was getting progressively worse. 'Oh God,' he cried. 'I wish they would take this pain away. I wish someone would tell me why I have to suffer this.'

He had asked that a thousand times since being told he had cancer, but had asked through anguish and despair, not with any expectation of an answer.

Not even Dr James could give him a ready answer when he visited him late in the evening. The reasons were manifold but he couldn't begin to explain coming like this to a man who had never thought about these things in his entire life. He was seeking an enormous bond of trust, which his position as a doctor helped achieve; what he hoped to do was help Ray Taylor to find a state of serenity where suffering no longer consumed him. He wasn't sure that Mr Taylor understood. He felt his attitude to healing, like that towards orthodox medicine was based on the material principle: of right to purchase whatever one had the power to purchase, believing that no effort was required, that one wasn't even expected to change one's lifestyle if that was what was making one ill, which was so often the case.

Dr James frequently encountered this attitude, though less with old patients who, through economic circumstances, had come to be more self-reliant and saw any help as a gift. He didn't refuse to help patients as a result of this attitude, and it wouldn't stop him helping Ray Taylor. All he appeared to do was sit on the bed and hold his hands, not saying anything, or doing anything dramatic until after about forty minutes the patient drifted off.

The staffnurse seemed surprised when she arrived at the bed and found Mr Taylor asleep. 'He hasn't had his injection,' she said. 'He can't sleep without it.'

'I shouldn't wake him up to give it him, Staff,' Dr James said. He was tired and drained from the level of concentration he had put in during this healing.

The patient wasn't miraculously cured when Dr James called to see him the following morning, but in his drowsy state from his pre-med injection he managed a wan smile, his first since being told his problem.

Dr James sat on Ray Taylor's bed and unselfconsciously held his hand. The morning business of the ward continued around them.

'I don't know what you did, doctor,' Ray Taylor whispered, causing Dr James to lean forward to hear. 'But I had a good night's sleep last night.'

'I didn't do anything, Mr Taylor,' he told him. 'You did it yourself.'

Ray Taylor seemed unsure. He gave the appearance of drifting off to sleep, then opened his eyes again. 'I keep coming back to that same question,' he gasped. 'Why does it have to be me?'

'Well, there is an answer,' Dr James said quietly. 'But you have to address the question to yourself. You've got to want the answer, and be prepared to deal with what you find.' He didn't know if he was getting through to him. Glancing up he saw two theatre porters come into the bay.

'You're going to theatre now.'

Fear and apprehension entered Ray Taylor's face as he looked around, as if for a familiar face, his wife perhaps, or his daughters. 'Will you come with me?' he whispered.

'Yes.' Dr James rose as the trolley was brought alongside.

'Hello, squire,' Trevor Holland, the porter, said cheerfully. 'Gotta put you on the trolley.'

Dr James stepped aside while they slid the poles into the canvas trolley cover that had been put under Ray Taylor, and lifted him on to the trolley.

The other patients watched him go, an old hand on the opposite side of the bay gave him a thumb up. He was familiar with patients' comings and goings, and said to the patient in the next bed, 'Poor old bugger. They're going to cut half his head away, they are. 'S cancer. 'S got it all down the right side of his face.'

'Yes, I heard that,' said the patient who had taken Bernard Reed's bed. 'Can you imagine that operation?'

'Amazing isn't it,' the old hand observed. 'What they can do for you nowadays is no one's business. 'S just bloody well amazing.'

The trolley with Ray Taylor, the two porters, a nurse and Dr James entered the lift like a burial party.

The doors closed. As the lift started to descend Ray Taylor's hand searched along the cover for Dr James's hand. The doctor held it all the way along the corridors that connected Nightingale with the new theatres.

In the theatre block the sister was concerned to maintain a sterile field and medical staff weren't encouraged to wander in with the casual ease of the older theatres. Dr James had to leave the patient at the sterile barrier to put on boots and theatre greens in order to stay with Ray Taylor right up to that last fearful look before he went under the anaesthetic.

Five hours thirty nine minutes after he had entered theatre for a head and neck resection the doors to the recovery room opened and a no longer recognizable Ray Taylor, the side of his face swathed in the swollen tissue of skinflaps, was wheeled out at a brisk pace by nurses and operating theatre technicians. The consultant anaesthetist, Dr Oliver Wade, and Nick Alderton, his registrar, were with the patient who was being ventilated via the trachea, and remained connected to the monitor, all of which came in from theatre with him, besides the blood transfusion and saline drip. A tired-looking Jessie Marvill followed them in. Unlike her colleagues, who had gone to the adjacent surgeons' room for coffee, she was concerned to see this patient come round in the recovery room.

As he was wheeled into position, a burst of activity followed as a final check through the monitors was made.

Tracings of his heart rhythms were running across the visual display on the ECG monitor.

After a moment Mr Passmore appeared and stood with Dr Marvill. 'It was a long stint, Jessie,' he said as though a rare privilege had been accorded her. 'You won't see one of those again in a while.'

Jessie Marvill said nothing.

He looked round at her. 'That's about as heroic as can be, the eye to the larynx.' He was proud of his part in this.

The electrocardiograph, which had been tweeping merrily away, suddenly ceased.

'His heart's stopped,' the recovery room nurse said.

This galvanized everyone except Jessie Marvill into action.

Although with modern anaesthetics heart failure was far from inevitable, Jessie Marvill accepted the patient giving up like this with a degree of inevitability. She watched, drained and emotionless, as the whole team swung into action to resuscitate the patient.

'0.15 mg of adrenalin. Intravenous, Nick,' Dr Wade said and immediately started cardiac massage.

The registrar anaesthetist injected the drug via the venous canula attached to the patient's arm.

Then they waited. There was no response.

'It's still a systole,' Mr Passmore informed them, checking the tracings from the ECG visual display. The heart had stuck at the point before the contraction which surged blood through the aorta and pulmonary artery. The blood was picking up none of the oxygen being pumped into the lungs.

'Let's try another 0.10 mg of adrenalin. I'll put it directly into the heart.' Dr Wade continued external massage until his registrar proffered the intra-cardial hypodermic. The consultant plunged it through the chest wall into the heart.

'He's turning blue,' the staffnurse said. Everyone in the recovery room could see as much.

Mr Passmore stayed with the tracing on the ECG. They were running in a straight line, despite the adrenalin into the heart, the external massage, the heart punches, defibrillation, the oxygen his lungs were getting.

Twenty minutes later Dr Marvill was still unmoving, the activity around her ground to a halt from exhaustion. There was nothing more to be done, though the consultant anaesthetist was determined to go on trying, even though there was little doubt about the extent of the brain damage if he did get the heart going again. Then at last even he gave up.

'What rotten luck,' Mr Passmore said. 'After everything we put into it.'

'Yes,' she said, 'rotten luck.'

He turned and went out through the theatre. Dead patients were of no interest, regardless of effort previously put in on them.

Finally Jessie Marvill turned away, leaving the electrocardiograph displaying its obvious message. Someone would eventually switch it off, she thought. Passing through the theatre, she glanced at the list board and saw there were seven more operations slotted in for this afternoon. Two of them were minor and she was to do those on her own.

In the surgeons' room Mr Thompson and David Passmore were discussing the lost patient. Jessie Marvill found it odd that the consultant hadn't entered the recovery room, even accepting that was the province of the anaesthetist. It disturbed her that he showed no apparent emotion at the loss of this patient on whom he had worked so hard. What worried her most was the possibility that one day she might be this detached, and she wondered again if in this specialty she had made the right choice. At times like this she also questioned her choice of profession: lost were the moments of pure enjoyment when she helped a patient; that feeling of power she had experienced early in her career when patients had deferred without question to her raw opinion; the trick was to remember those, and forget the Mr Taylors. But she wasn't sure that she would ever learn that trick.

Jessie Marvill was certain she had made the wrong choice when she heard her boss saying, '. . . Pity we lost him like that. The photographer I brought in got some excellent pictures. They'd have looked well in my book.'

'I daresay you could still use them, Marcus,' Mr Passmore said.

'Would have been more impressive had the caption read, "The patient survived and had a good year or two."'

Without a word Jessie Marvill turned and left the room, not caring at that moment if she never came back.

Book II

The medical establishment prefers
treatment to prevention.

19

Without doubt one of the biggest commercial growth areas currently was private health care. Bankers, industrialists, oil-rich sheiks, union pension funds, shopkeepers, all were quietly investing; while the government, through the National Enterprise Board pursued a policy of active encouragement, making available whatever parts of the NHS that could be sold without too vociferous a public outcry or political opposition. Good health was something most people wanted, and those who could afford to pay were ever willing, for paying meant merely digging into one's pocket, mattress or bank balance; it required no effort in changing whatever was causing the illness. Private health care was leapfrogging social, economic and political barriers as people sought the means of good health, erroneously believing private health care better than that available in the public sector; when the only real difference was that the fee-for-service mentality of medical staff in private medicine guaranteed treatment in more convenient, and somewhat more courteous packages: doctors being paid directly by the patient had to be deferential, and wouldn't employ a discourteous nurse; the clinics where patients paid at the door knew they'd get few recommendations if they weren't structured for patients' convenience. But few patients questioned whether this hotel-like service intruded on the clinical aspect, or considered how a doctor who was receiving a direct fee for service might increase the service, extend an operation or treatment beyond necessity in order to fatten the fee.

While private medicine expanded, the other side of the coin, public sector medicine, was shrinking in direct proportion. Everyone was entitled to treatment within the NHS, if they could find GPs to take them on to their list – there were too few doctors for patients in some areas, especially less attractive inner city areas, or if there was a hospital with a bed available, as more and more were being taken out of service as a result of public expenditure cuts. The NHS was over-stretched, with a shortage of doctors, nurses, ancillaries and facilities, but most of all a shortage of money, and nothing was likely to change while more money was being taken out of the service. This was partly due to the fact that the DHSS increasingly saw less need for public medicine with private medicine meeting so many needs.

Whatever their social, economic or political status, people tended to get the sort of medical treatment they deserved. It had the same universal standard both in private and public medicine, a standard that too frequently wasn't high, and wouldn't be any different while the process was shrouded in mystery and mystique, a situation that continued because patients refused to question the practitioners treating them.

Traditionally it was believed not good manners to question one's doctor, because he knew best; also there was the strong element of fear that often accompanied the patient, the fear of being unwell, of suffering, or dying, that this mysterious being could change. Patients willingly laid the magic mantle over doctors, and wanted to do nothing to lessen its potency. Doctors were pleased to wear that mantle, enjoying the status and power it brought them. They weren't about to encourage a process of questioning their position.

An area of medicine where cuts hadn't yet made an immediately noticeable difference was general practice. Here, as a result of GPs being unable to get more money per patient for those on their list, more and more found themselves having to increase their number of patients in order to maintain their living standard. At one time doctors' income was on a par with barristers', nowadays they were trailing solicitors, which was a source of annoyance to some. By accepting more patients than they could often reasonably cope with they had to shorten the time allocated to each patient; because of this, the tendency was to refer them to hospital, only to frequently discover they could no longer find them a bed. Part of this overwork-syndrome was that doctors reached for the prescription pad before the patient had sat down and started to relate the problem.

Dr Percy Thurson was no exception, yet curiously his patients seemed not to mind, their thinking in relation to other patients being: the quicker he gets shot of them the quicker he gets to me.

Dr Thurson's surgery, like the practice itself, was rather old-fashioned; there were wooden filing cabinets, some with patients' records going back to before he took over the practice – a receptionist looked after current records in another part of the house. Also in this room were two glass-fronted drugs cabinets, a high examination couch, a desk, with a desperate clutter of samples and promotions from drug companies around the periphery. Only the centre of the blotter was clear for his prescription block and medical certificates. At the bow windows heavy net curtains gave this former Victorian sitting-room a dark appearance. There was no aspidistra in the window bay, instead a table holding instruments, again with a slightly old-fashioned look to them, a sphygmomanometer for measuring blood pressure, a tendon hammer for testing reflexes.

Dr Percy Thurson could easily have been taken for older than sixty-five. Blood vessels in his pink, fleshy face had started to rupture, giving a broken reddish appearance, his white hair had started to fall at last; that once familiar avuncular manner that put patients so much at ease was strained nowadays. He was worn out and constantly on edge; he was a man who had given too much of himself too often. The pills he popped to get him through the day whenever he felt over-extended weren't helping much any more, neither were those to get him through the night.

He had come to the end with the young woman in the chair opposite his desk; he had listened to her story, and knew her problem, or believed he did. Reaching for his pen and prescription pad, he said, 'Chloë, you're getting yourself into such a state over this baby.' He was weary, but not unsympathetic. 'First you were convinced it would be stillborn; then that it was going to have spina bifida. Now you're worrying about going into hospital. You're a healthy young woman, and all your tests have shown that you're going to have a healthy and normal baby. I'm going to give you some more tablets . . .'

'Will they harm the baby?' she asked quietly.

He raised his eyes from the prescription block. 'You'll do it more harm with all this worry if your blood pressure goes up.'

Chloë Shallcross was a frail, over-anxious young lady who was six months pregnant with her first child. Although pleased, the root of her anxiety was her rejection from her own mother at birth, starting when her mother's nipples became abscessed. Chloë was afraid that with her own child a similar pattern of rejection might emerge, and so projected this fear on to her own baby. The fear before her current one was that the baby was going to be spina bifida or have Down's syndrome. The fears had started as a result of articles Chloë had read, as there was no family history of anyone being congenitally defective. However at sixteen weeks Thurson had arranged for her to have amniocentesis; the amniotic sac was punctured by a long needle through the abdomen wall and some of the fluid in the uterus drawn off. Genetic disorders could be discovered by chemical or cytological tests.

The tests in themselves did nothing to reassure Chloë Shallcross. This was an anxious time for her, as she had to wait until she was sixteen weeks pregnant before undergoing the test. Prior to sixteen weeks the foetus wasn't sufficiently developed to show up abnormalities; she had to wait another two weeks for the results, and like so many women she hadn't thought through the implications of a possible abortion. Chloë hadn't been entirely reassured by the results she had been given or freed from anxiety, especially not when she learned afterwards that the test itself could result in a miscarriage. In fact her tests had showed marginally elevated blood, and raised alfa-feota protein – which would later prove normal – but Chloë Shallcross wasn't given this information.

She wasn't reassured now. 'I'm not just anxious, doctor,' she said, instinctively not wanting more pills for anxiety. But she wasn't firm enough.

'Of course, Chloë,' he said with a sigh, wanting to get on to his next patient. He continued scribbling. 'I did speak to the community midwife, but she isn't happy about home-birth. I don't think anyone would deliver a first baby at home.'

'I don't want to have it in hospital,' she persisted in a subdued voice.

'You mustn't worry about what happened to your friend or anyone else, or anything you happen to see on television,' he told her, rising and coming round to her. 'I know Mum had some difficulties with you, but that was because of abscesses on the nipples when you were feeding. I don't think you'll have any problems like that. Anyway we can deal with those sort of things very effectively nowadays. So let's have no more worrying. You get these,' he said, giving her the prescription, 'they'll help you, and they won't harm baby.'

Chloë Shallcross got up awkwardly, getting an encouraging arm half around her shoulder from the doctor.

'Try not to worry, Chloë.' He smiled and opened the door for her, as though this was one more satisfied customer.

Percy Thurson no longer had space for those sort of thoughts, but buried in deep recesses of his mind were recollections of patients leaving his surgery a lot happier than when they arrived. He assumed that was still the case.

'Gets worse every time you come here,' a man in his thirties said in a complaining whisper to the woman next to him in the crowded waiting-room. He was Bernard Reed, who was still having problems after his second operation for an anal fissure. He was experienced enough to know that Monday wasn't the best morning to visit the doctor even with an appointment, but being unable to face work, like most of these patients, it was necessary.

'You're next – my appointment was twenty minutes ago.' He sighed impatiently as if that might bring the appointments back on schedule.

'She's been in there a long time,' the woman, Ethel Grant, said. 'He usually gets through them quicker than this.'

Patients in this large room were snuffling and restless, trying to absorb themselves in old magazines. Some held whispered disjointed conversations; a worn-down mother tried to restrain three noisy children, threatening to clout them, saying, 'That woman will be back in a minute and tell you off again.' She meant the receptionist, who had her desk by the door.

'I'd like to know how much longer she's going to be,' Reed said, glancing at his watch.

Everyone looked up expectantly as the door handle turned, but it was the receptionist, returning. She was a middle-aged woman with a sharp manner. Without warning she grabbed the eldest child who was charging about, but didn't consider how she was partly to blame for their restlessness.

'Why don't you be a good little girl for your mother?' she challenged.

'Sharron, behave! I won't tell you again,' the mother said, as if it was pointless.

'Here, take your little brother and sister along to the papershop and get some crisps.' The receptionist gave her fifty pence. That was the easiest way of dealing with that problem. She assumed that authority and gave the mother a thin smile, before sending in the next patient.

Dr Thurson lost track of the number of patients he saw each surgery, sometimes too many. Frequently of late he lost track of who they were, as faces, names and complaints all merged together, despite there being a stream of regular patients. Changing to an appointments system hadn't helped much, it hadn't helped contain the length of the surgeries; a patient would need more attention than the few minutes allocated, or telephone in great distress and be seen without an appointment, and lost time was never made up.

He knew the patient who came into the surgery, but couldn't recall her name or complaint, even though he had seen her within the last month.

'Hello Mrs . . .' the greeting trailed off as he found her card that his receptionist had placed on the desk along with the records of all the other patients with appointments that morning. He indicated the chair, and his thoughts wandered for a second or two as she sat.

'What's the problem, Mrs Grant?'

'Well, it's the usual, doctor.' Ethel Grant was in her early fifties, a mother and a grandmother, who had taken care of herself. 'I mean, the pain just didn't stop Saturday night. I almost called you out yesterday, I did.'

'Have the hot flushes returned?' he asked, glancing through his notes.

'I'd put up with those if I could only do something about this pain.'

'Just pop your skirt off, and get on the couch, Mrs . . .' Her name slipped his memory.

He reached for a piece of notepaper as the patient removed her skirt and slip and boosted herself on to the couch. He addressed the letter to Mr Philip Montagu, a consultant gynaecologist at St Clair's Hospital.

'I think you're going through the change of life, Mrs Grant. But I would like you to see a gynaecologist about the pain you're getting.'

He would examine her again, but this referral was a course he had decided on two visits ago. The reason he was only just getting to it wasn't that he was a bad doctor, or that he was old or past it, or over-stretched and needed to take on a partner. Things were rarely so simple. The rationale for his delay was his knowledge of Mrs Grant. Percy Thurson had the advantage of knowing most of his patients intimately, when the right aid to memory could be found; he knew the social and economic pressures that often had a direct bearing on their health; their fears and hopes, and although he could mostly do nothing about those, he could sometimes use that information when treating them. He knew for instance that Mrs Grant had an active and, he presumed, enjoyable sexlife, so resisted sending her for a course of treatment that might result in this coming to an end. But frequently him not doing what he ought to do was due to him being over-stretched.

He glanced at his watch as he rose to go across to the patient. He would need to do a thorough examination in order to write the referral note, that would put his surgery even further behind. But he would do it.

The couple who followed Mrs Grant didn't need treatment, a prescription or medical certificate, but advice about what action they might take against the hospital where the woman's mother had died of cancer five months ago. Gina Tong and her husband Roy had been told that her mother had died as a result of her treatment, which had been new and experimental.

'I'm not sure how best to advise you on this,' Dr Thurson told them after managing to calm Gina Tong down from the distressed state she had worked herself into. 'I think you really need a solicitor. You could sue the hospital, but it's a path full of pitfalls, and it could cause you both a lot of emotional pain.'

'But people do sue when something goes wrong,' Roy Tong said. He was unsure what good it would do, but felt he had to try something for his wife's sake.

'There have been successful lawsuits,' Dr Thurson said. 'But people don't often sue, Roy. It could prove costly, and I'm not sure that Mum died as a result of her treatment rather than the cancer.'

'But a nurse on the gynae ward told us they were trying out this new drug on Gina's Mum. Several women had it and they all died. It was some combination of drug and radium treatment.'

'Post-operative treatment for ovarian carcinoma often involves both chemotherapy and radiotherapy,' Dr Thurson told them. 'Nurses rarely see the whole picture. Believe me, drugs have to meet some pretty rigorous safety standards before they get to the public. Drug companies do every conceivable test imaginable on animals before they're allowed to test them on humans,' – as if this were a virtue.

There was an awkward silence.

'Well, what do you advise, doctor?' Gina Tong asked. 'Should we just forget it?'

'That would be my advice, Gina,' he said. 'But if you feel this is something you must go ahead with perhaps you should have a chat with the consultant gynaecologist or the radiotherapist, either might set your mind at rest.'

The Tongs were uncertain about this, thinking it would mean some sort of cover-up.

'I'll write to the consultant, Mr Montagu. I'm sure he'll be able to tell you just what happened,' he said. There was little more he could do for them. He would have preferred giving them some sense of satisfaction, but they were restless and impatient to leave. 'I'll write to the consultant today.' He knew what the answer would be.

The patients in the waiting-room were little closer to

being seen by the time David Soper arrived. He was well-groomed and wore mutton chop side-whiskers, but his suit was a shade behind the latest fashion. Soper held the door for a patient, whom he followed to the reception desk.

'Dr Thurson can't possibly see you today,' the receptionist was saying into the telephone, 'his appointments are full. You can come in at eleven o'clock and wait around, but he is running late.' The patient didn't favour that option. 'Then let me make you an appointment. Right, that's Friday the 15th at 9.50,' Mrs Joan Richards said. She replaced the phone.

'I've an appointment at 10.40,' the patient at the desk informed her.

'Did you particularly need to see the doctor, or is it a repeat prescription?'

'Well,' the patient hesitated. 'I'm having trouble with my back.'

'What sort of trouble?' Mrs Richards was quite adept at diagnosing from behind her desk; and often patients went away with a prescription or a certificate, pleased to avoid a wait.

'It catches me here whenever I bend down.'

'In the lumbar region. Any pain in the legs?'

'A bit in my right leg now and again.'

'Sciatica by the sound of it, Mr Hopkins,' she announced. 'I can give you a prescription. Do you need a certificate . . .?' She had a pile of certificates presigned by the doctor. Initially Dr Thurson had been reluctant to delegate, being the sort of doctor who made a point of seeing everyone and doing everything himself. But gradually the receptionist had got him to give some ground.

This patient wasn't sure. 'Well if I could just see the doctor,' he said.

'He is running very late,' she said brusquely, and dismissed him, turning her attention to the drugs rep.

'David Soper, Cavandish Pharmaceuticals,' Soper

reminded her with a jolly hand signal. He pulled a face about the patient, acknowledging his unreasonableness. This eased her embarrassment and made her feel more amenable. 'I was in the area. Thought I'd just drop in to see if Dr Thurson was coming to our little do at St Clair's next Tuesday.'

'He said he was, unless he's forgotten.' She took a telephone call. 'Dr Thurson's surgery . . . He can't make a visit this morning. He could between four and five this afternoon . . . I'm sorry, the doctor is very busy. If you bring him in at eleven, I'll ask Dr Thurson to see him.'

As if oblivious to how busy the doctor was, Soper said, 'Is it possible to have a little word?' – as the receptionist came off the phone.

'I'm sure he'll see you,' she said quietly. 'I'll slip you in between patients.'

'Does your waiting-room need any magazines?' He opened his case, producing a batch of glossies. Pharmaceutical companies bought up back issues of magazines cheaply to promote goodwill.

Joan Richards had been a doctor's receptionist long enough now to know how to treat drug reps, even area managers like Soper. She wasn't about to let him off so lightly.

'Do you have any starter dose antibiotics to spare?' She knew how to cadge for her boss, whose practice wasn't exactly the most prosperous.

'In the car. I'll get you some,' he said readily.

'And maybe some polythene examination gloves,' she added. These the doctor used all the time and had to buy for himself.

David Soper looked at her, accepting that this was the price of access to the doctor.

When the buzzer on the receptionist's desk sounded for the next patient, most of those waiting looked up as if believing they were next.

'I'll see if I can slip you in now,' Mrs Richards said quietly to David Soper, who had been quite generous. Often reps tried to get away with giving calendars, paperclip holders or things to scrape ice off car windscreens.

She led Soper out and across the hall to the surgery door. 'Could you spare Mr Soper of Cavandish's a couple of minutes?' Mrs Richards asked.

'A minute or two, if he's here.' Dr Thurson glanced at his watch, a couple of minutes wouldn't make much difference. There was something on his mind involving this rep's company only he couldn't remember what.

Mrs Richards pushed the door open and let the rep through.

'Morning, Dr Thurson,' Soper said, sounding his most unctuous. 'I hope this isn't too inconvenient.'

'I suspect I'm running behind,' Thurson said as if unsure.

'I'll be brief. I hope you're coming to our luncheon buffet at St Clair's next Tuesday. I didn't get a reply to our invitation.'

Dr Thurson glanced over the mess of letters and literature on his desk. 'It's lunch?' He was certain there was something else.

'A cold buffet. With an exhibition for two brand new drugs we're introducing. Oestraline has proved highly effective in clinical trials for treating dysmenorrhoea.' He produced a sample on cue. Then, while his case was open, he took out a six-inch box and an envelope. 'Now, sir which do you want? The box or the envelope?'

Dr Thurson was a total blank.

'You agreed to participate in trials for our new vasodilator, Vasculine-90,' Soper reminded him. 'What is required of you is five patients who you could prescribe the drug to, with three follow up consultations on each. There's a £75 cash fee attached, or a carriage clock valued at £140, whichever you prefer.'

This was a familiar practice of drug companies to get GPs

to test their products. The results where there was a direct fee to the doctor tended to be more favourable and less valid. Not many doctors objected.

'I'll take the clock,' Dr Thurson said.

'An excellent choice, sir,' Soper handed over the box. Although the clocks retailed at £140 they were purchased in quantities at less than half-price.

'You'll send us through the details on each patient concerned.'

'I'll get them off to you directly I prescribe the treatment,' Thurson promised. The chances were that he would forget, or miss one of the follow-up consultations.

'Thank you. We'll look forward to seeing you next Tuesday.' He shut his case with a feeling of satisfaction. This sort of GP made the life of a drugs rep much easier.

Dr Thurson wished he felt as satisfied with his morning's work so far. Before summoning his next patient he riffled through the drug samples littering his desk for something to help him through the rest of the morning.

20

Cavandish Pharmaceuticals wasn't the biggest of the drug companies, but was moderately large and broadly based, producing all sorts from over-the-counter relief for headaches and blocked noses, through broad spectrum antibiotics, antidepressants, cancer drugs; with miscellaneous dressings and appliances. Like their competitors they were a part of the 'me too' syndrome, finding it necessary to duplicate drugs that others had pioneered, while suffering similiar reverses when their drugs came out of licence. When an entirely new drug was invented the company concerned was given an exclusive fifteen-year licence, which often gave them huge profits. Cavandish tended to be fairly aggressive in the market place, but tax legislation prevented them being more generous towards doctors and pharmacists, as such expenditure was no longer deductible. However, their marketing people knew that money spent on such things as luncheon exhibitions paid dividends, and scarcely dented their profitability. The process was called product conditioning, and the more they were able to associate their product in the minds of doctors and pharmacists with a pleasant experience, regardless of how effective the drug was, the more it would be prescribed. And if used in hospitals it would be prescribed by GPs in the catchment area. The product name was also important, for a lot of doctors prescribed according to what they could spell without difficulty.

All doctors at St Clair's were invited to the Cavandish luncheon; there would have been no way of keeping them out as it was held in the doctors' dining hall at the medical centre with the folding doors to the adjacent sitting-room opened. Most of the junior doctors had brought their bleeps, which frequently went off, causing them to disappear to phone. The pharmacists, administrators and nursing officers had been invited too, along with local GPs. There were a hundred or so people present without the sales force of Cavandish. Waitresses in black uniforms moved among them with drinks and canapés. None of the food was simple: mussels in cream, potato croquettes, pressed tongue, egg clairmont, eggs *a la grècque*, and other cream dishes. Ironically Cavandish were active in producing cholesterol inhibitors. Pinned around the room were glossy posters proclaiming the two products currently being promoted: Milatine, a drug which militated against numerous unpleasant aspects of pregnancy, especially nausea; the theory being that women couldn't and shouldn't have to suffer this discomfort. Such was the philosophy that resulted in the thalidomide tragedy. Oestraline was a drug to 'treat' dysmenorrhoea, but this was more profitable than practical, as there was no effective treatment for difficult menstrual periods. Yet doctors kept prescribing such products. The fine print setting out possible side effects such as diarrhoea, depression, blood dyscrasia, was barely readable.

The room was a burble of conversation, between doctors and reps, people re-establishing contact. Dr Thurson had managed to make it and was enjoying the food, as indeed were most guests. Cavandish's had taken trouble over the catering. Carefully managing plate, fork and glass in the crush, he sought out Dr Jessie Marvill, whom he had spoken to on the telephone when trying to find beds for patients, and had in fact met before when seeing patients in hospital.

'Is your boss coming?' he asked.

'It's unlikely,' Dr Marvill said. 'I'm not sure he'd want to know about drugs that might cause women to have babies with congenital abnormalities.'

Fortunately, having come to the conclusion that she was wrong-footed in surgery, Jessie Marvill had found the courage to quit the specialty. This had been against the advice of most colleagues, with the exception of Dr Laurence James and Vernon Davis, who was now Mr Davis, having become a Fellow of the Royal College of Surgeons. To her surprise he had thought it better to be out of work than doing a job she didn't believe in. Her surgeon father had told her she was likely to be out of work for a long while; her GP mother encouraged her to try a GP's vocational training scheme; two years in various hospital specialties was necessary, then a year in a training practice before one could become a principal partner. Unable to find a GP training scheme, Jessie Marvill had decided to put her own together, and had managed to get a job on Philip Montagu's gynae-obstetric firm. The contract, like most that SHOs got, was for six months only, but would be accredited. To follow it she might be very lucky if she found another specialty in the same hospital to take her on, but usually junior doctors moved to wherever they could find a job.

'You're not impressed with Milatine?' Dr Thurson said.

'I'm sure their tests on rats were successful.' She had to speak loudly to make herself heard, and didn't mind if she was overheard. Her views were changing almost daily over the use of drugs. Seeing so much iatrogenic disorder in hospital she was coming to the view that drugs did as much harm as they did good. However, she couldn't entirely avoid prescribing because she, as much as the patient, was subject to conditioned response. She saw Dr Thurson's look. 'Their scoff is much better than from our kitchens,' she explained.

'Could you have a word about a young girl attending his antenatal clinic. Chloë Shallcross.'

'What's the problem?' Dr Marvill asked. She didn't recall the woman's name.

'Anxiety. She gets anxious at every report and rumour she ever hears. It's hospital delivery currently.'

'I'll have a word when she comes in,' Dr Marvill told him. She didn't say how she thought the young woman had reason to be anxious.

A sudden fracas rose from across the mess, a dish of food crashing to the floor instantly brought a roar from junior doctors, rather like school kids in a canteen when something got broken. At the centre was Mr Vernon Davis, the surgical registrar, who was protesting to a group of drugs reps.

'. . . I know Cavandish has a cosy arrangement with certain consultants here,' he said in an agitated manner, referring to their research unit at the hospital. 'But I think your product stinks. It's symptomatic of the whole rotten ethos of drug companies – treat the symptom, but encourage the cause. I'd like to throw the lot of you out of the hospital altogether . . .' Realizing that the entire conversation in the room had dropped, he stopped abruptly, and looked round at the wall of silent faces.

'Why don't you relax, Vernon,' a colleague advised. 'Enjoy a decent lunch for a change.'

There was no backing down now. 'Go to hell,' he said. He didn't go as far as throwing the money-lenders out of the temple, but decided to leave himself.

Mr Smith-Sampson, Davis's boss, had been following these proceedings with interest, convinced that his registrar was cracking up. Sir Randolph Spence, vice-chairman of Cavandish and also director of the hospital's research unit, was with him; so was Dr Reginald Cloutman, a consultant radiotherapist – this was the doctor who would arrange radiation treatment for tumours, after the radiologist had interpreted the X-rays. Sometimes radiotherapists were the most sensitive of doctors.

'Been working your registrar a little too hard, Ronald?' Sir Randolph said with a smile. He knew Davis's reputation for dissent and political activity; to him there was nothing between the two.

Mr Smith-Sampson chose to ignore the remark. 'Your company always puts on the best food at these things, Randolph,' he said, sliding some bacon and pasta in cream into his mouth. 'I suppose you must be making the most money.'

Sir Randolph gave a polite smile.

'Percy! Enjoying your lunch?' Dr Alan O'Brien, the District Medical Officer, said as he joined Thurson. He had something other than idle chit-chat on his mind. He had seen Thurson arrive and had waited for an opportunity to speak to him.

Dr Thurson glanced at his watch. 'I ought to be getting back.' He didn't want to talk to O'Brien, as if to avoid the problem he was associated with.

O'Brien hesitated, and made sure no one within earshot was listening. 'The GMC is going for a formal hearing on that complaint against you. It's going before the Professional Conduct Committee in about two months.'

Thurson nodded wearily, as if this was inevitable.

'I may have to withdraw from the committee on account of our relationship on the DMT.'

Thurson said nothing, but resisted looking at him.

'We'll see what happens,' O'Brien went on. 'I'm sure it'll be no more than a formality, Percy. They'll consider the prescription, take evidence from the dead child's parents. Might be an idea for you to talk to your Medical Defence Union, if you haven't already done so.'

Dr Thurson nodded again as if this was in hand. In fact he had scarcely thought about it since that tragic overprescribing of a powerful painkiller to a four-year-old girl.

'These things happen, distressing as they are,' O'Brien said. 'A lot depends on the chairman, Sir Jack Steadman. D'you know him? He's a decent sort.' He glanced around again. 'He's here. Perhaps I should introduce you. Can't do any harm.'

He gave Thurson an encouraging nod, and steered him across the room. The introduction would be casual, the conversation friendly. Nothing would be said about the professional misconduct complaint that was coming before the General Medical Council. But the meeting might help, the chairman would know what a well reasoning man Dr Thurson was.

A Kuwaiti, immaculately attired in Western style clothes, followed the equally immaculate Mr Philip Montagu, the consultant gynaecologist, through a long ward in the old Nightingale Block at St Clair's Hospital. He was Ahmed Hassad. His passive expression gave away nothing of his thinking; his manicured hands remained clasped in front of him as he waited for doors to be opened, either by his business advisor, Jameel Khaled, or by Sir Randolph Spence who was with them. Philip Montagu held doors for no one other than private patients.

'What this would become,' Philip Montagu was saying, 'is the most modern, well-equipped obs and gynae unit in the country.' He gave only an occasional glance to the Kuwaiti who offered no sign that he was impressed as he toured through this empty, but recently upgraded ward. 'This ward arrangement will substantially change,' Montagu continued. 'There'll be private units mostly. With a computerized nursing station.'

'I can see this is a commendable building,' Hassad said. 'But what progress is the scheme expected to make?'

'We'll meet our projected target date,' Montagu said. 'Medical politics is all a question of timing. Only when this block is completely empty can we start negotiations for it.' The block was far from empty yet, and progress in shutting the remaining wards wasn't as fast as he would have liked. He didn't tell his financial backer that.

'You are optimistic that this clinic can open in two years?' Khaled asked. He spoke with a faultless English accent.

Only his syntax was slightly odd at times.

'That won't change,' Montagu said. 'Depending how long before formal negotiations start. I doubt if we could acquire a more suitable site, not at the price we want to pay.'

'Why not talk directly to the government minister?' Hassad said, having found the direct approach the most satisfactory, even in Britain.

'Delicate business,' Sir Randolph Spence said, 'taking a hospital out of the public sector.' He believed that these foreigners didn't understand the nuances of the situation. 'There are no end of bureaucratic hoops. First it has to be shown to be of no earthly use to anyone.'

They came out of the ward on to a stairwell, which was old-fashioned and festooned with pipes. There was a centre lift, but they descended the stairs.

'This will all be remodelled,' Montagu explained. Although these proposals had been outlined before, this was the first time Ahmed Hassad, who was over for medical treatment himself, had actually toured the block they were proposing to buy from the DHSS. 'It'll accommodate two express lifts.'

'Your government is sympathetic to this type of investment,' Hassad pointed out, pursuing his tack.

'Entirely,' Montagu assured them, 'but democratic,' – this with pride. Philip Montagu felt ambivalent towards these people; he wanted and needed them, because he wanted his own clinic, but refused to be intimidated. 'With the current level of NHS cutbacks and closures, health care's become a sensitive issue. The Minister recognizes, indeed is on record as saying, that private enterprise has to meet the shortfall in public medicine. If we get our timing right we will be seen to be filling a real need.'

His smile was as polished as any politician's.

On reaching the lower ward, Philip Montagu said, 'This is one of my gynae wards.'

He led the party in, showing no concern at the intrusion the women here might have felt this to be. These were patients after all; he was the consultant; this was business.

21

Mothers-to-be in various stages of late pregnancy had to wait in antenatal clinics, which like most other clinics slipped gear. There were various reasons, a doctor failing to show up, or falling asleep between patients; enough time not initially being allowed for a thorough physical and psychological examination was another reason. Some pregnant women not only needed a proper examination, but time to be reassured by the obstetrician. Chloë Shallcross was one such. However the most common reason for long waits was that patients were given the same appointment times, the principle being that doctors' time was more valuable than patients'.

There were eleven other women waiting at 3.26 when Chloë Shallcross was seen for her 2.15 appointment. A couple of them were anxious about missing their children coming home from school and told the sister in charge of the clinic, but it seemed to make little difference.

This afternoon Dr Jessie Marvill was doing the obstetrics side of her gynae-obstetrics rotation. The two areas were very separate and it was simply convenience and physical geography that placed them under the same consultant. Ordinarily there would be a different SHO for gynae and obstetrics, and often two registrars within the same firm. The fact that there wasn't here didn't reflect Philip Montagu's status; on the contrary, he made sure that the best of everything came to his firm. It so happened that he ran two firms within the same District, one at Queen's which was a teaching hospital, the other at St Clair's which received less of his time. Jessie Marvill was doing both parts of the rotation because the firm was one SHO short, and although he certainly had his own reasons for not making a fuss about getting another, Mr Montagu didn't inform Dr Marvill of them, even though it meant her being more than usually stretched.

On the high couch in the small, modern well lit examination room Chloë Shallcross had her large belly bared, and Dr Marvill was feeling her uterus with her flat hand.

'Your GP tells me you're anxious about coming in to have baby,' Jessie Marvill said.

Despite the doctor's manner being friendly Chloë Shallcross felt intimidated, and sheepishly avoided answering.

'That's fine, Chloë.' She got the sphygmomanometer out and wrapped the band around her arm. The nurse had taken this reading earlier but Dr Marvill made a point of taking the b/p twice as pressure was often higher at the beginning of the examination. 'You'd prefer a home delivery?'

'I don't know,' Chloë Shallcross said. 'I suppose . . . well, I don't want it in hospital. I'm scared about having it at home, but it seems more natural somehow.'

Dr Marvill nodded. 'Doctors do tend to interfere if they get the chance. Did you try West London? They have a natural childbirth unit. You still go into hospital, but there's almost no interference. You're all on your own on the floor on a mattress with your husband. The doctor and midwife stay with you the whole while in case they're needed.' She smiled at Chloë. 'We don't have that sort of unit. But if everything is going well we will leave things entirely to you.'

'It's not the same, though,' Chloë said, a little bolder.

'No, but it does mean staff are on hand if there were complications. Midwives are sometimes a bit nervous about home delivery for a first child.' Jessie Marvill had a warm smile capable of putting most people at ease, but she felt she wasn't convincing this woman. As she considered her for a moment for some inexplicable reason she saw Chloë Shallcross's medical future mapped out as though set down in her record. She saw mental disturbance, then a complete breakdown. The fact that she had this vision worried her more than its content, and she shut it off, refusing to believe it. 'What if something went wrong at home and you lost the baby?' she asked, taking a firm medical line. 'How would you feel about that Chloë?'

Chloë Shallcross didn't say anything, but felt suitably guilty.

Irresistibly Jessie Marvill's thoughts went back to that vision of this girl's future, and she wondered if it was to do with her own increasing dilemma. Instinctively she felt that the sort of medicine she wanted to practise should evolve away from hospitals, but as a junior doctor she could do little to change that; yet despite her resistance she found herself being swung into line with the thinking of those doctors who readily meshed with the career structure in hospital medicine. Denying what she saw for Chloë Shallcross was part of the process. If she were to tell Laurence James about it he would be delighted for her. If she told Peter Lambolle, her registrar, he'd have thought her mad. She would tell neither.

'I promise you, Chloë, we'll involve you in every decision. No one's going to keep you from your baby. My boss puts great emphasis on the mother-child bonding. You can get dressed.' The sister helped her off the bed.

'Is everything all right?' Chloë Shallcross asked, more confident now.

'Fine. Your blood pressure's a little high. Try to relax and stop worrying, or you'll be in here for bed rest,' Dr Marvill warned her. 'Are you practising breathing?'

'Yes, at the antenatal classes. With my husband.'

'Does he want to be present?' Dr Marvill asked, sitting to write up her notes.

'Yes, he wants to.'

'I'm sure he'll be made welcome.'

She gave her another reassuring smile and left her to get dressed.

A woman in her late thirties, and four months pregnant, sat in the waiting area; she was totally distracted and neither heard nor responded to any of the conversations around her. She wasn't concerned about the delay or children returning from school on their own. She had no children. This was to be her first, the basis of her anxiety.

She started at her name being called, but didn't rise.

'Mrs Jakeman,' the sister said again.

Gwen Jakeman rose reluctantly, wishing she didn't have to see the doctor and hear what she knew would be bad news.

When the sister came into the examination room with Mrs Jakeman, Dr Marvill was asleep at the table, her pen poised over Chloë Shallcross's notes.

'Dr Marvill. Your next patient,' the sister said, touching her shoulder. Doctors frequently fell asleep on duty, especially in outpatient clinics.

'Hello,' Dr Marvill said, taking in Gwen Jakeman instantly. 'Sorry you were kept waiting. We got a little behind.' She glanced over the notes as Mrs Jakeman settled herself, and realized that she had an unpleasant task, one she suspected neither Dr Lambolle nor Mr Montagu had wanted.

'I'm sorry Mr Montagu isn't here,' she said, putting off the unhappy moment. 'He's at his other clinic.'

'It's positive,' Gwen Jakeman said without prelusive niceties.

'The amniocentesis was positive.' Dr Marvill was still ducking the issue. Finally she nodded. 'There's a probability of your baby having Down's syndrome.'

Gwen Jakeman stared into the middle-distance, avoiding tears.

'Mr Montagu recommends termination as early as possible, Mrs Jakeman.' Dr Marvill was reading his note in the file and beginning to feel angry. Not because the consultant had left this task to her, but because he made no allowance for the woman's feelings. 'We could fit you in this week.'

'It's certain?' she asked.

'We can't tell how handicapped it will be,' Jessie Marvill said. 'There's no doubt about some degree of mongolism.'

She sighed. 'Everyone said it was madness to start a family at my age.'

'If you decide to have your pregnancy terminated, then the earlier the better. You are eighteen weeks.'

Gwen Jakeman closed her eyes, but a tear slid from between the lids of her right eye and dropped on to her cheek. 'I'll probably have the baby anyway.'

A curious sense of relief settled over Dr Marvill. 'It is still a baby,' she said, then hesitated. Although she supported the abortion lobby because she believed that women should have the right to decide such issues for themselves and not be dictated to by the medical profession, the church, or laws devised by men, she doubted that people had the right to abort defective foetuses simply because society didn't want to deal with the resulting problems. She didn't say this. 'Before making your decision you might consider how little fun it could be for baby. It's just a thought.'

There was a pause.

'Perhaps it's better than no fun at all. I don't know,' Gwen Jakeman was a picture of confusion. She would eventually arrive at the decision to have her baby and wouldn't be persuaded from it.

Two days later in the same modern examination room where the antenatal clinic was held, Dr Marvill was wearing her other hat and holding the morning gynaecology clinic. In theory an SHO learned the problems of the specialty from the consultant or the registrar, but in fact there were no formal teaching sessions. Instead the SHO learned directly on the patients, seeking help with any difficult or unusual complaints.

Dr Marvill had been uneasy about a patient this morning and rather than chance upon the right course of action, she risked being thought incompetent and took the problem to the consultant, who was seeing patients in the adjacent examination room. Although there was no doubt that Mr Montagu was a very accomplished consultant, he was by no means an accomplished teacher. He tended to treat knowledge as power and was reluctant to part with it. Instead he assumed the pupil knew as much as he did.

As a result of Dr Thurson's referral letter Ethel Grant got an early appointment to the clinic. Having been examined a second time she was slowly dressing, not wanting to arrive at the point where she had to face the consultant.

When she finally emerged from behind the screen around the examination couch, Mr Montagu glanced up from scribbling his notes and gave her a tight smile. His opinion was a carcinoma of the body of the uterus.

'Do have a chair, Mrs Grant. I won't keep you.' He finished his notes. 'Now, I'd like to pop you in and have a closer look at you. Nothing very alarming,' he assured her in his brisk way of speaking.

She nodded. 'When would that be?' she wanted to know.

'That's a question I'm unable to answer. I'm afraid I don't have any spare beds at the moment.'

Mrs Grant nodded again, feeling relieved. 'Is it a growth of some sort?' The words almost didn't emerge. That fear had been with her since she first went to Dr Thurson with the problem.

'I know what you're thinking, Mrs Grant,' he said. 'But it's nothing to worry about. Ladies get lumps down there at your time of life. We'll probably do a hysterectomy while we're at it. You're finished with this little box now, so let's take it out. Then you can't get any trouble there.' This implied that she hadn't a carcinoma without him lying directly. He waited for some response, but there was only anxious silence, which he took to be assent. 'Good. We'll write to you when we have a bed.'

'Thank you,' Mrs Grant said, as though she had been done a favour.

When she had gone Mr Montagu passed her record to Dr Marvill, then went to wash his hands.

'There's a patient we'll probably see as an emergency, Jessie,' he observed. 'That's all that can come of this intolerable bed shortage.' He dried his hands on a paper towel. 'I'll be next door a while longer if you need me.' He went out.

The sister brought in a twenty-five-year-old mother with two young kids in tow. Their presence in the examination room wouldn't have pleased the consultant, and the sister was glad Dr Marvill was on her own again.

'Hello,' Dr Marvill said. She then asked the children their names, but they didn't answer. 'Don't you know?'

'Why don't you tell the doctor, Darryl,' the mother said to the eldest child, who was about four.

Shy silence from both the boy and his younger sister.

'I'm sorry,' their mother said, 'but I couldn't find no one to have them while I came here.'

'Not to worry, Mrs Cooper. Can you get chairs for them, sister,' the doctor asked.

'What seems to be the problem, Mrs Cooper?' Dr Marvill asked, glancing at the notes. 'I see. How long has your bladder been leaking?'

'Well, ever since I had Sharron really,' she explained. 'It's got worse, though especially when I cough or sneeze.'

'Getting you down, is it?'

'Well, a bit. It's ever so embarrassing if I go out anywhere.'

'Yes, it must be. Let's have a look at you. Slip your bottom things off and hop up on the couch.'

She knew what the problem was without examining her, what the solution was, and how remote her chances were of having anything done about it in the immediate future. Mr Montagu gave no priority to the type of corrective operation that this woman needed. The examination of the anterior vaginal wall, made with the hand from behind the patient, who lay on her left side with her knees up, was fairly brief. It confirmed an anterior prolapse.

'The pelvic floor is the problem,' she said, removing her gloved hand. 'The muscles stretch during pregnancy. They haven't returned to support the bladder.'

It was the result of poor obstetric care, but Dr Marvill wasn't about to tell Mrs Cooper. Increasingly her instinct was to defend colleagues over patients, even when they were unknown to her.

'Can anything be done?' Mrs Cooper asked. It didn't occur to her to question how it had happened.

'We can tighten the muscles with a few stitches. It's a simple matter.' She hesitated. 'I'm afraid it's not considered very urgent, Mrs Cooper. There's a waiting list for this type of operation.'

'How long will I have to wait? I mean, it's really getting me down,' she said. Wetting herself as she did was bringing psychological problems. She was getting not to want to leave the house.

'I know it's very uncomfortable, Mrs Cooper. But there's little hope of you coming in under six months.' Dr Marvill felt she was letting patients down when telling them such things.

However, Mr Montagu didn't mind pointing out those realities to patients. He wanted the public to know what sort of crises were being created through persistent cuts. But he was careful not to raise his profile by taking a public stand over the issue.

The next patient he saw was Vera Osborne, who was in a similar situation to Mrs Cooper, though for an entirely different reason. The non-urgent operation Mrs Osborne needed was for fibroids, but she wasn't about to tolerate a six month wait. In fact a little earlier she was complaining bitterly to a friend who came with her about her appointment being twenty minutes late, and planned to tell the doctor what she thought of this shoddy behaviour.

But when she finally got to see the consultant and was examined, she was completely charmed by him.

'This is so terribly uncomfortable, doctor,' she said, pulling her fur coat about her as if for protection in the chair opposite. 'At times I'm sure I'll bleed to death. I couldn't possibly put up with this for another six months.'

'I can assure you, Mrs Osborne, that you won't bleed to death.' He rose and came round the desk to her and took her hand. The rings she was wearing, like the coat, weren't imitation. 'Fibroids are very tiresome, but considered non-urgent. So what happens in the NHS is that the non-urgent cases are continually pushed back.'

She grasped his meaning immediately. 'One may never reach to the top of the list?'

'You will get on my theatre list eventually.'

'But this is scandalous.'

'Unless we're given more facilities, more doctors, the problem's likely to get worse.'

'Well, I can't go on like this. I'll have to get it done privately,' Mrs Osborne threatened. 'Would I be seen to quicker if I did?'

That wasn't a question Mr Montagu needed to ponder. He reached for his appointments book. 'I can only tell you that if you were to consult me privately – and I'm not advising that you should, of course – but were you to . . .' he ran his finger down the page. 'I could fit you in before my NHS list next Thursday.'

'Would it be terribly expensive?' she asked.

Money wasn't something he discussed with patients. Instead he asked, 'How much do you value good health, Mrs Osborne?'

'I have some BUPA insurance,' she said. 'But I was saving that should I need anything major.'

Mr Montagu smiled. 'You needn't worry about those details, my dear,' – the charm pouring out. Mr Montagu's position was quite clear in his division of time between private and NHS patients, and despite the indignation of some junior doctors over such practices, he felt no compunction. It was clearly better for this patient that she could get on an early list, not something to be stopped at all costs; he would have preferred such convenience being available to all patients.

'My secretary will telephone you tomorrow, and arrange when it most suits you to come in.'

'It will be you doing my operation?' she asked.

'Of course.'

The surgeon of their choice was what a lot of private patients were prepared to pay for, and in theory got; in practice the registrars did much of the private work.

'You'll be a picture of health,' Philip Montagu said as he walked her to the door.

The patient left the examination room smiling the sort of smile that Prince Charles brought to faces of middle-aged women.

'Where has the morning gone?' Mr Montagu said, when he stepped in to see Jessie Marvill a little later. 'I have another three appointments which perhaps you wouldn't mind seeing, Jessie,' he said, giving her no choice. 'They're mostly follow-ups. Oh, there is a Mrs Barnes coming in wanting a termination. I suppose she had better have one. But only on condition she agrees to being sterilized.' He considered the young doctor, wondering if that was a hurdle she would easily take. Had he time he might have set her clear about his policy. He wouldn't give abortions on demand to women who did nothing to help themselves. Making sterilization a condition of the operation meant that Mrs Barnes wouldn't be back within another three or four months. It was a familiar practice, one the consultant fully approved of. That type of mother he believed thoroughly irresponsible, and had few doubts about their children becoming dependent on the state. 'Perhaps you should ask Dr Lambolle to see her. I'll be in the Street this afternoon, if I'm needed.'

He removed his white coat, revealing his pale grey doublebreasted suit. He was ready to run off to Harley Street where he was holding a clinic this afternoon.

Dr Marvill thought about Mrs Barnes, and suspected that Peter Lambolle would be no more sensitive towards her than Mr Montagu. She decided to see the woman herself and try to discover what her real problem was.

22

Night calls were something most GPs disliked as it meant either their evening or sleep being disturbed, which often had the knock-on effect of tiredness, irritability or even neglect the following day. But patients rarely considered that. In most well-run practices doctors didn't take night emergency calls, but employed a covering service, which made the visits, and dealt with the out of surgery emergencies.

Dr Percy Thurson didn't employ a deputizing service and calls in the middle of the night were something he had learned to live with. He wasn't being reactionary, he had tried a covering service, only found his patients didn't like being visited at their most vulnerable, at night and medically in need, by a stranger, who often dealt brusquely with them or told them they were wasting his time.

The ringing telephone which was incorporated into Dr Thurson's dream, was so far out of reach that he had no hope of answering it, therefore no need to wake up. Finally his wife, who had woken the moment it started, shook him into consciousness but resisted answering the telephone or her husband would never have woken.

With leaden legs Percy Thurson sat round on the edge of his bed and pummelled his eyes, trying to wake himself up. The telephone on the night table had got him up as if in defiance of the array of pills next to it, most of which were sleepers, with one bottle of wake-up pills.

Edna Thurson lay in the bed next to her husband, watching him anxiously. Lately he was having more and more difficulty in waking up for these calls, and then more difficulty getting back off to sleep without lots of pills.

Finally she got out of bed and came round to answer the phone.

'Dr Thurson,' she said. 'What's the trouble with your wife, Mr Grant?' During their long marriage she had learned to conduct symptom-taking very competently; sometimes she gave advice in the absence of any response from her husband. She glanced at Thurson as she relayed pieces of information to him. 'She's bleeding badly.' The doctor's eyes closed. 'Can't she stop it with a sanitary towel . . . ? Just one moment, Mr Grant. You'd better speak to my husband.' She handed him the phone, bringing him awake again.

'How long has she been bleeding like that, Mr . . . ?' The doctor nodded off, his ear against the receiver. 'I see. I'd better come and see her. Yes, Mr Grant . . . That's all right.'

Dr Thurson put the phone down and closed his eyes again. After a moment his wife touched his arm.

'Percy. I'll make some coffee.'

He came awake with a start. 'I have a call to make.' He reached for a wake-up pill, and swallowed it. He thought about what might be ahead of him, then took another.

This wasn't a call merely seeking reassurance at two o'clock in the morning, but a real emergency. Mrs Grant was bleeding heavily from the vagina, in a way that might have led a night cover doctor, unfamiliar with the patient, to suspect she was haemorrhaging from a home abortion. There was nothing he could do to stop the bleeding, other than pack the vagina with cottonwool.

What Mrs Grant needed was a hospital bed, an emergency operation. What Dr Thurson got from the gynae SHO on call at St Clair's when he telephoned was resistance. He didn't disbelieve Dr Marvill when she told him there were no gynae beds available, but that didn't alter this patient's needs one jot.

'. . . I quite appreciate the bed situation,' Dr Thurson

was saying in the narrow hallway of the Grants' council house, 'but this patient has been seen at St Clair's. It makes sense for her to come in there.'

'Just how urgent an admission is she?' Dr Marvill asked, tiredness no less apparent in her voice. 'She may have to go to St Luke's.'

'If she's not admitted for an emergency operation,' Dr Thurson told her quietly, 'she may possibly bleed to death.'

'I'll have to wake the registrar. Can you hold on?'

'I'll hold,' Dr Thurson said. He leaned against the window sill and instantly nodded off.

An anxious Mr Grant woke him up on his way to taking a cup of tea to his wife. 'Is she going to be all right, doctor?' he asked fearfully, the prospect of being on his own looming.

Dr Thurson considered him, as if not hearing this question which he'd been asked a million times in similar situations. He was finding he could no longer answer with reassuring ease as he once had.

'If we can get her into hospital, Mr Grant,' Dr Thurson said. He didn't want this man to question him further as he was in no fit state either to lie competently or get involved on any emotional level.

'I'll take that,' he said, reaching for the tea. 'Your wife may need an anaesthetic.'

When Dr Marvill came back on the line she told him that Peter Lambolle, the registrar would see the patient, that they could admit her.

When twenty gynae beds held twenty gynae patients the only way another could be admitted as an emergency was by discharging a patient. But as it was the small hours of morning when Mrs Grant arrived this wasn't possible, and after her emergency hysterectomy a bed had been found for her on a general surgical ward belonging to another firm.

Ordinarily it might have been simple enough to discharge a patient the following morning and bring Mrs Grant into a gynae bed, but in fact Mr Montagu didn't allow junior staff to discharge patients, not even his registrar, and they had had to await his ward round. That wasn't what was on Dr Peter Lambolle's mind when he came on to the modern gynaecology ward on the new surgical block. Such things were never too far from his thoughts, for like most of his contemporaries he expected one day to get a consultant post, and so played those games which improved his chances. However, at the same time he chose to believe that he was independent enough to practise his own sort of medicine; it wasn't a coincidence that happened to fit with the firm's style.

Approaching the nurses' station in the centre of the ward, which was set out in an oblong around the centre block, Dr Lambolle's pace was even more brisk than usual today.

'Sorry to have called you up, doctor,' Sister Parker said from the desk, 'but there's a query on Mrs Downes's drugs dosage.' She produced the patient's record, which barely showed a clear space, so much had been written up on it. 'Is that meant to be 20 mg of Plastinim, or 200 mg as written?'

'Goodness, I would have said 20 gm.' Dr Lambolle's surprise bordered on alarm at such a large quantity of the cytotoxic drug. It could cause hepatic or renal dysfunction or destroy all the white blood cells. 'Who wrote that up?'

'Dr Lambolle did,' she told him as if talking about someone else. Sister Parker had an easy way with the medical staff.

'Oh well, even he can make a mistake,' he said lightly, to disguise his defensiveness. 'D'you have the protocol sheets?'

The sister produced a large black covered folder which held the data sheets produced by drug companies in treating cancer patients. 'She's been having 200 mg intravenous. I thought it seemed a lot.'

'It's 20 mg,' he said, reading through the sheets. 'We'd better take some blood. It's likely that her marrow will pack up.'

'Can you write up the change of dosage?' the sister asked.

'I wonder if she'd better stop altogether.' He thought about that. 'Try her on 10 mg.' He made the amendment on the card. 'How is she?'

'She's been vomiting a lot. Not that we can get her to eat much.'

'We'll try something new for the nausea.' Dr Lambolle wrote up a new antinauseant.

'I think going for radiotherapy upsets her more than anything. But that's all she ever complains about, the dear,' the sister said appreciatively.

'It's the side effects of the cytotoxic drugs,' Dr Lambolle said. 'Not the radiotherapy.'

The sister looked at him, wondering about the point of his remark. 'I can't convince her of that. Will you take the blood?'

'I'll ask Dr Marvill to,' he said, wanting to hurry away. Registrars mostly didn't take blood from patients, but had the most junior member of the firm do it. Sometimes they broke that rule, and certainly Dr Lambolle would have in these circumstances, but today he wanted to get back to a domestic problem. This morning his wife had told him that she was leaving him. Marital problems for junior doctors were often an occupational hazard.

'Well, could you have a quick word with Mrs Grant?' the sister asked, despite his haste. 'She's been asking about the results of her op.'

He looked at his watch. Then went briskly on to the ward.

'Hello, Mrs Grant,' Dr Lambolle said as he approached her on this six-bedded bay. 'What's the problem?'

'My operation, doctor,' she began uncertainly. She had been given no information about the operation over the last thirty-six hours, and had recovered sufficiently now to be worried. Her biggest fear wasn't that it was something that she might die of, but that she might do so without seeing her grandchildren again. 'Was it all right?'

'We removed your uterus entirely,' he said. 'It's possible the malignancy has spread to one of the ovaries and we'll have to operate again. But we may decide to treat this with radiation.'

The manner in which he stated this almost sent her into shock. Sister Parker was surprised, and thought his bluntness unnecessary; the 1st-year student nurse who was also present had to bite her tongue to prevent herself speaking, but almost burst into tears. She would be left to cope with this distressed patient.

'Mr Montagu will see you on his Thursday ward round,' Dr Lambolle added. 'We'll decide the next course of action then.'

With that he wheeled away and went out, followed by the sister.

Mrs Grant suddenly burst into tears.

Having been a nurse for only six months, Sandra French still found crying patients a bit shocking. She hadn't yet learned how to deal adequately with such situations and probably never would. Left with this woman who had been told she had not only lost her womb, but also had cancer, she neither knew what to do nor say, but thought it was unnecessarily cruel of Dr Lambolle to break the news to her as he had.

'But I won't see my lovely grandchildren grow up. I won't,' Mrs Grant sobbed, 'I know I won't.'

'Of course you will. We get wonderful results with radiotherapy,' the young nurse said. That was what she was being taught.

'How could he be so unkind?' Nurse French said later to Sister Parker, still not having got over her anger. 'Mrs Grant is desperately worried about not seeing her grandchildren grow up. He practically told her she won't.' She was taking sterile packs from the CSSD box and putting them in a cupboard.

'Upsetting yourself won't do any good, Sandra,' Sister Parker said.

'Why did he tell her like that?'

'Goodness only knows what goes on in Dr Lambolle's head. Possibly he thought it best.'

'But he doesn't have to be with her all day, sister.' That was the real issue, for whatever affected patients the nursing staff had to live with.

'No,' Sister Parker conceded, feeling guilty about not having said anything to the doctor. 'You pop off to your break. I'll have a word with Mrs Grant.' She smiled tightly. Her way of dealing with such problems was by ignoring them.

Looking worn out and crumpled in comparison with her colleague's earlier appearance, Dr Marvill came on to the ward to get some blood from Mrs Downes, the frail but cheerful seventy-year-old, in the bed opposite Mrs Grant. She knew nothing of the mistake in the amount of Plastinim she had been given, other than the effect she felt.

'Sorry if that hurt, Mrs Downes,' Dr Marvill said, drawing blood into a hypodermic syringe. 'It's done now.' She pressed a piece of cottonwool to the puncture and flexed the arm, leaving it flexed, from habit rather than hope of leaving no bruise.

'Oh,' the old lady said dully, looking at her bruised arm. She was very thin and sickly-looking and was suffering from alopecia as a result of the highly toxic drugs. 'It's not your fault, dear.'

'How are you feeling in yourself?' she asked, putting the blood into a bottle which she labelled for the lab.

'I wish you'd stop sending me down for that machine,' Mrs Downes said, 'that's all I wish.'

'What machine is that, Mrs Downes?' Dr Marvill asked. 'Radiotherapy, is that what you mean?' She had talked to Mrs Downes before about radiotherapy and recalled how unhappy she was about it.

'Mrs Downes doesn't like having radiotherapy much,' Sister Parker commented on joining them. 'She rarely complains, but she's becoming increasingly unhappy about the treatment generally.'

Dr Marvill considered the patient. 'Perhaps we should consider alternative treatment.' She had a notion what that alternative should be, but didn't know how she might persuade Mr Montagu.

She gave Mrs Downes a tired smile, determined to do something about an alternative for the patient. Any treatment that made a patient as unhappy as chemotherapy and radiotherapy were making this woman couldn't be doing any good. Although that wasn't entirely logical it was what Jessie Marvill was coming to believe more and more.

23

In an attempt to help make life marginally more tolerable for Mrs Downes, Dr Jessie Marvill raised the question of stopping radiotherapy with her boss, but not before she had discussed it with Laurence James. His ideas were quite radical, but would at least make the patient more comfortable, and certainly happier. Possibly she had chosen the wrong moment to speak to Mr Montagu, and mentioning Dr James didn't aid her cause; not only did he dismiss her suggestion, he made her seem foolish. Possibly there was little merit in the alternative she had suggested, but she would have accepted that had he given her an argument, thus making her feel part of his team; instead he appeared to see her suggestion as a challenge to his authority. Maybe she was being unfair to her boss, but he wasn't suffering with this little knock to his ego, but Mrs Downes was.

Dr Marvill felt a sense of guilt as she stopped by Mrs Downes's bed on the consultant's ward round.

'Is she asleep?' Mr Montagu asked. She gave that appearance.

'Mrs Downes?' Sister Parker put a hand on the old lady's bony shoulder.

'Oh, I wasn't asleep, dear. I was just resting my eyes,' Mrs Downes said, opening her eyes.

'How are you feeling, my dear?' He sounded condescending. When she didn't answer, the consultant turned to Dr Marvill. 'How has she been?'

'Not very well at all,' Dr Marvill said flatly, but noticed no flicker of interest from her boss. 'At the time of surgery she had nodules of tumour on the peritoneum. Since then she has been receiving a combination of radiotherapy and chemotherapy. There appear to be no new secondaries. We have the latest liver scan here. There are several necrotic ulcers which have become infected.'

'Could we just have a look, sister?' he asked.

The request got the curtains quickly drawn and the bedclothes pulled back.

'She's still obstructed,' Dr Marvill said.

'What has she been having?' Montagu glanced over her record. 'Gosh, just about everything,' he said lightly. 'You reduced the Plastinim.'

'There was some renal impairment, and her white count was only 1500,' Dr Lambolle said. 'I thought it best to reduce the dose.' He made no mention of his mistake in overprescribing, and Mr Montagu didn't pick it up.

'We don't seem to be having much success,' the consultant commented. 'How often is she going to radiotherapy?'

'Twice a week,' Dr Marvill answered, then hesitated. The consultant appeared to have forgotten their conversation yesterday about this patient. 'She's not happy with the treatment. She always vomits after it. Can't eat.'

'It often affects patients in that way,' Montagu said cheerfully, as if calculated to give offence.

Despite this Dr Marvill said, 'I wonder if in view of the psychological damage this treatment mightn't beneficially be stopped. Or an alternative found.'

The look Mr Montagu gave her clearly indicated that he remembered their previous conversation. He pulled out one of her liver scans and held it to the light. This was a series of small transparencies taken from the screen of the scanner following the injection of radiopaque dye injected into the liver. 'When were these taken?'

'Two days ago,' Dr Marvill said.

'We could send her to theatre and have something done about the bowel obstruction,' he said. 'I think that might be asking a lot of a seventy-year-old with these live secondaries.

I can't see that her current treatment is doing much for her. Let's try a high oxygenation chemotherapy, and step up the radiotherapy. Once we get her right we can clean up this necrotic debris,' indicating the ulcers, 'ready for skin grafting.'

There was no argument from the team around him, and Jessie Marvill felt more guilty about her silence, especially as she believed that the direction Laurence James had sent her in was right. The patient had dystrophic lesions which were caused by defective nutrition. First Mrs Downes didn't eat enough, then what she did eat wasn't metabolizing properly. This situation wouldn't improve all the while she continued with cytotoxic drugs and radiotherapy.

Mr Montagu appeared not to notice the look on Dr Marvill's face as he handed her the file, or if he had he assumed it was due to nothing more than tiredness. Peter Lambolle had noticed but knew when to keep quiet.

'I'm not confident we'll see much improvement. Perhaps we'll have to think about a place in a hospice for her,' the consultant told Mrs Richie, the social worker who was with them.

'What do you want to try her on?' Dr Lambolle asked.

'There's the drug Cavandish have developed here. Azalatine. See what they recommend in conjunction with each of her three weekly visits to radiotherapy.'

They moved on, with Mrs Downes no wiser for their visit, but still uncomplaining. Jessie Marvill was depressed at this patient effectively being written off. Somehow colleagues seemed not to allow such things to affect them, or coped better with the emotional impact. When she had talked to Laurence James about this he had suggested there was a simple choice, either to learn as most doctors did early in their careers to find emotional detachment through repression, or suffer from being in touch with your feelings and possibly being a better doctor for it. He didn't say it was an easy choice.

When they arrived back at the nursing station at the end of the ward round, usually there was a brief general discussion about patients; sometimes tea was available. To see Mr Montagu on the nursing station sipping tea and chatting amicably was to see the human side of him; mostly he didn't have the time to spare.

'Excuse me, Mr Montagu, Sir Randolph Spence telephoned,' a student nurse informed him. 'He asked if you could ring him before five.'

'Thank you.' He glanced at his watch. 'How's the move from the old block progressing, sister? Are we getting them across all right?'

'We're trying to – but we continue to get emergency admissions here. We still have that young woman from the RTA who miscarried in our intensive care bed.'

'But she died. Why is she still here?' He looked around at his team for information.

'There's no room on ITU,' the sister said.

'They're ventilating her for her heart or kidneys,' Dr Lambolle informed him. 'I can't remember which. She was carrying a donor card.'

'I see.' He appeared calm, but Mr Montagu was not pleased. 'Despite my waiting list being what it is I now keep cadavers warm for the transplant units.' One thing certain to infuriate Philip Montagu was the heart transplant unit besting him. As this managed to attract a lot of attention it therefore commanded a lot of facilities and finance, both of which Mr Montagu believed should come his way. In committee he argued tirelessly against cardiac surgeons expanding into transplants. He wasn't about to take this insult, and went to the phone and rang the cardi unit, telling them that he had patients queueing for beds, and that either they collected their body or he would phone the mortuary and get the body removed.

The rest of the firm pretended not to hear their boss's tirade against organ transplantation. The sister asked

Lambolle to write up Mrs Downes's treatment chart, which he did, after checking the recommended dosage of Azalatine.

'It's a shame her having to have more cytotoxic drugs and more radiotherapy,' the sister said, keeping an eye on the consultant. 'I'm sure none of it's doing her a bit of good.'

'She's hope and prayer territory, sister,' the registrar told her as he handed back the written up chart.

Jessie Marvill almost asked why they didn't simply hope and pray for the patient then. She hated that sort of glib response so familiar to registrars, and all it did was help to convince her that she was right in the choice she knew she would have to help Mrs Downes make. All she hoped was that the old lady would be able to stay the course.

24

Coming more and more, as she did, to doubt the efficacy of a lot of her actions, Jessie Marvill increasingly relied on Dr Laurence James for support as she explored alternatives. Fortunately as far as her career was concerned he didn't advocate that no change could take place without first destroying the old system. His commitment was to changes within the present structure. That was as well for although she leaned on him emotionally – they made no attempt to hide their love affair from colleagues – and accepted that there were faults in the present health care set-up, she believed there was no alternative worth tearing this one down for.

Having bleeped Dr James to go to lunch – they didn't spend all their breaks together, but often found themselves among the same crowd – she told him about Mrs Downes as they walked to the medical centre.

'Mr Montagu's not the only consultant to go wrong-footed up the wrong path, Jess,' Dr James said. 'My boss often thinks he's absolutely right treating cancer patients with radiotherapy or chemotherapy. I suppose they are right if one accepts the object is to live as long as possible. He's probably doing her considerable damage with the current combination.'

'I think we've run out of ideas for this patient.'

'You discussed the possibility of stopping her treatment altogether?' Dr James said.

'Mr Montagu wouldn't even listen to that.' She remembered how foolish she had been made to feel for mentioning it. 'He said the present option was the only one.'

'Doing nothing is an option. Healing is another. I don't

say Mrs Downes will pick up her bed and walk. But she might,' he added lightly. 'It could help her to become well in mind and spirit. That would be a big advance on her present position.'

'I feel inclined to advise her to refuse the treatment. Life is becoming more and more miserable for her.'

Dr James nodded. 'Be careful you don't upset your boss, Jessie. I'd've said he's not the sort of man to easily forget. Why not tell Mrs Downes what the drugs will do to her, especially Azalatine? Goodness knows how many cancer patients are being killed off with that wonder. There's no doubt that high oxygenation chemotherapy makes cancer cells sensitive to radiation. But it sensitizes too many healthy cells to be of real value. They haven't as yet solved that problem despite their claims for Azalatine. Patients like Mrs Downes too often get used as human guinea pigs. You know the history of this particular drug?'

'It was developed here in the research unit,' Dr Marvill ventured.

'That unit's run by Sir Randolph Spence, who also happens to be deputy chairman of the company marketing it.'

'Didn't the ethical committee make any comment about the drug?' Jessie asked.

'They wholly endorsed the findings of the clinical trials. Then Sir Randolph is the committee chairman.'

Their conversation didn't stop when they entered the dining-room, but it did drop as other doctors were around.

From the serving counter, which ran almost the length of the dining-room, with the mess kitchen for heating food situated immediately behind, Dr James collected a salad, brown roll, a piece of fruit, and some juice. Without hesitation nowadays Jessie Marvell went for the same.

'Would you see Mrs Downes, Laurence?' she asked.

'Not unless your boss says it's all right. You talk to her, Jess, try and persuade her not to have that awful combination therapy,' he said. 'Write her up a diet instead, include some of her favourite foods. You have to get her to change her attitude about living, if that's what she wants – she'll be a different woman in three months. If not she'll certainly be dead,' he added on a lighter note.

It was evening and the ward had settled down after the visitors' departure when Dr Marvill arrived, bringing Mrs Downes's record with her. The old lady was lying quite still, staring up at the ceiling. Neither her daughter nor son-in-law had been to see her.

'Hello, Mrs Downes,' Dr Marvill said quietly, as if trying not to disturb her. 'How are you this evening?'

The old lady was a bit startled, and for a moment thought she had a visitor. 'Oh, hello, dear,' she said.

'Did you have any visitors?' she asked.

'No,' she replied. 'They don't come, my family. They don't visit me. I don't want them.' She sounded bitter.

'How are you managing your pain?' Dr Marvill asked.

'Oh, it's no good grumbling, is it. It's not the nurses' fault.' She hesitated. 'But I do feel bad after that electric treatment.'

'I'm afraid it's not very nice.' Dr Marvill paused, feeling momentarily uncertain about saying what she planned to say. She drew up a chair. 'I'm not even sure if it's doing you much good.'

'Oh, I'm glad you said that, dear.' She sounded relieved. 'No one tells you much. They think because you're old and ill you don't understand. They're afraid to tell you the truth, that's the trouble.'

Jessie Marvill took the old woman's hand in hers. It was only bone covered by cold, yellowish skin.

'I've always said what's meant to be is meant to be. My husband died nine years ago. He had a lot of pain, but never complained, he didn't. Some men are such babies about a bit of pain, but not my Syd.' She paused, remembering the way her husband was. 'I wanted to stop having this treatment, but everyone was taking so much trouble. I didn't want them to think I wasn't grateful.'

'You shouldn't worry about that, Mrs Downes. We're here to do whatever we can.'

'Oh that's very good of you, dear,' the old woman said. 'But you don't know what's for the best, do you?'

'What I think you should try to do, my love,' Jessie Marvill said, stroking her hand, 'is decide yourself if it's worth going on with. If you want to put up with this uncomfortable feeling the treatment is giving you.'

'It's not doing me any good though, is it,' the woman in the bed said. 'I wouldn't mind so much if it was.'

'Part of the problem is that the operation you had for the primary tumour was so late, the spread that had occurred couldn't be operated for. This is why you're having your present treatment, to kill those malignant cells. Unfortunately it damages healthy cells as well, particularly in the liver and kidneys. That makes you feel miserable.'

Dr Marvill's hands stayed in contact with Mrs Downes's during the silence that followed. Finally Mrs Downes gave a resigned smile, showing no sign of distress. 'You're more than just a doctor,' she whispered, as if not wanting anyone else to hear what she had discovered.

Dr Marvill didn't reply.

'I'm glad you explained, dear,' she said. 'No one ever did. That Dr Montagu's always in such a hurry, I don't like to bother him. I suppose they keep him busy.' She smiled again. 'Well, there's not much hope for me, is there.'

'That depends on you, Mrs Downes, how much you're prepared to fight. There are alternatives to radiotherapy and surgery. I could help you to find another way, if you're up to it. If you want to.'

'I don't want to put you to that trouble, dear . . . Oh, don't think I'm not grateful. But there's other people who could do with it. That lady there, Mrs Grant, she's got cancer,' she confided in a whisper to Dr Marvill. 'She's only fifty-three, poor thing.'

'All the effort would be yours, Mrs Downes. You should never stop wanting to be well.'

'Oh I'll do anything you say, dear,' the old lady said. 'You'd have to tell me what to do. I wouldn't want to let you down.'

Dr Marvill smiled, feeling she had won a small victory.

25

It was with great reluctance that Percy Thurson had telephoned his medical defence Union, and with equal reluctance he had gone to see them to discuss the matter of his fatally overprescribing a powerful painkiller to a four-year-old. He had felt no easier within himself that the legal adviser there had told him his defence seemed reasonably sound, and that they would support him as they were obliged to, being one of the two insurance companies that doctors had to take cover with before they were permitted to work. They had given him the choice of solicitors, and as an option informed him that he could ask his own solicitor to represent him before the Professional Conduct Committee of the GMC.

Sitting in the small reception area of the solicitor's old-fashioned-looking office, Dr Thurson avoided thinking about the incident that had brought him here. Instead he was thinking about the application he had made to the Medical Practices Committee to take on a partner, and how if he had been allowed to take on the right sort of person he might have avoided this.

The telephonist, who served as a receptionist, emerged from her cupboard-like office. 'Would you come this way, Dr Thurson?' she said, 'Mr Forster is free now.'

Dr Thurson rose wearily and followed the girl out. She knocked on the door opposite and opened it.

'Percy. How nice to see you,' the solicitor, Charles Forster said, rising and shaking his hand. 'Let me take your coat. Sorry to have kept you waiting.'

'Hello, Charles,' Thurson said. His manner was flat by comparison.

'We'll have tea now, Shirley,' Forster said. It was earlier than he usually had tea in the afternoon. Charles Forster was older than Thurson, but more spry and looked younger.

'How serious is this problem you find yourself with, Percy? As I told you I've never represented anyone before the General Medical Council. But your defence union has put me in touch with one or two young barristers who've had some experience in that area.'

'Whether I'm responsible or not,' Thurson said, 'the child's death weighs heavily.'

'Of course, Percy. My questions might be difficult for you,' the solicitor said sympathetically. 'The charge of misconduct resulted from a complaint that you caused the patient's death by overprescribing?'

'She was suffering from an infection of the middle ear. I gave her an antidiarrhoeal and a painkiller, DF118,' he said with a sense of remorse. That drug was in itself ill-advised as it wasn't recommended for young children.

'What was the amount you gave, Percy?' Forster asked.

'Well for young children, like that four-year-old, it would be a small amount, 15 mg,' Thurson said. 'It's claimed the amount on the prescription was 60 mg. The adult dose.'

'Would that represent a lethal overdose, Percy?' the solicitor asked. 'For a four-year-old?'

'Not necessarily,' Thurson said. 'If one was unlucky. Perhaps mother gave baby an extra tablet because it was feeling particularly miserable. Most people do exceed the stated dose, you know. Baby fell asleep and vomited and inhaled its own vomit.'

'Did you make out the prescription for the correct dose?' Forster asked.

Thurson hesitated. This was something he was less than sure about. 'I don't know, Charles. I did alter the prescription,' he confessed. 'From 60 mg to 15 mg. But it's claimed that I made the alterations after I'd recovered the prescription from the chemist.'

'After the child's death, in fact.' Charles Forster considered him for a moment. He was an old friend whom he didn't wish to offend, but there were conclusions he had to arrive at. 'Did you in fact alter the amount on the prescription after you had retrieved it from Simmonds the chemist?' That was the question to be considered by the GMC, precisely when he had made the alteration.

For a moment Percy Thurson was tempted to question what difference it made at which point he had altered the prescription. Whether his mistake or the chemist's, the child was still as dead. Instead he said, 'I can't remember. To be honest, things have been getting on top of me lately. I think the alteration was made when I wrote out the prescription.'

'What would be the usual procedure in a case of misprescribing?' the solicitor wanted to know.

'One would reduce or stop the dose immediately the mistake was discovered,' Thurson told him.

'Are there no safeguards against errors in prescribing?'

'Safeguards? None that I'm aware of,' Thurson said. 'How could there be?'

'Mightn't the chemist ring you up and say that he thinks the prescription is wrong?' the solicitor suggested.

'It's not for chemists to question the prescribing habits of doctors,' Dr Thurson said. 'Unless the prescription was obviously wrong. Then he has a duty to.'

'You had no difficulty retrieving the prescription? The chemist didn't find it an unusual request?'

'One pops in and out occasionally to leave prescriptions for patients that one's phoned the chemist about. Or to alter prescriptions if he hasn't a certain drug in stock.'

After a moment the solicitor said, 'What was your thinking when you recovered the prescription from the chemist, Percy?'

Thurson took a long time to answer. He tried to

penetrate the fog that seemed to surround the incident. Finally he shook his head, it was a gesture of abject defeat. 'I don't know.'

'Do you have the prescription now, Percy?'

After a moment, as if to think about that, the doctor said, 'No, I don't. I have misplaced it in my surgery somewhere.'

'There is no doubt that this child died from the overdose of painkiller?' the solicitor inquired.

That had been clearly established at the inquest, and no matter what was said or done now, how well or badly he was represented, nothing would change that. It was something he would have to live with.

The distractions caused by four-year-old Victoria White's death, regardless of actual guilt, went with Dr Thurson to his next appointment. This was a meeting at St Clair's hospital of the District Management Team where he spoke for the GPs in the district. The DMT, which came together on a regular basis to help formulate practical policy, was chaired by Basil Hart, the District Treasurer. Also present were Stephen Morwell, the District Administrator; the District Nursing Officer Lesley Dickson; and Dr Alan O'Brien, the District Medical Officer, each of whom were paid officers. Dr Cloutman, a radiotherapist, who represented the consultants, and Dr Thurson were paid only expenses.

Being stretched and demoralized as he so often was, Dr Thurson sometimes thought about giving up his seat on the committee. Frequently he didn't have the energy even to get to the meetings, but when he did he found it a relief being there, discussing problems in general. That, combined with lassitude and the memory of how active a GP he had once been, were what prevented him resigning.

With thoughts on an entirely different plane, only occasionally did Dr Thurson manage to follow what was being said around the table in the boardroom.

'Are we all agreed then?' Basil Hart asked, looking to bring the item under discussion to a close. 'A strict limitation on locum registrars to replace those on leave?'

'I'm not entirely sure the junior doctors' committee will let us push that one through, not even with Region's backing,' Stephen Morwell said. 'Dr Davis – I beg your pardon, Mr Davis is threatening to make it a BMA issue.'

'I doubt the BMA will prove very effective,' Dr Cloutman said. The BMA was the best the doctors had in the way of a union, but its infrequently flexed muscles had all but atrophied.

'They're complaining that this will mean working excessive hours to provide cover.'

'I suppose there is some truth in that,' Dr Cloutman allowed, but didn't feel it valid enough to lend his support, despite the view being taken by some parliamentarians that it was valid. 'We did it in my day, didn't hurt any of us.'

'It could mean a one in one, certainly a one in two, rota for SHOs in some specialties,' Dr Thurson pointed out. He was in total sympathy with any over-stretched doctor regardless of the level of responsibility.

'In theory,' Hart said casually. 'It's unlikely to happen in practice.' This man had faith in the theory of management; in theory he was capable of fitting eleven patients into ten beds.

'In my experience not only is it likely to happen,' Dr Thurson said firmly, 'it very likely will. As a result you'll find some junior doctors under great pressure. Mistakes are likely to become legion.'

'They can call on their consultants,' Morwell said. That theory rarely worked in practice. Consultants were supposedly always available to make decisions outside the junior doctor's experience, but rarely were, and if they were called it got the junior doctor a black mark; registrars were left to cope with most problems.

'And what happens when the SHO on call has no registrar available because he's on leave without a locum replacement?' Dr Thurson asked, finding a clear line in his thoughts.

'Oh, you're being too cautious, Percy,' Basil Hart said. 'The potential saving makes this really worth pursuing.'

Dr Thurson's resistance collapsed with a shrug when he saw the rest of the DMT nodding.

'The next item on the agenda,' Hart said moving quickly on. 'Rationalizing of beds *vis-à-vis* Nightingale Block. How is the move progressing?'

'In fits and starts,' Lesley Dickson, the Nursing Officer informed them. 'The gynae ward's completed its move. The medical ward is half empty. The geriatric ward hasn't begun.'

'Are these wards being upgraded?' Dr Cloutman asked.

'Philip Montagu has ideas about that,' Morwell said.

'Do we take that to be a serious proposal? His wanting to turn the entire block into a gynae unit?' Basil Hart asked.

'He's made no formal proposal in the consultative document as yet.'

'He has been actively lobbying,' Dr Alan O'Brien said.

'I know, he talked to Region, which I thought presumptuous.'

'We have quite enough gynae beds in the District,' Lesley Dickson said. 'Geriatric beds are more urgently needed.'

'It's immaterial what sort of beds are most needed,' Stephen Morwell said. 'The fact is that unless these savings could be made elsewhere, closing Nightingale is a necessity.'

'Then what is item 6A on the agenda?' Dr Cloutman asked, slightly puzzled. 'This application to Region for a capital grant of £540,000 to upgrade those two wards? Two wards that we're closing?'

'They would qualify under the Capital Grants Scheme. Money's available at Region for such grants,' Morwell said. 'But regardless of whether our application is successful, it will help mollify the unions. They threatened to oppose closure other than for upgrading.'

'Will these two wards in fact be upgraded?'

'If we got the Capital grant,' Morwell told him. 'It would make sense having upgraded wards that could at some point be brought back into service.'

'If a grant isn't available?'

'That's what we'll report back to the unions.'

'I must say it disturbs me,' Dr Thurson told the meeting, 'saving money by chopping off bits of the services.'

'We're not chopping off services,' Stephen Morwell argued. 'We're looking for the five per cent cut in expenditure that has been asked for.' This large cut in the running cost of the Districts had been called for by Region, which in turn was trying to meet the government's cash limits. It was a struggle, especially for those in the front line. It was doubtful whether the five per cent target could be reached, but hopefully the deficit would be kept under the figure they were permitted to carry forward into the next financial year. 'Nightingale's closure would go a big way towards meeting that target.'

'But GPs already have difficulty getting hospital beds for patients,' Thurson said, pursuing his tack.

'There is no question that savings have to be made if we're to stay open at all,' Basil Hart put in.

'You cut off a patient's arms,' Dr Thurson said with an increasing feeling of alienation, and close to giving up, 'he remains alive, but he functions less well.' He looked at his watch. He had a home visit to make and was late. But it seemed like an excuse. 'Just before I go, could I raise the question of prescriptions from outpatient clinics being dispensed outside, rather than in the hospital pharmacy? Is this practice to continue?'

'Well, it's an economic measure,' Stephen Morwell replied, ignoring the chair.

'It's no sort of economy, Stephen,' Thurson said. 'It costs

the NHS three times as much to dispense prescriptions in the High Street.' He caught Dr O'Brien's eye and his own problem with a chemist flooded back.

'But it's a worthwhile saving to the hospital,' Morwell responded. 'I think we must confine ourselves to our own budgeting and not worry about the FPC's.'

Dr Thurson saw no point in arguing against such bureaucratic idiocy. He gathered his papers, made his excuses, and left, feeling deflated. There had been a time when he left these meetings with a sense of achievement; now he felt as though he had been going through the same hoops rather too long.

That feeling was accentuated by his first patient of the afternoon, Betty Parrish, who cheerfully showed him into the sitting-room of her ground floor council flat. She was a big lady who was disabled with rheumatoid arthritis but managed to get around in her wheelchair.

'Have you got time for a cup of tea?' she asked. 'The kettle won't take a minute.'

'I had some a little while ago,' he said, sitting on the arm of a chair. 'How are you?' He took her wrist, and checked her pulse. 'Any dizziness when you get out of the chair?'

'There was when they examined me at the DHSS offices last Tuesday,' she said, becoming tearful just thinking about that.

'How did you get on?' He opened his case to take her blood pressure.

'They won't give me a mobility allowance, doctor. They said I wasn't disabled enough.'

'Didn't they read my letter?' he asked, angry at the injustice of it. Mrs Parrish was disabled, and as immobile as could be without coming to a stop.

'I think so, doctor. I wouldn't mind, I mean, I can manage without the allowance if I'm careful. But they practically accuse you of cheating, that's what hurts my feelings. I'm not trying to cheat anyone,' she sobbed. 'I managed to walk a few paces. If I was cheating I would have pretended I couldn't. I expect they'd have given me one then. When I got giddy and fell down they looked at me like I was pulling a fast one, trying to get something I'm not entitled to.'

'Don't upset yourself, Mrs Parrish,' Dr Thurson told her. 'I'll write to the DHSS again, we'll get you a tribunal hearing.'

'Oh I don't want to be humiliated like that again, doctor. I'd sooner not have their money.'

'I know how you feel, Mrs Parrish, but it's your money. You're entitled to it and we won't let them bully you out of it simply because you can walk a few paces on a good day.' He put his head in his hand as he became totally abstracted. He was too tired to think out his next move, and in such moments his mind went blank. 'I'll write to them again, Mrs . . . We'll see what can be done.' He rose without taking her blood pressure, but seeing his bag open he took out his prescription pad.

His next house call was to a fourteen-year-old girl with excessive vaginal bleeding that set off vague alarm bells in him. It was the possibility of what had caused this rather than the volume of blood that concerned him. After examining her and diagnosing accurately the cause, he gave her a 1 ml intramuscular injection of Ergometrine to try and control the bleeding.

The girl's mother hovered in the room, which was festooned with posters of pop stars, and unnecessarily straightened school books on the tidy desk. It was displacement activity for anxiety, but her presence irritated the GP, who wanted to question the girl.

'Would you get some water, Mrs Attwood?' Dr Thurson asked, taking some tablets from his case.

'There's a carafe on the table, doctor,' Mrs Attwood said.

'Ah yes,' – as if he hadn't seen it. 'Just take these, Bernice. They'll help the pain.'

Unquestioning Bernice Attwood swallowed the tablets.

'Could you dispose of those?' He offered Mrs Attwood the spent hypodermic and a dirty disposable glove which he had turned inside out and then wrapped in a bag.

The mother seemed a little surprised, uncertain about leaving the room. 'Yes, of course.'

The doctor closed the door after her, then turned and considered Bernice.

'Is there anything you feel you want to tell me, Bernice?'

She hesitated, then shook her head.

'Are you sure?' This was friendly rather than interrogative.

'I got knocked at school, in hockey. I just started to bleed. Honestly,' Bernice said. 'I did.'

Dr Thurson nodded and squeezed her hand. Bernice was plump and very pretty, with long blonde hair and soft blue eyes; she gave no impression of sexual maturity, unlike a lot of girls, due to over-protective parents. Certainly from her appearance Thurson wouldn't ordinarily suspect the current problem. Bernice had a vulnerability that invited reassurance; it didn't occur to him that this might have been a ploy, but instead he accepted the invitation and squeezed her hand again, telling her not to worry, that they'd stop the bleeding at the hospital.

'Is it serious, doctor?' Mrs Attwood asked. She was waiting in the austerely tidy hallway.

'Have you noticed anything unusual about Bernice lately, Mrs Attwood?' He set his bag on the hall table.

'I don't think so. But then she's been staying in her room a lot, with all her studying for her O-levels,' the mother said. 'We're confident she'll get very good passes.'

Thurson nodded thoughtfully, then his mind went blank and he needed a moment to find his thread again.

'I can't stop the bleeding,' he said. 'I think she'll have to go to hospital. I'll try and arrange for a gynaecologist to see her right away.'

'Well, what brought this on, doctor?' Mrs Attwood

wanted to know.

Thurson considered this over-anxious mother. 'I don't know, Mrs Attwood,' he said, preferring not to tell her his suspicions yet. 'Let's see what they say at the hospital.'

By the time he had spoken to Dr Marvill at St Clair's and arranged a bed for Bernice and had visited another patient, Dr Thurson was late for evening surgery. There was nothing unusual about that. When his car drew up outside the house where his surgery was, he didn't stir, but remained behind the wheel as though unable to face the evening ahead. He sat there for a while, wondering if his efforts were worthwhile. Lately he seemed to have no space at all to think about what he was doing, and when he did it sometimes seemed totally pointless; so few people relied on themselves, but instead relied totally on him, expecting him, with the help of drugs, to put right years of self-abuse. Tonight there would be a surgery full of patients, who if told what they must really do with themselves in order to be well, wouldn't believe him, or wouldn't be prepared to do it. Tomorrow there would be another full surgery, and the next day, possibly the same people for all he knew. He stopped thinking about that. To have continued might have resulted in not holding a surgery, and more depressing was the fact that probably no one would be any the worse for it. He sighed deeply and climbed out of the car.

Dr Thurson let himself into his surgery and straight away pressed the intercom button to his receptionist; he hung up his coat, then riffled through his sample box for a pill to keep him going.

'Sorry I'm late, Joan,' he said when the receptionist brought him his mail and messages. 'Are there many waiting?'

'A few. Some complaining,' she told him. 'Mrs Castle's daughter phoned to say her mother's pulled out her catheter again, and could you call in there sometime after surgery. I told her to ring the district nurse. Apparently she's been twice today already.'

'Was she cross about it?' Thurson asked.

'She did say she had better things to do than changing wet bedding.'

He glanced through his mail, and without opening any of it, slid it on to the desk where it would be lost forever.

'Chloë Shallcross rang. She has a temperature and feels too ill to come into the surgery and wonders if you could call out. The Gerrard boy isn't any better. And Mr Reed phoned with his usual problem.'

'Give him a prescription or a certificate.'

'He's phoned back twice. He wants to speak to you,' she said. 'He was threatening to make a complaint. He even threatened to change doctors!' The phone that was switched through to the surgery started ringing. 'That's probably him again.'

'I don't want to speak to him,' Thurson said, suddenly exasperated. 'There's nothing more I can do for the man, he'll have to learn to live with his leaking bum.'

The receptionist asked the caller to hold on. 'It's Dr Marvill at St Clair's. About the Attwood girl.'

'Oh.' He seemed surprised, and took the phone. 'Send the first one in,' he told the receptionist. 'Thurson. Hello, doctor,' he said into the phone.

From the small office in the A and E department at St Clair's Dr Marvill said, 'It's a post partum haemorrhage the Attwood girl has. The uterus has failed to contract.'

'Ah,' Dr Thurson dragged Bernice Attwood back into his thoughts. 'I suspected she had had a baby, but I couldn't get much out of her. Especially not with the mother there.'

'Yes, the mother became hysterical. Her husband arrived a short while ago. He's as difficult. They seem more concerned with how it will have affected her exam results.' Dr Marvill took the coffee the staffnurse had brought her and absentmindedly drank some before realizing there was milk and sugar in it.

'When do you estimate delivery occurred?'

'Within the last twenty-four hours. The girl seems vague, but is no longer denying it,' Dr Marvill said. 'Is there a history of mental disturbance, either with the girl or the family? The father seems rather obsessive – anything more than that?'

'I don't think so,' Thurson said, trying to recall the Attwoods' medical history. 'The mother said Bernice has been under a lot of strain with exams.'

'I think there's a more serious problem here.' This was an opinion Dr Marvill had formed both from talking to Bernice and observing her. 'She flushed the placenta down the loo. I suspect the same fate might have befallen the baby were it not so big.'

'Is she saying what happened to it?'

'She refuses to talk about that. My suspicion is that she's hidden it in the house, either that or buried it in the garden. She seems to have set up an effective block against it.' Dr Marvill hesitated. 'Look, any chance of your going to the house with the Attwoods while they look for this baby?' She didn't like asking that of him, but he was the obvious choice.

'Oh Lord, I've a surgery full of patients. Couldn't you get a social worker to go?'

'I think it might be better if it was someone they knew. I'd go myself, but I'm on call.'

'I could probably get there after surgery,' he said after thinking about it. 'It won't be before about half eight.'

'Could you call in here first?' Dr Marvill asked.

'I think I'd better. Thank you, doctor,' he said and put the phone down. Almost as a reflex action, rather like some people reached for cigarettes, Dr Thurson reached for another pill. The visit to the Attwood house was something he would sooner have left to the police, but Bernice possibly needed psychiatric help, and bringing the police in at this stage wouldn't be the way to help her.

He glanced at the first patient's card on his desk. 'Come in, Mrs Taylor, take a seat.' He sat behind the desk and automatically brought forward his prescription pad. He knew what was wrong with this patient without her telling him. Having lost her husband with cancer seven months ago, she hadn't managed to get out of the depression she had slipped into. The pains she complained of, mostly in the chest, were symptomatic of that.

The hunt for Bernice Attwood's baby started and ended in her bedroom. Dr Thurson waited with Frederick Attwood, while Mrs Attwood went through cupboards and drawers, searched boxes and clothes. The cardboard bootbox under the bed made her apprehensive. When she stood up with it and opened the lid her worst fears were confirmed.

'I can scarcely believe this,' Mr Attwood said. He was a schoolteacher and very rigid in his thinking, which was reflected in his tense body. 'It's like a particularly nasty dream.'

'Why don't you go downstairs,' Dr Thurson said, taking the box. 'I'll have that. Go with your wife.' He ushered them from the room. He wanted to examine the dead child, and thought it too distressing for them to witness.

The baby was quite dead and not from any cause that might have been remotely described as natural.

When he told the Attwoods they were blank with disbelief.

'I think Bernice will need some professional help,' Dr Thurson said, taking tablets from his case in the Attwoods' sitting-room.

'She has been under a lot of strain with her O-levels,' Attwood commented, as if in mitigation. 'She sat five mocks.'

'I daresay she may have been working too hard,' Dr Thurson said. 'Too much pressure can cause people to behave quite inexplicably.'

'Bernice's behaviour is certainly that.' Attwood thought it intolerable.

'Here, take these, Mrs Attwood,' Thurson gave her Dicynene tablets instead of Valium. His mind was still on treating the daughter. 'I think the problem goes deeper. Baby appears to have been smothered.'

'I refuse to believe this. Bernice has had every educational advantage,' her father said, becoming agitated.

'It's a shock for you both. These things are often difficult to come to terms with,' Dr Thurson told them. 'There'll be a postmortem. I daresay we might get to the truth eventually.' He noticed Mrs Attwood hadn't moved, it was as though she had frozen in shock. For some reason Dr Thurson looked at the bottle of pills he still had in his hand and realized his mistake. 'I'd better have those back.' He put the tablets back in the bottle and found the Valium. 'These will help you over the shock. They'll help you to sleep tonight.'

That might have been the answer.

26

The prospect of becoming a father pleased Brian Shallcross more than he believed possible. His first response to the news that his wife was going to have a baby had been that they were too young to be burdened with children, but that had been transitory, and as soon as he had got used to the notion he enjoyed it more and more. Chloë's anxious mood states had confused him, and initially he didn't know how to cope and had become anxious and angry himself until he realized things were best left, that the cause of her anxiety would soon pass if he didn't react.

The anxiety he felt now was as real as the cause: his wife was having a miscarriage; she was in pain and bleeding.

In the hallway of their modern house Brian Shallcross was on the telephone trying to summon help at this early hour. Dr Thurson was the first person he thought of, but he wasn't answering the phone. It had been ringing for ages. Finally someone answered.

'Hello. Hello, Dr Thurson?'

'This is Dr Thurson's wife,' Edna Thurson said. She had eventually answered the phone when she realized her husband couldn't wake up.

'Could I speak to Dr Thurson?' Shallcross said. 'It's very urgent.' He sensed no urgency in the response.

'Oh, he's asleep, I'm afraid,' Mrs Thurson told him. 'I don't think I can wake him. Is it urgent?'

'My wife's having a miscarriage.' he said. 'I think she's having a miscarriage.'

'I can't wake him.' She was confused, and unsure what advice to give.

'She's having a miscarriage . . .' he repeated, fear and

frustration bringing tears to his eyes.

'He's taken some pills. He's been out visiting half the night, he couldn't eat supper, he was so tired. He can't go on like this, you know. They must let him take a partner this time. But I don't know if they will, you see. That's the problem . . .'

Brian Shallcross slammed the phone down, shutting out Mrs Thurson's troubles. He hesitated, then ran up the stairs, deciding to take his wife to hospital rather than try to get an ambulance.

When on call Dr Marvill made a point of not going to bed before twelve midnight as crises seemed to happen more frequently before rather than after then. Only tonight had disproved her theory, as she had had two calls around one o'clock and expected to have to go to one of the women again.

In her tiny cluttered room at the hospital Dr Marvill had fallen asleep with the light on, the medical book she had been reading was propped against her.

The phone woke her with a start, and she grabbed it instantly, her thought process taking a moment longer.

'Dr Marvill . . .' She listened, understanding enough of the problem in order to respond. 'Yes, I'll be along directly.'

She replaced the phone and got out of bed, but her pace suggested she would arrive there anything but directly.

After the nurses in the Accident and Emergency department had wheeled his wife away into the theatre, Brian Shallcross felt that time didn't move. It might have helped had someone come out and said what was happening, but no one did. He thought about phoning Chloë's mother, but decided it was too early. He tried to sit, he tried to read, but couldn't and pacing up and down didn't help. The A and E department was deserted, even the porter on the desk had disappeared. Brian Shallcross watched the dawn arrive, and sometime after, he didn't know how long, an old lady came in wearing an overcoat. She made herself at home in the waiting area, obviously familiar with the place.

The porter who was earlier manning the reception desk returned with a cup of tea. He knew the woman, and Brian Shallcross followed their conversation as a means of distraction.

'Hello, dear,' the porter said, 'you're about early.'

'I've got an aggravating knee,' the old lady replied.

'Couldn't you sleep?' These weren't responses to questions, as neither seemed to listen as people mostly did when observing the rules of conversation.

'I got an aggravating knee. It seems to hurt more above the knee than below. It hurts more above the knee than below.' She rose and went across to him.

'You've got a bit of fluid there, dear,' the porter diagnosed from behind the desk.

'It hurts more above the knee than below it,' she repeated.

'You want to put it up,' he advised. 'But don't bind it above or below the knee.'

'It hurts more above than below the knee.'

'Try a hot water-bottle on it.'

'I've got an electric blanket,' she announced.

'You try a hot-water bottle.'

With that she shuffled back to the bench, there to rest or kill time rather than wait for a more expert opinion.

Dr Marvill appeared from the A and E theatre along the corridor.

'Your wife's fine, Mr Shallcross,' she said. 'She's had what's called an ante partum haemorrhage. The bleeding occurs from the uterine wall, where the placenta is attached to it.' No one was ever sure why this bleeding occurred, but she didn't tell him that. 'It should settle down all right.'

'Is the baby all right?'

'It's fine,' Dr Marvill reassured him with a tired smile. 'We'll keep your wife in for a couple of days to make sure. You can go and see her.'

She indicated where he should go, then shuffled away, wondering what the chances of getting back to sleep were, whether it was even worth trying to.

In fact she didn't return to bed, it was too late to make that worthwhile. Instead she took a hot bath, and felt more alert immediately afterwards. But by the time she got across to the medical centre, for breakfast of black coffee and toast, tiredness had seeped through her again. Her eyes focused blearily on the newsprint before her, and she took in little of the information she was reading.

At an adjacent table Roger Crick was trying to persuade a surgical registrar from ENT to remove some of his moles. Jessie Marvill listened to the conversation for a moment.

'I can't say when I'll be able to pop them off, Roger,' the ENT surgeon told him. 'But present yourself in theatre sometime. You think they're problematic? They look okay to me.'

'I'd sooner not take that chance,' – was Dr Crick's position.

Dr Marvill smiled to herself, and turned the page of the *Sun*. Roger Crick must have had more moles removed.

'I hear you're not happy in your work,' Vernon Davis said as he joined her. 'Congratulations. Maybe we should form a club.' Despair tinged his humour.

Jessie Marvill folded the newspaper and considered him. 'Unless there's another SHO appointed soon I won't stay the course.'

'The junior doctors' committee is still batting on that one, Jess,' he told her. 'We won't let them get away with it. We should go for a complete withdrawal of services. I doubt we'll get any backing from the BMA. I think we should go ahead without it. I'm sure you've got it about right, heading for general practice.'

'Have you ever considered changing, Vernon?' she asked. Although he had a difficult time because of his views, she believed he tended to be slightly self-pitying. This reminded her of Roger Trentham, her former boyfriend. She thought of Laurence James, who coped very well, despite having no less difficulty as a result of his beliefs.

'To go where?' Davis asked. 'I have eleven months to run on my contract. Smith-Sampson won't give me a reference – he said as much. All I can do is outlast him.'

Jessie looked at him, but didn't say anything.

'At the rate he makes mistakes, someone other than me will find him out, Jessie. He can't get a circumcision right nowadays,' – his voice rose in anger. 'I had to re-do a young lad yesterday whom he'd sewn up too tightly.'

Jessie Marvill nodded. That was as far as she could go this morning. She finished her coffee.

'My boss has an early start.' She rose offering him the *Sun* like a consolation prize.

The reason Mr Montagu was starting his theatre earlier than usual was because he was fitting in a private patient before his NHS work. With private patients he made a point of seeing them prior to their being anaesthetized. It reassured them that their money was well spent.

Wearing theatre greens and a Jeyes cloth cap, with a blue Johnson and Johnson mask draped at his throat, Mr Montagu entered the anaesthetic room, which was adjacent to the modern gynae theatre. Mrs Osborne was on the trolley, wearing the type of theatre gown NHS patients were put in; the equipment was the same, as were the techniques employed. The deferential attention both before and after the operation was all that private patients paid for.

Dr Ian Lawson, the senior registrar anaesthetist, was present, along with a bright smiling nurse.

'Good morning, Mrs Osborne,' Mr Montagu said. 'How are you feeling?'

'A little nervous,' she managed drowsily.

'A little nervous?' he said, not quite anticipating her. 'No need. You can have absolute confidence in Dr Lawson.' He indicated the senior registrar anaesthetist, whom he had made a point of using. 'I have only the best on my team. In a little while it'll be over and finished with. No more discomfort. No more bleeding.'

He held her hand while Dr Lawson looked for a vein in the other hand to put the needle in.

'What polite little veins,' he said, making it sound like a compliment. Her nervousness had caused the veins to constrict. 'Just relax, my dear, relax. A slight discomfort, that's all. There, you barely felt that.'

He was good at his job and got the needle in immediately. Some anaesthetists needed two or three tries which reflected their own nervousness.

Mrs Osborne drifted off immediately. The oxygen bag was connected to the endotracheal tube in her mouth and the anaesthetist squeezed it several times. The muscle relaxant he had given her had stopped the breathing reflex.

By the time Mr Montagu was scrubbed and in gown and gloves, Mrs Osborne was on the operating table, on her back with her knees bent up and just dropped apart. Dr Marvill passed a catheter to empty the patient's bladder. Then everyone was ready for the surgeon. The theatre sister, who was scrubbed, assisted by a staffnurse, who would alternate with her throughout the morning, made final adjustments to the patient's sheeting, and checked the instruments. The anaesthetist constantly monitored the patient's breathing, and checked her blood pressure.

'I'll do a Pfannestiel, sister,' he reminded her, and added unkindly, 'Even at her age she wants a neat little scar.' This she would get in the pubic hair line.

Drs Lambolle and Marvill joined him.

'Can I have this up a little more, Danny?' he said to the Operating department assistant, indicating the table. Curiously males weren't permitted on the gynae wards as nurses, but there was no objection to male ODAs in gynae theatres.

The porter cranked up the table to the surgeon's preferred height. Dr Montagu asked for some more antiseptic to be painted on the patient. Then without further explanation he made his first incision across the shaved pubic line. He quickly reached the anterior wall of the uterus, which he cut through with scissors.

Pushing his hand into the opening, his fingers explored the uterus.

'Ah,' he intoned as if in surprise. He had anticipated doing a myomectomy, which was the excision of the fibroid tumours with part of the uterine muscle, while leaving the uterus virtually intact. 'There are more of them than I had hoped. I'll have to take the box out' – referring to the womb.

'She won't be happy about that,' Dr Lambolle commented.

'She'll thank us for it later.'

'What about leaving her ovaries?' the registrar asked.

'They're not much use to her now,' Mr Montagu said, 'She might express some emotional attachment if given the choice.' He would remove them at the same time and so reduce the risk of cancer. Some surgeons thought in terms of removing anything that was even remotely prone to cancer.

Taking a scalpel he went into the opening, severing the first of the blood vessels to the uterine wall. He handed the scalpel to the scrubnurse and took a stitchholder with thread for tying off. There was a lot of tying off to be done on this very bloody operation.

As Dr Lambolle swabbed the wound, a vessel burst and bled profusely. He called for a large swab.

'There are no large swabs in the gynae packs,' the scrubnurse told him.

'This is intolerable. We were running short on my last list,' Montagu said.

'I have ordered them, several times,' the theatre sister

said, anticipating him.

'I'd better have a word with Alice Inglis myself,' he said. She was the Nursing Officer responsible for theatres. He assisted Dr Lambolle with small swabs. Then said, 'Kocher's' and was handed the forceps. Conversation around the table was low and muffled by their masks, hearing was difficult and sometimes the wrong instrument was proffered.

After clamping a vessel he offered the forceps to Dr Marvill to hold out of the way. She didn't respond as she had nodded off to sleep.

'Are you falling asleep, Jessie?' Mr Montagu said. 'This is a private patient you know.' It was one of his rare stabs at humour, and because of its rarity no one recognized it for what it was. 'Someone take her out and get her some coffee.'

'Sorry – I'm all right,' Dr Marvill said.

'Coffee,' he insisted. 'We've a long list this morning.'

Dr Marvill went out with the theatre runner, who would make her coffee and talk to her to prevent her falling asleep again. Junior doctors nodded off in theatre not infrequently.

The consultant took another clamp and set that on the vessel, then pushed it out of the way while he tied off.

'Have you decided where you're going yet, Ian?' he asked Dr Lawson.

'I thought perhaps I might try Saudi Arabia.'

'A firm offer?'

'I haven't explored seriously,' Dr Lawson said. He had to look elsewhere in the hope of advancing his career as consultant posts were becoming scarcer.

'I'm putting a firm together for a private unit in the not too distant future,' Mr Montagu told him, as his hands explored the cavity. 'Perhaps you'd care to join us.'

'Will there be a consultant post?' the anaesthetist asked.

'There certainly will.

'I'd be delighted to,' Dr Lawson said.

'You'll be part of a first rate team.'

Dr Lambolle continued to swab. He felt no less frustrated

at his career prospects, but he didn't get an offer. Like most of his contemporaries he would have to put up with the situation and all its frustrations. Perhaps one day those organizing the career structure would acknowledge that this situation wasn't good for the doctor, so ultimately it wasn't good for the patient either. However, the chances were that even if that fact was acknowledged, still nothing would get done about it, because ironically, patients weren't that much of a consideration.

27

Although falling asleep at work was something that happened to most junior doctors, even in theatre, and had almost certainly happened to consultants in their time, that was no reason for them to tolerate it, or be sympathetic, for most had the happy knack of forgetting they were once junior doctors.

Dr Marvill didn't expect her boss to be particularly understanding. He had bleeped her and when she phoned him his secretary informed her Mr Montagu wanted to see her right away. She believed that was overreaction to her closing her eyes for a moment, even if they had been operating on a private patient.

Entering the outer office where Mr Montagu's secretary was typing from a dictating machine, Dr Marvill was told to go in. The woman didn't smile and didn't stop typing. Uncertain what her attitude meant, Dr Marvill hesitated and knocked on the door first. Mr Montagu was in his Turnbull-Asher shirtsleeves, removing papers from the glass fronted book cabinet in this comfortable office.

'Shut the door,' he said without prelusive niceties. 'You do realize I could have your contract terminated.'

'I'm sorry,' she began, surprised by his attitude. 'I had been up on calls most of the night before,' she said in her own defence.

'What? Oh . . .' He realized that she was on another tack. 'I'm not concerned about your falling asleep in my theatre – serious as that is, it happens to the best of doctors. I'm more concerned about Mrs Downes. She's refusing radiotherapy or the drugs I prescribed. It seems you're to thank. Perhaps you'd care to explain yourself?' With patients, because of his position – the knowledge it gave him and the fear they brought him – Philip Montagu was supremely in control. He enjoyed the power his role gave him over women, that was a subconscious reason for becoming a gynaecologist. Similarly, he was able to dominate Jessie Marvill. But his grip here was less sure, for he recognized an independent will and saw by her actions with Mrs Downes a challenge to his authority. This resulted in his repressed anger.

'Well, sir,' Dr Marvill began uncertainly, 'I believed I was doing what was best for the patient.'

'You presume to know more than me about that?'

'No sir,' she found herself saying, despite having talked this through with Laurence James. He had encouraged her action, and helped convince her of its correctness, despite it being professionally wrong.

'That's reassuring, doctor,' he said. 'I don't enjoy having my judgement undermined by junior members of my staff.'

'I'm sorry.' Dr Marvill felt the ground slip from beneath her. 'Mrs Downes was desperately unhappy with her treatment. I simply explained to her what was happening, what its shortcomings were.'

'Experience tells me that most patients are best left in ignorance of these things. If they knew better than consultants they would be treating themselves and not queueing up for treatment.' He paused and stared at her, expecting her to break down. 'Any change of policy regarding a patient I would appreciate you discussed with me.'

'I did in fact raise the matter with you, Mr Montagu,' Dr Marvill ventured as an alternative to tears.

'I clearly recall the conversation. Do you consider a change of diet and attitude a practical alternative for a patient with carcinoma of the ovary, with numerous secondaries?' he asked as if believing her action an idiosyncratic whim.

'I think the value of cytotoxic drugs and radiotherapy extremely limited with this patient. A more nutritious diet with a change of outlook would certainly help make her more comfortable,' she suggested, knowing that a working relationship had to continue for another three months.

Not expecting her to defend her action, and realizing he had run his own argument into a cul-de-sac, he said, 'I won't discuss this matter further. When Mrs Downes dies, which she certainly will, and quite unpleasantly, the responsibility will be yours alone, Dr Marvill. That's all.' He dismissed her.

Had anyone else spoken to her like Philip Montagu had, especially in her currently exhausted state, Jessie Marvill would certainly have cried, but was determined not to now. Having clashed head on with medical chauvinism, she did not enjoy the experience, but accepted that it was one likely to be repeated, especially if she sought to practise any form of alternative medicine.

No sooner did Dr Marvill go out of the office than Mr Montagu's secretary came in.

'Mr and Mrs Tong are here, sir,' she said.

'Show them in, Janet,' Montagu told her, reaching his jacket from a hanger.

The charming exterior, so closely following his emotional scene with Dr Marvill, fitted him as readily as his jacket.

'Do come in, have a seat,' he said, shaking their hands, before sitting behind his desk. 'Now. How can I help?' This made them uneasy. He knew why they were here.

The Tongs looked confused. Somehow they had expected this doctor to be on the defensive.

'It's about Gina's mother, Mrs Robertson,' Roy Tong said on an uncertain tack. 'She died in hospital here, six months ago. She had cancer. The thing is, we were told she died because of her treatment. It was sort of experimental.'

'That doesn't sound very realistic. Patients aren't guinea pigs,' Montagu said sincerely; despite that, in fact, that often was their true role. 'Your GP wrote to me about your unease. Do you know what therapy your mother received?'

'She had radium treatment and some new cancer drug. We were told that was the most effective treatment after her operation.'

'That often proves so, Mr Tong,' the surgeon told them. 'Mrs Robertson's tumour couldn't be removed entirely, because of its spread. On examination, deposits were found in the peritoneum and the omentum.' He didn't explain where these were, believing that sort of information was of no use to them. 'After removing as much of the carcinoma as possible, the next course of action was to eradicate what remained. As a matter of interest, who told you this combination of treatment killed your mother?'

The Tongs avoided his eyes. But were silent.

'I see. Do you know what drugs your mother was given?'

'I don't know,' Mrs Tong said in a whisper.

'We were told it was a new drug being tested. They had to ask her permission,' Roy Tong said.

'Not quite true, Mr Tong,' Mr Montagu told him. 'It was a drug called Azalatine, developed in this very hospital. It's one we can be justly proud of. I don't know if you are aware of the stringent safeguards laid down by the Committee on Safety of Medicines. These are very strict, and absolutely adhered to. It's in everyone's interests that they are. The drug companies would have it no other way. They are absolutely scrupulous in these matters.' The consultant let them ponder that fact. He might not have been aware that his partner, Sir Randolph Spence, was not only deputy chairman of Cavandish Pharmaceuticals, the company whose research unit was attached to St Clair's, but was also Chairman of the Medical Ethics Committee. This body vetted research projects involving patients, and approved clinical trials, first satisfying itself that enough ground work had been done with tests on animals. 'The cytotoxic drug that we had on clinical trial here last year passed the requirements. In fact we're using it quite successfully.'

There was a pause. The Tongs were uncertain where to take their argument. It seemed unreasonable to challenge this reassurance from such an eminent specialist. But despite himself Roy Tong said, 'Well, something went wrong for Rose. We thought if we could find just what went wrong, maybe we could sue the drug company or the hospital.'

Mr Montagu concealed his smile. 'I can understand your distress. But I honestly think you'd find that unsatisfactory. Let me explain a little about high oxygenation chemotherapy, which is the treatment your mother had. It's not entirely new. What happens inside tumours is that malignant cells are less well oxygenated than ordinary, healthy cells. They're anoxic. In other words they are deficient in oxygen. Without oxygen malignant cells are less sensitive to radiation. What a drug such as Azalatine does is help the tumour cells to absorb oxygen, so that radiotherapy is more effective. Nothing went wrong with the treatment, the real problem for Mrs Robertson was that she was detected so late, as her medical record shows. This is often the case with carcinoma of the ovaries. Have you seen a copy of Mrs Robertson's medical record?' he asked as if it were possible for them to have easily done so.

'No. The hospital administrator told us we could get it only through the court.'

'Yes, well there's nothing sinister in this,' Mr Montagu said. 'It's a question of maintaining confidentiality.'

'But it's her Mum's record.' Roy Tong felt slightly angry. 'We are her closest family. I mean, she's been dead six months.'

Gina Tong began to cry.

Mr Montagu nodded sympathetically. 'The fact is, medical records belong to the Secretary of State, so the administrator is not empowered to hand them over. I wish it were otherwise at times like this.' He paused, 'Does any of this help you at all?'

'Well, it's good of you to explain, sir,' Gina Tong said.

'Not at all. I wish I could have been of more help.'

'Thank you for seeing us,' Roy Tong said.

'If there is anything else troubling you, don't hesitate to get in touch.' Mr Montagu gave them a tight smile as he rose, clearly indicating that the meeting was at a close.

'Do you think the Tongs'll try to sue the hospital?' the administrator asked Philip Montagu when the consultant called by his office later that afternoon.

'I think they are less confused about her death than they were. Basically they didn't know how to deal with it.'

'Not many do,' Needham commented.

'I talked to Reggie Cloutman before coming here,' Montagu said. 'He thinks it may have been one of his technicians who talked to the Tongs.' The consultant had taken a lot of trouble on this case, which had interrupted his busy day, and not out of fear of his reputation, or for the Tongs' sake. This was done as a favour to Roy Needham, who Montagu wanted as an ally when he made his move for Nightingale Block.

'There's no evidence to suggest the treatment was responsible for her death?' Needham closed the patient's record.

'All treatment is partially responsible in such cases,' Montagu allowed. 'We've had successes too. The Ethics Committee was satisfied with the results of the clinical trials. I fully explained to the Tongs why treatment didn't always succeed. They seemed reasonably consoled.'

'Thank you, Philip.' Needham felt grateful to him for the trouble he had taken, but did not question why he had been so helpful. 'Let's hope this closes the matter.' He rose to show the consultant out.

In the outer office Chris Hogan was waiting with two shop stewards. Needham hadn't forgotten they were coming, but the visit from the consultant gynaecologist had left him unprepared for this bi-weekly meeting.

'I'll be ready for you in two minutes, Chris,' Needham said, and dived back into his office to whip out his notes.

There was a lot on the agenda, some of it added for horsetrading and point-taking. The familiar chestnut, restoration of porters' overtime, was raised early and dealt with, Roy Needham promising once again to take the matter up at Region. But there was no pressure to do so as the portering was functioning despite the regular overtime ban. But it wasn't something Chris Hogan would let go of.

The matter of the ancillary workers' rota was raised with the unions about management wanting to change over to a three eight-hour shift system throughout the twenty-four hours, which would rotate either weekly or monthly, similar to police shifts. This was to avoid the influx of labour during the early part of the day, trailing away to almost nothing at night. Although it was a sound idea the union avoided it because the membership didn't like nightwork, and they knew the move was really aimed at the nurses, who management didn't want to fight. Most nurses liked night duty even less, and there were often difficulties finding enough qualified nurses to keep the hospital running at night – student nurses had no choice in the matter.

There was trouble in the linen room, where staff had been moved because the linen budget was overspent, which was why the gynae theatre had run out of large swabs. The obstetrics theatre had run out of small towels; the deficit had to be made up so that more towels and swabs could be bought.

Little satisfaction and progress had been made by the time Needham's secretary interrupted with some tea. There were no biscuits on the tray, as the DMT had decided that biscuits being handed out at such meetings were adding unreasonably to the annual catering bill.

'Thank you, Wendy,' Needham said. He rose and poured tea for Chris Hogan and his two shop stewards, being fairly placatory towards them. The deputy administrator and the senior nursing officer had to pour their own.

'Help yourselves to sugar,' Needham said. 'I'm sorry there aren't any biscuits.'

'We'll have to start bringing our own bickies, Roy,' the deputy administrator said.

'To return to the linen room for a moment,' Needham said, 'all I can do is repeat what I've told you, Chris. There are no plans for closing the dressmaking department. In fact that's the last section I'd want to see close. It does the long-stay geriatrics good to have decent clothes.'

'In that case there should be no problem reinstating the seamstress who was downgraded,' Hogan said. He was wearing a suit and tie for this meeting.

'What's happened is they've overspent on the linen budget. They're trying to rationalize the linen department. I'll take it up with the Domestic Manager,' Needham promised, making a note. 'In fact I don't think the lady in question had been made up to seamstress grade.'

'She was doing the job though. That brings us to Mrs Appleby,' Hogan said, consulting his notes. 'She's the ancillary moved from men's medical on Nightingale when it closed. She wants to go back on ward work.'

'She has been offered another ward,' Mrs Kay, the deputy administrator put in. 'It means taking the late shift.'

'Well what about her family, Mrs Kay? You can't penalize her for that,' Hogan said. 'That's what you're doing.'

'It's only temporary. She can go back on days as soon as there's a shift to suit her,' Roy Needham informed him.

'When's that going to be? She'll want to know.'

'Just as soon as we get this question of shifts sorted.'

'What about Nightingale, Chris,' Roland Morley, a shop steward, asked.

'Yes, what's happening there?'

'Didn't you receive copies of the consultative document?'

'All we've got to say about that,' Hogan informed him, 'is we'll stop it from closing permanently.'

'There's no question of permanent closure. We've been consulting on the basis of the block being put to better use for a single specialty. For geriatrics, or as a psychi' unit.'

'It's like the thin edge of the wedge. Wards that close for any reason seem to have a habit of not opening again,' Hogan said.

'The immediate plans are clear, Chris. We want to empty the remaining wards in order to upgrade them. It isn't likely that would happen if we were shutting the block permanently,' Needham argued.

That seemed logical, even though in healthcare, logic was no proof of anything.

Whatever they were told either here in these meetings or in the consultative document, which was got out by the DMT to consider everyone's views, Chris Hogan decided his union should keep a close watching brief on Nightingale Block, lest the few remaining beds there were closed never to open again.

28

Although money for healthcare in the public sector was tight, there being only a limited amount for the whole range of services, there was no fixed sum for any one specialty, and usually a case had to be made for each financial allocation. How much spending power accrued to any specialty within a district was often dependent on how good a case they made. Lobbying in the health service by consultants wasn't confined to District, which had no direct source of income, only the power to decide where it was spent, but often taken to the Regional Health Authority, with capital grants within its gift, regardless of the recommendations of district management teams. Few consultants were more aware of the value of lobbying than Philip Montagu, who cultivated productive relations at all levels. Despite the DHSS's policy documents giving psychiatric and geriatric patients priority of resources, what in fact determined priority in any specialty was its acuteness, reflected in turnover. This partly explained why in reality geriatric and psychiatric medicine trailed in the priority tables. The equation was simple: cash for hardware and facilities followed surgery, which resulted in turnover; so the dictum was cut as often as possible. Mr Montagu actively pursued a policy of surgical intervention in both his gynae and obstetric units.

Looking to his own interests, Philip Montagu had gone to see George Christian, the regional administrator. The meeting was informal, but even so Rex Dundobbin, the treasurer, was also present in Christian's modern office in the RHA block. The stark space was large, with comfortable furniture, but gave the impression of its occupant being impermanent.

'Attractive as specialized units in the District may be, Philip,' George Christian was saying in response to Mr Montagu's proposal, 'I'm not sure we could get your scheme on.'

'The DHSS have their priorities wrong,' Montagu informed them. 'Consider the number of gynaecological procedures my firm has carried out within the last twelve months, together with my waiting list. Also consider the concern expressed over perinatal mortality at the last DHA meeting. One begins to get some indication of priority.'

'No one doubts the importance of the specialty. But it all comes down to money. There just isn't enough to turn Nightingale Block into a gynae unit.'

'The heart surgeons at Queen's have submitted a similar plan,' Rex Dundobbin said, as if to purposely anger Montagu. He was in his late fifties, and about ten years older than the regional administrator. 'Mr Latham has put forward a scheme to take over the block for a heart unit, with emphasis on transplants. I must say it's attracting wide support.'

Anger exploded in Philip Montagu's brain, but he clamped it off. 'That whole business is obscene. I saw a photograph of their latest candidate in Tuesday's *Mail.* They might have dealt with his weight problem before giving him another heart to abuse. It's all self-aggrandizement. I daresay these operations will continue, and with more tabloid headlines, which are quite offensive to our profession. How would this unit enrich the community we serve? On cost alone the procedures are scandalous. £20-£25,000 per operation. Healthcare should be broadbased, giving the greatest service to the largest number of patients.' That wasn't his true philosophy, but it suited his current argument. 'I would rather see Nightingale Block taken out of service than given to those self-publicists.'

'In reality, Philip,' George Christian said, 'I think permanent closure is on the cards. Despite the DMT seeing it as a viable part of the District.' It might have been an indiscretion saying this to other than Philip Montagu.

'Even assuming that the block can be kept functioning, I'm no longer sure my colleagues would be prepared to put up with beds there.' The consultant was manoeuvring to the position he wanted. 'The facilities are inadequate. The block might be suitable for long-stay geriatrics, I can't see anyone else seriously considering it.'

'Plans are in hand to upgrade the rest of the block,' Rex Dundobbin informed him.

'It seems a bit woolly-minded,' Montagu said dismissively.

George Christian considered the gynaecologist, a smile brushing the corner of his mouth. 'What is it you have in mind, Philip?' he asked bluntly.

Staring straight back at him, Montagu said, 'Were the closure made permanent, the consortium that I'm a part of might be interested in either buying or leasing the block for a gynae-obstetrics unit.'

Both of the RHA officers thought about this proposal.

'That possibility wasn't overlooked,' Christian said. He turned to his colleague for an estimation of the financial position.

'It would mean a very real saving,' Rex Dundobbin said. 'Assuming the unions were agreeable.'

'The biggest hurdle to get the unions over is permanent closure,' George Christian pointed out. 'After that I don't suppose they'll much mind. Are you making a formal proposal?'

'I'd like to see the outcome of the consultations on the block,' Montagu said. 'I'm trying to gauge the sort of reception an offer is likely to get.'

'You might not be surprised to learn, Philip,' said George Christian, 'that you'll meet very little objection.'

Rex Dundobbin was nodding, as if speaking for the whole Authority.

After inconclusive discussions between the various parties concerned, the management at St Clair's, the unions, the Community Health Council – which acted as a consumers' watchdog over the hospitals in the District – the DMT, the full medical committee, the proposal for permanently closing Nightingale Block was put on the agenda at the next District Health Authority meeting. The proposal was a red rag to a bull as far as the unions were concerned.

NUPE had briefed Councillor Bill Williamson, who was one of the twenty members of the Authority seated around the rectangular table arrangement in the too small boardroom at the DHA offices. Officers of the DHA had briefed the police, warning them that there might be trouble, but their presence was over-kill outside the building and up in the boardroom reception area as they almost outnumbered the members of the public present. Councillor Williamson protested at their presence but was ruled out of order.

'The permanent closure of Nightingale Block is unacceptable to almost everyone concerned, not least a large section of this Authority,' Councillor Williamson said from his seat. No one rose when speaking. On principle he opposed any closure within the NHS, especially where it meant private medicine taking up the slack.

'What was put forward as a temporary panacea for a perennial complaint, shortage of finance, is now being offered as the final solution,' Councillor Williamson went on. 'I know there are financial shortfalls. We've suffered cuts, cuts and yet more cuts, these I've persistently fought both within this Authority and within the council chamber. But shutting 120 beds, i.e. one quarter of St Clair's, which the closure of Nightingale Block represents, for the saving of £560,000, i.e. one twentieth of that hospital's expenditure, makes no logical or economic sense.'

The proposed closure, representing as it did a single focus for the many shades of political thinking, from those supporting government/DHSS policy to those violently opposed to it, brought an unusually well attended DHA meeting. All the members had shown up this evening, each with an array of papers before them. Stephen Morwell and Basil Hart were to the right and left of the DHA Chairman, a Dr Clarence Vine, a local GP; Dr Alan O'Brien was there also. Crowding the too few public seats were union members, including Chris Hogan. Because of the limited room public seating was cramped in the double doorway and spread back into the adjacent room, so in effect only about four people could follow the proceedings adequately.

'The saving is taken for the District as a whole, not just St Clair's,' Stephen Morwell said. He was reluctantly supporting the closure, and was likely to jump back over the fence if he saw his District suffering. He had no vote on this Authority, but was there to give information. 'It was decided on balance that the five per cent saving would be less damaging here than if it were made up of piecemeal cuts across the board.'

'But what you're doing,' Councillor Williamson said, changing tack slightly, 'is eroding community-based care by closing part of this hospital. There are people desperately in need of beds, beds which GPs can no longer find for them. This closure will mean some people living in abject misery. I think it's time we said no to the erosion of these very basic services.'

'It does seem to me, Mr Chairman,' said Councillor Lloyd, a man of different political shade, 'that there is an unfair burden on our resources with people from outside our District coming here for treatment. Are there any figures on this?'

'I don't have any before me,' said the deputy district administrator, who was older than his boss and sat on his right. 'There is a teaching hospital within this authority. So we must expect a fairly high intake from across the country.'

'Enough to fill 120 beds?' Councillor Lloyd asked.

'In fact, if I might come in here, Mr Chairman,' Dr O'Brien ventured, 'the teaching hospital within our District takes over fifty per cent of its patients from outside those boundaries. As Queen's has over five hundred beds, Nightingale Block could be filled several times over.'

'That's just as I expected,' Councillor Lloyd said as if he had found the solution.

'It is perhaps worth pointing out, if these teaching beds weren't available, consultants would go elsewhere. We might suffer more from a decline in standards.'

'There's no escaping the need for cuts, as unwelcome as these may be,' said Dr Vine, the chairman. 'We are running at a substantial deficit due to wage settlements in excess of the government's cash limits. The medical staff settlement earlier this year of nine per cent has so far cost £260,000. This deficit must be met from the current budget; the fact is we cannot do that at the present level of expenditure.' He glanced around the room, hoping there were no more points to be raised. 'I'll hear from the Community Health Council, then I would like to take a vote. I believe everyone's had a chance to speak. Mrs Forks?' he said to the chairwoman of the CHC, who was sitting at the side of the room with several members of her council.

She was a short, sturdily built grandmother in her mid-fifties. She had a strong personality, but had to stand to be seen. 'When we were consulted about the temporary closure of some of the wards on Nightingale, the CHC was opposed to this because of the urgent need of geriatric beds. This situation hasn't changed, yet now we're talking about closing the entire block. There are many elderly patients who are at risk and should be brought into hospital. Often beds can't be found because consultants in other specialties won't risk the chronically sick blocking beds. Unless more beds are made available for this type of patient the Health Authority is failing to meet its statutory requirements. With almost no extra expenditure Nightingale Block could provide many worthwhile long-stay geriatric beds. We accept that cuts are a way of life, but they should be more evenly spread.'

'We are also failing as an Authority if we can't provide a broadly-based service,' Clarence Vine observed. 'Now I'd like to take a vote . . .' he saw the hand of an insistent councillor, but ignored it. 'We must take a vote.'

'But I haven't spoken,' the lady councillor said.

'Well if you could be brief.'

'Yes, I can make my point quite briefly. My point is this,' she began. 'I have been treated all my life with homoeopathic medicine. I think we must put forward a well thought out argument to Region to enable them to take up a homoeopathic programme with the Department. This, I have on good authority, would result in substantial savings to our District, and to the Region. This would make available money to meet the priorities for geriatrics as set out in the Department's policy document. There is a strong economic case for homoeopathic medicine. What we mustn't do is be caught out by sloppy argument.'

'Thank you, Lady Ryder,' the Chairman said, dismissing both her and her argument. 'Can we take a vote then? All those in favour of finding some way of keeping the block open?'

Seven hands were raised. The District administrator took the count.

'Those in favour of closing Nightingale?'

'Is this permanent or temporary closure?' a councillor asked.

'Well either,' Dr Vine told him.

'We really ought to separate that vote, Mr Chairman.'

'No, I don't think we can. Or we'll have to take another vote on how temporary the closure should be,' the Chairman ruled.

'We were promised it was only closing for upgrading,'

Chris Hogan called out. 'What about the people what need those beds?'

'We've been sold out all the way down the line on this,' Roland Morley, a union shop steward said angrily.

'I can't take these sort of arguments from outside,' the DHA chairman told them. 'I must take a vote. All those in favour of closing Nightingale Block? I'm taking the vote now. Those in favour?'

Nine hands went up. Only the elected members of the DHA had a vote, not the paid officers. Among the latter was Stephen Morwell, who was shaking his head, disapproving of the vote.

There were four abstentions, and Dr Vine pronounced the vote carried in favour of closure.

This brought a roar of objection from the NUPE members, who were crowding the double doorways. This item on the agenda was their only interest, and now it had been dealt with far from satisfactorily, they started protesting, none of them unaware of the police presence.

Councillor Bill Williamson got out of his chair and went after Hogan, catching him in the adjacent chamber as he was leaving.

'Chris!' Williamson said. 'The voting was very close.'

'They've really taken us for a ride,' Hogan complained. 'All that consultation was ballocks.'

'We've got to keep up the pressure for the sort of healthcare we want at St Clair's,' Williamson said lamely.

'Oh, we will, don't worry about that. They won't get away with this,' Hogan promised. He didn't intend letting the block close, even if it meant his lying down across the doorway. But he believed there were more effective means at his disposal.

29

Having a baby delivered in hospital, where all the latest technology to assist the birth was available, had a lot in common with white sliced bread. That was all Chloë Shallcross could think about as her husband drove her in at the start of labour. She had heard a hospital doctor say that in a television discussion about the merits of home birth to hospital birth. Inevitably she had been worried, more so for the fact that she ate sliced white bread. The doctor had said that neither was beneficial. Why she remembered this rather than something happy or exciting she didn't know.

Most births were normal and required no medical assistance, she reminded herself. That was another piece of information she had recently picked up. Then why was she going into hospital? she found herself asking. Such questions assailed her throughout the journey and with each came a new doubt. But she seemed unable to say anything to Brian, who kept making cheerful, reassuring remarks to let her know that everything would be all right. Chloë knew that if she told him she didn't want to go to the hospital after all, he would have assumed she was having an anxiety attack, and would have taken her anyway. That was how it had been ever since her doctor had confirmed she was pregnant. It was as if she could no longer take responsibility for herself, much less her baby; everyone else knew what was best, or thought they did. She only wished she had had the courage to say no.

It was 8.15 A.M. when they reached the nursing station on the first floor obstetrics ward at St Clair's. The urgency and sense of panic that Brian Shallcross had been managing to contain suddenly slipped away. He had got his wife here safely. She was in expert hands now.

The ward clerk took the details of her admission in an unhurried way. She addressed Brian Shallcross, as if he was a more reliable source of information.

'Can we contact you during the day?' she asked him.

'Yes, at work.' He gave her the phone number. 'At home all other times. I'll be at home, or here.' His answer indicated how nervous he was.

'How are you feeling, Mrs Shallcross?' inquired the large West Indian ward sister when she joined them. She was called Ali Heathwall.

Without thinking Chloë automatically said, 'I'm fine, thank you. I feel a bit sick when I have my contractions.'

'You should be able to control that with your breathing,' Sister Heathwall told her. 'How often are the contractions, honey?'

'Oh about ten minutes, aren't they, Brian?'

'Yes, almost exactly.' He looked at his watch, anxious to prove his usefulness and not be moved on.

'Oh, we've lots of time yet. Let's get you settled. You can have a nice bath and an enema,' she promised, leading her on to the bay.

'But I've had diarrhoea for the last two days,' Chloë explained, meaning loose motions and expecting that to make some difference.

'We'll give you an enema anyway. Then ask doctor to look in.'

'Is it all right if I come?' Brian Shallcross asked.

'She won't want you around, doing this business,' Sister Heathwall said. 'There's lots of time. You'd be better off going to work and coming back.'

That wasn't what either Chloë or her husband wanted, but both felt intimidated by Sister Heathwall.

Around 9.30 Dr Marvill made her first visit to the obstetric ward, which was in small units, with single labour rooms and nursing bays of four beds. She found Staff-midwife Bella Gruneman, another West Indian, on the nurses' station where she had each of the records of the five women who were in labour laid out for instant assessment.

'Are you on this morning?' Staff Gruneman said. 'I thought it was Dr Charles.'

'He's gone on study leave.'

'Lucky him,' the midwife commented, as if believing he was on holiday.

'Have we any problems?' Jessie Marvill asked, glancing at the records.

'With Mrs Jakeman. She's one of the two spontaneous labours what come in over night. She's been in labour eighteen hours, she's stuck at seven centimetres.'

'You'll be delivering her over the weekend by the sound of it,' Dr Marvill joked. Then she saw the note on Mrs Jakeman's record and remembered her. She had been advised that her baby would have Down's syndrome, but had bravely, Dr Marvill thought, decided to have the baby rather than a termination.

'Has she had any Syntocinon?' the doctor asked, and was told the patient had been having the drip for three hours. 'When was she last examined?'

'About half an hour ago,' the midwife said.

'How frequent are the contractions?'

'Every three minutes. Dr McElroy said if she didn't make ten by this morning she would be for the chop.'

'I'd better have a look at her.'

'And Mrs Shallcross, who came in this morning. There's some foetal distress.'

'The waters haven't broken,' Dr Marvill observed from her chart. 'I might have to rupture the membranes.' She remembered Chloë Shallcross's anxiety about intervention from the antenatal clinic, and wondered if she could avoid speeding up her labour. But she would have to if there was foetal distress. 'I'd better see her first.'

Chloë Shallcross was on the pre-labour ward with three

other women, all of whom were relaxed and doing exercises, one reading; one was knitting baby clothes. Chloë wasn't reassured by any of this.

'Do you have any special problems, Chloë?' Dr Marvill asked, taking her blood pressure. 'You got over your doubts about coming in?'

Chloë shrugged, finding it difficult to say she hadn't when everyone was so nice. 'No one seems to tell you what's happening.'

'Well I'll try not to leave you in the dark,' Dr Marvill said. 'After all, it's your baby. Sometimes things happen so fast there's no time to explain.' She released the screw on the sphygmomanometer and listened through her stethoscope to the pulse in the brachial artery.

'Your blood pressure has gone up, Chloë,' the doctor told her after a moment. 'I think we might have to give you a little help after all. You might need an epidural. I'm sorry.'

'Oh do you have to?' Chloë was obviously disappointed.

'For baby's sake and your own it might be a good idea, Chloë,' Dr Marvill said. 'It will help bring down your blood pressure. What happens is we'll pop you into the delivery room, then I'll break the membranes and release your waters. Then we'll put up a drip to help stimulate contractions. I'll ask the anaesthetist to pop in and see you.'

The slight problem with artificially rupturing the membranes was that the umbilical cord sometimes slipped under the baby, and caused the oxygen supply to shut down causing foetal distress, which was the very thing they were trying to avoid by speeding up Chloë Shallcross's labour. The risk was small and Mr Montagu, being technology-orientated, believed symptom-management worth it. Although she was coming to like this sort of medicine less and less, Jessie Marvill was paradoxically resisting it less and less, and that worried her more. One day she envisaged herself arriving at a point when she didn't, but adopted institutionalized medicine as if it were second nature.

'We'll make everything as comfortable as possible for you.' She gave her an encouraging smile and went to scrub up, leaving her with Staff-midwife Singh, who was smiling and cheerful and in her late twenties.

'It'll be all right Chloë, you'll see,' the midwife said. 'Is your husband coming in?'

'He's here somewhere,' Chloë said.

'Good. We'll take you next door and get things started. Everything will be very nice.'

Chloë Shallcross didn't respond.

Having scrubbed and wearing gloves, gown and mask, Dr Marvill made a vaginal examination of Mrs Jakeman on the labour bed.

The staff-midwife in attendance was hooking up a new bottle of the synthetic hormone used to stimulate labour where uterine effort was inadequate. Few people questioned the use of this drug, whose principal constituent was oxytocin, even though there was substantial evidence that it was responsible for the huge increase in the number of hospital delivered babies with jaundice.

'Not having much luck, Mrs Jakeman,' Dr Marvill said. She had been in labour for eighteen hours and looked hot and exhausted. 'You're still only seven centimetres. I think you're going to need a Caesarean.'

At that prospect Mrs Jakeman, who had more pressure on her during this pregnancy than most women, broke down and started to cry.

'It's the best way, honey,' Staff-midwife Gruneman said, taking her hand. 'You don't want anything to interfere with your lovely baby coming safely,' she added without thinking.

There was no resistance left in Mrs Jakeman, and she found herself sobbing and agreeing.

''Course you don't, honey. You'll have your baby real soon.'

'Can you ask sister to bleep Dr Lambolle,' Dr Marvill said to the student midwife. 'We'll get you delivered very soon, Mrs Jakeman.' She pulled off her mask and gave her a warm smile.

'Mrs Shallcross is ready,' another student midwife said, coming into the labour ward.

After re-scrubbing Dr Marvill inserted a pair of long, roundnosed scissors through Chloë Shallcross's dilated cervix, and nicked the membrane. The waters in the uterus ran into the bowl the student midwife was holding.

Staff-midwife Singh set up a Syntocinon and glucose drip, but was permitted to go no further; a doctor had to put the venous canula into the arm.

'What we're going to do, Chloë, is monitor baby's heartbeats. You'll be able to hear everything is okay on the monitor. Won't that be fun, listening to your baby!'

The foetal monitor, which was attached to the baby's head through the cervix, was a spring-loaded bow-shaped needle that was pushed through the baby's scalp.

'This is the foetal monitor, Chloë,' she said. 'You won't feel it.'

'Will the baby?' Chloë asked.

'Only a slight prick,' Dr Marvill said as she hooked the needle into the scalp one-handed, then attached the two-strand flex to it.

Staff-midwife Singh turned up the monitor. 'Mrs Shallcross,' she said, 'that's baby's heartbeat.'

Chloë beamed with pleasure at the loud, clear beat, as if for the first time her baby had become real and living to her. A light flashed to the heart's rhythm, its pace shown on a dial.

'Baby sounds nice and strong,' Dr Marvill told her. 'I'll just connect the drip.'

She opened the sterile pack and inserted the venous canula into a vein in Chloë's arm. She connected the drip and adjusted it.

'How does that feel? Not too uncomfortable?' she asked.

Chloë nodded. Apart from the inclination to vomit, which she seemed able to control, she was coping with her contractions despite the pain. 'Can Brian come in now?'

'Of course. I'll ask sister to send him in.'

'Thank you, doctor,' the midwife said, as Dr Marvill left for the maternity theatre.

The staff-midwife fetched a rubber belt to attach around Chloë's middle to monitor her contractions. 'Can you roll over a little, Mrs Shallcross?' She helped her. 'That's good.' Laying the belt under her, she rolled her back and fastened it over her middle. This monitor gave a paper printout.

Dr Dilys Simons the anaesthetist, breezed in and introduced herself and told Chloë she had come to give her an epidural. Her manner was at once open and friendly yet intimidating; it might have been offensive to suggest she would do anything against the wishes of the patient. So despite being horrified, Chloë passively accepted the drip being planted into her spine.

'I'm going to leave you for a little while, Mrs Shallcross,' Staff-midwife Singh said after the anaesthetist had gone. 'If you get into difficulty you press this.' She gave her the call bell hanging over the bed.

Chloë Shallcross was on her own for the first time since arriving at the hospital. As she looked at the high technology surrounding her, she was more frightened than reassured. She started thinking about the drugs her baby would be getting, then about what she would do if one of the monitors stopped. She reached to make sure the call bell was close to hand.

Each time she helped in a Caesarean section Jessie Marvill thought about her family dog, a bitch who became accidentally pregnant for the first time late in life and had to have her litter by a Caesar. When she awoke from the anaesthetic and was confronted by five little strangers, with whom she could make no connection, she had killed each of them. Although nothing as extreme had ever happened as the result of a child delivered by a Caesar, she felt the same principle applied. A mother should be consciously involved with the birth, even to the point of not taking drugs.

Having delivered Mrs Jakeman's baby through the opening in her abdominal wall, Dr Lambolle held it by its feet while Dr Marvill clamped the umbilical and cut it. Dr Lambolle laid the baby on the operating table, handing over responsibility to the paediatric registrar. A paediatrician was present for all Caesarean sections and forceps deliveries, but would have made a point of being there anyway for Mrs Jakeman's baby.

'It's spina bif' as well as hydrocephalic,' Dr Arwyn Jones announced when he took the baby on to the examination trolley. The infant wasn't yet breathing.

'I had noticed,' Dr Lambolle said casually, as he removed the placenta. 'Is it worth the neuros popping a valve in?' he asked. At one time doctors didn't question that procedure, it had been a matter of course. Not any more. The burden of such children on both the parents and the medical and social service resources made the effort not worthwhile. That applied to any number of babies born with a variety of congenital defects.

'I think perhaps the simplest solution is not to encourage it to breathe,' he said, wrapping up the still child.

'It'll solve a lot of problems.'

This wasn't something Dr Marvill had newly encountered, yet each time it happened it surprised her. Especially now for knowing what Mrs Jakeman had gone through with her decision to have the child.

'Putting the baby through a whole series of operations would be intolerable,' Dr Lambolle said, glancing up at his colleague.

Jessie Marvill was too angry to say anything, and so said nothing. But she hated herself for remaining silent.

In the kitchen on the obstetrics ward Dr Marvill drank

tea which Sister Heathwall had made for her, and distractedly ate the expensive biscuits from the tin that she had put in front of her, as if anticipating her mood. She felt flat, and beaten, beyond the familiar tiredness. It wasn't solely to do with Mrs Jakeman losing her baby, but also the fact that Laurence James had phoned to say he had got the job he had been after at Northwick Park hospital. She was pleased for him, but it meant he wouldn't be around to give her his support. The medicine she was practising more and more seemed to conspire to defeat her.

'How often do you see Mr Montagu on the ward?' she asked as she sipped the too strong black tea. She had recently given up milk, accepting that it wasn't logical to stop eating meat yet support the beef trade by using milk which was a by-product. Laurence James's influence was apparent. The diets he worked out for patients who were looking to change their lifestyle and the course of their illness contained no meat. Jessie Marvill felt she couldn't make such recommendations to patients like Mrs Downes without changing herself.

'He never come,' Sister Heathwall said. 'Unless he deliver a private baby.'

That was typical, Jessie Marvill thought. The consultant laid down all the ground rules about high technology and was never around to see the effect. The midwives in the unit were the most demoralized about doctors delivering so many babies, which they had to when forceps were involved and they were used more often as a result of drug induction.

'He seems to influence everything?' Dr Marvill observed.

'He always get the best for his Mums,' the sister said, as if pleased with her consultant's achievements.

Dr Lambolle appeared. 'Ah, in time for tea.'

'You always in time,' Sister Heathwall said, and rose to get him a cup.

'All quiet after our emergencies?' He glanced at Dr

Marvill, but avoided what he knew was troubling her. He was clear in his mind about not encouraging congenitally defective babies to breathe, and believed the decision shouldn't be left to parents, who couldn't cope.

'I hope it stays quiet for the weekend,' Sister Heathwall said.

'We try to oblige. Are you on?'

'Not till Tuesday, doctor.'

'Any more difficulty with Mrs Shallcross, Jessie?' Dr Lambolle asked.

'Some bradycardia. The FH seems to have settled down all right. But her blood pressure is still high. She's not very happy about the epidural.'

'Thank you. More presents from grateful mums.' Lambolle took his tea and some biscuits. 'We do everything to manage labour, make it efficient, convenient, painless,' he said dismissively.

'That's part of the problem, I think. Process,' Dr Marvill said. She wasn't about to discuss the question of their managing births like a goods inward office, as she knew nothing would change. It would merely strain their relationship further.

'A bit remote, I grant you. But what it does mean is we're all here if there are problems. Try a prolapsed cord in the middle of the night. The baby's lost by the time everyone is called,' Dr Lambolle said, justifying his role.

'I'm not very sure about this priority given to reducing perinatal death. When none is given to saving congenitally defective babies,' she found herself saying.

'You can't be serious, dear girl?' His manner was condescending.

'The mother/child relationship is for life,' Jessie Marvill said.

'A lot of effort is put into bonding nowadays,' Lambolle responded.

'I know.' She took another biscuit. Bonding had been

taken up as good obstetric management, but Jessie Marvill didn't bother to point that out.

'Giving birth is a passionate affair. I'm sure mothers are inhibited on the labour wards. They're so public. Most mothers haven't met half of the people present.'

'When baby's arriving most of them are so relieved they wouldn't care if it was Piccadilly,' Dr Lambolle said with absolute assurance.

Dr Marvill wasn't impressed, but didn't pursue her argument. Instead she sipped the tea, which had a heavy taste of tannin.

A student midwife put her head into the kitchen. 'Sister,' she began; then saw Dr Marvill. 'Oh, doctor, Staff Singh wants you. Shallcross's monitor shows type II dips,' – already having learned how to be remote from baby and mother. Dr Marvill responded, followed by Dr Lambolle.

'We might have to give her the chop,' Dr Lambolle observed, from the depressed state of the foetal heartbeat shown on the monitor.

Dr Marvill said nothing, but knew that a Caesar was about the last thing Mrs Shallcross hoped for.

'Certainly if the bradycardia worsens,' Dr Lambolle said. 'We might manage with forceps.' He addressed the midwife. 'Try changing her position. It might help the placenta.'

Foetal distress was sometimes caused by lack of oxygen, from the weight of the uterus bearing on the large blood vessels in the mother's back.

'Just ease on to your side if you can, Chloë,' Staff-midwife Singh encouraged. 'That's it.' Both she and her student were struggling to lift her over. Back trouble was an occupational hazard of midwives, not obstetricians.

Almost at once the baby's heartbeat picked up.

'Oh good show!' Dr Marvill was cheered by this.

'I'd still go for a forceps when she's fully, Jessie,' Dr Lambolle advised.

'I'd like to give her a little longer.'

Dr Lambolle looked at her, but didn't press his advice. 'How much Syntocinon is she getting?'

'20 mls a minute. A drip every three seconds,' the student midwife said.

'Take it down to 15. No, make it 10,' Dr Lambolle said.

Chloë Shallcross had another contraction and cried out with surprise. She hadn't so far had any as painful.

'Breathe,' the midwife told her. 'Go on now, don't fight it.'

'That looked painful,' Dr Lambolle said. 'Is the epidural working properly?' Then to Chloë, 'Do you feel nice and numb, Mrs Shallcross?'

'You're doing really very nicely, Chloë,' Dr Marvill said encouragingly as she did a vaginal examination after the contraction.

Chloë indicated not. 'Is Brian coming?' she wanted to know, believing she was getting close to having her baby.

'Yes, your husband,' the midwife said, having forgotten to ask Sister to find him.

'I'll be around if you need me,' Dr Lambolle said and went out.

'Baby's trying hard, Chloë. Keep up the good work.' Dr Marvill gave her a smile. 'I'll give her another twenty minutes, Staff,' Dr Marvill said. Knowing the way Chloë felt, Jessie Marvill wanted her to get there on her own, but didn't know how long she could hold off full intervention.

A student midwife came into the labour room. 'Could you come to Mrs Hodges, doctor? Staff thinks we're going to need forceps.'

Dr Marvill went out.

'They're not going to deliver my baby with forceps?' Chloë had read all about forceps delivery and didn't like the idea at all.

'Not if I can help it, Chloë,' Staff-midwife Singh said. 'The doctor's given us a while longer. You're not quite fully dilated yet anyway. You need to go a little further before they could use forceps. We'll get you there.'

'Staff!' The student midwife brought her attention to the dip in the FH on the monitor. 'Shall I get the doctor?'

'We'll give it a moment. Just move her again.'

When they turned her the foetal heart picked up. The midwife smiled at Chloë; she had a vested interest in delivery without intervention, and was determined it should happen that way.

30

Chloë Shallcross's contractions got stronger and were more even, there was a sharp increase to them and gradual decline. The graph running up on the machine was no longer returning to the base line. She hadn't delivered within the target time given her by Dr Marvill, even though that had been subsequently extended. Brian Shallcross was eventually called in, and the midwife left. He gave his wife what support he could, but got a little panicky when her pain didn't decrease. He massaged her thighs, hoping that would help.

'I'd better call the midwife,' he said finally, and reached for the bell push. He began rubbing her thighs again, but it seemed to give his wife no relief. He touched her belly and she cried out for him not to. He moistened her mouth and rubbed ice across her forehead.

A white midwife appeared with an unfamiliar student.

'Hello,' she said, 'I'm Staff-midwife Watson. I'm going to deliver your baby for you.'

'Where's Staff Singh?' Chloë was surprised. She hadn't seen this midwife before. She had built up a rapport with Midwife Singh and had come to trust her.

'Gone home to her family,' the midwife explained. It was a common enough occurrence. 'Now let's have a look at you.' She pulled on gloves and mask to do a vaginal examination. 'What d'you think it's going to be? D'you have any preferences?'

'No,' Chloë said hoarsely.

'You're almost there now,' she announced. 'You'll soon know.'

With Chloë's permission she let the student midwife do

an examination. In fact Chloë wanted neither of them doing this, but was afraid to tell them not to.

Chloë had another very strong contraction, during which the examination stopped.

'Why don't you massage her spine,' the midwife told Brian Shallcross who watched helplessly. 'D'you want a little gas and air?'

Chloë shook her head.

'I think it would be a good idea,' the midwife said. She was the sort of decisive lady who knew what was best for everyone.

The foetal heart dipped after the next contraction.

'We're going to change your position, to help baby.' The midwife checked the monitor as they turned Chloë. Nothing happened, the FH didn't pick up.

'Find Dr Marvill, tell her there's a bad type II,' she told the student.

'Is there something wrong?' Brian Shallcross asked, his anxiety increasing.

'Nothing for you to worry about.' The midwife shut down the drip. 'Let's put you over on your other side,' she said, turning Chloë again with her husband's help.

The foetal heart picked up.

Chloë had another contraction, and her breathing started to race.

'Slow down,' the midwife told her calmly. 'You're breathing much too fast. Slow down. Don't overbreathe.'

Dr Marvill arrived, followed by Lambolle and the anaesthetist, Dr Dilys Simons.

'The foetal heart recovered?' Dr Marvill noted.

'Just before this contraction, doctor,' the midwife said. 'When we changed her position.'

'Is she fully?' Dr Marvill referred to the cervix being fully dilated.

'She's at nine centimetres still.'

'Is she stuck?' When Dr Marvill did a vaginal examination,

her index and middle fingers not quite spread in the cervix told her how much it was dilated. 'She seems to be stuck at nine.'

The anterior rim of the cervix was showing around the baby's head.

The foetal heart dipped again and didn't pick up.

'We'll try getting it out with the ventouse, Jessie,' Lambolle informed her. 'Otherwise she'll need a Caesar. Can you top her up?' he said to the anaesthetist.

'I daresay I can manage that,' Dr Simonds said.

'We're going to deliver your baby, Chloë,' Dr Marvill explained. 'You'll be awake so you'll know what's going on.'

'Could you wait outside,' Staff-midwife Watson said to Brian Shallcross, who was a bit confused. She gave him no choice.

Dr Marvill passed a catheter and emptied Chloë's bladder, while Dr Simons topped up the injection through the tube left in the spine. The epidural had brought about loss of sensation from the waist down, and the uterine action was slowed initially, but then the uterus relaxed between contractions. The main drawbacks, which no one pointed out to Chloë, were that she would be unable to control her legs, so delivered in stirrups, and have no movement in her legs for two hours after; the umbilical cord would have to be clamped immediately; the placenta wouldn't be delivered naturally, as there was an increase in the risk of haemorrhaging. Further, anaesthetics given to mothers were believed to decrease the affection they displayed towards their children.

The monitor was disconnected from the foetal head. Then the rubber suction cup of the ventouse extractor, which was about the size of a small saucer was placed against the baby's head, and the air was drawn out of the space between cup and scalp. Dr Lambolle gently pulled on the handles of the extractor, but the vacuum broke without pulling the baby through the cervix. He started again.

'Can you feel your toes?' Dr Simons asked. 'Excellent,' – when Chloë found no feeling there.

'That's got it,' Dr Lambolle said, as the suction held fast this time to the baby's head. 'Jessie?'

Dr Marvill performed an episiotomy with scissors to facilitate easier passage. The sound of the perineum being cut was like a knife through canvas.

'Can you bear down,' Lambolle said. 'Bear down.'

'Push,' the midwife urged. 'Come on now push into your bottom, dear. Harder. Harder. Harder.'

Chloë did so, calling for her husband, who had been left outside.

Dr Arwyn Jones, the paediatrician, arrived as Dr Lambolle pulled the baby clear. Immediately the clamps went on to the cord, which Dr Marvill cut. She would have preferred laying baby on Mum's belly to let them make contact, to have the staff withdraw, leaving Mum, Dad and baby together. That wasn't to be.

The mucus was sucked out of the baby's airways while Dr Lambolle released the extractor. The baby began grunting, this sound indicated intercostal recession.

'It's a little girl, Chloë,' Dr Marvill said. 'Can Mum hold her baby?'

'What did the latest scan indicate?' Dr Jones asked. He was concerned that it was premature.

'Fairly mature, thirty-seven weeks plus. Almost no deviation from the EDD,' Dr Marvill replied.

'I'd say it was a bit younger than thirty-seven weeks. There's some intercostal recession,' Dr Jones told her. 'Let's pop it into the Resusitair.'

This was a piece of equipment like an incubator but made primarily for resuscitation. When the baby was made stable it was wheeled through to the Special Baby Care Unit.

'Can I hold my baby?' Chloë asked, not realizing she had gone.

'In a moment,' Dr Marvill said, trying to reassure her. 'Everything is fine, Chloë. Let me deliver the placenta and put in some stitches.'

Dr Marvill took seven minutes to stitch Chloë Shallcross, and knew that must have seemed a lifetime for this mother who hadn't so much as touched her baby.

'Why can't I touch my baby?' Chloë said. 'She's got brain damage, hasn't she . . .' All her fears had surfaced by this time.

'Don't be silly,' Staff-midwife Watson told her. 'She's a lovely little girl.'

'That's it,' Dr Marvill announced, with the last stitch. She left the midwife to clean her up.

'Why can't I have my baby, doctor?'

'I'm just going to find out, Chloë. Baby was a bit premature, it seems. It was having slight difficulty breathing. I don't suppose the drugs you had helped it much. I'm just going to find out what's happening.'

'Doctor,' the midwife said, following her to one side. 'Telling mothers that sort of thing alarms them.' She knew the consultant disapproved of such a practice.

Jessie Marvill looked at her. 'Wouldn't you say she has a right to know?' She turned away into the Special Baby Care Unit.

'Is my baby all right?' Chloë asked the midwife.

'You'll have her in no time. Let's just get you tidied up. You don't want your husband seeing you like this.' Being unmarried the midwife had no understanding why a husband shouldn't mind seeing his wife like that.

Dr Marvill felt angry when she came into the adjacent Special Care Baby Unit, believing it was wrong to have so little regard for the mother, notwithstanding the urgency of the situation, but when she saw the work that had been done on Baby Shallcross she shifted ground. The baby, who was in an incubator, with electrodes fixed to her head, and a drip up her nose, was breathing satisfactorily. Swift action had without doubt saved her from brain damage, if not saved her life as well.

'We'd better let the mother have a look,' Dr Jones said.

Chloë Shallcross was brought through, but seeing her baby for the very first time in the perspex incubator startled her.

'There she is,' Staffnurse Owens said. She was southern Irish, with a plump, smiling red face. 'Isn't she gorgeous?'

Chloë didn't respond, but stared dully at the baby.

Jessie Marvill remembered the family dog who couldn't relate to her litter of pups because of surgical intervention.

'You can be putting your hands through and touching her, so.' Staffnurse Owens demonstrated.

Chloë was unsure. She hesitated, but finally didn't.

'She'll be in the incubator a day or two, Chloë,' Dr Marvill told her. 'Then you'll be on the ward together.'

'Won't that be grand,' Staffnurse Owens said. 'It will of course.'

Chloë Shallcross was confused, her feelings about this whole experience remained in turmoil.

Baby Shallcross was in the incubator for a day and a half, then allowed on to the special 'nesting' ward, rather than the general post labour ward. Chloë Shallcross was encouraged to bond with her baby through breast feeding and having it with her most of the time. But this didn't work. She had a difficult time, the infant didn't seem to want the breast, and Chloë took this as further rejection.

'That's nothing to worry about, Mrs Shallcross,' a 2nd-year student nurse told her as the baby rejected the breast yet again. 'There's difficulty sometimes after being on the Baby Unit. I'll give her a bottle.'

Chloë watched the nurse successfully bottle feed the baby. That was something she regretted, and the feeling of resentment she had towards the child began to increase. It preferred anyone to her.

The relationship didn't improve throughout their stay, and the prospect of going home with the baby loomed frighteningly, especially as Chloë had realized the truth; about that she had decided to keep quiet for now.

Although his wife was acting strangely, Brian Shallcross kept cheerful, believing things would be okay when she was home with their baby and fully occupied. Unlike his wife he was delighted when that day arrived. He whistled merrily as he pushed into the nesting room, carrying a grip bag.

He found Chloë on the edge of her bed, still in her nightdress, the baby was crying in its cot.

'Hey, what's all this for, my little darling,' he said, and quietened the baby by picking her up. He turned to his wife. 'Come on, love. I thought you'd be ready. Come on,' he said encouraging her. 'It'll be all right.'

She didn't respond.

'What did the doctor say?'

'She said we probably wouldn't want to have intercourse for ages because it will hurt me,' she informed him, as if she had learned that by rote.

'Oh,' was his response. 'What did she say about not wanting to go home with the baby?'

Chloë shrugged. 'We'll get over these difficulties. I should talk things over with my GP. She doesn't want me, Brian. She goes to everyone else.' She remained distant and blank.

Her husband put his arm around her, not really understanding how she felt, or knowing why she didn't share his excitement. 'Come on,' he said. 'It'll be all right.'

'I don't want to, Brian.' She hesitated, then found herself saying, 'I don't think she's my baby. I think they swapped her over.' She hadn't meant to tell anyone, but the words slipped out.

'What?' That surprised him, and he felt cheated for a moment. 'Don't be silly. That's silly talking like that. It's stupid,' – his tone getting firmer. 'Now come on, Chlo'. Come on.'

He was taking his wife and baby home, and there was an end to this nonsense.

31

The chamber of the General Medical Council was a tall imposing room, hung with portraits of founder members. It had the atmosphere of a courtroom, and during the few days of the bi-annual Professional Conduct Committee hearings had that hushed reverence and unrehearsed air. The committee which heard evidence against offenders comprised eight members of the general council, all of whom were doctors, all but one male, none younger than forty-five, and all white. Quite a high number of Asian doctors appeared before the committee. The chairman was Sir Jack Steadman, whose height, at six foot three, topped with snow-white hair, gave him an impressive presence. On his left on the bench was the deputy registrar, who summoned the erring doctors and read the charges; a legal adviser on the opposite side made sure the council didn't get egg on its face.

At tables on either side of the room beyond the committee were legal representatives: Donald Farrington, a barrister brought in by the solicitors representing the council, a solicitor from that firm and a clerk.

Across the chamber was Dr Percy Thurson, with his barrister and solicitor. Bernard Brian QC sat taking notes throughout the twenty minutes that Donald Farrington took to present the facts of the case. He told how on the night of 9 November last year Dr Thurson mistakenly prescribed 60 mg of a powerful painkiller, DF118, along with an antidiarrhoeal, Lomotil, to a four-year-old child, Victoria White, who was suffering with an ear infection. The child who had been severely dehydrated at the time, had died of heart failure after vomiting and inhaling her vomit. Subsequently Dr Thurson had visited the retail chemist and retrieved the prescription and altered it to 15 mg. As far as the council's barrister was concerned the retrieving and altering of the prescription was clearly professional misconduct. The fact that the coroner had returned a verdict of death by misadventure had no bearing.

'We have the child's parents here, sir,' Donald Farrington said, addressing the chairman, 'in case you should want to examine them. But unless you do we don't propose calling them.' Their emotive testimony wouldn't impress this committee, and might serve to remind them how difficult a doctor's job was made by such parents. The one salient aspect of their evidence, at what point the prescription had been altered, wasn't reliable. A more reliable witness was the chemist who had dispensed the prescription. He was Ian Simmonds, who took the oath at the witness table at the opposite end of the room.

'Is it normal practice for chemists to hand prescriptions back to doctors when they call in to request them?' Mr Farrington asked him.

'It happens not infrequently,' Simmonds responded. 'It's the doctor's prescription after all.'

'What reason did Dr Thurson give for the request?' Farrington asked. 'Did he in fact give one?'

'He said he wanted to check the dosage prescribed.'

'You didn't find that suspicious?'

'No. Dr Thurson is well thought of in the area,' the chemist replied. 'I've been here for fifteen years, we've always had an excellent relationship.'

'Would you think very carefully about my next question, Mr Simmonds,' the barrister said. 'Had the prescription for the drug DF118 been altered when you returned it to Dr Thurson. Like this in fact?' He offered the amended prescription, which an usher from the Service Corps took across to the witness. 'From 60 mg to 15 mg?'

'No, it hadn't,' Simmonds was quite certain.

That level of certainty made Bernard Brian slightly uneasy. This man would impress the committee. When it was his turn to question the witness he followed the same tack. 'If it had been altered before being presented at your shop,' Mr Brian said, 'that would mean you had made the mistake, not Dr Thurson.'

'It hadn't. I didn't make a mistake,' Simmonds said, becoming defensive. 'I'm quite certain.'

'You're familiar with the drug, DF118, Mr Simmonds?'

'It's called for from time to time.'

'You have no difficulty in supplying it?'

'No, sir,' the chemist said.

'Being familiar with this drug as you are, did it not occur to you to question the amount, especially if, as Dr Thurson maintains, and I see no reason to doubt this, he had altered the prescription? Did not 60 mg of a powerful painkiller seem rather extreme for a child, especially as the manufacturers advise that it isn't recommended for children?'

'Had I been alarmed about the amount I would have telephoned Dr Thurson,' Simmonds said. 'Pharmacists have a statutory duty to do that, no matter how well respected the doctor.'

'But 60 mg is a very large dose for a child,' Brian said.

'With respect, sir, if I might come in here,' Mr Farrington said to the chairman. 'Nowhere on this prescription does it indicate that the drug was for a child.'

'Yes, I see. Thank you, Mr Farrington,' Sir Jack Steadman said.

Whatever the rights or wrongs of the arguments going on in this chamber, none of it was giving Dr Thurson any comfort as he sat listening. It was a great effort to rise and cross to the witness table, his limbs were leaden. His swearing to tell the truth was meaningless. He didn't know what the truth was, and was no longer even sure what he believed it was.

Bernard Brian took the doctor through the details of the

incident that had led to the child's death last November, how the father had twice telephoned the surgery about his daughter's pain, and how the doctor had eventually gone out to her.

'The parents had been in a fairly agitated state, had they not, Dr Thurson?' the council's barrister asked when it was his turn.

'Well, fairly,' Thurson responded listlessly. 'Most parents are in those circumstances.'

'And there was no doubt that this child was suffering?'

'No,' Dr Thurson said; remembering was unpleasant.

'The parents were very distressed about this?'

Again Dr Thurson agreed. Also when the barrister suggested in such circumstances he might easily have written 60 mg of DF118 instead of 15 mg.

'Could you possibly expand on your intention when you went to Simmonds the chemist and recovered the prescription?'

Dr Thurson hesitated, his mind was a blank. 'I'm not sure,' he said. 'Possibly I wanted to check that I had prescribed the right dosage.'

'The drug in question isn't suitable for children, is that not so?' the barrister said.

'Oh, it's not recommended by the manufacturer, that's all. Manufacturers recommend drugs also, some that do a lot more harm than good.'

'When you discovered the mistake on the prescription at the chemist's shop, you took the opportunity to alter it, did you not?'

'Sir,' Dr Thurson's barrister said, rising, 'my learned friend is overreaching in this line of questioning. It is neither established that Dr Thurson overprescribed the fatal drug, nor that he altered the prescription retrospectively.'

The chairman agreed and Mr Farrington didn't push the point. Sir Jack Steadman then invited Dr Thurson to add anything. He had no wish to.

In his concluding remarks Bernard Brian QC said how honest, open and forthright Dr Thurson was, qualities he had displayed by the evidence he had given to this hearing; how hard he worked, how highly he was thought of by patients. '. . . Without doubt in the thirty-nine years that Dr Thurson has been in practice he has given service to the community with little or no consideration either of reward or his own health. Rarely has he denied comfort or a kind word to patients; in fact, he has given so much through unstinting service all these years that at times he has worn himself out. As you have heard, he has applied several times to the Medical Practices Committee to take on a partner, only to be told he can't unless he increases his list, thereby increasing the very burden he is seeking to ease. Perhaps if a mistake was made by Dr Thurson in overprescribing the drug DF118 to Victoria White, then fault lies equally with the MPC. Nothing at this stage will return Victoria White to her parents, but perhaps something can be gained from this tragedy.'

During this Mrs White, who was in the public gallery at the end of the chamber with her husband, got up and quickly went out. The three reporters covering these hearings didn't know who she was, so didn't pursue her.

There was a brief silence in the chamber after Bernard Brian had concluded.

'The strangers will withdraw,' the chairman announced.

Strangers meant everyone with the exception of the council members, the adviser and deputy registrar.

When Dr Thurson emerged from the chamber on to a corridor, his wife was waiting. Other people emerged to wait around, mostly lawyers. The press tended to wait upstairs ready for the bell to summon them back in when a decision had been reached.

Edna Thurson caught her husband's arm as if to reassure him.

'You mustn't keep blaming yourself,' she said quietly. 'It won't look good.'

He looked at her, but didn't say anything.

'Percy,' Charles Forster said. 'I can imagine how you feel.' He glanced at his watch. 'Brian thinks they'll be a while, so we'll have time for coffee along the street.'

It wasn't usual for the defendant to leave the building at this stage, but the solicitor saw the state his client was in, and there was nowhere in the GMC building for them to go.

The chamber was finally cleared of all but the nine members of the professional conduct committee, who remained sitting, and didn't measurably relax. One doctor picked his nose, as he had done throughout the hearing. The chairman reiterated the facts, then took comments. The process was quite swift.

'Do we have a measure of agreement? Do we?' Sir Jack Steadman concluded. 'Do we find the case of professional misconduct that resulted in the death of Victoria White proven against Dr Thurson?'

What existed was a measure of disagreement.

Cutting through this Geoffrey Twiddy, the legal adviser said, 'I don't think you can find on that, Mr Chairman. If we took this case at its most simple, i.e. overprescribing, what this amounts to is no more than bad judgement by Dr Thurson. Neither he nor any other member of your profession is answerable for that.'

'But the man quite obviously retrieved the prescription and altered it,' a member of the committee, Dr Hyde-Thompson said. 'Very likely to disguise his incompetence.'

'That's what this committee has to determine,' the legal adviser said. 'Whether Dr Thurson altered the prescription after it had been dispensed in order to disguise his own culpability, then removed it from the chemists and failed to produce it to the coroner. These are the only two counts of professional misconduct.'

'Then could we take a vote on that?' the chairman said. 'Those who find it proven?'

'With respect, Mr Chairman,' the legal adviser said. 'I think those two points should perhaps be put separately.'

As this was the first time Sir Jack Steadman had chaired this committee he had no objection to being corrected.

'Thank you, Mr Twiddy,' he said. 'Then is it found proven that Dr Thurson altered the prescription after retrieving it from Simmonds the chemist?'

The lone hand of Dr Hyde-Thompson went up.

'Then the second point. Is it found proven that Dr Thurson failed to produce the prescription to the coroner, Dr John Bristow, at the inquest on Victoria White?'

Eight hands went up. There was no doubt about that.

'Does anyone have anything else to add? Any further points? Dr O'Brien?' the chairman said, turning to the District Medical Officer who didn't in fact withdraw on account of his knowing Dr Thurson.

'I would like to say a word on behalf of Dr Thurson,' Dr O'Brien said. 'In view of the tremendous pressure of work on him at the time I urge this committee to support a recommendation that no action be taken. Especially in view of his having applied to the MPC yet again to be allowed to take on a partner, Mr Chairman.'

'With any more hope of success?'

'Perhaps this hearing will serve to highlight his need.'

'Any objections to Dr O'Brien's recommendation?' the chairman asked.

'I feel it wouldn't be right for this committee to make such a recommendation in view of the seriousness of the complaint,' Dr Hyde-Thompson said. 'I would like to recommend that Dr Thurson be reprimanded.'

There were one or two nods of agreement. But no such public announcement was made when strangers were allowed back into the chamber.

The chairman simply stated that the case was concluded.

The only effect the result had on Percy Thurson was to leave him with a sense of disappointment. Had the case been proven and suspension followed it might have forced him to retire. He realized work was a habit, one which at times he hated. He hated the shortcuts necessary to get through each day, the stupidity of those patients who came back time and again with the same complaints because neither they nor he could do anything about the cause; he hated himself for not being able to stop himself putting one foot in front of the other, which he would do until he dropped or made so serious an error that he would be compelled to retire. He didn't look forward to that, but believed he couldn't avoid it.

32

The doubts and fears that Chloë Shallcross had had in hospital over taking her baby home, and which she refused to speak to anyone about, were borne out. She couldn't cope. Not when it needed feeding or changing, not when it cried, and certainly not when it screamed. She didn't physically abuse the child, but couldn't respond to it. Brian Shallcross took time off work or looked after the baby when he came home in the evening; his mother sometimes visited during the day and helped.

No one considered that Chloë might have a problem that she needed help with, instead of being nagged, despaired of, or asked in vain what was wrong, as she became more depressed, had an increasing feeling of lassitude, and saw no point in going on.

The health visitor was the first to acknowledge that Chloë and her baby weren't progressing as was reasonably expected.

'Have you decided on a name yet?' the health visitor asked as she bustled along the hall.

Chloë Shallcross responded flatly, 'No. We haven't thought of one.'

'Well, there's time yet. But you must register her within six weeks. How about breast feeding? Getting any better?'

'No.' Chloë's whole manner was apathetic.

'Are you persevering, Chloë? You must try, you know,' – on a firmer note.

'She's not interested. There's not much milk anyway,' Chloë told her as she brought her into the sitting-room where the cot was.

'How long has baby been hot like this?' the health visitor

asked, examining her.

'Don't know. I thought she was supposed to be warm.'

'She has a temperature. I'd better ask doctor to look in,' Mrs Adlard, the health visitor said. Although she heard no alarm bells, she was sufficiently concerned, especially now that the baby was running a high temperature, to bring the situation to the doctor's attention.

Despite the publicity that had surrounded his appearance before the GMC, both Dr Thurson's morning and evening surgeries were as full as ever. Either there was no stigma attached to that hearing, or patients – like most smokers' attitude to lung cancer – believed it couldn't happen to them. It had been a busy morning, and he had inevitably got behind. No one who came to his surgery ever expected to be seen without a wait, yet still they came.

The eighty-year-old patient sitting on the other side of the desk, seemed younger than the doctor. Henry Staples, who looked sprightly, despite his large size, was keen to get going. If asked how he kept so relatively fit and active he would have said it was due to three things, keeping an allotment garden most of his life, cycling everywhere, including here this morning, and having a good wife. The problem Mr Thurson was treating him for was a vascular disease, which was a common enough complaint in the aged.

'What about tablets, Mr Staples? How are you getting on with them?'

'I can't say as I do, doctor,' the old man said. 'But it don't do to grumble.' Patients often prefaced a great grumble with that.

'How are they affecting you?' He was marking a questionnaire from Cavandish Pharmaceuticals, for whom he was conducting this trial on their new vasodilating drug, Vasculine-90.

'They might be keeping me circulating, but I get giddy and sick every time I take them,' Henry Staples said. 'I thought I was going to fall off my bike one day when I took one. I've not fallen off since I was a nipper.'

'We'll keep on with them for another fortnight. If the side effects are no better, we'll try something else,' Dr Thurson said, finding himself moderating his written comments. 'Perhaps you should stop riding your bicycle for a while.'

Henry Staples didn't say anything. He would have sooner not taken the tablets than stop using his bike. He had a sit-up-and-beg Raleigh, but in his younger days he had had Rudge racers. 'I'll come back in two weeks shall I, doctor?' he said.

'I'll see you in two weeks,' Thurson told him as if neither one was hearing the other. He gave him his prescription. 'You mind with that bicycle now.'

'She looks after me. My missus,' the old man said as he shuffled out. 'She takes good care of me.'

Dr Thurson shut the door and glanced at the clock, which Cavandish Pharmaceuticals had given for helping try out their new vasodilator. The clock had stopped at 8.16. He took it to his desk to wind it, and left it amidst the confusion.

'Mrs Adlard is here,' the receptionist said through the intercom. Then added as a memory jogger, 'The health visitor. Do you have a minute?'

'Yes,' Dr Thurson replied. 'How many more patients do I have?'

'Six. One's left for another appointment.'

The health visitor came in with quick birdlike movements, as though trying through her actions to take up less of the doctor's time than necessary. 'I'm a bit worried about Mrs Shallcross,' she said. 'She's having difficulty coping with the baby.'

'I saw her last week, I think.' He rose from his desk to get the file, which the health visitor held out to him. 'I gave her something for depression.'

'I'm not sure that it's helping her,' Mrs Adlard said, without implying criticism. 'Do you think you could pop in? Baby's running a temperature.'

'She's no longer managing to breast feed?' the doctor asked, seeing his note on the patient's card.

'I'm not even sure that she's trying.'

'I ought to leave it till this evening when the husband's there,' Dr Thurson suggested. He already had half a dozen calls to make before lunch.

'Yes. That might be best,' the health visitor agreed.

Baby Shallcross was screaming when Dr Thurson eventually arrived at the house. Brian Shallcross was trying without success to comfort her. Usually she quietened immediately for him. He was a little upset that she didn't respond, and worried in case there was something seriously wrong.

'There doesn't seem much wrong with her lungs now,' the doctor said. 'Well, young lady, what's all this for?'

The baby was unimpressed.

Dr Thurson started his examination and found the child was very hot. 'How long has baby been like this, Daddy?' he asked. Referring to parents as Mummy and Daddy was a habit he no longer noticed.

'Most of the day,' Brian Shallcross said, looking at his wife. He had managed to extract that much information.

'Pop her down, Daddy – on the table. Let's have a proper look at her.'

Baby Shallcross was laid on the dining table, still screaming. Dr Thurson uncovered her and ran his hands over her tiny limbs, looking for breaks of any kind, but found none. He took her temperature. He looked into her ears and throat, then listened to her chest with his stethoscope during a pause in her screaming.

Chloë Shallcross watched passively. This might have been someone else's child.

'She has a chest infection,' the doctor announced finally.

'I'll give her antibiotics, they should bring her temperature down.' He took a sterile hypodermic pack from his bag and a small needle. 'If she's not any better in the morning, you must telephone me, Mummy. We might have to pop baby back to hospital. Now you will do that, Mummy?' he said, eliciting a nod from Chloë.

'Is it serious, doctor?' Brian Shallcross asked.

'Nothing to get unduly concerned about,' Dr Thurson told them. 'But after her previous difficulties let's be safe. I won't be available after 9.30 this evening but my locum will be on duty. So if you have any difficulties in the night, you be sure to ring him.'

Life had been only slightly easier since using a night-time deputizing service, for rather than have a stranger come out to them in the middle of the night patients tended to hang on till the following morning. But it was early days, and he hoped they would get used to the idea. They would have to, as there was no other way he could manage now that the Medical Practices Committee had turned down his second application for a partner; again on the grounds that he hadn't a sufficiently large practice.

'You might just want to look away if it distresses you, Mummy,' he said as he gave the baby her injection.

The antibiotics had little effect, or none Brian Shallcross noticed as he nursed his daughter through the night. She screamed almost unremittingly, sleeping for no longer than fifteen minutes. The baby was still screaming at two o'clock in the morning, and Brian Shallcross decided to phone the doctor. He got no joy from the deputizing service, only a message that the doctor on duty was out on a call and would ring back when he returned. Brian Shallcross left his name and number with a helpless sense of frustration. When he returned to the bedroom his wife was sitting up in bed, but doing nothing for the baby.

'. . . I can't get the doctor, he's out on a call,' he said. 'Why don't you try comforting her? Why don't you just try,

Chlo'?' His fears were compounded by his wife's apathy.

'I can't . . . she won't,' Chloë said. She was totally confused about her own feelings rather than not knowing what to do.

Brian Shallcross picked up the child, and tried to comfort her again. Anxiety was grinding him down.

'All right, sweetheart. Baby's going to be all right.' His words weren't convincing. He rocked her in his arms, which only seemed to make her worse.

'I'm going to take her to hospital,' he announced. 'There's something wrong. There's got to be. I'll take her down there.'

Having made that decision, getting his wife to go with him needed threats and pleas. But finally she agreed to.

Delay seemed interminable in the Accident and Emergency department at St Clair's. Brian Shallcross first had to give the nurse on duty all the details, repeat them to the casualty officer when he arrived from bed, then tell his story yet again to the paediatrician who was called. Despite the delay Brian Shallcross believed they had at last got someone who knew what was what.

From then on Brian and Chloë Shallcross simply waited. Slowly the time moved on and around 6 A.M. the casualty department became active when a motor cyclist who had had an accident on his way to work was brought in. There were distant cries of a child, possibly it was their child. No one came and told them anything. An hour or so ago the staffnurse had told them where to get tea from a machine and Brian Shallcross had brought some and drunk it out of habit. A gulf existed between these two, as it did between Chloë and her baby, one which was getting wider. Brian Shallcross couldn't understand his wife's attitude, or her problem; why she couldn't respond to the child or why she got depressed, while Chloë felt she had failed, and knowing Brian was blaming her made her feel worse.

Dr Arwyn Jones, the paediatric registrar, approached

from along the corridor.

'Sorry it's taken so long,' he said, 'but we have to get these things right. She has an infection in her left lung.' He thought it could be an abscess that might result in the lung collapsing, but didn't tell the parents. 'She'll have to stop in, we'll pop her back in an incubator.'

'I don't see that . . . I mean, how's it happened?' Brian Shallcross was confused and upset and afraid. 'I mean, she's had enough problems. It's not fair.'

'Babies pick up these things very easily, Mr Shallcross,' Dr Jones said. 'Possibly she got the infection here in the hospital. Fortunately we've diagnosed it early. We'll get her treatment started right away.'

'She's got to go in now you mean?' Brian Shallcross was further confused.

'That's best. We'll get her started with antibiotics. We can take her up to paediatrics right away,' – assuming their consent. 'We'll fix you up with a bed. I'm sure you'll want to stay with your baby, Mrs Shallcross.'

That wasn't something she wanted, not even for just one night.

Rushing home from the hospital – having got off work early to visit his daughter – Brian Shallcross called his wife as he entered the house. He was more hurt and upset about not finding her at the hospital. He came into the living-room where Chloë was staring at afternoon television.

'Chloë! What are you doing? Why aren't you at the hospital? I went there. I thought you were staying with Oriole.' That was the name he had decided on, giving no thought to how it might affect her later in life.

Chloë shook her head. 'I can't. I can't bear to see her there,' she said in a subdued voice. She had simply walked out of the mother-and-baby unit. 'I don't want to see her there any more.'

'That's silly. You're being silly,' he told her, still not

understanding her problem. 'It's not the hospital's fault. Those doctors are working like anything to make her better.'

'I don't want to go. I don't. I can't . . .'

'You must. You're her mother!' He was getting angry. 'You should be with her.'

'I can't!' she screamed. 'Why don't you understand. You're stupid. Stupid.'

She suddenly ran, up to the bedroom, rather than have this confrontation.

He pursued her, finding her sobbing on the bed. This caused his anger to subside, leaving him confused and exasperated.

'Chloë. What is wrong? What is it?' he asked. 'I mean, she's your daughter.'

There was no response.

'Why don't you stop being depressed,' he told her irrationally. 'You've no reason to be. I mean, you've got a nice house, you've got a lovely daughter. She's going to be all right.'

'I can't.' Her words barely emerged.

'Then why don't you go and see Dr Thurson? He'll give you something to make you feel better. Oriole's going to be all right, she is.' He waited, hoping for a response. 'Look, go and see the doctor. That's best,' he suggested. 'I'll phone for an appointment.'

From Chloë Shallcross's visit, which extended through the next patient's appointment, Dr Thurson got an indication of the size of her problem, and knew it wasn't something he could deal with in his present set-up. Ideally he should have been the person to help her, but knew it would be at the expense of so many of his other patients. Instinctively recognizing the fallacy of that argument he closed off the thought.

'What would you feel about going along for a chat with a psychiatrist, Chloë?' the doctor suggested. 'It might help.'

Chloë didn't respond. She was pushing a crumpled tissue under her nose, and looked herself much like a crumpled tissue.

'There's nothing very unusual about what's happening to you,' he told her. 'It's a common enough problem when Mummy and baby are separated immediately after birth. What we have to do is prevent the problem becoming so large that it's unmanageable. This is why I think it would be useful if you saw the psychiatrist.'

Chloë shrugged, feeling apathetic. 'There doesn't seem much point,' she mumbled.

'I think there is. You'll get over this difficult patch and establish a worthwhile relationship with baby. What you're experiencing is guilt basically. You think you've failed, because you were unable to have a perfect baby. But that's not reality. The psychiatrist will help you recognize what is real and what isn't.' He rose and came round the desk. 'Now dry those tears, they're smudging your make-up.' He gave her a fresh tissue and she cleaned off some of the make-up with it. 'That's better. I'll write to Dr Hendrix at St Clair's. They have an excellent day centre there. Meanwhile I'll give you something for your depression. You'll see that life can be worthwhile, Chloë,' he said. He went back to his chair and drew his prescription pad forward, as if all solutions were reachable. This, and a referral to the specialist was all he could do, despite his inclination to do more.

33

On the gynae ward lunch was a meal, like all other meals, that Mrs Downes at one time had had no interest in. Now she watched the tall stainless steel trolley come on to the ward with an air of anticipation and expectation. Over the past month or so she had come to look forward to her meals as to no other event in her day. Furthermore, since she had stopped having radiotherapy and chemotherapy she had been able to eat all that was put in front of her. But this may have had something to do with the food that she now had being a lot better and in accordance with the strict diet Dr Marvill had set out. There had been a lot of resistance to such things as raw vegetables, not from the patient but the dieticians, and where the diet called for bran, they had tried putting the patient off with bran supplements such as All-Bran. Jessie Marvill had insisted that they organize what the diet called for, knowing that they tended to look upon her as a little crazy.

Mrs Downes felt a sense of impatience as one of the two ancillaries removed a tray of food from the trolley and passed it to her helper to take to a patient.

There were five other women on Mrs Downes's bay and none of them had been there longer than a week. She had seen a number of patients come and go during the twelve weeks she had been in hospital, and not all go home either. The ancillary pulled out a tray and nodded to Mrs Downes's side of the ward. Mistakenly her colleague started towards Mrs Downes. 'No, she has her special. That's for Miss Marshall. Don't suppose she'll eat it.'

Miss Marshall had shown no interest in food or anything else since coming into hospital.

The ancillary at the trolley pulled out the special lunch from the bottom rack and took it across to Mrs Downes. It was comprised entirely of raw vegetables, apart from coarse wholemeal bread. For dessert there was muesli with fruit juice on it and sliced banana, the same as she had for breakfast.

Getting raw muesli had been another struggle for Dr Marvill, proprietary brands with cooked cereals, sugar or dried milk had been offered; the argument put forward was that it was cheaper to buy such brands than use the labour intensive home-made variety, notwithstanding the nutritional benefits of the latter.

'There you are, my dear,' the ancillary said disapprovingly. 'Doesn't ever change, does it.'

Mrs Downes, who was looking strikingly well, wasn't deterred. Whatever her diet lacked in apparent variety was more than compensated for by her having been taught to chew her food until every mouthful was liquid; that way she tasted the flavour of each vegetable. 'What about my glass of Guinness?' She sounded cross. She was given a drink both at lunch and supper.

'The nurse'll bring you that,' she said, and pushed the trolley out of the bay.

When the sister brought the drink five minutes later Mrs Downes was well into her meal and so refused it.

'You know I'm supposed to have it before my meal,' she chided.

'It won't hurt this once, my dear,' the sister said.

'It will. Drinking with your food dilutes all the stomach juices,' she said, quoting Dr Marvill.

'Just as you say, my dear,' Sister Robertson said patiently. She couldn't deny how much better Mrs Downes was looking, even if she was tedious about her food. 'Have two before supper then. I'll bring you a cuppa later.' Sister Robertson wasn't one to forget or dismiss patients' need under pressure. She brought the old lady weak black tea later that afternoon, even though there was a consultant's ward round. She brought Dr Thurson with her.

Dr Thurson tried to keep in touch with his patients in hospital, especially the elderly like Mrs Downes, who had been abandoned by their families. But such visits weren't frequent occurrences.

'You have a visitor, Mrs Downes,' the young Scots sister said.

'Is it anyone I know?' Mrs Downes asked, almost staring the doctor in the face. She was more interested in her tea.

'You ought to. It's your GP,' the sister said.

'Oh, I know him,' Mrs Downes said, 'known him for years, I have.' He might not have been present from the manner of her response.

'How are you, my dear?' Dr Thurson asked as if intruding on a private conversation.

'How do I look, doctor?' she responded, pleased with herself. 'I'd say I look an absolute picture.'

'You certainly do,' Dr Thurson agreed.

'I feel wonderful,' she said. 'Haven't felt better for years.'

Since stopping her treatment and changing her regimen, she had put on weight, and a lot of her pain had disappeared. The pain that was left was bearable.

'Will you wait and have a word with Mr Montagu? He's due on the ward any time now,' Sister Robertson informed him.

'I'm going off on holiday,' Mrs Downes announced. 'Convalescence down in Clacton by the sea.'

'No, I only popped in as I was bringing a patient to hospital. I like to keep in touch with my patients,' he said. Then he thought about Mrs Downes and her family and decided he should wait and see what plans the gynaecologist had for her.

He waited, though got little more from the consultant when he arrived than he could have got from the young ward sister. Mr Montagu invited him to join them at the patient's bedside. The reason for this was that until reminded by his junior staff he wouldn't know what the position was with the patient.

The arrival of the consultant and his team at Mrs Downes's bed caused her to wake with a start. She had been napping and thought for a moment it was the ancillary worker with the afternoon tea.

The latest liver scans showed no sign of the secondary cancers having advanced in Mrs Downes, although they had by no means disappeared. Mr Montagu held the transparencies to the light and nodded his approval, before passing them to Dr Thurson to see, as if this patient, despite the clinical evidence, was a personal triumph.

Dr Lambolle, Dr Marvill, a hospital social worker and Sister Robertson, plus a nurse pushing the records trolley were present.

'The two things don't seem to add up,' he said generally, indicating the cancers shown on the liver scan and the patient in the bed. 'There's no remission, yet she appears in excellent health.' He waited for the GP's opinion.

'Yes, it's a remarkable change,' Dr Thurson said. 'She's like a different person.'

'We certainly seem to have found the answer for you, my dear,' Montagu said with no sense of shame. 'You're a new woman.'

'I know I am,' Mrs Downes declared proudly.

'She's had no cytotoxic drugs?' he said, glancing over the file.

'She's had no drugs at all,' Dr Marvill informed him. 'Not even sleeping tablets.'

Mrs Downes enjoyed this attention, and concentrated hard on the group of people around her bed but couldn't in fact hear what they were saying.

'Excellent. It looks like we'll be passing her over to your care before long, doctor,' he told Thurson. 'We can think about discharging her. Any problems, Mrs Richie?' he asked the social worker.

'There is some difficulty about going home. There's a son and his family, who aren't keen to take her back,' she said, getting the details wrong.

'It's Mrs Downes's daughter in fact,' Jessie Marvill said. 'But she doesn't want to go back to live with them.'

'There has been a bit of a problem with Mrs Downes at home,' Dr Thurson said. 'The daughter is hypertensive and apt to get very impatient with her mother.'

Hearing just enough to take the drift of this conversation, Mrs Downes piped in, 'I'm not going back there. It was them who made me ill in the first place.' She firmly believed this. She had found their resentment of her presence very tiring.

'I don't think it would be a good idea to have her away entirely,' Mr Montagu said. 'I'd like to keep an eye on her. Can she go to Part III?' This was a section of the Health Act, which dealt with sheltered provision for the elderly run by the local authority social services.

'There was talk of her going to convalescence,' Mrs Richie said.

'Good. We'll try to fix her up with a geriatric bed on her return.' He handed the file to Sister Robertson. 'You're to be congratulated,' he told the patient. 'Well done.'

'Mrs Downes did work jolly hard to change her attitude and her diet,' Dr Marvill said.

Mr Montagu didn't wish to know about such whimsical things as his SHO tried introducing to his specialty. Instead he was busy, busy, busy. 'A change of diet would do none of us any harm,' he said glibly, patting his stomach. 'Keeps the tums down.' He gave her no further opportunity to expand on Mrs Downes's current treatment.

'Nice to see you again, Dr Thurson,' he said. 'If there's any more information you need about the patient please don't hesitate to contact me, or one of my staff.' With a polite smile he moved away.

The firm passed the next bed, with, 'Mrs Holder is in for her hysterectomy tomorrow,' from Dr Lambolle. There was no need for Mr Montagu to see her.

'Doctor,' Percy Thurson said to Jessie Marvill, who was the last to leave Mrs Downes's bedside. 'Could I have a word about Mrs Grant?'

'Yes, of course . . .' she responded at once, bewilderment quickly following. 'Mrs Grant? I'm afraid she died. The beginning of the week.' She said this as if breaking the news to a relative, and almost added, I'm sorry.

'Oh, did she.' The news shocked Dr Thurson. He wasn't especially well equipped for dealing with the emotional implications of death for all his time in medicine. He felt he should have been informed. Possibly he had been and the information had slipped past him. Feeling confused and upset and inadequate as he did, he still thought that perhaps he should go and see the family.

Jessie Marvill watched him turn and shuffle out of the bay. For a moment she thought he might topple over and was about to offer him a chair. An inclination to go after him welled through her, but she was aware of her boss going on with his ward round, which she was needed on. At times she had seen her mother fairly beaten from contact with patients, but never as beaten as this GP was. The image of Dr Thurson, who she thought thoroughly decent on the occasions they had made contact, would affect her profoundly.

'Miss Marshall has been confirmed as having malignant deposits, probably ovarian in origin,' Dr Marvill said out of the patient's hearing. 'Cytology was positive.'

Montagu thought about this, then nodded to himself as he considered the course of action. 'She should come to theatre tomorrow. We'll have a close look,' he said.

He went along the side of the bed to the patient. 'Hello, Miss Marshall. How are we this afternoon? We'd like to pop you into theatre tomorrow. We'll tidy up your insides. Then we'll probably pop you on a course of drugs combined with radiotherapy. That should help solve your little bit of trouble . . .'

The parting image of Dr Thurson sped across Dr Marvill's mind's eye as she heard her boss say this. It was followed by one of Mrs Grant who had had a similar complaint; then Mrs Downes. But Jessie Marvill was too tired to draw any conclusion at that moment.

Book III

Health should be judged by the quality
of life rather than its quantity.

34

Some days seemed born of disaster, and no one knew why; on such days there were numerous traffic accidents, endless industrial and domestic accidents; on such days people who were usually reasonable boiled up, placid people exploded; doctors' surgeries and A and E units filled up with people trying to get help, or hide until the day passed.

This was one such day and the casualty department of St Clair's was doing brisk business, with a lot of people seeking or needing treatment, most of them having to wait; there were follow-up patients who also had to wait.

One of the emergencies was Henry Staples, an ordinarily robust eighty-year-old who, on this particular day, had suffered a Stokes-Adams heart attack on his bicycle.

Such days were a strain on the medical and nursing staff. A staffnurse was finding difficulty coping this morning as she went to a cupboard to collect a handful of canulae, for intravenous input; the fact that she had to go for them at all added to her stress; they should have been readily available in the cardiac arrest trolley, if anything went wrong as a result of them not being there. She hurried back towards the examination room, ignoring the cries for help. As she went she signalled to a 2nd-year student nurse to answer the telephone, whose persistent bell was wearing everyone down.

In the waiting area a drunk obsessively picked off flecks of dried sick from his encrusted jacket. He had wandered in looking for respite from the pressures of panhandling. He would find it until the end of the day when someone would get around to him. A patient with his arm in a sling wasn't about to wait any longer.

'Nurse! How much longer must I wait? – the doctor told me to come back at nine,' he said. It was 10.45, but he didn't secure the staffnurse's attention. He would later, when his rising blood pressure caused a CVA.

The staffnurse went into the treatment room where Henry Staples lay and drew the curtain, wishing that she could shut the pressures out as easily. But there was as much pressure inside the room.

Henry Staples was on the high examination couch, where the registrar cardiologist was working on him, in the absence of the crash-call team. Dr Satish Kumar, a thirty-eight-year-old Indian, was helped by Jessie Marvill. She wasn't on the cardiac arrest team, but had responded to the call for the geriatric SHO. No member of the cardiac arrest team, which had been called initially for Henry Staples, had arrived this day, even though it consisted of five doctors. Sometimes they all responded or like today, each one relied on someone else getting there. On such days patients sometimes died. Dr Kumar couldn't get the electrodes from the electrocardiograph machine to stick to the mat of grey hair on the patient's bare chest. The A and E sister moved in quickly with a pair of scissors and snipped the hair away. The patient was breathing, and his heart was now functioning, having responded to the sharp blow Dr Kumar made to the precordium, but the crash-call porters who had brought the defibrillator waited. Dr Dom Zammit, the Maltese casualty officer, was also there, observing, using this as a way of avoiding the problems piling up beyond that curtain. Mr Staples's magnificent twenty-nine-year-old, brightly polished brown boots were on a chair by the bed, and commented on by everyone who came in.

'How is it going?' Dr Kumar asked in his easy, unflappable manner. He was grateful to the geriatrician, and realized this pace wasn't what she would have been used to.

Having taken one of the venous canulae from the

staffnurse, Dr Marvill was having difficulty fitting it into the old boy's arm as his veins were collapsing.

'D'you need any help?' Dr Kumar asked, implying no criticism, despite the delay compounding the problem.

'I'm getting it now, I think,' Dr Marvill said.

'I don't know who last checked this crash-call trolley,' Dr Kumar said. 'There should have been canulae in the drawer.' It was an observation.

Dr Marvill switched the saline drip through the valve attached to the intravenous needle.

'How much Isoprenaline?' she asked.

'The usual concentration. Give him 3 or 4 mg a minute,' Dr Kumar told her. 'I think he will need pacing.' He was checking the electrocardiogram rolling across the machine.

'There isn't a spare pacemaker,' the sister said, adding to their problems. 'The crash-call last Tuesday took the only one we had. It went up to the ward and wasn't returned.'

'Oh,' Dr Kumar said. 'We'll see how his rhythm is for an hour or so. I think we should try and locate one.'

The 2nd-year student nurse pulled the curtain aside. 'Sister, there's an overdose on the bell.'

'It's going to be one of those days,' the sister said, raising her eyebrows. Morning o/ds were unusual.

'What did she take?' Dr Zammit asked, automatically assuming that the overdose victim was female. 'Does anyone know?'

'They think Valium.'

Although Valium wasn't particularly dangerous in o/d, it was often combined with other drugs, so action needed to be prompt.

'Sister, would you try to borrow a pacer? Cardiology at Queen's ought to have one,' Dr Kumar suggested as she went out.

'I'll do my best, doctor,' she said.

Sister Blythe tried first through her own contacts to locate a pacer; the stores said they hadn't got one; the ward where a pacer went with the patient last Tuesday told her it was no longer there. She had no luck in borrowing one from the medical wards, and finally handed the problem to Roy Needham, the administrator, and returned to more pressing problems.

The pacer wasn't forgotten by Sister Blythe as she attended to other patients for she knew that if she didn't pursue it there was a good chance that it would be pushed aside by other priorities.

A little later when she returned to the office to check with admin, Sister Blythe found Dr Zammit there reading *Medical Emergencies, Diagnosis and Management*, the section on overdose procedures. Numerous doctors had to rely on that little book, and the casualty sister had even known doctors excuse themselves from treatment rooms to go and read up something.

'Did she arrive yet?' Dr Zammit tried to conceal the book.

The sister knew he meant the overdose. 'No. Did admin phone back about the pacer?'

'No one telephoned,' he said.

'Would you look at the man with burns, doctor,' she said as she picked up the phone. That was as close as she came to giving him a direct order. She didn't know quite what this doctor's problem was, but he seemed only able to cope with one emergency at a time, unlike most A and E doctors.

'Burns?' Dr Zammit thumbed through his book in vain for a reference.

'This is Accident and Emergency,' the sister said into the phone. 'Did Mr Needham manage to find a pacer?'

'His deputy's on to Queen's now,' the secretary told her.

'Well, the patient's hanging on by his fingernails.'

Exaggerating sometimes helped.

'She is trying,' the secretary snapped. She was another one affected by this day and its non-stop problems.

The deputy administrator, Jenny Rogers, who had been in the job only three days, was having no success locating a pacemaker. Not being able to find one in this hospital, she got on to Queen's stores manager, who wasn't forthcoming.

'I wouldn't be phoning you if there was one in this hospital, Mr Prince,' she said, feeling a sense of frustration.

'I do appreciate your difficulties, Miss Rogers,' the stores manager sympathized in his ponderous manner. 'But I've only one left in stock. I have to hold that for an emergency.'

'This is an emergency,' she told him.

'I realize that, Miss Rogers. I was talking about an emergency at this hospital. The problem is we can't buy in any more.'

'Queen's and St Clair's are part of the same District. The District budget buys equipment for both hospitals,' she explained as though he wasn't aware of this. 'The fact that you have a pacemaker and we have the emergency is incidental. The problem is solved by your putting it on transport over here.'

'Can't do that, Miss Rogers,' Charlie Prince said.

Whether or not this was seen as failure, Jenny Rogers decided she couldn't pursue the pacer any further at this level. 'Then I'm going to get Mr Needham to ring the District Administrator and have him telephone you.' She disconnected the call, and took the problem to her boss.

Roy Needham was amused at the thought of his deputy trying to reason with the stores manager. In future she would know there was a better way to such equipment, the medical grapevine.

'I should have warned you about Charlie Prince, Jenny,' Needham said as he picked up the phone. 'He can be an awkward bugger.'

'I told him how urgently the pacer was needed.'

'They always are.' He turned to the phone. 'Is Dr Robinson there? Roy Needham at St Clair's.' He waited. 'We'll see if we have more luck on the medical grapevine.

Peter,' he said to the consultant cardiologist on the line. 'We've a slight problem. The crash-call team has a patient who needs pacing, but no pacer. I was wondering if you could help.'

'Well, I don't have one myself,' Dr Robinson said. unhelpfully. 'Only pacemakers with patients attached. What do you suggest, that I disconnect a patient?'

'There is one in the stores over there. If you were to call for it, I could arrange transport.'

'And if we have an emergency meanwhile, Roy? If you people would only leave the purchase of medical equipment to medical staff,' Robinson suggested, 'we wouldn't have these constant hiccups.'

Needham made sympathetic noises, but didn't agree in fact. He knew what would result from such purchasing, all the equipment would go to the most attractive specialty.

'What are you offering in return for this enormous favour?' Dr Robinson wanted to know.

'I would have said you were a consultant who had just about everything, Peter.'

'I don't have a parking space at St Clair's when I hold my clinic.' He held a clinic there one afternoon a week.

'I think we can find a space for you. I'll get the works department to paint your name on it.'

Satisfied with the trade, the consultant said, 'If you send transport I'll beg a machine for you. But we would like it back.'

'Best sackcloth and ashes,' Needham said to his deputy on replacing the phone.

That was but one of the hoops he was prepared to jump through to keep his hospital functioning.

Henry Staples opened his eyes for the first time in the treatment room and blinked. He was confused. He thought about his bicycle, which had been his means of transport for as many years as he could remember. He rarely went on buses, but welcomed them because it meant the disappearance of trams and tramlines, which bicycle wheels could get stuck in.

'Where's my bicycle?' he whispered.

'You took a spill,' Dr Kumar told him. 'You'll be fine. We're giving you something to keep your heart going.'

Without interest Henry Staples shut his eyes and drifted away again; he had asked about his bicycle.

'Is there any word on a pacer?' Dr Kumar asked the sister as she slid back the curtain and entered the treatment room.

'Yes. They're sending one over from Queen's now,' Sister Blythe said.

'Oh good,' Dr Kumar said. He checked the ventricular arrhythmias from the electrocardiograph. There were fewer now. 'How old is he?'

'There aren't any details,' Sister Blythe said.

'He looks fit. I'd say he might have a few years yet.' Dr Kumar had difficulty persuading colleagues in radiography that it was worth pacing an old man, but had emphasized how robust he was. He would insert the pacer wire through an intravenous catheter and into the right ventricle of the heart under X-ray control. He tore off the paper ECG reading, folded it and clipped it to the patient's notes. 'He can go across to X-ray immediately after lunch. Thank you, sister.'

'You're welcome, doctor,' she said.

'Are you going to lunch, Jessie?' Dr Kumar asked.

'I've a patient to see on G2,' Dr Marvill said, looking at her watch.

'I don't think she will be going anywhere,' he said with a smile. 'Have lunch first.'

Jessie Marvill was easily persuaded, as Satish Kumar was a more sensitive soul than a lot of her colleagues, and she missed such company since Dr Laurence James's departure.

The klaxon that heralded the ambulance was something the staff in A and E were keyed up to. Certainly they all reacted to it, if only to pause and consider either running to lend a hand or avoiding the problem.

Sister Blythe went to meet the ambulance as it arrived outside.

The student nurse came after her with a stretcher trolley. The patient was brought out of the ambulance conscious, but groggy and unaware of what was happening as they wheeled her up the ramp and through the glass doors.

'Did anyone come with her?' the sister asked. 'What's her name?'

'Mrs Taylor,' the ambulance attendant read off her call sheet. 'Brenda Taylor.'

'Mrs Taylor?' the sister said, when they got her on to the examination couch. 'How many tablets did you take, Mrs Taylor? D'you know? D'you know what they were? How many tablets did you take, dear?'

There was a groan from Mrs Taylor. Sister Blythe wasn't hopeful of a coherent response, the questions helped prevent the patient slipping into unconsciousness.

'Where's Dr Zammit?' she asked.

'With the burns patient,' the student nurse told her.

'Find him,' Sister Blythe said. 'How long ago did you take the tablets, Mrs Taylor? Do you know?' Then to the lady ambulance attendant, 'Who found her?'

'A neighbour,' she said. 'She wouldn't come with her, didn't want to get involved.'

'Stupid,' the sister said impatiently. She inserted her fingers into the patient's mouth, then an airway.

'Ah she come,' Dr Zammit said – his reading-up on drug overdose wasn't in vain. 'Was it Valium she took?' He lifted her eyelids and looked at her eyes with a torch. 'How long you take tablets? Long time?'

'Mrs Taylor?' the sister said. 'How long ago did you take the tablets, dear? Was there any evidence of what she took?'

'Well, the police found a couple of empty bottles,' the ambulance attendant said. 'They were coming in.'

'Mrs Taylor? Did you take anything else with the tablets?' Unable to get any response the sister turned to the doctor for the next move.

'We'd better put up an IV line,' he said. 'We need blood and urine samples.'

'Does anyone know who her doctor is?'

Mrs Taylor was able to answer, and said in a slurred, barely audible way that it was Dr Thurson who, when contacted, informed them she was suffering from depression as a result of losing her husband the year before last. She had been prescribed Valium, and Parnate.

With all immediately available information to hand Dr Zammit was still unsure what to do, so decided to pump out the patient's stomach. At worst the procedure would make her uncomfortable. Quite often there was no point in gastric lavage due either to the small amount of tablets taken or time period which had elapsed since the overdose, but medical teams frequently performed a stomach washout anyway, as the unpleasant procedure made the patient think twice about a repeat performance.

Dr Zammit aspirated the stomach contents by means of an orogastric tube, which he passed via the patient's mouth. He started the procedure, but as washing out the stomach was a long and messy process, which had to be repeated an overdose was to give her only three days' supply. It was done Mrs Taylor's problems were only beginning. She was destined to return again to the accident and emergency unit. This was something that the staff were aware of, but were all too much under pressure to think about. Dr Zammit touched on the problem when he saw her later on that day.

'Feeling better, Mrs Taylor?' he said, entering the examination room. 'The soreness will soon go. Your daughter is coming to collect you. You think it be good for you to see the psychiatrist here, Mrs Taylor?'

'I'm not mentally ill,' Mrs Taylor said. 'I don't need to see a psychiatrist.'

'I can't make you see, Mrs Taylor.' He didn't pursue the matter. 'You can leave when your daughter gets here,' he told her. 'I'll give you something for your depression. Help you to sleep.' He wrote a prescription for Valium on her notes; it would be dispensed at the hospital without any question.

'I'm not depressed,' Mrs Taylor managed.

'You should go to your doctor,' he advised her. 'I think that best.'

Brenda Taylor went rigid with frustration at no one recognizing her problem. 'I'm not suffering from depression,' she mouthed.

'No,' he said. 'See your GP.' Like so many doctors he misprescribed Valium and his answer to her having taken an overdose was to give her only three days' supply. It was simpler than trying to deal with a problem that would eventually take her to Coldbrook mental hospital.

35

A bed had been found for Henry Staples on one of the two medical wards that were in the modern part of the hospital. The average age on the six-bedded bay, like the rest of the ward, was seventy, which made it seem more like a geriatric than a medical ward. But then most medical problems increased with age.

Patients here were CVAs, myocardial infarcts, plus some with chronic bronchitis with acute chest infections. A stroke patient in the bed opposite Henry Staples was unconscious, one next to him was also connected to a pacer, but unlike Mr Staples was on top of the bed in a dressing gown, with his legs crossed.

Fay Godwin, the sister, came on to the bay with another woman and uncrossed the heart patient's legs. 'Mr George,' she rebuked. 'You know that's not good for your circulation.'

'Sorry, sister.'

They went along to Mr Staples.

'How are you feeling now, Mr Staples?' she asked in a loud voice.

'Oh, pretty good. Ready to go home for my dinner.' He knew he had had a spill, a little setback, but had no notion of his problem. 'Where's my bicycle?'

'We mustn't rush things, otherwise you'll be in here for a long stay.'

'I feel fine. I just want to go for my dinner,' he said.

'That's good. We'll see what the doctor says. What we need now is some information. This is Mrs Morris,' she said. 'She does our admissions.'

'Hello, Mr Staples. Could I get a few details, love, we've

only got your name. What's your address?'

'38 Grove Dwellings, Block F. That's Fairfield,' he said, clear as could be.

'How old are you dear?' She wrote up his card.

'You guess.' He was proud of the way he looked, and enjoyed having people trying to guess his age.

'Twenty-one,' Mrs Morris said.

'He could almost pass for twenty-one,' Sister Godwin said.

That pleased Henry Staples even though he knew it was silly. 'Eighty-one on 27 May. Eighty-one years old. Does that surprise you?'

'It certainly does. You look wonderful, I must say.'

'My lady's seventy-nine next birthday,' he announced.

'That's your wife?'

'Fifty-eight years we been married.' He was interested in telling his story. 'She's looked after me. I've looked after her.'

'What's her name, love?'

'Joan. My wife's Joanny. Fifty-eight years we've been married.'

'Has anyone told her you're here?' Mrs Morris asked, as if he might know.

'Oh I don't want her told,' he said. 'That won't do.'

'Won't she worry?'

'She'll start to worry. It's nothing, is it? Nothing to worry my lady about,' Henry Staples said. 'I'll just slip home on m' bike.'

Mrs Morris and Sister Godwin both smiled.

'Your wife might like to know where you are, Mr Staples.'

Henry Staples began to get anxious. 'I don't want her upset. She'll tell me to stop riding that bike of mine.'

'But she'll have to know where you are, dear.'

'Don't you worry, Mr Staples,' Sister Godwin said, taking his hand. 'I'll ask a hospital social worker to see your wife. She can bring her to visit you.'

Mr Staples was unsure. 'But I only fell off my bike. I didn't break nothing.'

'You had a heart attack, dear,' she said. 'Don't you worry. I'll ask the social worker to go and have a word.'

That set Henry Staples worrying: he knew his wife, they didn't. His Joanny would rush to the hospital as soon as she heard; she would take on too much and make herself ill, then she would be the one in hospital.

Rambling and overanxious he tried later to convey this to Mrs Richie, the hospital social worker. But he wasn't sure that she understood when she left to go and see his wife. Henry Staples worried about his wife now and would continue to do so until he was reunited with her. The basis for his worry was partly his realizing that he had to stay in hospital and couldn't simply get on his bicycle and go home.

There was no reply when Rita Richie knocked at the door of the flat in Grove Dwellings. Block F was an age-blackened, inner city tenement, with a dark stairwell climbing through the centre. At each level of the four storeys there was graffiti. Some attempt had been made to scrub it off the Staples's wall.

Mrs Richie rang the bell again. Finally a woman in her fifties poked her head out of the next flat.

'She's not there, love,' she said. 'She's gone to the hospital.'

'Oh, she knows!' Mrs Richie was surprised.

'Silly girl – wouldn't wait. I told her my Arthur'd run her up there. I blame m'self, I should've took her.'

From the out of kilter conversation the social worker gathered something had gone wrong.

'Missed her step, hurrying for the bus,' the neighbour explained. 'She's done her hip in.'

'Which hospital was she taken to?'

'St Clair's. They'll be together, won't they,' she said,

having a romantic notion about hospitals. 'They're a lovely couple. Does you good seeing them together, it does.'

'Is there any family?'

''S a son in Australia. Lost their other two boys in the war, they did,' the neighbour said. 'How is Henry?'

'Oh, he's fine. He'll be up and around in no time,' Mrs Richie said. 'Could I come in and have a quick word?' She could fill in a few details from the neighbour, even though it wasn't good social work practice.

Having been admitted to St Clair's with a question mark against a fractured skull and broken hip, Mrs Staples was found to have a slight concussion and, surprisingly, a dislocated hip; in the aged the bones were so thin and brittle that the force required to throw the hip out of its socket almost always fractured the femur. The orthopaedic surgeons were a long time accepting what she had wrong with her, suspecting instead a hairline fracture near the hip joint. But finally they slipped the hip back into its socket; that was the easy part. The dislocation could be as bad as a fracture and take as long to heal, but if rested the patient would fully recover. Inactivity would be the most difficult thing imaginable for Mrs Staples, who had kept busy every day of her life.

'Mrs Staples – dislocated hip,' Trevor Holland, a theatre porter, announced, arriving on to the women's orthopaedics ward in the old Nightingale Block. A 3rd-year student nurse was with the patient. 'Where's she go?'

'By the door,' the Chinese ward sister said. 'Hello, Mrs Staples. Are we awake?' she asked as they manoeuvred the trolley alongside an empty bed. 'Not quite with us still.'

'I thought you was emptying this ward,' Holland said, glancing around the ward, which was in the slow process of being closed for upgrading as there was nowhere to transfer these patients to.

'We took ladies from the bus crash outside the gate last night,' the sister told him.

'You'll be filled up again at this rate.' He spun the empty trolley away from the bed.

'We send them home as quickly as we can.' The sister was very short, and had strong, bowed legs.

'Tell you what, I won't bring you no more, sister,' he said humorously and went out, leaving the sister puzzled.

'Mrs Staples, can you hear me?' the sister said.

Mrs Staples opened her eyes. Although conscious she was drowsy and confused.

'That's the idea. We just going take your pulse and blood pressure.'

Mrs Staples didn't understand why her husband wasn't here, remembering only that someone had told her she was going to the hospital to see her husband. Everything else that she remembered happened a very long time ago.

She had enjoyed being a little girl, she recalled inaccurately. Most of her recall now was from her distant past, and inaccurate, and would remain so for a while.

'Nurse!' Henry Staples saw the uniform flit past the open doorway.

The nurse didn't see him.

'They're never still long enough.' He was feeling a little exasperated. He wanted to get out of bed, but was hemmed in by apparatus.

'You have to use this, old fellow.' The man in the next bed indicated the call button. He was about sixty-five. 'That signals to the operator, and she'll buzz the nurses' station.' He nodded, encouraging Henry.

The disconnected voice from the console operator responded almost immediately, startling Henry.

'Yes, what d'you want, Mr Staples?'

Henry Staples looked about him, confused by this system.

'Tell her what you want,' the neighbour urged. 'Tell her what you need.'

'My lady,' Henry Staples said uncertainly, not knowing where to speak. 'Is she all right? Is she . . . ?' He saw a nurse in the corridor. 'Nurse! Nurse!' he called in slight panic.

The nurse came on to the bay, flicking down the location indicator by the door.

'What can I do for you, Mr Staples?' she asked.

'My lady. How is she?' he expected her to know who he was talking about.

She didn't.

'She's never been in hospital before – she won't know what's happening.' He was worried about this. 'Can I get this doo-dah out, and go and see her?'

'Does it need emptying?' The nurse checked the urinal attached to the catheter.

'It's nowhere near full, Mr Staples.'

'I'm not a dirty old man. I'm not going to wet the bed.' Henry Staples was too embarrassed to make too much fuss. 'I don't want it in.'

'We'll have to see what the doctor says,' the nurse told him.

'I want to see my lady.' Henry couldn't imagine going there attached to a pee bag. They hadn't even seen each other naked in a very long while.

'We'll see what doctor says, Mr Staples,' she said, tucking and tidying his bed.

Later on in the central nursing station when Dr Roger Crick was writing up a patient's treatment sheet, the middle-aged ward sister brought up Mr Staples's much repeated request. 'He's wanting his catheter out so he can go across to Nightingale Block to see his wife,' she explained.

'He could take his urinal with him,' Dr Crick said.

'You don't know Mr Staples!'

Dr Crick was thinking about the real problem. 'Queen's will want his pacer back before long. What we have is a choice of not returning it and keeping him here, or sending him home without a pacer – possibly to die.' That was a dilemma and one that presented itself more and more. 'What's his wife in with?'

'A dislocated hip, and concussion.'

'It can't be! Didn't she fracture the femur?' Dr Crick asked.

'Apparently not,' Sister Godwin said. 'He's a nice old man. Seeing his wife is the only thing that will settle him, I'm thinking.'

'I'll get Dr Lang to look at him and maybe pop the catheter out. Then you can send him across. Kim!' He saw an Asian surgeon go along the ward and went after him. 'You're in theatre tomorrow,' Dr Crick said.

'Not much time, Roger,' Dr Kim said, anticipating him.

'Could you pop me in on your theatre for ten minutes? I have these sinister looking moles on my feet,' – having achieved the removal of the moles from his face. Although by no means unusual in his hypochondria – most doctors imagined themselves with the disease of the month – Dr Crick was unusual in that he sought treatment, especially surgery. Generally doctors would die on their feet of things which they daily assured patients were treatable.

There was no hurt involved for Henry Staples when the medical SHO removed his catheter, other than to his pride. He squirmed with embarrassment at the young female doctor holding his penis and sliding the tube from the urethra.

'I didn't need this,' he said crossly.

'Perhaps you didn't, Mr Staples,' Dr Lang replied. 'Some do, it's just a precaution.' She didn't tell him it was a nursing convenience also. 'There. You're all set to go and see your wife. I should wait for the porter,' she added as he tried to get out of bed.

He was impatient for the porter to arrive, like a child waiting for Christmas morning.

'D'you know we've been married fifty-eight years,'

Henry Staples told the porter for the third time as he took him across to Nightingale Block in a wheelchair.

'Soon be having your diamond wedding,' Chris Hogan's answer was the same each time. ''S not many go that far nowadays.' He knew that from bitter experience; he was divorced; so was his son, while his eldest daughter was in the process.

'She was just a slip of a girl when I married her. As slim and pretty as you like. Wore a pink dress, she did. Belonged to my older sister. She's gone now. She was eighty-eight.' These details were as clear as could be to Henry Staples.

'Eighty-eight? 'S not bad innings, Henry, is it,' Hogan said, pushing him out of the old lift and on to women's orthopaedics. 'You're not doing bad yourself.'

'We've never spent a single night apart,' the old man said. He was exaggerating, but that was what he believed then.

'Is that right? It won't be for long,' Hogan assured him. 'They'll put you together in a nice side ward when you're both well again.'

With thoughts swimming and eyes flitting over the patients, not pausing long enough to focus, Henry Staples failed to see his wife or the staffnurse who approached.

'Mr Staples,' the staffnurse said. 'You've come to see Mrs Staples.' She was in the bed almost directly opposite them.

Joy bubbled out of the old man when his eyes finally settled on his wife. He started out of the wheelchair, but was calmly restrained by Hogan, who pushed him to the bedside.

Henry looked back at the nurse, not knowing how to express himself. 'Is she all right?' he asked.

'She's doing nicely, Mr Staples,' the staffnurse said. 'She's sleeping that's all.'

'Oh I won't wake her. She'll need her rest.' He took her slightly arthritic hand in his.

'Is Nurse Guenin on duty?' Chris Hogan asked.

'She's in the office,' the staffnurse said.

'I'll just have a word. You in the union, Staff?' he enquired. He never ceased trying to recruit people to his union, nor would he until there was but one union for all healthworkers.

'The RCN,' she said with a note of superiority.

'Well, I hope they stand by you when the going gets a bit rough.' It was a veiled warning. 'The door's always open,' he added as he went along the ward, leaving the Staples alone together.

Although there were other patients around, some taking an interest in the visitor, Henry Staples was completely unaware of anyone else. He was reassured for seeing his wife breathing and with no sign of injury, apart from the yellow bruise that was spreading along her grey hair line. All Henry wanted was to go on being with his lady. He saw no cloud on the horizon. In a few days when they were both fully recovered from their spills they would go home and everything would be as it was before. He had absolutely no doubts.

36

Health care management was only second best for Jenny Rogers, the deputy administrator. She would have preferred being a doctor, but hadn't the stamina. Although she had taken a degree course at university, she preferred practical lessons, which was what she got with Roy Needham. He was immensely helpful as there wasn't a thing he didn't know about running a hospital, or man-management. That was where her inexperience showed. She approached people with the wrong attitude to get the best from them, especially the porters, who she knew were illegally reporting sick. She would have had a hospital doctor examine them rather than their own GPs, as most GPs issued certificates for the asking. Her boss had advised that it would create too much ill feeling; at the moment the porters' hostility was centred on District, rather than local management, which bore the brunt of the inconvenience their absenteeism caused.

Jenny Rogers knocked on her boss's open office door.

'Come in, Jenny,' Needham said. He left his door open unless holding a meeting. 'Finding your feet?' During this breaking-in period he invited general discussion about hospital management. He expected she would be here no more than two years before moving on to increase her experience.

'I do have a slight problem,' she said. 'The porter on the incinerator has gone sick.'

'Oh, it's his turn, is it?'

'He has produced a doctor's certificate,' she explained. Despite being relieved that Roy Needham was here to fall back on, she sometimes resented having to bring problems to him, and even wondered if he didn't purposely nurture such dependence.

'Oh yes, I bet. If District restored their regular overtime it would prevent all this nonsense.'

'Shall I move someone else on to the incinerator to do his job?'

'You'd better have a word with the NUPE branch secretary,' Needham told her, but then had second thoughts. She would be no match for Chris Hogan, who would take advantage of her inexperience. 'Leave it with me. I'll have a word.'

'You could put Yassar Arif on the incinerator, Mr Needham,' Hogan said when they met that afternoon and he had listened to the administrator's proposal. 'But he is only grade 3. You can't really have a grade 3 man incinerating limbs. That's a grade 4 job.'

'They burn just the same, Chris,' Needham said. They were sitting opposite one another at the Formica topped table in the canteen.

'You don't want to be too sure.' There was no suggestion of mirth from Hogan.

'Then can we make him grade 4 temporarily, while Charlie Trollis is off sick?' Needham suggested.

'That means Yassar doing grade 4 work,' Hogan pointed out. 'I'd say he was capable all right. When Charlie returns Yassar'll go back down to grade 3?'

This drew a nod from Roy Needham.

'That's hardly fair, Mr Needham. I mean, a man capable of doing grade 4 work must be grade 4.'

'I can't make him up permanently,' Needham said. He could have done, but they had their quota of ancillaries at that level.

'Then I can't see that he can take responsibility for incinerating limbs,' Hogan said, following his own logic.

'All right.' Needham rose. He could have asked this as a personal favour, but didn't think that was a good idea. 'I'll find someone else.'

'So long as he's grade 4,' Hogan said.

Needham knew just the person to cope with the incinerator, but wouldn't ask himself as his intervention hadn't been a success; he would pass it back to Jenny Rogers.

A Ford hearse with two scruffily dressed undertakers stopped at the roller shutter of the mortuary, which was situated at the far end of the new pathology block. One of the undertakers rang the bell, while the other opened the hearse for the elm coffin with its solid brass handles.

The shutter door opened on to the refrigeration room which was spartan and spotless, and had a bank of five fridges with four-shelves each, plus one deep freeze. As the undertaker brought the coffin in on the trolley, Andy Betts, the large, red-faced mortuary technician, slid a shroud-enwrapped body on to a hydraulic trolley, which he lowered.

'You cremating her in that?' Betts asked as one of the undertakers opened the coffin and took out an embroidered cassock.

'I wouldn't have thought so.' The ginger undertaker, who had two days' stubble on his face, thought Betts was referring to the elaborate coffin. 'She'll go in veneer.'

'Going in that cassock, is she?'

'No. It's in case the relatives want a look.'

'I'll give you a hand.' Betts unfurled the shroud to reveal a parchment-like old lady, who had been crudely stitched from her crotch to her throat.

'She'll take a lot of gas,' the undertaker said. The less bodyfat there was meant the longer the body had to stay in the gas flame in order to combust.

They fitted her into the cassock.

'She have a postmortem, Andy?' the ginger undertaker asked. It was a meaningless question that helped get them over their awkwardness.

'What d'you think that is up her front?' – indicating the

stitching. 'A zip?'

'D'you get on that horse I give you?' the other undertaker asked.

'I didn't get a chance,' Betts said.

'You did yourself a right favour, Andy, my son. It's still running, I think.'

'That makes her look a bit better,' – having got the cassock on her. 'What age was she?'

'Ninety-three?' Betts said, checking her wrist band, as if it made some difference. 'Yes, ninety-three. Ready? One, two, three.'

They lifted her into the coffin.

Betts rubbed the woman's name off the numbered fridge space on the blackboard. There were seven other names up on the board which hung opposite the fridges plus 'leg'. This was being kept for histology. The mortuary technician felt an inexplicable revulsion for separate limbs which he never felt for bodies.

In the office where Betts's lugubrious assistant, Peter Marwick, was making tea, Betts passed the ginger undertaker the signed cremation form, then opened the large mortuary ledger and indicated where he must sign, even though he had done this a thousand times before.

'You got another one for us, haven't you?' he said. 'An Alfred Thompson?'

'He's having a postmortem this evening,' Betts informed him.

The undertaker peeled off a pound note and gave it to Betts. It was a practice observed by all the undertaking firms.

'Cheers, Andy.'

Jenny Rogers arrived, still trying to sort out the problem of the incinerator porter being off.

'Mr Betts.'

She followed him into the refrigeration room where he proceeded to remove a body from a fridge to the postmortem room – to impress his visitor, knowing she was likely to be unfamiliar with corpses.

'Mr Needham wondered if you could spare someone to work on the incinerator?' she asked, trying to escape her queasiness by avoiding looking at the body.

'What do you mean, someone? Someone? I bloody well like that,' Betts said bullyingly. 'There's only ever been me and Marvel man,' – referring to Marwick.

'Yes, well he's grade 4. We'll find you someone else to help in here,' she ventured.

'That was G2,' Marwick said, stepping through from the office. 'They've a body they want bringing down.' He went to the fridge room to get the milk for tea. Hanging inside the cabinet were a number of chickens, plus a litre of white wine to help Betts through the day.

'We won't be able to collect it, we're too busy. What's wrong with the porters?' This was to do with his own sense of importance, rather than the fact that it was ordinarily the porters' job to bring the bodies off the wards.

'Sister wants a nice capon. Not too large,' he said, without thinking, in front of the deputy administrator.

'That'll be another bloody postmortem,' Betts complained.

'Well, why don't you phone geriatrics,' Marwick said, 'and tell them to stop dying?' Despite his manner he had occasional flashes of wit.

Andy Betts gave him an unappreciative look. 'She wants you on the incinerator.' He was unconcerned about losing his assistant, as he could manage on his own, but on principle, he said, 'I'd better get someone to help me. I've got three to open up for the pathologist.'

'I'll find you some help. Thanks. It's only temporarily.' Jenny Rogers left quickly in case he changed his mind.

'I know the sort of help I'll get.' Andy Betts shook his head in dismay. 'Fancy saying that about capons in front of her.'

'Her boss had one at Christmas,' Marwick said.

'You're as silly as a goat, Peter.' He shook his head again. 'Get the box. Let's collect this one from G2.' His rationale was that he would sooner have the body when it suited him rather than when it suited the porters. He ran a tight, efficient ship.

'We going to have our tea first?' Marwick said as he pulled out the trolley with a hinged aluminium box.

'Let's have our tea first, Peter,' Betts said as he selected a capon, which he popped under the lid on the trolley.

The nurses on G2, which was an old open plan Nightingale ward, briskly drew the curtains around the twenty-eight occupied beds. This was a ritual to deny death whenever a body was collected, but one frequently repeated on the geriatric wards. On cue Andy Betts and Peter Marwick made their appearance, and an agency staffnurse opened the curtains around the bed in which the old lady had died. She had been washed and wrapped in a sheet.

Betts handed over the capon to Sister Webberburn, who paid him. He had a reputation for fresh chickens, but was amused at where he hung them, that people bought them unquestioningly, showed the same polite response they showed to death.

'She's a heavy one,' Betts said when he joined Peter Marwick and lifted the body on to the trolley.

The lid came down over the corpse and they started out, the sister handing over the record. The whole procedure was well rehearsed, and took only five minutes. Curtains were drawn back as if nothing had happened. Most people being unable to readily come to terms with death, the evolved policy was that it mustn't be seen. It was considered demoralizing both for staff and other patients to leave dead patients on display in wards; some of the patients on this ward weren't sufficiently aware to care, others were a bit confused, some were frightened by the ritual itself.

'Where's she gone?' an old lady asked, seeing the empty bed.

'She's gone, you silly old woman,' her neighbour, who was as old but much sharper, informed her.

'Gone? She didn't say goodbye.'

'She can't now. She's gone to the library.'

'I haven't read a library book in years,' she said.

'You don't want to be reading books at your age.'

Dr Marvill came on to the ward, watched by old ladies who had nothing else to do except watch any movement about the ward like that across the television screen.

The geriatric wards depressed Jessie Marvill slightly, particularly the miserable conditions the patients often existed in compared to the conditions that pertained in her previous job. What struck her most was how little the aged were thought of, shown in the absence of flowers and chocolates on their wards. She had practically lived off gifts of chocolates from ladies on the obstetrics wards; there people were so grateful to the medical and nursing staff for helping new life into the world, while no one was grateful for delaying the old in leaving.

'You think Mrs Kent may have had a CVA?' she said to Sister Webberburn, who was twenty-seven but looked eighteen.

'She ate her lunch all right,' the sister explained. 'But vomited soon after. She spat her teeth across the ward.' She handed her the patient's record. 'There seems to be a weakness on her left side.'

At the bedside of the woman in coma, Dr Marvill tried to rouse her first by calling her name; then rubbing hard on her cheek in front of her ear. Painful stimulus sometimes brought the patient to consciousness, but there was no response. With her torch Dr Marvill tested the reaction of the pupils to light. There was almost none.

'She's been unconscious since lunch?'

'Yes. We've tried several times to rouse her but haven't had much luck.'

'I think you're right. She's had a massive stroke,' Dr

Marvill said. She lifted and dropped all four limbs in turn; the tone of the muscles was poor. Moving the knees and the elbows, she found them stiffer on the affected side.

'Is that a spare bed?' Dr Marvill asked, seeing the bed being stripped by an auxiliary. She began to test the tendon reflexes: elbows, wrists, knees, ankles.

'I haven't returned it yet,' the sister said. Vacant bed returns were made from the wards three times a day. 'Dr Ravi asked me to try and hold a bed. A bit of a cheek, but when he turns on his Indian charm . . .'

'Hasn't Dr Bayliss a patient coming from orthopaedics? A Mrs Staples.'

'I don't think she is after all. They're hoping to get her mobile.'

'Oh, I see, we'll get her if they fail.'

That was the usual pattern. No one wanted bed-blocking patients, the acute specialties least of all; anticipating such cases arising they tried dumping them on the geriatricians. Since joining this firm, as part of her GP vocational training, Dr Marvill was aware of adopting what most other doctors considered to be the geriatricians' paranoia, the main symptom was the belief that they got the bad end of everything.

'We've been warned we might have to take more patients here if they succeed in closing the geriatric unit on Nightingale Block. I wish someone would tell me how.'

'Is the work-in continuing?' Dr Marvill asked. She had been asked if she would be prepared to join the picket line to stop the closure. She had said she would, but no doctors had so far.

'Have you heard anything more silly? We need more geri' beds, not less,' the sister complained.

'Maybe you should join the work-in,' Dr Marvill suggested. 'We'd better put up a drip, give her some fluids to stop her getting dehydrated. Does she have any relatives?'

Dr Marvill continued her examination with the plantar responses on the patient's feet. She ran the pointed end of the tendon hammer along the soles, causing the big toe to go up instead of down on the affected side.

'They come in nearly every day,' the sister said. 'They're one of the few what do. Seems such a shame.'

'They ought to be warned,' was Dr Marvill's conclusion.

The family would be warned that this woman could die at any time, and so given open visiting.

'It's such a shame.'

Dr Marvill didn't comment. There was nothing she could constructively add, so turned away to get a canula from the drawer and put up the intravenous drip. Despite the conditions, she enjoyed working with elderly patients. They seemed so thankful when helped towards some relief. Because they lived so close to death they forced upon her such an awareness of death that she wondered about the purpose of what she was doing.

That was a path Jessie Marvill's thoughts were travelling along more and more, but each time she found herself there, like now, she instead moved on to a practical function which extended the patient's life just a little.

37

The full Medical Committee for the District of which St. Clair's was a part, comprised of every doctor holding a consultant post, and met on a regular basis. In theory every consultant was entitled to attend, but in practice only a familiar coterie did, mostly to help formulate policy which reflected the interest of their own specialties. If a consultant who didn't ordinarily attend showed up, it was often because something on the agenda directly affected his or her specialty.

All things were discussed, but a topic often dominating meetings was the loss of beds due to closures, lack of nursing staff, shortage of money. Taking up a lot of time at the meeting in the boardroom this afternoon was the imminent closure of Nightingale Block; which had brought howls of protest from all areas of health care, and had caused the work-in by the staff in the one remaining functional ward, which was for chronic female geriatrics. This accounted for the fact that four of the eight consultants present were geriatricians. Mr Smith-Sampson, the senior consultant surgeon, who chaired the meeting, had invited Stephen Morwell the District Administrator, and Basil Hart, the District treasurer, as they were believed allies in avoiding closure rather than instruments in achieving it.

'What might the Authority's next move be?' Dr Carl Bayliss asked. 'Assuming Nightingale isn't closed as ordered?' He was a geriatrician whose beds were at St Clair's.

A geriatrician from Queen's Hospital, one twenty years younger, said, 'More to the point, are we going to allow this perfectly useful unit to be closed?'

'That's what we're discussing, Dr Cambell,' Mr Smith-Sampson said, in a mildly censuring way, 'even though I'm not sure it's part of our brief.' He didn't want to be part of any presumption that this committee would rubber stamp moves to prevent the legal closure of Nightingale.

'Whether it is or not,' Dr Cambell argued, 'we should have some clear policy. Personally I hope this committee will endorse the sacrifices being made by some staff members over this issue.'

'I think the moral support of consultants would prove valuable,' Stephen Morwell said. He had resisted the closure when it had been taken up by Region as a means of saving money, but he didn't know how long he could avoid implementing that decision now. He was rather hoping his committee would approve the closure, so that his principled stand could be seen to be overwhelmed by the opposition. 'I'm not sure how it will relate in practical terms. Region has overruled us. District's failure to implement closure could result in several courses of action. One would certainly be a financial embargo.'

'Could District finance the unit?' asked Dr Ghullam Ravi, the geriatrician from St Clair's.

'Up to a point,' Basil Hart told him. 'But only within this financial term. To run that twenty-two-bedded unit costs on current estimates, £290,000 per annum. This takes no account of inflation. Being funded from Region, there's no question of our meeting such a shortfall, not without closing some other department. That basically is the choice we are faced with.' He felt no attachment to any particular area of this hospital, Queen's or any of the other units within his District. Accepting the need to save money, he saw shutting Nightingale Block as a rational move.

'This is avoiding the critical issue, Mr Hart,' Dr Bayliss said. His sole concern was for patients. 'What are we to do with the twenty-two chronic patients occupying those beds?

The problem won't disappear with the closure of this unit as Region seems to imagine. There are no spare beds for them.'

'I am aware of the situation. It's for those reasons I haven't implemented closure,' Stephen Morwell said. 'All of these arguments have been put to Region.'

'But this whole saving is made nonsense of by the fact that the equivalent sum, in the form of a Capital Grant, is to be spent upgrading this ward,' Bayliss said angrily. Although he argued frequently that his patients should have no fewer facilities simply because they were old, he believed passionately that it was better for them to have beds on an old ward rather than no beds on a smartly upgraded ward.

'That does seem a monumental waste,' Mr Barry Sunderland, a vascular surgeon, suggested. 'Especially as there won't be finance available to run these upgraded wards.'

'The main plank of Region's argument, as I understand it,' Mr Philip Montagu ventured, 'is that there are sufficient geriatric beds. I'm inclined to agree.'

This brought protests from the geriatricians, none of whom attended regularly or were as skilful in committee as Philip Montagu.

'I've never heard anything so outrageous. I see no shortage of gynae beds, Philip,' Dr Bayliss said. 'Most major medical problems occur in the elderly, without their attracting anything like major financing.' This was a sore point with Carl Bayliss, who became increasingly frustrated at seeing most of the available funds going to the more glamorous specialties.

'I quite agree, Carl. The aged are a serious social problem,' Mr Montagu responded. 'But it will not be solved by increasing hospital beds. Many of these old people aren't medical problems at all. They should be looked after elsewhere.'

'Alternative services suffer the same fate,' Dr Ravi said. 'They are having money taken out of them.'

'These sort of patients should be looked after by their families,' Mr Montagu said, ignoring his colleagues' anger.

'Indeed?' Dr Bayliss appeared enlightened. 'The fact that that doesn't work is part of a much larger problem. We're dealing with a relatively new phenomenon. The old, one might say, are a medical success story. However, what's been neglected in the process is learning how to cope with the old in such numbers. Often the young and the middle-aged resent and fear their dependence, and don't want them as part of their family. Sometimes it's simply that they've moved away to new neighbourhoods and the councils in those boroughs won't take on these elderly people.'

'To some extent the situation will improve as unemployment increases,' Montagu suggested as if that was an equitable solution. 'There'll be more female relatives at home to take care of the elderly.'

'That doesn't alter the fact that we seem unable to deal with the aged as a social problem,' Bayliss said.

Philip Montagu shrugged. He was pleased not to be dealing with the aged himself.

'I fear things are going to get worse in this area,' Morwell said after an awkward silence, 'especially if the government succeed in changing the financial arrangements of the NHS.'

'What alternative action is open to Region should the closure continue to be opposed, Stephen?' asked Dr Cloutman, the radiotherapist. He was a friend of Mr Montagu's, and often supported him in committee.

'They could physically remove the patients.'

'Then we'd better warn the staff on Nightingale,' Dr Cambell said. 'Have them strengthen the picket line.'

Although Dr Cambell said that with a smile, it embarrassed the chairman. He wanted to somehow divorce himself from the remark, while at the same time avoid showing his bias. 'I think we've detained Mr Morwell and Mr Hart long enough,' Mr Smith-Sampson said. 'I suggest this committee calls on them to make further approaches to Region for a stay of execution on Nightingale's geriatric unit.'

There was general agreement except from Philip Montagu, who believed that keeping the block open served no beneficial purpose. It did however delay the plans for his clinic, which no one here knew about, not even Reginald Cloutman. Montagu wasn't sure how much longer he should delay pursuing alternative sites. After his meeting with George Christian, the Regional Administrator, Montagu was optimistic that the block would be closed, but now it appeared the battle was likely to drag on.

The week had been frustrating for George Christian, who had been seen to lose face several times over Nightingale Block. Determined that this situation shouldn't continue, he had invited Stephen Morwell to discuss the position. But despite this reasoned approach to the District administrator, he still wasn't prepared to meet him even halfway.

Stephen Morwell simply restated his position. His District Management Team saw Nightingale as a viable part of St Clair's. There was a real need to expand the service rather than contract it. Stephen Morwell believed that there was a determination on someone's part to reduce the size of the District, and this was something he would stridently resist.

'Is it a question that having declared your position you don't want to be seen to go back on it?' the Regional administrator asked. 'Or do you feel unable to give that instruction to sector?'

'There's no question of that,' Morwell said from the opposite side of the desk in the comfortable but cramped office. 'If I told Roy Needham to arrange the evacuation of the chronic geriatrics I'm sure he'd give the orders. But I have little expectation of it happening. The unions would refuse. They've indicated as much.'

'This is arrant nonsense. Hospitals aren't run for their benefit,' Christian said. He didn't openly display anger, but the observant might have noticed a set in the jaw, the ridging of his neck and shoulders with tension.

'What I'm less certain about, George, is where these patients would go,' Morwell said.

'Oh come on, Stephen, you know there's always a corner they can fit into. Mightn't some be sent home?' Christian suggested. He agreed with Philip Montagu, that a lot of the patients occupying geriatric beds shouldn't be in hospital.

'With respect, George,' Morwell said, 'that's a decision for the geriatricians.'

'There's an urgent need for rationalization. Geriatricians, along with everyone else, must be made to realize this. We are approaching a deepening financial crisis,' he said, repeating his earlier argument. 'Nightingale Block has to close. If you can't organize it, Stephen, then I'll do it myself.'

That ended the discussion.

Implementing that move personally was what George Christian was finally brought to, and then met nothing but opposition, from ward staff to ambulance service control officer whom he telephoned to arrange transport.

'How many ambulances have you available for this afternoon?' Christian asked. His impatience and his tension were increasing with each negative response.

'None, I'm afraid, Mr Christian,' Peter Cheney, the control officer said, staring from the window of his small office at the twelve ambulances parked in the yard.

'None?' Christian didn't attempt to disguise his disbelief. 'Are you suggesting that if there was an accident outside here you couldn't send an ambulance?'

'The position changes from hour to hour, sir,' Peter Cheney said uneasily. 'Could be I'll have ten vehicles come available in the next fifteen minutes.'

'Then let us assume that some vehicles will be available,' Christian said labouredly. 'Would you muster all you can spare at Regional offices at 2 P.M. to evacuate twenty-two patients from a block we're closing.'

Peter Cheney hesitated. 'At Regional offices? I'll see what I can do for you.' Rather than put that to his drivers and have them refuse to cross the picket line, he would make sure they were all on calls.

'At two o'clock,' George Christian confirmed. 'Thank you Mr Cheney.' He replaced the phone believing he had won a battle at least.

However he waited in vain. Two o'clock arrived without any ambulances. Tension built up in George Christian's neck and shoulders bringing him to the point of screaming; he felt foolish waiting on the steps of the building for the ambulances to arrive, as though not trusting the commissionaire to inform him, believing he was part of some conspiracy. Adding to his intractable feelings of isolation were the looks he received from people going in and out of the building. He was convinced they were laughing at him over his plan being thwarted. That made him more determined.

'It's the unions, George,' said Francis Yeldham, the small, slightly effeminate Regional Nursing Officer, as he joined Christian in the entrance of the modern building. 'They've stopped the ambulances. The drivers are refusing to transport patients from Nightingale Block.'

'We'll see about that,' Christian said. 'We'll get private ambulances. That unit is going to be closed. We'll have some of the office staff go with us and dismantle the equipment.'

The situation was getting to be ridiculous, but he didn't for a moment consider withdrawing.

Helped by both the Regional Nursing Officer and the Treasurer, he phoned all the private ambulance firms within a radius of twenty-five miles. Most were pleased by the inquiry from the Regional Health Authority, and those whose vehicles were required elsewhere regretted not being able to accommodate the authority at such short notice. Not one baulked at the nature of the job.

A fleet of fifteen ambulances was cobbled together, vehicles varying in shape and size and ranging from VWs to Vauxhall estate cars, but all bearing the legend ambulance. Arriving outside Nightingale Block, which was a former workhouse and like a separate hospital within St Clair's, they encountered a picket of nurses, technicians and ancillaries. Their hastily penned notices read: 'Beds Not Bureaucracy' 'Patients Before £s' 'The Old Have Rights Too!'

Variations of these were chanted at George Christian and his gang as they entered the building. No one tried to forcibly stop them, though some wanted to.

Despite having agreed in theory to the move, in practice the Regional medical officer disapproved, but came along to make sure no patient suffered physically in the move; however, he wouldn't have cared to give an opinion as to their mental and emotional states as a result.

On the female geriatric ward pandemonium descended as the few patients who could walk were led away, some in day-clothes, others in their night-clothes; others were wheeled out on anything with wheels, wheelchairs, beds and trolleys; some of them left without any of their personal effects; some patients wouldn't see those again. The patients were totally bewildered as office workers proceeded to wreck the equipment, barely giving them time to get clear before turning over beds and lockers, ripping down curtains. George Christian was making certain that this ward couldn't be re-occupied in a hurry.

'You ought to be thoroughly ashamed of yourself, Mr Christian,' Sister Adams said. She was fifty, and in all her time as a nurse she had never encountered anything so disgraceful.

George Christian simply turned away, not about to debate health service economics.

Trembling with anger, Sister Adams came near to hitting this man with the potted plant she had managed to rescue. Instead she hurried along the ward to help a patient.

With the patients out of Nightingale Block the problem of what to do with them remained. This mostly fell to the deputy administrator, and the bed allocations officer, Maureen Day, who knew from her chart that there were only seven available beds in the entire hospital, none of them geriatric. This meant Jenny Rogers trying to juggle and rearrange beds to create space. Two hours intensive effort resulted in space being found for seven patients.

When Jenny Rogers returned to the administrator's offices hot from running around, and far from a solution, the secretary extended the telephone to her. 'Jenny, bed allocations.'

'Good news, I hope.' She went into her adjacent office and dropped the folders on her desk.

'Maureen,' she said, picking up the phone. 'Have you found some more empty beds?'

'Two on the surgical wing – they're sending two patients home,' she said, pleased with herself.

'These are long-stay geriatrics,' she reminded her. 'What about the other thirteen?'

'There are only two beds available anywhere,' Maureen Day said. 'Mr Thompson's not pleased about having them used for geriatrics, not even for one night.'

'Oh well, we'll have to squeeze more beds on to the acute geriatric wards. Thanks, Maureen. I'll come back to you.'

That was the only solution. But neither the patients in transit, those on the geriatric ward nor the staff were consulted. The geriatricians expressed disbelief when the scheme was put to them, both at the fact that anyone could show such insensitivity towards patients, or that more beds could be got on to their wards. But because they were caring people, and couldn't display similar insensitivity, they had no option but to agree. But not without resentment for an authority that could allow this situation in the first place.

38

As a result of pressure by the vascular surgeons budgets were rearranged at District so that more pacemakers could be purchased. The consultants didn't care how the money was found and despite protests from the administration they didn't believe that such a relatively small amount of money couldn't be found, and threatened to talk to the media if it wasn't. Whether because of the prospect of tabloid headlines: 'Patients Sent Home to Die' or the reality of that, District yielded, and the pacemakers were purchased. But an order for two pieces of X-ray equipment was subsequently cancelled.

The misfortune of those who would suffer yet longer delays in the X-ray department meant that Henry Staples could have a permanent pacemaker fitted into his chest. This was done for him under a local anaesthetic by Mr Barry Sunderland.

'You didn't feel that, Mr Staples?' he said as he made his incision.

'No,' Henry Staples said as he felt a sharp, prickling sensation.

'Soon be done now.' He slid the internal pacemaker, which was the size of a small pack of playing cards, through the chest incision.

'What's this for?' the question popped out of Henry Staples's silent thoughts when he was only vaguely aware of the surgeons talking to each other.

'Didn't Dr Crick explain?' the surgeon asked. He glanced at his SHO. 'We took the hat round and managed to buy you a permanent pacer – it'll give you a new heart, Henry. Don't you want that?'

'What I want is a new bike,' he said for something to say. He knew more or less what the pacer did, but no one had explained why he should have it.

'Not our department, old man,' Mr Sunderland told him. 'Who would fit him up in that area, Jack?' he said to his SHO.

'Callisthenics, I imagine,' the SHO said, joining in the joke. 'I think there's an enormous waiting list.'

''S not natural, all this stuff,' the old man said, following his own thoughts.

'Why's that, Henry?'

'Stands to reason when you wear out it's time to go,' Henry Staples said. 'When I was a young man I could lift a three-hundred-weight anvil. Now I can't do in a week what it took me a day to do then.'

'You've a few years yet, you old rascal,' Mr Sunderland advised him.

Henry Staples's thoughts drifted back to when he was a young man and all the things he had been able to do then. He had dug roads for the Gas Board, kept three allotments, entered and won all sorts of road trials on his bicycles. It was at times like this that he regretted being old. The only thing he didn't regret was that his lady was still with him.

Back on the ward his activity increased and he was impatient to get out of hospital. But the nurses made him slow down, and he noticed how tired he became.

Henry was on his bed dozing, half-dreaming about cycling to Brighton and back comfortably in a day when the Medical Unit Nursing Officer, Sandra Flockhart, appeared on her ward round with the sister.

'Everything all right, Mr Staples?' She preferred to assume it was, rather than listen to patients and went on without awaiting his reply. 'That's good. I think you should share your secret – how you look so fit.'

'Mr Staples has his pacemaker fitted,' Sister Godwin said. 'It's settled down nicely.'

'I'm missing my lady,' Henry Staples said as if he were part of the conversation. 'Why can't she come here with me?' Someone had suggested that, but nothing had happened.

'Oh, I can see you'll be leaving us very soon,' Sandra Flockhart joked, dismissing his question. At one time a husband and wife could have shared a side ward, but the hospital was too short of beds and staff at present to organize that.

'Mr Staples's wife dislocated her hip,' the sister said.

'Ah yes, she's on orthopaedics.' A seventy-eight-year-old with such an injury was unusual enough for the NO to be aware of.

'I think she's gone to geriatrics. Now Mr Staples is more mobile he can visit her.'

'Good idea,' Miss Flockhart said. 'It'll cheer her up.'

The porter who wheeled Henry Staples across to the female geriatric ward was Spanish and had little in the way of conversation, despite the old man's valiant attempt. When they couldn't find Mrs Staples, Henry assumed he had been brought to the wrong ward. His spirits, which had risen at the prospect of seeing his wife, sank as the porter pushed him on to G2. The geriatric ward was so crowded, there was barely space between the beds.

Tears came to Henry Staples's eyes as he stared around the ward while the porter went to find out where Mrs Staples was. He became depressed at the thought of his wife being here; those unfortunates who were here looked as if they were waiting to die. Until then he hadn't associated death with something anyone waited for. He never had, and all his family had died in harness.

'They make mistake,' the porter announced when he returned. 'She not come from orthopaedics. We go there.'

'She's on the other ward?' Henry Staples said, his spirits lifting at once. 'Oh, on another ward, is she, you say? On the other ward still?' He clapped his hands together.

'We find. Don't worry.' The porter spun his chair round and pushed him out.

A depression settled over Henry Staples again when he found his wife on the modern orthopaedic ward. The reason was that she was confused and didn't seem to know him. She had been confused when he had seen her here before, but only a bit more than she had been at home – forgetting his name, or what she was saying halfway through. Like many old people the Staples both suffered from mild dementia and had coped with it untroubled until this upset, which brought them to the notice of people able to diagnose the complaint. Now they would each get progressively worse.

'My husband's down his allotment,' Mrs Staples said lucidly, but like she was talking to a stranger. 'Keeps us in vegetables, he do . . . lovely and fresh. Why I've never had to buy vegetables.'

'Joanny, I give up m' allotment four year ago – it got too much for me,' he told her. But she wasn't listening.

'He keeps us in vegetables. I don't know what we'd've done without it. Dig for victory, they said on the wireless. You should'a seen them onions he grew, got prizes they did. Got prizes.'

Henry Staples smiled at the recollection. 'I won the local show three years on the trot. '56, '57, '58,' he said, not without pride. 'There was some stiff competition them days. They didn't watch telly all the time like now.'

'That was before the war.' Mrs Staples paused then suddenly said, 'He died in the war, he did.' The memory might have been an old photograph long ago tucked away and rediscovered.

'Don't be daft, Joanny,' the old man chided, starting to lose patience. 'I'm here. It was our two boys what died. Henry and George what died.'

'We lost two boys,' the old woman recalled. 'Mrs Simpkins lost one of her'n. And Mrs Watson. Got a telegram this morning.'

'Joanny, that was 1942.' Henry Staples remembered as though yesterday. Their son Henry had been a sailor on HMS *Edinburgh*, which had been fatally damaged in action in the North Sea on 2 May with the loss of thirty lives. George had been killed a year later in North Africa.

'Overnight her hair went white. The shock you see.' She stopped and looked along the ward. 'They'll bring round the tea soon. Bit of bread and butter, a bit of jam sponge. 'S hard to get hold of jam what with rationing. We make our own, when there's a bit of sugar spare.'

The confusion was no different throughout the entire hour of his visit with her, and it was as much as Henry could do to hold back his tears. He no longer could on returning to his own ward. He felt too upset to eat his supper, and so distressed that he didn't want to go on with life. No one explained to him why his wife had gone a bit daft. Having progressed so well himself, he expected her to make equal progress.

Long after the main lights on the ward went out, Henry Staples lay awake crying, though he made no noise. He wished his son Albert was here instead of in Australia, as he needed someone to talk to, family rather than a doctor or nurse.

Henry Staples vacantly watched the black male charge nurse check on a coma patient in the bed opposite, turning him with the help of a student nurse.

Noticing Mr Staples's restlessness, he came across. 'What's the matter, Henry?' he asked. 'Can't sleep?'

Henry Staples didn't want to talk to this nurse, but felt even he was better than no one.

'What's the problem, man? Your pacemaker troubling you?' The immediate assumption of medical and nursing staff was that any problem was physical – that was easier to deal with.

Henry Staples shook his head. 'She don't know me,' he

said. 'My wife. Fifty-eight years we been married.' There was a heaviness in his words. Right then he would have liked to have closed his eyes and let go himself.

'She will. Give her time,' the charge nurse told him. 'They sometimes get confused after a bump on the head, even the young ones, Henry. The anaesthetic probably jumbled things up for her a bit more. It often plays people up, especially when they're getting on.' He wondered about telling this patient that.

'She thought she was back in the war,' Henry said.

'I've seen that happen. Someone should have warned you,' Charge Nurse Thomas said, annoyed that the staff on orthopaedics hadn't done so. 'It could last a week or two. Then she'll settle down.'

'She didn't know who I was.' At that moment Henry Staples was like a child who refused to be consoled.

'I'll see about getting you something to help you sleep,' the charge nurse said, resorting to the familiar solution.

39

One more effect of cuts in health care spending, though one generally unnoticed, was that appointments to consultant posts were becoming less frequent; this was another source of frustration for junior doctors, and despite protests to the Regional Health Authorities no change of policy was imminent. There was nowhere for newly appointed consultants to go anyway. The only clear opening for a junior doctor to be appointed to a consultant post was if the incumbent retired. Then the competition was desperate and it by no means followed that the senior registrar of the firm would be appointed. Now that Mr Smith-Sampson was retiring, Vernon Davis, his senior registrar, had been short-listed, but with no expectation of being appointed; not because he hadn't jumped through the required hoops, or published enough papers; even though he despised the former practice, and knew the latter was for the surgeon's prestige rather than the advancement of medicine.

The Regional Health Authority was the sole arbiter of a consultant post appointment except in those made within a teaching district, which St Clair's was part of. Here fellow consultants had a lot of the say about Mr Smith-Sampson's successor and vetted the candidates' social suitability through the consultants' sherry party. Every consultant in the District was invited to this, along with the junior doctors who had reached the short-list.

Not all the consultants attended the party held in the mess at Queen's, but most of the cutters did. The four short-listed junior doctors had made a special effort with their appearance, even Vernon Davis, who knew this gathering was a charade, that the choice had already been made through the lobbying by consultants. This social function was the prelude to the rubber stamp of the appointments board.

Mr Ronald Smith-Sampson was being treated very deferentially by everyone, and especially the other three candidates. These were Mr David Passmore, Mr Daniel Steele and Mr Charles Buckingham. Although eminently qualified, having got his Fellowship to the Royal College, which entitled him to Mr rather than Dr, Vernon Davis felt that his presence was tokenism; they were being seen to be fair in short-listing him, but in fact he believed this was Mr Smith-Sampson's way of humiliating him, by showing that he could influence his career badly right to the last. Nothing dissuaded Vernon Davis in that view and the bitterness he felt towards Mr Smith-Sampson began to surface, aided by his fifth glass of dry sherry.

'I read your paper on vertebral reconstruction after laminectomy,' Marcus Thompson was saying to a candidate with some impressive papers to his name. 'Did you find any significantly increased neurological deficit resulting from the procedure?'

'Not much,' Mr Charles Buckingham told him, feeling flattered by the attention of this surgeon. 'It's relatively early days. But it certainly seems to be more successful than straightforward excision coupled with needle biopsy.'

'I would quite like to take a dekko at what you have,' Marcus Thompson said.

'Most of it's been published,' Buckingham said. 'But you'd be welcome to see the patient follow-up.'

'I wouldn't have thought general surgery was the ideal place for you,' Mr Thompson said. 'You seem to have a leaning towards neurosurgery.'

'Not really, sir. I see myself specializing in major malignancies. This post seems logical enough.' He smiled, having every expectation of pleasing this consultant for wanting to enter his own specialized field.

Illogically feeling a sense of threat, Marcus Thompson gave him an abrupt nod. 'I wish you luck,' he said, and went to seek out another candidate, having decided not to support Buckingham, preferring his own man instead.

Having reached the mandatory retirement age, Ronald Smith-Sampson wasn't entirely giving up his involvement with the hospital, but was remaining on several committees. His current interest centred less on the candidates' ability, which he took for granted, than their politics. There were altogether too many radical elements creeping into medicine, to the detriment of patients, he believed.

Despite knowing that David Passmore was sound in his thinking, Smith-Sampson said, 'That was an unpleasant business at the geriatric unit the other day.' He was referring to the work-in by staff faced with the ward closure, and the general support they received within the hospital.

'It's quite extraordinary what junior staff concern themselves with nowadays,' Mrs Smith-Sampson said passively.

David Passmore glanced between them, looking for another clue before committing his opinion. He had met Mrs Smith-Sampson socially several times, and she always seemed to talk as an adjunct to her husband. 'Yes, quite extraordinary.' He was on safe ground, he thought, though he didn't believe junior doctors were on the picket.

'If there's a need to close uneconomic units then it must be done without anyone interfering. That kind of political activity won't improve a junior doctor's career prospects,' Mr Smith-Sampson said. 'Not if I have anything to say about it.'

Thinking about Vernon Davis's involvement with the junior doctors' committee, David Passmore was glad he had taken no part himself. 'Yes, I agree,' he said. 'There's scarcely enough time for one's clinical work.'

The Smith-Sampsons were smiling now, as if at a son's

good exam result.

'This sherry party's a bloody charade,' Vernon Davis said in an agitated fashion to Mr Barry Sunderland, whom he almost fell against. He realized that consultants in the surgical specialties were conspicuously avoiding him. 'I know the appointment's decided long before we get to this. I'm not going to be appointed, I know I'm not,' he insisted, as if being given an argument. 'I've nothing to lose from speaking frankly. Smith-Sampson's had it in for me ever since I was foolish enough to criticize him. He's a vindictive man who won't admit his mistakes . . .'

'I think you're imagining things,' Mr Sunderland said. 'Everyone thinks highly of your work. Excuse me.' He tried to walk away, but Davis held him.

'I'm not imagining it. He was past it years ago. I deserve this post, if only for putting up with his bile, covering up his mistakes. He won't even give me a reference, that's how vindictive he is. I forced him to retire . . .'

'Look, they're signalling for me,' Mr Sunderland said, extricating himself from Vernon Davis.

That left Vernon Davis in limbo, unable to control his facial tics as familiar feelings of paranoia closed in on him. He was aware that people were talking about him. He finished his sherry and grabbed another from a waitress, who came past with a tray. He looked around the room for someone sympathetic to hear his story, but people seemed to avoid his eyes. His gaze fell upon Mr Smith-Sampson who held his look for a moment. Knowing that the consultant was talking about him, enjoying the prospect of the humiliation he was about to make him suffer, Vernon Davis decided to take the initiative.

As he approached Mr Smith-Sampson, his unsteadiness was due more to tension than booze. He seized the consultant's hand and shook it, causing him to spill his drink.

'Congratulations on your long overdue retirement, sir,'

he said, making a spectacle of himself. 'Jus' to show there're no hard feelings.'

'I think you're drunk, Mr Davis,' Smith-Sampson said, mopping the sherry off his hand.

'This whole bloody thing is a farce,' Mr Davis said. 'I don't want this bloody appointment . . .'

'You won't get it,' the consultant said in a fit of pique.

A smile of triumph sped across Vernon Davis's face, but the feeling it brought was too tenuous to build on.

'You're retiring not a moment too soon,' he managed before Dr Mathias interrupted from across the room.

'Ladies and gentlemen,' he said, quietening the burble. 'If I might just deflect from the main purpose of this worthy gathering. I would like to remind you about the recently launched children's liver transplant fund. As most of you are aware, our target is half a million pounds. To help towards this figure Mr Sunderland has generously agreed to raffle one thousand pounds' worth of his services for cosmetic surgery. This will lift a face, or a tummy, or even a bottom, I'm reliably informed.' There were polite ripples of laughter. 'I hope you'll all take lots of tickets and sell them to your friends. I don't need to remind you how worthy the cause is.'

There was loud applause, both for the cause and the surgeon's generosity. In this current enthusiasm no one remembered a similar launch eighteen months ago for a renal dialysis unit. Or possibly some of those present weren't aware what had happened to the unit. It had stopped taking patients because District could no longer afford to run it. The unit was paid for entirely out of public donations; however, after the initial enthusiasm that got the target figure raised, there was no fund to run it, and no willingness on the part of the public to run it by subscription.

The same fate would befall the children's liver transplant unit. The mother who had started raising money after her child had died from a liver disease had been encouraged by the clinicians; the belief was that once the unit had been set up and donated, the District would then be obliged to go on funding it. It was an erroneous belief.

Turning around in order to harangue Mr Smith-Sampson some more, Vernon Davis found both the consultant and his onion-nosed wife had gone; so he pursued a waitress for a drink to console himself over his poor career prospects.

Coincidentally there was a party at the medical centre at St Clair's on the same evening as the consultants' sherry party. This was to send two doctors off to Western Australia.

The party was necessarily a noisy, boisterous affair, with lots of booze and child-like games, all of which were sex-orientated. They were mostly doctors present but some nurses had been invited, and some of them, like the doctors, were still on duty. Four couples each with a balloon between them, tried to rise off the floor without losing contact with the balloon to blaring music, clapping and cries of encouragement. A loud roar went up as one couple almost achieved this before someone with a lighted cigarette burst the balloon.

Jessie Marvill watched with mild amusement, being too tired to enter into the spirit of this, and the wine she had drunk wasn't helping. She was no more amused by an earlier game that had entailed pouring Rice Krispies down the necks of participants, who shook them out while drinking a pint of beer – no mean feat. Although childish, she knew the games helped doctors shed a lot of their tension, which was something they most needed to do, herself included. All too frequently alcohol was the means of relaxation, and there were times when Jessie Marvill recognized that she drank too much both for her own good, and that of patients, were she to be called out. Drinking for need was a habit that often started in post-graduate medical school where one tended to be overcrammed with information, both theoretical and practical, but taught not at all how to deal with the emotional problems that the job threw up. Jessie Marvill remembered her first encounter with death as a medical student; the registrar who had taken her and four other students to a death on the ward had them look through the dead woman's eye with an ophthalmoscope to examine the blood vessels. This had meant her putting her cheek almost against that of the corpse. That experience, like many others, had left an uneasy impression. At her teaching hospital fellow students participated in the Charing Cross Country Club. Twenty were allowed to belong at any one time, and once a month they drank themselves absolutely blotto. The one who was deemed the most sober at the end of the session had to resign and another took his place. There were no shortages of students waiting to join, and Jessie understood why. This was a familiar pattern, one hard to break; booze or drugs were used to sublimate unresolved emotions. At one time she had picked up men and gone to bed with them as a means of avoiding her feelings. She thought about doing that now, but told herself she had grown out of that. She had a yearning for a worthwhile sexual experience, which casual sex didn't satisfy. Not having a steady relationship created sexual imbalance, which brought emotional imbalance; she thought of Laurence James at Northwick Park, and wondered about looking for a job that way herself. But in reality she would take an accredited job for her vocational training scheme wherever she could get one. Moving around so much on short-term contracts often created difficulties in relationships, and contributed to the high incidence of broken marriages.

She stopped herself thinking about that when Roger Trentham approached her with a two-litre bottle of wine, and she let him refill her glass. Later she would inevitably go back to his room with him. That wasn't the result of her former boyfriend getting a contract at this hospital. The odd occasions before when she had agreed to meet him usually ended with their sleeping together. Each time Roger Trentham hoped it would mean the resurrection of their relationship; for Jessie it was another bad habit, one she knew was preventing her forming a permanent relationship elsewhere.

Striding across the darkened hospital, drawn towards the party noise like a moth to candlelight was Night Nursing Officer Connie Price. She was a grandmother in her early fifties who had gone back to nursing after her family had grown up; this made her a more tolerant administrator.

Unlike doctors who punched out a code to open the door, her means of entry was by ringing the bell. Eventually the door was opened.

'Ah, matron,' the drunken doctor at the door said expansively. 'Glad you could come. What are you drinking?'

'No thank you, doctor. I came to ask if you could bring the noise down a wee bit. There have been complaints.' She knew there was probably little point in telling this doctor, but at least she had tried.

'Of course. Just a wee bit,' he said, mocking her accent. Behind him was a loud roar as a couple got up off the floor without bursting their balloon.

Most complaints and problems at night found their way to Connie Price, other than strictly medical problems, and sometimes even those when the medical staff weren't around. As was the case when later that night Mrs Staples attempted to get out of bed on the orthopaedic ward and had some sort of fit when the nursing staff prevented her.

Dr Philip Assersohn was the SHO on call, but he didn't respond. Dr Sainsbury, the registrar, wasn't available either. Probably both were at the party, which took Connie Price back to the social club. Both had been there, but no longer were. She was told Dr Assersohn had gone to his room.

Connie Price wondered if the doctor would be in any fit state to see a patient as she went briskly along the top corridor of the doctors' block. She rapped softly on Dr Assersohn's door so as not to wake others who might have been sleeping.

'Dr Assersohn?' She rapped again. 'Dr Assersohn, are you awake?' She knocked once more, louder now. 'Dr Assersohn.'

Finally the door was thrown open by the confused SHO, who was both drunk and naked.

'I believe you're on call tonight, doctor,' the woman said. 'You didn't answer your bleep.'

''Sright,' slurred Dr Assersohn. 'I'll come right away.' He started into the corridor.

Connie Price smiled at the notion of him going to the ward like that, but was too kind to allow it. She steered him back to his room. 'Don't bother, doctor. I'll find someone else.'

In the entrance of the block she met Jessie Marvill, who was returning to her room, having avoided the assumption by Roger Trentham that she would spend the night with him. The Night Nursing Officer explained the problem and asked if she would see Mrs Staples.

At first her reaction was to say no, she was tired and she wanted to go to bed, and this was an orthopaedic call. But she knew that wasn't realistic. As she went off to the ward she felt anxious as her tired thoughts tried to come to terms with her first instinct being to say no, fearing she was becoming that sort of doctor.

Dr Marvill thought the old woman had suffered a CVA. The stroke had been mild and wouldn't be incapacitating, there would be perceptible slowing in movement and possibly some speech difficulty. During the examination she realized that this was the patient they had at one time been expecting on the geriatric ward, and wondered if they would now get her as this set-back would delay her departure from hospital.

Returning to her room she met Satish Kumar, who had been to a crash-call and looked terrible, Jessie thought. He greeted her formally.

'Were you called from the party?' she asked, not having noticed him there.

'No, I was asleep,' he told her. 'It is a great shock to the system, even when the sleep is troubled.'

Having once done a stint on the crash-call team, Jessie Marvill could sympathize. Even the sound of someone else's crash-call bleep had set her running for months after her stint was finished, and still her heart would contract whenever she heard one. Worse than the starting was the returning in the middle of the night, when one was expected to go back to sleep. Some doctors found that impossible after a life-or-death struggle for a patient, one they became involved in, regardless of professional detachment. This was Dr Kumar's problem, Jessie Marvill realized, when they reached her room on the first floor corridor. The man was tense, on edge, in need of talking out. Offering him coffee seemed the least she could do.

At first he declined, and Jessie was glad to be able to get to her own bed, but she pressed him, suspecting he was being polite. Unlike a lot of his male colleagues, he assumed nothing, he even seemed embarrassed about being in her room at two o'clock in the morning, whereas most might have interpreted coffee as a prelude to her bed. The small room wasn't made for entertaining, and he had to sit on the bed while she made coffee in the electric percolator.

'I don't have any milk, Satish,' she said.

'That is quite all right.'

'Was your patient okay?'

'I think I will get another call tonight.'

'Are you on tomorrow?'

'Yes. But it makes no difference, whether I am or not called again,' Dr Kumar said. 'I cannot sleep after I am woken up. I try to avoid taking Mogadon.'

'Very wise.'

While she made the coffee he talked with alarm about the numbers of doctors who took drugs to help them sleep, then more drugs to help them wake. He spoke about his work in the hospital, and how difficult he found relating to people who often weren't truly ill, or had knowingly invited their illness.

That was a dilemma most doctors had to learn to live with and she wondered if he wasn't being unrealistic, especially as he wasn't particularly young.

'What do you plan on doing eventually?' Jessie Marvill asked.

'I will return home and practise medicine. Not the medicine we practise here. We have not such advanced technology outside of the cities. I would not want that. I will go into the interior with my wife when she has qualified. She is studying in Bombay. There is a need of doctors who can treat people by holistic methods, and help to educate them.'

'That sounds worthwhile,' Jessie Marvill said. She was becoming less sure by the day of what she truly wanted to do, and admired those who did know. 'Is that what you've always wanted?'

'No. I wanted an important practice with rich patients. But experiencing what is available here, and seeing how medical technology is often used to counter material debauchery, it made me realize that my country should not be striving for this.'

'I often wonder about the expectations of third-world doctors in the West,' Jessie said.

'Conditioning makes most want the same technical advancement for their own countries,' Dr Kumar said. 'That is a desirable goal until one considers how unsuitable to third-world culture high-technology medicine is. Also what its ill effects are.'

This wasn't new to Jessie Marvill, but was something she avoided thinking about.

'Sometimes I think this is the underdeveloped society. In India we still have God, after all. Science is all the time trying to find cures for disease, while food technologists are inventing new ways to cause disease. Unfortunately my government wants all this because of the prestige it brings. But soon the treatment becomes part of the disease. Because treatment is so widely available people think they are doing entirely as they wish with their health.'

'I'm not sure everyone is like that,' Jessie Marvill said, instinctively defensive about her profession rather than with a deep belief that he was wrong. 'I do know the feeling.'

'Yes, I possibly exaggerate.'

'Could the medical advances in your country be arrested?' Dr Marvill asked, knowing that nothing could be uninvented. 'Isn't the sort of medicine that's demanded directly related to the patient's awareness of what's available?'

'Only here is that true. Gandhi once said: "Earth provides enough to satisfy every man's need, but not his greed". Ironically good health is incompatible with high-technology medicine.'

They talked till past five o'clock when Dr Kumar was bleeped to his patient with the cardiac arrest. At this abrupt end of their conversation Jessie Marvill felt it should have just been starting. She envied the man his clarity of purpose, and wondered briefly about joining his barefoot medical practice in some remote region of India. Had he suggested that she would have committed herself at once. Almost any alternative was preferable to the battering she felt she was getting in the present system.

The Consultant Appointments Committee, which met in the boardroom at St Clair's to appoint the successor to Mr Smith-Sampson, comprised an outside assessor, who was a professor of surgery from the University of London; a lay member of the Medical School Council; a representative of the Royal College; the vascular surgeon, Mr Barry Sunderland; a consultant from Hammersmith who was invited as the RHA assessor to help ensure impartiality.

Those who had arrived on time for the 3.15 meeting, like those who were late, were given tea while awaiting the arrival of Dame Dorothy Blackwell, a local councillor and member of the DHA, who was in the chair.

Mr Marcus Thompson arrived late, and was surprised that they hadn't started.

'I thought we'd have been underway by now,' he said.

'She's even later than usual,' Barry Sunderland said and glanced at his wristwatch.

'I hope we're going to get started quite soon.' Thompson looked at his own watch, then helped himself to tea.

'Are we going to appoint your man, Marcus?' Sunderland asked. He was unconcerned who got the consultant post, with the exception of Vernon Davis.

'I've done enough work on the telephone on his behalf,' Thompson said.

'Trevor Preston from the Royal College is questioning whether one of his jobs was accredited,' Sunderland said, lowering his voice as he glanced at the acerbic-looking man in the clerical grey suit sitting at the table. 'He's trying to appoint the chap doing cancer research at Hammersmith.'

'Buckingham's published some decent papers,' Marcus Thompson said. Then added unkindly, 'but I think he reworked a couple of Hans Taber's papers in Germany. It's fairly cut and dried.'

'Good afternoon, gentlemen – sorry I'm late,' Dame Dorothy Blackwell said as she bustled in. She was short, round and in her late fifties. 'I think we should get straight to business. I'm determined to appoint someone today.' Having said this she went and got herself tea, before greeting people individually.

Dorothy Blackwell was the only person present who wasn't a party to lobbying; however, in a private meeting she had had with the District Administrator she had been advised who the consultants preferred. She would make the recommendation to Region, who would in turn rubber stamp it.

40

Objectivity was a state which Mr Michael Ort, the forty-nine-year-old consultant orthopaedic surgeon, believed he achieved in all decisions about patients. In fact he was emotionally detached and totally judgemental. This position didn't affect his skill as a surgeon – some might have argued that it improved it; those patients he had judged more deserving of an operation because of their occupation or position in life, got with that decision implicit belief that he was doing some good.

In a small office Mr Michael Ort's firm was checking through the patients' lists with the physiotherapist and the sisters from the orthopaedic wards. Mrs Staples's case was currently receiving their attention. They had hoped by this time to have had her up and moved on to convalescence, if not home, but her stroke had put her back.

'What sort of progress is she making, Philip?' Ort asked.

'It's a bit slow. She's still confused,' Dr Assersohn, the SHO said. 'We're not sure if this is due to her stroke or her original condition.'

'Just how confused is she?'

'She's mildly demented, but she knows who her husband is most of the time now. Though she's not entirely sure why she's here.'

'She keeps trying to get out of bed herself,' the Chinese sister said. 'She's a determined lady. We have cotsides put on her bed.'

'Could she go home?' Ort wanted to know.

'I'd guess that her hip would be all right, if she rests. I'm doubtful about her ability to cope while these confused states continue. We've changed her medication. That might help,' Dr Assersohn said.

'Is there a bed for her on geriatrics? She might be better off there now. Have a word with Dr Bayliss, Alan.' He suspected there might be some resistance. He passed the file to his secretary. 'Who's top of the waiting list for hip replacement?'

'Well somehow we find ourselves with four patients in equal first place,' Dr Sainsbury, the firm's registrar, informed him. There was an almost static waiting list for hip replacements. Sometimes a patient jumped it by needing an emergency operation, usually as a result of an infected prosthesis. They tried clearing the list at the rate of one a week, the recipient being chosen on a points system according to need.

'All with the same number of points?' Ort said. 'How did that come about?'

'I'm not entirely sure.' Dr Sainsbury looked along the list as if for an answer. 'Mrs Kent in G2 has been floating around near the top for about two months now. She's seventy-four of course,' he added as if that were a reason for not replacing her arthritic hip. 'There's also Mrs Weston. She's been waiting two years.'

'She's only a housewife,' Ort said, meaning that she had no standing in the economic order of things. 'No one's been waiting longer than anyone else?'

'Not that I can see.'

'Perhaps we'd better draw to see which I do this week,' he said, not wishing to be too unfair to Mrs Kent and Mrs Weston. 'Have two, just in case one doesn't present well.'

He might have had prior knowledge about Mrs Kent, who was the winner of the draw.

When Dr Sainsbury went to the female geriatric ward to give Mrs Kent the good news, he found the place deserted of nursing staff. Dr Marvill was in the cluttered office writing a report. She interested him. She was attractive and very bright, though tended to keep weird company.

However, he didn't hold that against her, and would like to have had her on his roster for the weekend cutting jobs that he organized in Belgium.

'Hello, Jessie. Sister not around?' he said.

'She's gone for her meal break,' Dr Marvill said, glancing up from a patient's notes.

Alan Sainsbury moved some files from a chair and made sure it wasn't dusty before sitting. He was a modern, fashionable dresser under his open white coat. On his lapel along with his name tag was a badge saying 'Resist'. He waited for Jessie Marvill to finish writing.

'You've a patient here, Mrs Kent?' he said. 'Is she well enough for surgery?'

'Hardly. She died yesterday evening.'

'Oh what a pity,' Dr Sainsbury said. 'She won the draw – for a hip replacement.'

'You left it a bit late.' She didn't disguise her distaste for medical treatment arrived at in such a random fashion, however fair those involved pretended it was.

Without missing a beat Dr Sainsbury went at the next hurdle. 'Does that mean you have a bed spare for Mrs Staples?'

'I don't know,' she said wearily, and closed the folder. 'You'd better check with Dr Bayliss.'

Sensing he wasn't making much headway he changed tack. 'I didn't see you leave the party.'

'I was on call,' she lied.

'What a good girl you are, Jessie,' he said. 'Everyone else left their bleeps at home.'

It got a smile from her.

'Did you hear who the consultant post went to?' It was idle curiosity. 'Could anyone resist Vernon Davis?' he said with a smile. 'Did you hear about the total spectacle he made of himself before the Appointments Committee? He wigged out completely. Someone will lock him away soon.'

Although Vernon Davis was becoming less and less

rational, Jessie Marvill thought this comment unkind, but said nothing.

'David Passmore's been appointed, subject to Regional approval – he's a freemason,' – as if that explained everything. She simply looked at him. 'You must know about the freemasonry here. Special handshakes, secret initiation rites – they meet in the boardroom.'

'It can't be very secret,' Dr Marvill said.

Dr Sainsbury smiled. 'Most of our consultants are masons.' It was another tack that was taking him nowhere. 'Would you like to go to a party on Saturday? Mostly the same crowd.'

'It got a bit childish,' she said as they left the office.

'You know doctors. It's all sex with them. That's why I wear this.' He indicated his 'Resist' badge.

'Oh, I thought that was political.' She truly did.

The move across to the crowded G2 ward added to Mrs Staples's confusion. She was coherent, and aware of time and place, but only with those closest to her, namely her husband and the physiotherapist. It threw her back a week.

She was in bed dozing after lunch, waiting for the next highlight of the day, afternoon tea, when her husband walked in. She woke with a start and became alarmed at seeing him in street clothes.

''Ere, what you doing out of your chair, Henry?' she asked as he squeezed along the narrow space between the beds. 'Do they know? You haven't done nothing silly?'

Surprise scrabbled his senses and it took him a moment to recover. He had been under his own steam for the past week. 'I'm better, Joanny. I'm all right now with the little doo-dah in me,' he reminded her patting his chest. 'You remember. I even been helping get the teas on the ward.'

'I was having a nice doze and I thought I saw my Henry walk in. I thought, it can't be, he died in the war. You look so much like him, Henry.'

'Don't you think about that, my lovely, that was a long time ago,' he told her, trying to shut out his own memories. 'They're sending me home soon.'

'You can't manage,' she declared. All of her married life she had taken care of her husband's every need and would have it no other way. 'How will you manage without me?'

'I don't know, I really don't. You're all I've got.' He held her hand.

'They'll have to fix up a home help,' she said. 'Not that they're much good. They never do a proper job. I'll have to come out m'self,' – as if believing she was in hospital for no good reason. 'You'll be all right with me there.'

'You stay and get well – you're on the mend. That's why they moved you in here.'

'This place,' she said in disgust. Anger exacerbated the effects of her stroke and she couldn't get her words out for a moment. ''S enough to put years on you. That poor dear there. She's half blind, can't talk, no one visits her. This one next door. I don't think she'll see the night out.'

'You'll soon be home, Joanny,' he said, trying to cheer himself as well as her. He was a little frightened about going home on his own. 'I'll be in every day to make sure you're all right. I don't have nothing else to do without you.'

'You keep off the bicycle,' she said. 'What about at night? What if you took queer?'

'The social worker's fixed up for the neighbours to look in. There's always Dr Thurson. They can get him on the phone.'

'He's an old man, Henry,' she reminded him. 'He can't keep going much longer.' They had been on Dr Thurson's panel since he had first practised in their neighbourhood forty years ago. As though it were yesterday she clearly remembered how young Dr Thurson had been then. She had no perception of becoming old herself during the intervening years; however Henry was, so she supposed she was too.

'I'll be all right. I'll be all right,' he reassured her. 'They're doing the teas out there now.' He nodded along the ward.

She straightened his shirt collar, pulling it from under his tie. 'You make sure you get enough to eat. And don't go riding that bicycle, d'you hear? You won't get half enough to eat. Them Meals on Wheels don't do a proper dinner. I seen some of the scrimpy meals they do . . .' Her speech went again and she lost the train of thought.

'I'll be all right,' he repeated without much assurance. 'I'll manage.' He looked round towards the clatter of tea cups. 'I'll just help with the teas.'

Although Dr Thurson was old, patients kept coming to him, and not simply those who had grown old with him, but their children, and grandchildren, and people who had moved into the area and couldn't find another doctor. All of which meant that his practice was still larger than he could cope with, despite now using a night deputizing service. His appointments system usually fell into disarray by his second or third patient each morning, he grew increasingly short-tempered with them; for the past year he had camped in vain on the doorstep of the Medical Practices Committee over the issue of taking on a partner, but suspected that they preferred him to retire when they would divide up his practice. He feared the redundancy of retirement and got angry whenever the question was raised. He wasn't able to let go, he needed to be wanted, if only by stupid or unthinking people who continually abused themselves.

Despite feeling sorry for the woman in the chair opposite him, Dr Thurson's impatience was increasing. He wanted to say that her problems were mostly of her own making, that she needed to be a little tolerant and yielding, and learn to relax. Instead he let her talk while he pumped up the sphygmomanometer to take her blood pressure. He noticed the handbag she was clutching tensely on her lap, and he took it from her.

'. . . I can't cope any more, doctor. I just can't. Everything's getting me down,' Ann Roberts said. The problem was her mother, Mrs Downes, who was back living with her and had been for nearly a year. Mrs Downes had astounded the medical profession by staying alive and active all this time; her daughter had only agreed to her returning home in the belief that it wouldn't be for long.

'It's all her fault, doctor. I've done my best. It's not as if I haven't. Even my Roy's been got down by her. We can't take much more. We shouldn't have had her back home. I never dreamed it would be this long. She's getting so dirty. She hides bits of whasitcalled in her room,' she said, meaning shit. 'And bits of food. 'S wonder we're not overrun with mice. She lies about it when you tell her, doctor. She's getting such a liar. She'll have to go back to the hospital, 'fore I end up in a loonybin. She's my own mother, but I can't have much more of her. She'll have to go back in . . .' Mrs Roberts finally ran out of steam.

The doctor completed the b/p reading. 'It's not easy finding places for old people in hospitals, Mrs Roberts. There aren't places readily available for those who are not ill.'

'She'll make me ill, then they'll have to find a place for me, doctor,' she said.

There was a tense desperation about her, and Dr Thurson wondered if it might not be easier to find a hospital bed for her.

'The situation isn't helping your blood pressure, Mrs Roberts. It's quite high again,' he said. 'We'll try some new tablets. We need to get it down to a manageable level.'

'There's only one thing'll do that, doctor,' she said.

The doctor sat wearily at his desk and wrote out the prescription. 'I can only suggest that I write to the geriatrician at St Clair's about your mother, Mrs Roberts, see if she can go in as a social admission for a month. They may find her a bed as she was a special interest patient. Try not to let the situation get on top of you. We want to get your blood pressure down.' He gave her the prescription along with a smile.

'Thank you, doctor.'

'I'll see you in a fortnight, Mrs . . .' Her name slipped his memory.

'A fortnight?' she confirmed, acknowledging this contact with hope.

'Make an appointment as you go.' He opened the door for her. Ordinarily patients had to find their own way out, and he didn't know if his gesture was from guilt or to make sure she left.

'Thank you, doctor,' she said again and hovered in the doorway as if there was something else.

The telephone ringing was an excuse to close the door.

'Mr Hillman from the Family Practitioner Committee is on the line, Dr Thurson,' Mrs Richards, the receptionist said when he picked the phone up. 'I thought you'd want to speak to him.'

'Yes, put him through, Joan . . .' He felt a tremor of apprehension.

'Hello, Dr Thurson? This is Hillman, FPC. I thought it best that I phoned you personally. The Medical Practices Committee has turned down your application to take on a partner. When you last wrote in with your proposals we did advise you at the time that this area is closed. I'm sorry.' The voice was impersonal, and carried no feeling of regret.

'I can't cope with this size of practice,' Thurson said earnestly. 'I need a younger man. What if I became ill?' This decision was a nonsense, he thought fleetingly, an act of persecution; they were trying to force him to retire.

'This area has been closed for sometime,' Hillman said. 'There is your deputizing service.'

'But I can't handle my present work-load.'

'I'm sorry, doctor. That was the decision of the MPC. You can appeal of course. If you intend to appeal it must be sent in within one month.'

Dr Thurson stopped listening, realizing there was no arguing with this sort of bureaucracy.

'We will be writing to you in due course . . .' the voice was saying.

Finally Dr Thurson replaced the phone. He remained unmoving, his gaze in the middle-distance. After a moment his eyes flitted across the tray of drug manufacturers' bumph spilling off the end of the desk. On the top was an inviting advert for Anafranil, promising to relieve all stress, depression and anxiety. Rising painfully he went and rummaged through his drugs samples cupboard. Some of the products had been there for years, dating from those heady days when companies had deluged GPs with everything they manufactured. He found a suitable calmer and swallowed a couple of capsules to get himself through the morning.

41

Despite the Inderal capsules and diuretics the doctor had given Mrs Roberts her hypertension subsided not at all, nor was it likely to. She was tense and edgy and allowed herself to be overwhelmed by every minor irritation; a lot of this amounted to self-centredness; she related everything to herself, seeing most incidents as a personal affront. If her husband dropped his dirty shirt on the floor it was to purposely annoy her rather than because he was messy; her son's untidiness she believed was directed at her; her mother's illness was part of the same pattern, and none of these slights washed over her, but instead penetrated her defences causing her to blow up and get headaches as her bloodvessels constricted.

At home in her council maisonette this evening Mrs Roberts cooked dinner as she did every evening for her husband, her late teenage son, and her mother, who was still in her room.

The fact that neither husband nor son would eat all the food set before them would put her more on edge – after the trouble she had taken to cook it – but not before she had lost her temper with her mother, who was more insulting for not even acknowledging her effort by coming to table.

'Is she coming down to have this now I've cooked it?' Mrs Roberts said, bringing in her own dinner. Her mother's food was cooling on the table. Her husband and son were eating. 'Did you call her?'

''Course I did,' her son said, not taking his nose out of *Motor Mechanic.*

'Why not let her have it upstairs?' Roy Roberts suggested, looking for an easier existence.

'I'm not having any more food poked down behind that bed. Made me feel bloody ill. 'S not all I found either.'

'Ah shut up!' Tony protested, having heard before what was down behind the bed.

'Don't you talk to your mother like that,' Roy Roberts said.

'Well, I'm having m' dinner.'

'You don't have to clear it up,' Mrs Roberts said. 'It's bad enough having to clear up after you two.'

'Make her clean it up.' Roy Roberts's attention went back to the TV that was on in the corner of the room.

'She can't even clean herself. She's not had a bath in a fortnight. I can't keep on wasting food if she's not going to eat it.'

Her husband and son exchanged a weary look and went on chomping as Mrs Roberts marched out to the hall door.

'Mum!' she called. 'Are you coming down for this food? Or is it going to waste again?'

In her small bedroom, which was crowded with relics of her past, seventy-one-year-old Mrs Downes sat in her chair in her stained quilted housecoat – not having dressed this morning – nodding and shaking her head in mocking response to her daughter's questions. She had heard her and could have replied, but chose not to, knowing that irritated her daughter more than anything. Mary Downes's life was a misery and she saw no reason to accommodate the person who was making it so.

Finally Ann Roberts came up the stairs. 'Have you gone completely deaf, or what?' she challenged. 'Your dinner is downstairs getting cold.'

'I'm not hungry. I had a bit of cheese 'n' pickle,' the old lady said, without looking at her daughter. 'Anyway, I'm to have a special diet.'

'I can't take this any more, Mum, I'm becoming a nervous wreck. You'll have to go back in hospital – you're making me ill. The doctor's given me tablets,' – as though that proved the rightness of her case. 'You'll have to go back in.'

'It won't take me long to pack,' Mrs Downes said, completely undermining the younger woman, who retreated, slamming the door.

Because she had survived so long with a major malignancy of the ovary, with liver secondaries, the clinicians at St Clair's were generally interested in Mrs Downes; therefore Dr Thurson had less difficulty in getting her a bed. Beds for social admissions, especially geriatric beds, were hard to come by, and GPs had to present the old as an especially interesting problem; the rest were often regarded as mere old crumble, blocking beds.

Dr Marvill, who examined Mrs Downes when she arrived on G2, was especially interested in her, and delighted that she remembered her from the gynae ward almost a year ago.

'I couldn't forget you, dear,' Mrs Downes said. 'I'd still be having electric treatment if it wasn't for you. Will that other doctor be coming to see me again?'

When Dr Marvill told her about Laurence James moving to another hospital Mrs Downes seemed genuinely disappointed. But it wasn't enough to dampen her buoyant mood over being back here.

On making her examination Dr Marvill found that the carcinoma hadn't remitted, but there was no indication of further spread.

'I'm doing all right, aren't I,' the old woman said.

'You're doing very well,' Dr Marvill confirmed with a smile. 'I think we'd better send you for some X-rays to make sure.' She felt confident that the scans would reveal nothing too adverse.

Seeing the woman in this condition gave Dr Marvill a lift, a sense that what she was doing was maybe worthwhile after all. It was not so far removed from the feeling she had had as a medical student when she had first come into contact with patients. That ability to still fears and reassure patients that they were going to get well was what got one from day to day. The feeling soon evaporated when she got a phone call from the casualty officer, who said they had a piece of crumble in the A and E department that was a possible geriatric admission.

The casualty officer wasn't around by the time Dr Marvill arrived at the casualty department or she would have said something about his referring to old patients as crumble. The expression – which related to their fragile state – she found offensive when used generally, and especially so about particular patients.

Sister Sellers was slightly embarrassed when Dr Marvill approached her. 'Oh, now we've cleaned off some of the filth, he doesn't seem to be injured after all.'

'What happened?' Dr Marvill asked.

'His son brought him in. Said he found him collapsed on the floor,' Sister Sellers explained, lowering her voice as the son was waiting nearby. 'I think it's a case of trying to dump Dad.'

'Well if he could find a space in this hospital, he'd be welcome,' she declared. Although old age wasn't something Dr Marvill found depressing, what did depress her was the way in which people tried to abrogate responsibility for the aged. She knew the answer was for society to be more caring, but she didn't know how that might be achieved. At times it seemed that everyone was trying to off load old relatives on to state care; but as hospitals were the most obvious place for this, she accepted that she probably saw the worst aspects of parent-dumping. But it made her no less depressed. 'I'd better have a look at him.'

In a treatment room, two nurses, both wearing rubber aprons and gloves, had just finished washing the dried excrement off the naked man on the couch.

'Hello, Mr Long,' Dr Marvill said, glancing at the admissions sheet. 'How are you? You had a fall? Did you? Did you fall?'

She examined him for a stroke. This hadn't been done, and judging by the filthy state Sister Sellers said the man had been in Dr Marvill understood why. It was odd that society tolerated children leaving aged, incontinent parents in their own filth, she reflected, but parents doing the same to young children might have meant Care proceedings.

'Can you grip my finger?' she asked.

'Have I got to come in, doctor?' old Mr Long asked.

'Let's see if there's anything wrong. This one,' – inviting him to grip with his right hand which wasn't so good. 'Do you feel any weakness here?'

'I can't get up steps like I used to,' he said. 'I can't get up the steps properly.'

'Do you remember falling?' Dr Marvill asked.

'When?' he wanted to know. 'I never had no fall.'

'Didn't you? Just before your son brought you in?'

'He's just telling them that.'

'How old are you?'

'Seventy-seven. I'll be seventy-eight in October,' he said.

'Do you know what the date is?'

'19th September. No, it's not, it's the 20th.'

'That's fine,' she said. It was the 19th of October. She smiled warmly at him.

The young Mr Long, who was in his late forties, wasn't so accommodating when he saw his plan set for a reverse.

'He's ill, I tell you,' he insisted. 'That's why I brought him in. He's not well.'

'Your father may have had a mild stroke, but it's not bothering him, Mr Long.'

'You gotta keep him, check him properly. The trouble is you lot are always too busy scribbling on bits of paper to find out what's wrong with people. I want a second opinion. I'm out at work all day, I mean, what if he fell on the fire, he could burn to death. I can't have him at home any more.'

'But there's nothing wrong with him.'

'I'm not fucking taking him back,' young Mr Long said, suddenly changing tack. 'You can take care of him now. I've had him for fifteen years. I got my own fucking life to lead.' With that he rushed out.

'Oh well,' Dr Marvill said.

'Oh dear,' Sister Sellers said. 'I had a feeling he was one of those. It's a familiar story. We had a woman who used to bring in her mother every week saying she couldn't cope. We couldn't take her as social admission or the daughter would never have taken her back. After the old lady died suddenly, her daughter was brought in; she had taken an overdose – loneliness, I suppose. I'll call the social work department, get them to take him home.'

'Thank you, sister,' Dr Marvill said.

That freed her from the immediate responsibility, but it was no answer.

'Rita,' the social work senior said, stepping from her cupboard-like office. 'There's a Mr Long who's been dumped in A and E by his son. Could you look into it?'

'Is it just a question of taking him back?' Mrs Richie said, covering the mouthpiece of the phone she was holding. 'I'm off at three.'

'I think so.'

Rita Richie scribbled the name on her pad and looked at her watch. If she had less clients and more time she might have been able to do something more constructive than dump the man back on his son.

She was at her desk in St Clair's social work department in the old part of the hospital. They were grossly short of space and the eight social workers, their senior and typists had to slither between desks and filing cabinets.

Turning back to the phone as the Home Help superintendent announced herself, Mrs Richie explained the needs of Henry Staples, who was going home. 'He does have a wife, but she's in hospital. He's ready for discharge provided he gets home help.'

'Where's the flat?' the Home Help superintendent asked. She wasn't encouraging.

'Block F, Grove Dwellings . . . sounds awful doesn't it,' Mrs Richie commented.

'Well, what we're talking about at this point is two hours help a week,' the woman informed her as if making a generous offer.

'Two hours? Goodness, this is an eighty-year-old man who's never had to look after himself before.'

'We'll do an assessment. But that's all I'm able to offer at present.' It might have been her personally who was doing the housework.

'Then what's the point of an assessment?' Mrs Richie didn't disguise her frustration.

'D'you want it or not, Mrs Richie?' the Home Help superintendent said sharply.

'I suppose it's better than nothing. When can you look at the flat?' She expected her to say in the morning.

'Tuesday week.'

'Goodness. Not before? He's waiting to go home.'

'I could do it this Thursday at 2.30,' – now pressed.

'Thursday will be fine,' Mrs Richie said, consulting her diary. 'Thank you, Mrs Bronson.' She replaced the phone. It seemed like a lot of effort for small return, then that all too often was the case.

42

The theory behind every modern drug ever marketed was thorough validation through laboratory tests – mostly on animals – then on human guinea pigs; only when conclusive satisfactory results were obtained did the product reach the general public. The theory was fairly sound, but the practice of validating marketable drugs was another matter. Other factors became a consideration, not least economics. A company which had spent thousands of pounds developing a new drug inevitably preferred a financial return, so was reluctant to abandon products or have them be shown to have little if any value. To that end they sought to control the tests as anyone controlling the data could make figures prove almost anything. The way drug companies often gained control was by financing the research units in hospitals, and thereby having their products developed and tested exclusively. Cavandish Pharmaceuticals funded the unit at St Clair's, where because of lack of finance, the hospital management was glad to have them.

One or two doctors doing research at the hospital weren't entirely happy with this arrangement, but that was a minor consideration.

Having got a foot in the door, it wasn't simply a case of Cavandish, or any other company, shovelling their products on to unsuspecting patients. Before that happened the new drugs had to go to the Medical Ethics Committee, which closely assessed all the data. Once the Committee was satisfied, controlled blind or double-blind tests could be started with consenting patients. The Medical Ethics Committee usually comprised consultants from the hospital, but no drugs company, which had gone to the trouble of setting up a research unit would allow its data to be interpreted coldly; instead they did a considerable amount of lobbying; life was made easier for Cavandish by virtue of the chairman of the Medical Ethics Committee being Sir Randolph Spence, who was also deputy chairman of Cavandish Pharmaceuticals. No concern was expressed about that, as Sir Randolph was motivated by the highest ideals; those people aware of the possible conflict of interest were mostly too polite to suggest that Cavandish might withdraw financial support for the unit if Sir Randolph were asked to resign.

The committee met so infrequently that it didn't have its own office, but borrowed one on the consultants' floor in the new part of the hospital. On those occasions it called upon individual researchers to expand and explain further their proposals contained in the data they had earlier presented, along with written theses.

One of the doctors asked to further explain his proposals was the American research physician Tom Bielicki, who wasn't optimistic about being given the go-ahead. Dr Carl Bayliss, the consultant geriatrician, who was a member of this committee, had told him as much in a private meeting, despite his own interest in the particular subject.

'Would you come in, Dr Bielicki?' the secretary said, opening the door.

Pushing his folder of papers under his arm, Dr Bielicki followed her into the room to face the three-man committee.

'Have a seat, doctor.' The chairman indicated the chair opposite the table.

It seemed more like the star chamber than an explanatory talk.

'We've considered your proposal very carefully. But this is not a matter we feel we want to deliberate on quickly. Indeed I for one feel a sense of disquiet,' Sir Randolph said, pre-empting the committee's decision. 'What you've proposed is a scheme to study the distribution and spread of Hela cells introduced intravenously into geriatric patients; the subsequent response of the body's immune system, and the effects of recently developed chemotherapy. The hope is that a more effective inhibiting treatment might be found for carcinoma, even in the late stages of the disease.' He considered before him the two thick folders of papers, which he hadn't had time to read in detail. 'Would you care to go through your scheme and explain more fully?'

There were over seven hundred pages of written and assembled material, and Dr Bielicki wondered what more there was to explain. 'Yes, thank you,' he said disappointed at this response, despite his forewarning. 'I think we're all aware of the current position. There has been almost zero progress in this field, certainly no major breakthrough. Beyond the body's natural immune system, to date we still have no defence against malignant neoplasia. We have found with animals that we can help their immune system defend them against carcinogenic structures. But what these animals' immune systems are dealing with are the tumours we've given them, which are mainly sarcoma, while the majority of human cancer is carcinoma. That is why I believe that research limited to animals isn't giving us the results we're looking for.'

'Your thesis suggests that animal experiments are pointless,' Sir Randolph said, defending a huge vested interest.

'My point is that we're not looking for a cure for malignancy in animals, but humans,' Bielicki said. 'Results of animal experimentation don't translate to human metabolism. The differentiation of cancer cells in humans suggests that all experiments on animals have given us is a body of untranslatable knowledge, in the technique of handling cancer cells. We're particularly adept at identifying and isolating cells, if we weren't I wouldn't be making this proposal. The time has come for us to move on to what Papworth described as the human guinea pig.'

'Geriatric patients in other words?' Dr Bayliss said.

'Well, sir, I worked with convicted prisoners in the United States, and they responded well. But they were mostly young, healthy Negroes, and it's assumed that their own immune systems were dealing effectively with the foreign cells. Also I'm sure "nothing to lose" psychology played a large part. Most of the evidence from cancer patients who have had a complete remission of the disease suggests a strong change of attitude. You'll appreciate that cancer is an age-prone disease, and the aged tend to be less emotive and less wilful.'

'Are patients expected to give their consent?'

'Yes, sir, they are,' Dr Bielicki said. 'Those able to.'

'Those who aren't?' Dr Bayliss asked.

'I would hope to approach their families.'

'Tell me, doctor,' Professor Mathias, the third committee member, said. 'Do you truly feel justified in what you're proposing? Patients who have suffered major illness, which is why most of them are here, will be subjected to experiments that may be of no benefit to them and could subject them to grave risks, resulting in death earlier than might otherwise be expected. You feel completely justified in this?'

'An argument could be made against ever moving from lab to patient,' Dr Bielicki suggested.

'You're proposing to introduce Hela cells not only to cancer patients, but those free of the disease. What if these cells were to replicate?'

'Sir, we must look at this in the broader context,' Bielicki said.

'If I might put in a word or two here,' Dr Carl Bayliss said with that gentle smile so familiar to his patients. 'There's no evidence to suggest that they will replicate, or even that what is proposed will be particularly detrimental to patients. I think that's an assumption we're making. I feel that were this research to continue it will add to the body of knowledge, not especially about the elderly, but generally.'

'The ethical dilemma troubles me, Carl,' Sir Randolph said.

'How does one draw the line?' Dr Bayliss asked. 'After all we have a research unit attached to this hospital which is pursuing a not dissimilar tack.' He glanced at Sir Randolph, but didn't comment on his position. 'The answer is simply that we don't. Without such theses as this one, medicine wouldn't have progressed as far as it has.'

'I feel unable to support this programme on the evidence presented. The benefits to these patients seem minimal set against the obvious risks,' the consultant physician said.

'I'm deeply concerned about the ethical implications, yet I don't want to be seen to stand in the way of progress. I think we need more information, and further time to consider this,' the chairman said ironically. This was a course he wouldn't dare to have pursued with his own company's research programme, despite their researchers preferring human guinea pigs.

Although after further deliberation the Medical Ethics Committee finally turned down Dr Bielicki's proposals, Carl Bayliss still thought them innovative and worthy. He knew that if imaginative leaps weren't made then medicine would cease to advance, which would be bad news for geriatric medicine. He invited Dr Bielicki to his office for another informal chat. 'I'm sorry the committee turned down your programme finally,' he said.

'Oh, I guess I expected it. But thanks for your support,' Dr Bielicki said.

'What are your plans?'

'I guess maybe I should join Cavandish Pharmaceuticals.'

'Yes, it is rather unfortunate that the chairman of the Ethics Committee should be director of the research unit,' Dr Bayliss told him.

'I guess their future would be secure if they cracked that

nut,' Dr Bielicki said.

'I think they do all right. Would you care for some coffee?' He switched on the electric percolator. 'If you wish to proceed with your experiments on a limited basis, I could find you a number of patients.'

'You could?' Bielicki was surprised. 'You're prepared to override the Committee?'

'Let me put it this way, I think we made the wrong decision, possibly for the wrong reason,' Bayliss said, 'I would want my name on your research paper.'

'No problem.' At this stage that seemed like a reasonable trade to Dr Bielicki, who was concerned to get on with his research uninterrupted. 'What about patients' families?'

'It might be simpler if you used patients without any family,' Dr Bayliss told him.

'Right.' Dr Bielicki nodded approvingly. That would make things less complicated. 'Thank you, sir.'

'Let's hope for some worthwhile results.'

Later, during his ward round with Dr Kenti, his African registrar, and Dr Marvill, the consultant made a mental note of patients who'd be suitable subjects for Dr Bielicki's research; some with little hope of making a recovery and being returned to a normal existence, even if that was only the loneliness of one unheated room and one insufficient meal. Some of the patients he chose he was genuinely fond of, like the seventy-five-year-old Mrs Haywood who had suffered a stroke and was aware of little. He didn't quickly pass her by, but spread the notes out on top of her when he squeezed along between the beds, and took comments from both Drs Kenti and Marvill as though there was real chance of getting her going again. The whole manner of this ward round was low key, almost furtive compared with those on surgical wards. Here everyone from the occupational therapists to student nurses took notes of some sort.

'Has there been any change, sister?' Dr Bayliss asked. The patient was on her side, unmoving. She had a nasogastric tube in.

'No. We try talking to her, sometimes there's a flicker of response,' she said.

'As long as there's that it's worth keeping on. Space is a bit difficult, I know, but perhaps you could move her bed to the opposite corner of the ward,' he suggested. 'She's blind in her right eye and her left is facing the wall. If she sees something going on in the ward it might help. Good.' He handed the file back.

'Mrs Roundtree,' the sister reminded him.

'Oh yes, she wanted a word.'

He approached Mrs Roundtree, who was out in a chair, and crouched to her.

'What can I do for you, my dear?' He took her hand.

'My nose, doctor,' she told him, pointing delicately with her fingers. 'This hard stuff up it. What in the old days we'd call bogeys.'

'Bogey-wogeys, hey,' he said. 'We'll put some cream on it and soften it. That should do it. Anything else troubling you?'

She looked around then beckoned him closer. 'My son doesn't come any more,' she whispered.

'We'll see what we can do about that as well,' he said, rising and patting her hand.

'Can you get a smear of Benzoin up her nose, stop it drying out,' he said to the sister. Then asked generally, 'Do we know why her son no longer visits?'

'He's gone to work in the Middle East,' the social worker said.

'Oh, I see.' He threw up his hands, as there was nothing to be done about that. He glanced back at Mrs Roundtree wondering if she would be suitable for Dr Bielicki's research. 'Has she been to Queen's for another brain scan?' he asked, checking for a note in the file. She had a brain tumour.

'She's going in the morning,' Dr Marvill informed him.

'Is there any hope of getting her back to the old people's home quite soon?' He addressed the ward sister. 'I think she'll start rapidly downhill unless we get her moving.'

'I don't think she'd cope back at the home yet,' the physiotherapist ventured.

'Lime Trees won't take her back because she's too incapacitated,' Mrs Richie said. 'But unless she goes back within two weeks they won't keep her bed.'

'Is she getting mobile?'

'She can't walk unaided,' the physiotherapist said. 'She's weak on the right side.'

'That's consistent with her lesion.' He passed the file to the sister mentally adding this patient to the list for Dr Bielicki. They moved on to the next bed. 'Mrs Staples. Our success story.'

'A very determined lady,' Dr Marvill said. 'She's no longer confused; the speech difficulty after her stroke has more or less been overcome. The problem now is getting her to rest. She's trying to do too much too quickly.'

'What's the situation about her leaving us?'

'It was decided she should go home,' Mrs Richie said. 'But we're having difficulty getting a home help. Her husband's at home of course.'

'He's only recently out of hospital himself,' Dr Bayliss commented. Then to the OT, 'Perhaps you could do a home assessment. See what help they can manage with.'

'I do think she'd be better off in her own home,' the OT said. 'And quite soon.'

There was general agreement.

The consultant didn't even consider this patient for Dr Bielicki.

'This business of Social Service back-up for patients leaving hospital is an enormous problem, Jessie,' Dr Bayliss said as he and Dr Marvill headed for the geriatric department after the ward round. He had invited her to walk with him, but it wasn't to discuss general problems with her. 'It's mostly inadequate and sometimes non-existent.'

'There doesn't seem to be much co-ordination,' she commented.

'Not even within the hospital. Look at this,' he said pointing out spores of litter gathering against some broken furniture in a paved area between buildings. 'Did you ever see such a shambles?'

Dr Marvill didn't respond, being familiar with this obsession of his.

'Like the fabric of this hospital, the old are on no one's list of priorities. It's silly when one considers that they take up more than fifty per cent of hospital beds.'

'Has any decision been reached about Nightingale Block?' Dr Marvill asked, thinking he might have more up-to-date information than the junior doctors' committee received.

'District has pledged continuing support for a psycho-geriatric unit. It's needed urgently,' Dr Bayliss said, 'especially now they've succeeded in closing the chronic unit. I no longer place much faith in such promises.' He paused. 'You're quite decided on your branch of medicine when you finish your rotation, Jessie?'

'I keep telling myself that I have,' she replied in a half-hearted way. 'But it appears the problems are as bad in general practice.'

'Worse, I would have said. That's why so many are referred.'

'The notion of structured, orthodox medicine is so unappealing,' Jessie Marvill said. The restlessness she felt for some alternative had been stirred by Laurence James, but she assumed she must have been ready for that, not to have resisted like most doctors. All that she saw happening in the present set-up confirmed for her that she was right. 'I find it very frustrating, recognizing the cause of the problem as we sometimes do, but only being able to treat the symptom. I have been thinking about some sort of barefoot alternative. I'm not sure what.'

'I'm not sure there is any real alternative, Jessie,' he told her reasonably. 'Far better that we try to make the present system work. Especially as it's all we have.'

They passed through a door on to a corridor which seemed about three miles long and was a shambles of electrical conduiting, water pipes; walls were in need of both plaster and paint; some floor tiles were missing and old furniture had been dumped there. Each time she saw this corridor Jessie Marvill knew how her boss felt. He had probably looked at this mess for years.

'The time will come when geriatric medicine will be taken seriously, Jessie. It won't always be a dumping ground,' the consultant said with confidence. 'As the aged population increases, greater priority must be given them. There will be chairs in geriatric medicine. I mention this, Jessie, because the specialty needs people with a sense of commitment, rather than doctors filling in until they can get a better job. I don't like having to admit it, but that's how we get so many geriatricians. The situation is improving now that cuts are meaning fewer jobs for doctors. We can be more choosey.' He paused. 'There will be an opening here for a registrar when Dr Kenti returns to Africa,' – finally getting to the point. 'I think you'd be right for the job.'

The offer held a certain appeal for Jessie Marvill as she enjoyed working with old patients, and the registrar post was a two-year contract, which meant she would be settled for longer than she had ever been settled as an SHO, changing jobs as she had every six or twelve months. But she sensed that she would be trapped on an institutionalized path she was no longer sure she was sufficiently committed to. 'It's kind of you to think of me,' Dr Marvill said.

'Don't decide right away,' he said quickly, 'or you won't take it. Wait till you've had a string of successes like Mrs Staples. Then it all seems worthwhile. Dr Kenti will be here another two months, God help us.' His winsome smile turned sour as they reached some broken beds parked in the corridor. 'Look, those beds have been broken for three months now. It's just not reasonable. It's an absolute shambles.'

All Jessie Marvill could do was agree.

43

The first thing that struck visitors to the Staples's over-crowded flat in Grove Dwellings was mess and confusion. Nothing had been cleared up by Henry Staples since he had come out of hospital. Used crockery was left on every available surface, some of it had fallen to the floor and broken; the contents of drawers and cupboards were spilled; there was litter and dust and coal ash. Henry Staples had never before had to care for himself, he had been the sole provider while his wife kept house.

Being only half-dressed, unwashed and unshaven, he looked a mess when he opened the door to Janet Stoop, the occupational therapist who had come with Mrs Richie to assess what was needed in the way of handrails and such for when Mrs Staples returned.

The two women were amazed that one person had got into so great a mess in such a relatively short while. They saw immediately that a full-time housekeeper was needed.

'She didn't do nothing, the home help. Said there was too much to do,' Henry Staples explained, by way of an apology.

'I should think there is,' Mrs Richie told him.

'Is my lady coming home soon?' he asked, cheered at the prospect.

'She can't to this mess,' Janet Stoop said. 'We'll have to get you sorted out.' She had a brisk, efficient manner, and a habit of moving in on people and organizing them.

'When's she coming back?' Henry asked.

'Will you be able to manage? Mrs Staples won't be very mobile at first.'

'I can't manage without her.' He didn't really want to try.

'It'll be all right when she's back, she'll keep me on the straight and narrow.'

'That's the spirit, Mr Staples,' the occupational therapist encouraged.

Right then Henry Staples was most concerned about how long these women would take to tidy the flat, which was why he believed they were there. He had to get to the hospital for afternoon visiting.

Faced with the expectation of going home, Joan Staples's excitement was matched only by her impatience. She wanted to get going right away, never having been in bed so long, not even during confinement. She had given birth one day and was getting her husband's dinner the next – as she recalled things. She thought it silly that they would let her up only twice a day for exercise, and yet sillier that she had to walk with a frame.

She had been up for exercise soon after her mid-day meal, but hadn't been allowed to stay up in a chair like her neighbour, Mrs Downes, whom she had become friendly with. Mrs Downes was helping with the teas; that was something Mrs Staples felt she could do better. For she believed, also about the fat West Indian auxiliary who was coming round with the trolley, that Mrs Downes hadn't a clue about a good cup of tea. But this was partly to do with resenting Mrs Downes's mobility, and her being allowed to wear her own clothes.

'There you are, dear, a nice cuppa,' Mrs Downes said as she brought the tea across. Away from her family she was enjoying life once more; her daughter hadn't allowed her to do anything at home, not because she didn't need help, but because she didn't want a mess. 'You want a biscuit, dear?'

'I got chocolate biscuits what my Henry brought – I can get them,' she said when Mrs Downes started to look for them.

'Look at that poor old dear.' Mrs Downes indicated a CVA patient in a chair by the bed near the door. 'She's been like that since dinner time.'

The stroke patient was desperately waggling her finger at the floor as if trying to communicate something. No one was attempting to understand her.

'Poor old girl,' Mrs Downes said. 'I feel so sorry for her. No one cares about her. Never gets no visitors.'

'Your people coming in?' Mrs Staples said, slyly scoring a point. Mrs Downes had confided her family problems.

'I'd say not. I'd lock myself in the bathroom.' She adjusted Mrs Staples's bedtable. 'Now you enjoy your tea, dear. I expect Henry'll be in soon.'

Suspicion loomed in Mrs Staples at this familiarity. Had she been mobile she would have thought nothing of it, but being in bed made her helpless and there was no telling what a lonely old woman like Mrs Downes might try on.

'He's a charming man,' Mrs Downes commented.

'You keep your eyes off my husband, thank you very much,' Mrs Staples said. 'And take that tea away – I know what you're up to.' There was no telling what she might have put in it to prolong her stay in bed, Mrs Staples decided.

'You silly old woman,' Mrs Downes retorted. 'You ought to be ashamed. I got very friendly with a gentleman from Brighton earlier this year when I was convalescing. I'll probably be getting married.'

'At your age, dear?' Mrs Staples said, as though the idea was ridiculous. 'You take that away. The darkie'll bring my tea.'

Without arguing Mrs Downes took the tea across to the CVA patient, who was still waggling her finger at the floor.

'There you are, dear,' Mrs Downes said, thinking she was being helpful bringing her tea. 'What you trying to say? Have you wet your knickers?' She saw water on the floor by her feet.

'Mrs Weitz can't manage tea on her own,' a nurse said as she approached.

Mrs Weitz wasn't waggling her finger as a result of her stroke, but at water seeping through the ward.

'Oh my God!' the nurse said, making the connection with the patient who had evacuated her lunch in her bed and had been taken for a bath ten minutes ago.

Rushing to the bathroom and throwing open the door, she found the patient sitting naked beside the bath, delighted at the water overflowing from the open taps.

It was one of many minor crises that were part of the daily fabric, but which had left no trace by the time Henry Staples arrived. He was one of only three visitors to G2, and patients who were aware of time and place looked hopefully to the door, but no more visitors arrived.

'How are you, my lovely?' Henry Staples asked, excited at seeing his wife. He was presentable now, having washed and shaved, though bits of whiskers had been missed.

'I'm getting fed up with being in this bed,' his wife said crossly. 'I could've done them teas earlier.' She glanced furtively at her neighbour. 'The staff have got enough to do.'

'You'll be coming home soon,' he told her, almost weeping. 'Just as soon as they fix up the flat with rails for you to grip on. Then you can move about without no trouble.'

'Well, I wish they'd hurry up. This place puts years on me.'

'Don't you think she's looking well, Mr Staples?' Sister Webberburn said when she stopped at the foot of the bed.

'She's looking an absolute picture, sister.'

'She's a naughty girl. She's trying to do too much,' the sister admonished. 'She'll be in here all the longer if she doesn't rest.' Henry nodded while his wife shook her head and clucked her tongue at this nonsense. That was the way it had always been. She had always done too much, and nothing he said or did changed that. So he said nothing for fear of upsetting her.

The night duty staff started at nine o'clock, which meant getting in at a quarter to for the handover from the day staff. The night shift continued until 8 A.M., so it wasn't surprising that few qualified nurses wanted that duty. Student nurses had no choice and agency nurses were employed when there were no others. The practice of some day staff moonlighting strengthened the argument for a compulsory rotating eight-hour shift system similar to the police, but it came no closer to reality.

At each change of staff the nurse in charge made a report on each patient, saying a few words about them, when the nurses coming on duty would take notes for their own reference.

Sister Webberburn did the report for the two night staff, an agency staffnurse in a brown uniform, and a 3rd-year student called Barbara Stolton, who was thin and grey with fatigue and had bad skin.

'. . . Mrs Staples is progressing nicely. She's expected to go home tomorrow or the next day,' she said and flicked to the next page in the Kardex file. 'Mrs Sullivan responds when talked to. The Friends have been finding visitors. Talking to her seems to bring her out of the coma.'

'Is anyone coming in tonight?' the staffnurse inquired.

'No. So if you get a minute, stop and have a word.' The card went over. 'Miss Woods is getting more deeply unconscious. She's only having water through the naso-gastric tube to stop her dehydrating. She's not expected to last much longer.' Turning the card, 'Mrs York died this evening. I'm afraid her family haven't been in,' she said, as if handing them an unpleasant job. In fact her family had never been to see her. 'I doubt if they will bother, so call the porters and have her taken to the mortuary.'

She was a patient Dr Bayliss had found for Dr Bielicki, and one of several who would appear to die from a viral infection that their immune system was unable to deal with. The pathologist would determine that death was the result of viral pneumonia.

One of the two cadavers Andy Betts and his partner, Peter Marwick, were working overtime on this evening had died of the same cause. It was unlikely that any sinister connection would be made between these deaths unless a connection was pointed out. Before that happened Dr Bayliss would decide that Dr Bielicki's research programme was less than useful and abandon it. Betts sewed up the front of the cadaver, having put the intestine and organs in the chest cavity in a plastic bag to prevent unpleasant seepage. As Marwick wiped the body down, Betts retrieved the name tag which had fallen on to the floor. Then he collected up the pituitary glands that weren't returned to the two bodies and popped them into a large jar of formalin with others.

'When I'm off sick tomorrow, Peter,' Betts said, coming through to the fridge room, 'when you open up for Dr Pidgeon, make sure you keep back the pituitaries.'

'How long you gonna be off?' Marwick said, not looking forward to coping on his own.

'I'll take m' full week. I'm entitled.'

'You want me to send them off?' Marwick asked, thinking about the pituitary glands. He shared the money paid for them.

'Depends how many pms there are.'

The laboratory in Cambridge where the glands went to be ground down for hormone extraction for diagnostic tests preferred them in batches of fifty as it made accounting easier.

Dr Bielicki would unwittingly help the mortuary technicians achieve that target figure.

Stumbling through one minor crisis to another on G2, all of which were made worse by the edginess and uncertainty of the agency staffnurse, who wouldn't be still for a moment, Nurse Stolton was grateful when her meal break arrived.

The dingy, deserted canteen, with its sticky formica-topped tables, was almost pleasant to be in. Another 3rd-year student, Trish Donaghue, plump and spotty, was with her. She was eating the fried food that was all that was available at night. Nurse Stolton had coffee and a cigarette instead. Although these young women were physically very different, each had the same tawdry, tired appearance.

'I can hardly stay awake on G2,' Nurse Stolton said. It had nothing at all to do with the pace on the ward but the lack of sleep during the day.

'You still with the old ladies?' Nurse Donaghue said. 'I wouldn't mind being there tonight.' She chewed the last of her sausage like she wasn't enjoying it.

'We haven't stopped all night hardly,' Nurse Stolton said. 'It's a real drag. Oh, you'll never guess what happened. The doctor asked that agency staff to change a patient's IV line. She went and took out the whole track.'

'What happened?'

'He went absolutely spare – said how he'd spent half an hour putting it in. Her trouble is she wants to keep on the go the whole time.' Nurse Stolton took out some knitting. 'Did you do all your exam?'

'No, I missed out quite a bit. D'you?'

'I couldn't do half it. What's a Jacquemier's sign?' Nurse Stolton asked.

'I put down miscarriage as a result of amniocentesis.'

'I'd never heard of it. I said it was brain damage after heart failure.' Neither had since looked it up to discover that it was the purplish colour of the vaginal mucosa which was a presumptive sign of pregnancy. Possibly because it no longer made any difference to their exam result. 'I'm gonna fail my final. I haven't done half enough work.'

Nurse Donaghue pushed her plate away and lit a cigarette. 'I was thinking of taking next week off to do some studying.'

'I was thinking of that. Only Del'll only want to go away, 'l do.'

She looked at her watch. It was time to go back, and she wished now that she had stayed on the ward and used her meal break to sleep. But the staffnurse would only have called on her to help if she had.

On returning to the darkened G2, Nurse Stolton found the staffnurse in the office checking the card index, familiarizing herself with the patients. She wouldn't do the same when the staffnurse went for her break, but would curl up in the armchair on the ward.

'Oh you're back,' the staffnurse said, looking at her watch.

'You going for your break?' Nurse Stolton asked.

'We ought to turn the patients first,' the staffnurse said, punishing herself. 'Oh, we'll do it when I come back,' – deciding to go easy on herself. But found that she couldn't. 'No, let's do it now.'

'Someone's getting out of bed,' Nurse Stolton said, looking down the ward. 'Mrs Staples!' This galvanized her into action.

Thinking she was at home, Mrs Staples had started out of bed to go to the bathroom, but finding her legs wouldn't support her, she had collapsed in the narrow gap between the beds, bumping her head and shoulder. She was unconscious when the nurses reached her.

'Is she all right?' the staffnurse asked Nurse Stolton, who was bent over the old woman.

'I can't feel her pulse.'

'I'm not going to take the blame,' the staffnurse said. 'She shouldn't have got out of bed. Get her back into bed, quickly,' – as if that might right the situation.

They lifted her on to the bed and covered her up.

'Shall I call the doctor?' Nurse Stolton said.

The normal procedure was to summon the doctor who

was on call. Sometimes it reflected on the nurse in charge if the doctor was called unnecessarily. It would be the same doctor the staffnurse had run foul of earlier when she had removed a patient's IV line by mistake.

'Mrs Staples? Can you hear me, dear? Mrs Staples?' the staffnurse said with an anxious edge.

After a moment Mrs Staples moaned, and the staffnurse heaved a sigh of relief.

'She'll be all right. Won't you, Mrs Staples? You'll be all right, dear. Had a bit of a shock, didn't you. You shouldn't've got out of bed, you're a naughty girl. Now we're going to have to put the sides up.'

From the patient's vacant look Nurse Stolton wondered if she wasn't in shock. 'Maybe we should just get Dr Kennedy-Martin to look in,' she suggested.

'I'm in charge of this ward,' the staffnurse reminded her. 'There's no need to bother the doctor. Let's get on and turn the patients.'

Nurse Stolton considered her colleague, then the patient, but remained unconvinced.

The morning found Mrs Staples unconscious, and with very troubled breathing. Dr Marvill was called.

'How long has she been like this?' Dr Marvill asked as she started her examination.

'Almost half an hour,' Sister Webberburn said. 'Like that anyway. The night staff reported her drifting in and out of consciousness.'

There was no treatment written up on the patient's chart, which Dr Marvill found slightly odd. 'She has pneumonia,' she said. 'I'll give her some antibiotics. She'd better have an IV drip. She may need oxygen.' She had accelerated respiration.

'It's such a shame,' the sister said. 'He was so looking forward to her going home. Her husband,' she explained.

Dr Marvill made no comment, which didn't reflect lack of feeling for this patient or her husband. Although their lives had probably reached no great peaks she did admire them for having worked at their relationship and kept it going as they had, especially when most people gave up at the first sign of trouble, herself included. The longest she had had a relationship for was fifteen months.

Feelings of regret and disappointment deepened in Dr Marvill each time she was called to Mrs Staples throughout the day and evening. Her mood wasn't improved when she learned how badly Henry Staples had taken the news of his wife's setback. Finally when Mrs Staples started to take on a bluish-grey pallor Dr Marvill decided to send her across to intensive care.

There Mrs Staples died in the small hours of the morning, and for all its advanced technology, intensive care couldn't hold the life in her, much less restore her to health.

44

It was ironical that on the day of Mrs Staples's death two carpenters from the council arrived to fix handrails to help her about the flat. Henry Staples was pleased to see them and made them a cup of tea. Their arrival convinced him that his wife's setback was minor, that she would in fact be home quite soon.

'These are for my lady,' he said as he followed them about the flat. 'She's in hospital.'

'She's coming home soon?' a carpenter said.

'Oh, any day now.'

'These'll help her get around, they will.'

The information he had been given about his wife contracting pneumonia and being seriously ill had deeply shocked Henry Staples; it had made him feel sick and breathless, and he hadn't been able to stand up. It had taken him a few hours to recover, and as he did so the reality about his wife had become more remote. At first his mind blocked against her illness, then parcelled it off in a far corner, where it wouldn't be considered.

On visiting his wife as usual the day after her setback, he had been very distressed to find her unconscious. He had sat with her for two hours, holding her hand and talking to her as though she were listening. Eventually he had been asked to leave, for his own sake, and when he had refused, Mrs Richie came to the ward and took him home. She had told him she would collect him today and take him to the hospital.

All that Henry Staples could put his mind to was going to the hospital to see his Joanny. From his chair in the living room his attention alternated between the clock and the road in front of Grove Dwellings as he waited for Mrs Richie. Time hung heavily, the clock hands seemed not to move, and Mrs Richie didn't arrive for two o'clock as she had promised. There was no telephone in the flat; his neighbour occasionally took phone messages, but she was out; he had seen her cross the forecourt and catch the bus.

As he waited Henry rubbed the back of his hands to get them warm. The chill he had felt ever since coming from the hospital yesterday wouldn't leave him. The clock hands had moved on only a few minutes since he had last looked and he wondered if it had gone wrong. Finally he got up and went to ask the carpenters the time.

'Almost five to three, m' old mate,' the carpenter said. 'Off up the hospital are you?'

'Yes,' Henry said, deciding not to wait for the social worker. There was no need, he could easily catch the bus. 'Pull the door to when you leave.'

'Got your key?'

He had.

Coming on to G2, Henry Staples immediately saw his lady sitting up in bed. His heart fluttered with excitement as he approached, but it wasn't until he got closer that he realized his mistake.

'Oh, I thought you was my lady,' he said, embarrassed. His eyesight was ordinarily good for his age. 'She's coming home today, she is.'

The old lady looked at him blankly.

'She's gone to the library,' another said, watching everything. 'I haven't read a book in years,' she added.

'Where's my lady?' he asked the black auxiliary who was polishing the floor. 'She's coming out today.'

'The lady who am in that bed?' the woman said. 'She been sent to intensive care. You stay there, honey. I go and get sister.'

'She's coming out today,' he said to disguise the fear that rose through him.

He decided not to wait for sister, in case she tried to stop him being with his Joanny. Instead he would find her himself.

On the intensive care unit, where because of life support equipment, the patients were barely recognizable, a staff-nurse shook her head in response to Mr Staples's inquiry.

'We've no Mrs Staples here,' she said. 'Are you sure she was brought here?'

Tears clouded Henry's eyes, and he had difficulty getting his words out. 'That's what they told me on the ward. Yesterday they told me she was coming home today.'

'Perhaps she's gone home,' the nurse suggested. 'I should go back to G2 and make inquiries.' She led him off the ward by the arm.

Weary, and sick at heart he shuffled back to the female geriatric ward. Thoughts creeping from those inner recesses were trying to alarm him, but he denied what they were telling him. Totally confused he stood in the corridor on G2 and waited for someone to tell him where his wife had been moved to. At that moment there wasn't a nurse in sight. One or two of the old ladies nodded knowingly, not about to let him into the secret.

A 1st-year student nurse came out of a side ward with a compressed paper bedpan, and stopped in surprise.

'D'you know where my lady is?' he asked her. 'My Joanny. We've been married fifty-eight years.'

'I don't know anything about it,' Nurse Angela Fernyhough said, feeling confused. She hurried into the sluice.

In an adjoining room, a bathroom which had been converted to a laundry room for those old ladies capable of washing their own clothes, the new ward sister was explaining to a patient how a machine worked.

'Sister,' Nurse Fernyhough said. 'Mr Staples is here looking for his wife.'

'Oh dear,' Sister Wyld said. She had taken over from Sister Webberburn, who had started a fortnight's leave. 'I think that's how you work it, Mrs Levison. Can I leave you to it now?'

'I've got the hang of it all right, dear,' Mrs Levison said. When the sister went out she turned the washing machine programme dial the wrong way, breaking it.

Sister Wyld approached the old man in the corridor with a jolly smile which belied her reluctance to deal with this. 'Hasn't the social worker been to see you, Mr Staples?' she asked, feeling embarrassed.

'I came in to see m' lady,' he mumbled, less sure of his position. 'She's supposed to come home, but I can't find her. She can't have gone home yet.'

'Come and sit down, Mr Staples.' She gave him a chair in the office, then crouched before him and grasped his thick, liver-spotted hands. 'I'm afraid your wife left us early this morning,' the sister said, this difficult task made more so by his unwillingness to grasp the truth.

'She isn't at home,' Henry said, taking her euphemism literally.

'Your wife developed pneumonia, Mr Staples. She had a fall.' The nursing sister hesitated, wondering if she should go on. 'I thought Sister Webberburn had told you before she went on leave. The pneumonia worsened, I'm afraid. Your wife died in the small hours. I'm sorry. I'm so sorry.'

'But I come for her now,' he said. 'They've fixed up the flat. Where they took her?'

'I expect she's gone to the mortuary, Mr Staples. I'll take you.' She got her cloak from a cupboard, and helped him up. 'Come on.'

The chapel of rest was empty, which only further convinced Mr Staples that his wife wasn't dead.

'She's not here,' he announced as if he believed the truth was coming around.

'I can see she's not,' Sister Wyld said. She knew that the bodies of patients didn't reside here, but were pushed through from the back of the mortuary. 'Wait here a moment. I'll find out where she is.'

Leaving him in the chapel she went across the corridor to the office. Finding it deserted, she ventured through to the fridge room.

'Mrs Staples?' Peter Marwick said in response to the enquiry, as he put one away. 'She's gone, I'm sure of it,' he said, turning to check the names on the board.

'Are you sure?' Sister Wyld said.

'Pretty sure,' Peter Marwick said, not seeing the name on the board. 'She was collected by the undertakers this morning.'

'Where's she gone?' Sister Wyld asked.

'To be cremated, I think,' he said. 'I seem to remember seeing the cremation form.'

'Are you sure there hasn't been a mistake?'

'We don't make them sort of mistakes, sister,' Marwick said with a confident laugh as he went to the office.

'Mr Betts runs a tight ship.' He opened the huge ledger and ran his finger down the column. 'She'd been hanging around for days . . . Here we are, Ethel Staples, eighty-seven. Come off G4 . . .'

'No, no, Joan Staples . . . she died last night.'

Peter Marwick was suddenly flustered, and wondered how Mr Betts would react if he had made such a mistake. He was about to insist that she was mistaken when he saw the name. 'Oh yes, here, Joan Staples, seventy-eight, off ITU. You know what it is, sister,' he confided, 'it's them black porters. They don't like coming here at night, in case they get the old evil eye. They shove 'em in any empty fridge and don't bother to chalk the name up. You want to have a look do you?' he said, indicating the chapel.

'We're going to see her now, Mr Staples,' Sister Wyld said, when she returned to the chapel.

Mrs Richie arrived a moment later, flushed from haste and awkward with embarrassment. 'I'm sorry, sorry. I'm so sorry, Mr Staples. I couldn't get to you, someone crashed into my car . . . I'm sorry.'

All this was going over Henry's head. He stared vacantly at the curtain in front of him, no awareness penetrating that dense curtain in his mind.

A whirr of an electric motor preceded the low rumbling of the conveyor. The curtains swished back. Apprehensively the sister brought Mr Staples forward. Mrs Richie was close at hand, regretting that this awful scene should have to take place.

No one said anything as Henry Staples stared at the shroud enwrapped body on the plinth, the sheet drawn back from its shrunken face. Finally he looked away, almost disinterestedly.

'Mr Staples?' Mrs Richie inquired after a moment.

Clearing his throat, Henry Staples said finally, 'That's not my wife. That's not my Joanny.'

'I don't know about that, old son,' Marwick said, imitative of Andy Betts. 'Joan Elizabeth Staples,' he read from the yellow death notice attached to the body. 'It's there in black and white.' He tucked the notice back into the sheet.

'It's not her,' Henry said. Who could argue with the man who had been married to the woman for fifty-eight years?

There was confusion now. Marwick looked to the sister for support, but she didn't know Mrs Staples, so turned to the social worker, whose recollection of the old woman wasn't clear enough to argue.

'Look at her closely, Mr Staples. Are you absolutely sure?' the sister said. She pulled an ominous face at the social worker.

'It's not,' Henry insisted.

'You're upset. It's been a shock for you,' Mrs Richie said, deciding to stick her neck out. 'I think it is Mrs Staples.'

'It's not my lady.' Henry Staples was getting angry now. 'I know what my wife looks like.'

'Don't upset yourself, Mr Staples,' the social worker said

calmly. 'What we should do is go home and see if we can find a photo of her. That's best.'

'There are a few bits and pieces of her'n,' Marwick offered.

Mrs Richie nodded, indicating that everything would be all right. 'Come on, Henry.'

Back at the flat there wasn't a photograph of Mrs Staples less than forty years old, so none that was of any practical use to Mrs Richie. However, for the old man each one brought a flood of memories as it showed that his wife hadn't changed one little bit. She was still as pretty as a picture, he reflected, as reality was held safely at bay.

He found some photos of his eldest son in naval uniform.

'That's my boy,' Henry said, showing Mrs Richie a photo. 'He was a stoker, he was. He went down on the *Edinburgh*. I remember hearing the news like it was this morning. They was torpedoed by a German U-boat. It knocked the stern right off, it did. Three days later they abandoned ship. As soon as we heard it on the wireless, my lady said, "He's gone, Henry," she said. She had this feeling. She had a dream about him that night, in the morning her hair was all turned white. We still got the telegram that come. And the one that come about our boy George. That's Albert.' He showed her an old colour photo. 'He went to Australia in 1951. He's got a grown-up family now. We haven't seen them, but they'll be coming over one of these days.' That was what Henry chose to remember instead of the card at Christmas signed with 'Regards from Albert and family'.

The first shafts of sunlight crept into Henry Staples's flat, catching him in his armchair where Mrs Richie had eventually left him yesterday. He had slept only in odd snatches and had dreamed of his wife and himself when they were young. He didn't move as the room, with the morning brightened. Eventually his neighbour let herself into the flat with a key and was startled on finding Henry Staples.

'Oh, Mr S, you gave me a turn there for a moment. I thought you was . . .' She tactfully didn't finish the sentence. 'I was going to get your breakfast. But you're up.' She came over to him. 'Haven't you been a'bed? You'll be the next one in hospital.'

He wasn't listening, thinking about his wife getting his breakfast, when his thoughts suddenly jumped track. 'I think she's still alive, my Joanny,' he said quietly. 'There's been a mistake made. That's what's happened. A mistake's been made, it has.'

'Oh you poor man,' the neighbour said softly. 'You're going to give yourself such grief.'

It was almost like a prayer.

45

Emotional batterings were something that Jessie Marvill found herself taking more and more, but possibly because she was able to take them less and less. For that reason there was nothing she wanted less than to become involved with Henry Staples's problems. She had seen him yesterday when he had again arrived on the geriatric ward looking for his wife, and he had cried as she sat with him and he had told her about his wife as a young woman. Although expressing himself clearly he had been confused in time and believed his wife was still a young woman. Jessie Marvill had been upset for the man's future as well as his immediate loss. She could anticipate the sequence of events, and knew that he was likely to end up in a psycho-geriatric unit. The inevitability of that depressed her, the fact that he was on his own without any extended family to support him, depressed her further. It was compounded by the fact that Dr Kumar had earlier called to see her to tell her he was returning to India – she had almost said if there was a vacancy she would like to have joined him and his wife. But as though reading her thoughts he had given her his address in Bombay. Then rather foolishly she had discussed the idea with Roger Trentham, who had simply said the whole prospect of her going barefoot in the third world was a nonsense, which made her feel worse. That was the sort of reaction she knew she would get from her father.

She was seeing patients at the geriatric day hospital when Dr Bayliss phoned and asked her to cope with Henry Staples, who was at the mortuary, refusing to accept that it was his wife they had there. She had said she couldn't spare the time as there was a room full of patients waiting but Dr

Bayliss had told her that old people had nothing else to do. Her boss hadn't given her a reason why she couldn't see Henry Staples, but tangentially he had given her one more reason why she would eventually turn down his repeated offer of the registrar post.

Entering the mortuary with an almost crippling sense of reluctance, Jessie Marvill found Mr Staples in the chapel viewing his wife's body. Andy Betts, who had returned from sick leave, was in the doorway keeping one eye on the old man, while the other flicked across the pages of the *Star*.

'Hello, Mr Staples,' Dr Marvill said, stepping into the chapel. 'No nearer to resolving the problem?'

'That's not my lady,' he said.

'Oh, I think it is,' she told him. It looked like Joan Staples, though in the face of Henry Staples's denial, despite what she believed was his mental state, she didn't want to be dogmatic. It might not be after all, and her insisting otherwise could do more harm than good. Dr Marvill turned to Andy Betts. 'Is there any possibility that two bodies could have become mixed up?'

'Not likely, doctor,' he said with absolute assurance, even though he hadn't been around. 'We had an Ethel Staples in when I was off, but she went, didn't she?'

'What happened to her?'

'Collected by the undertakers.'

'He seems convinced that this isn't his wife. He ought to know. Do you have details of the other Mrs Staples's arrangements?'

The man sighed impatiently. 'Only the undertakers. The death clerk's office made the arrangements.' He showed her the details in his ledger, as though they were irrefutable proof.

'Ethel Rose Staples, aged eighty-seven,' the deputy administrator read from a file in her office, when Dr Marvill pursued the inquiry.

She felt the situation was ridiculous, and wondered about this caring profession where no one knew patients well enough to state categorically that a dead woman was who she was supposed to be; whether her husband would be satisfied with the answer was another matter. Pursuing this first through nursing, then general administration, was, Dr Marvill found, like wading through mud. She was getting angry with everyone generally and herself in particular, for she had treated Henry Staples's wife, but couldn't be any more sure herself.

'She was Dr Ravi's patient,' Jenny Rogers continued. 'She died of viral pneumonia. There was no next of kin, but she made a will expressing a wish to be cremated.'

'That doesn't help Mr Staples,' Dr Marvill said.

'Perhaps you should ask Dr Ravi to try and identify her. Or Dr Cullen, as he has more dealings with the chronics,' the administrator suggested. Beyond that she wasn't helpful; the paperwork was in order, but that told them nothing.

Giles Cullen, Dr Ravi's registrar, was forty-three and obviously at a dead-end in his career. That was something Jessie Marvill might have admired had it left him with a vital interest in what he was doing, but he had none; geriatric medicine was the only job he could get. His appearance, like his manner, was jaded – he was wearing yesterday's soiled shirt with a button missing at the collar, which his tie didn't quite hold together. To see a doctor like this after the arduous process of qualifying, depressed Jessie Marvill but she was curious to know what caused him to lose the drive he presumably once had. She wondered if it was to do with the disenchantment she felt with institutionalized medicine, the constant no-win battle against ignorance, apathy and stupidity, all of which seemed compounded by the state; the reasoning that spent millions of pounds treating an aged population for chronic bronchitis rather than actively discouraging people from

smoking seemed stupid in the extreme. But she felt no urge to get closer to Dr Cullen.

'I signed Part 2 of the cremation certificate,' he said as they stood in the fridge room and looked at the woman's body. 'But I'm buggered if I can tell whether this one was our patient or not.' He lit a cigarette which got him a frosty look from Andy Betts. 'I don't think she was. Mind you, I find that one piece of crumble looks much the same as another.'

'Mr Staples doesn't think so.' Jessie Marvill knew she would get no further on this tack.

'I can't see it matters, does it,' Dr Cullen said. 'She's dead, after all. Why doesn't the old boy take her away and bury her?'

That was what Andy Betts wanted to happen, and almost everyone else who was involved, and Dr Marvill wondered if the simplest course wouldn't be to let the matter drop, have the social services arrange the funeral, and let Henry Staples cope the best he could with what he believed about the woman. However, someone somewhere would eventually have to deal with the effect of that on Henry Staples.

Jessie Marvill didn't let the matter drop, but instead pursued it with Dr Pigeon, who had performed a post-mortem on both women.

'I'm not sure I'm able to verify which Mrs Staples it is in the mortuary,' the greyhaired pathologist said. He had a sincere smile, yet a complexion like a butcher's. 'They both died of a similar pulmonary infection. Though I suspect in the older of the two women, Ethel Staples, her condition was exacerbated, if not caused, by the introduction of Hela cells.'

'Hela cells?' Dr Marvill was a little surprised. 'Why would anyone introduce those?'

'Cancer research. Some of these elderly patients had been participating.' It was Dr Pigeon's turn to be surprised. 'I assumed you knew. Dr Bayliss helped set up the programme. I think perhaps you'd better discuss it with him,' he said, closing the line of inquiry. 'I'm sorry I can't help you further.'

Dr Marvill approached her boss uncertainly, wondering if in fact the pathologist hadn't got his geriatricians mixed up as Ethel Staples had been Dr Ravi's patient.

'No, that's right,' Carl Bayliss said candidly. 'Dr Ravi found one or two patients for these tests as well.'

As if unsure of what she was hearing, Dr Marvill sat and stared at the man, thinking perhaps she had missed something and now misunderstood what she was being told. 'But wouldn't they throw the body's immune system into complete turmoil?'

'The point of the exercise is to stimulate the immune system into acting against foreign cells,' Dr Bayliss explained. 'It's early days, but the results aren't as encouraging as one might have hoped.'

Depression had settled over Jessie Marvill by the time she left her boss's office, and all the indications were that that feeling wasn't going to lift in a hurry. Here was a consultant whom she had counted among the good guys, despite his obsession with litter, and he was treating patients as though they were laboratory animals on whom a cure for cancer could be tested. The fact that her colleagues could do this, and do it presumably unchallenged, precipitated a crisis in her career, one that started her seriously considering whether she should leave medicine altogether; the crisis that would immediately follow when she came to the point, was whether she was in fact strong enough to leave medicine, for the commitment, the investment of her time and energy, to say nothing of her emotions, was too great to easily walk away from. However, a possible alternative, she feared, was that if she stayed, she might end up like Dr Cullen, without belief in herself and what she was doing, or perhaps worse, like Dr Bayliss, convinced in the assumption that he could do as he would to patients.

All of this, as revealing as it was to Jessie Marvill, brought her no nearer to knowing whether the Mrs Staples in the mortuary was the woman Henry Staples had been married to. The consensus seemed to be that it was, which was all she could tell the social worker. She also advised her to keep close tabs on him as he would probably be in need of help himself quite soon.

Henry Staples was outside the mortuary when Andy Betts arrived on his bicycle, which he parked in the toilet off the postmortem room. He brought with him a Marks and Spencer carrier bag with his sandwiches, a bottle of wine, and a carton of milk.

'Come to have another look at your missus?' he said. 'You might as well come through here.' He led the old man into the fridge room, taking his carrier bag with him.

'That's not her,' Henry said quietly after Betts drew the tray from the fridge and flicked back the sheet.

'Well there's no one else, old son. That I assure you,' Betts said, putting his lunch away in another fridge.

He wasn't sure how long this could go on – him pulling out Mrs Staples, with the old man saying it wasn't her – but supposed it would until they locked Henry Staples in the loony bin. The sooner they did that the better, he thought as he went to the office to phone Jenny Rogers.

'Is Mrs Richie there?' the deputy administrator said into the phone. 'It's Jenny Rogers.' As she waited, she thought how silly this situation was getting. If Mr Staples didn't take his wife and bury her, finally the hospital would have to make the arrangements, she supposed, and there would be an end to it. 'Ah, Mrs Richie. Our friend's back at the mortuary. That body's been in and out of the fridge so often I imagine even she's fed up with it.'

'Well I don't know what the answer is.'

Mrs Richie was perhaps the most sensitive to Mr Staples's predicament, if partly out of a sense of guilt, and didn't want to have to steamroller him into a decision. But she was afraid it was coming to that.

'I do feel sorry for him like everyone else,' the deputy administrator said. 'But short of offering him another body, I don't know what to suggest. We've checked and double-checked. I mean, this can't go on. Could you pop across and try and sort something out.'

It was a bright dry November morning, and sitting out of the wind the sunshine was warm. Mrs Richie had taken Henry Staples into the hospital garden, only a small part of which was still tended. The old man talked knowledgeably about the floribunda roses that had hung on.

'My Joanny didn't go a lot on flowers,' he said. 'She loved the vegetables. She loved them all right.' He fell silent a moment, then suddenly said, 'I don't know what happened to her. Something did. I keep wondering where they got her. They could have her on one of them old people's wards, with one of them food pipes in her. They keep a lot of people in there like that. They won't let their families take them home. I think that's what's happened.'

'No, I'm afraid that's not the case, Mr Staples,' Mrs Richie said firmly. 'Look, don't you think we ought to make some arrangements about the funeral?'

'She's not my lady,' he whispered. 'I keep telling them. I can't bury someone who's nothing to do with me.'

'You'll make yourself ill if you go on with this,' she warned him. 'You don't want to go back in hospital – have people think you're barmy?'

After a long silence Henry Staples dabbed a neatly folded grubby handkerchief to his watering eyes and said feebly, 'It's not her.'

'Come on, Henry,' she encouraged gently, 'don't distress yourself. I know it's upsetting, but let's be realistic. C'mon. Let's go to the canteen and get a cup of tea and talk about the arrangements for the funeral shall we?'

He didn't respond at first. But then rose slowly off the

bench, his joints feeling suddenly stiff. He shuffled off, resigned to the notion of burying that woman who they were saying was his wife. They were quite mistaken, he told himself, for he knew it wasn't his Joanny, and he would keep returning to the hospital until he found her.

Book IV

Mental hospitals are an institution whose primary function isn't to cure the sick but defend a society based on privilege and injustice.

Quietly and without fanfare, [illegible] had [illegible] ago [illegible] hospitals [illegible] because [illegible] remained [illegible] hadn't been [illegible] goes starting [illegible] local groups [illegible] like custodians [illegible] treatments and [illegible] found for patients was [illegible] sought rather than [illegible] were discharged from the hospital [illegible] halfway houses [illegible] the [illegible] Surprisingly, these [illegible] they were back [illegible] frighten children. [illegible] the [illegible] would be [illegible] integrating incoming mental patients [illegible] to that end [illegible] hospitals. But [illegible] once the psychiatrists [illegible] assessment [illegible] from a disturbance which [illegible] particularly [illegible] therapeutic community.

This progressive movement [illegible] been made possible [illegible] patients, although mental health workers [illegible] for their patients [illegible]

46

Quietly and without much notice being taken, a revolution had occurred during the last decade in most mental hospitals; those vast, bleak Victorian loony bins had become freer, more tolerant, less restrictive. Bars had been removed, doors left unlocked, patients, some of whom hadn't been off the wards in years, were able to come and go as staffing ratios increased; the atmosphere became more liberal, patients more human, the staff more sensitive, less like custodians, who contained rather than helped. New treatments and experiments were tried, stimulation was found for patients who before had vegetated, turnover was sought rather than stagnation passively accepted; patients were discharged from the hospital or went to hostels and halfway houses run by the health or social services. Surprisingly these patients didn't break down the moment they were back among society, didn't create disturbance or frighten children. The theory then had been that one day the bins would be run down and eventually closed, integrating incoming mental patients into general hospitals; to that end psychiatric units were set up within general hospitals. But with beds only readily available in the big old bins the psychiatrists tended to send patients to them for assessment; the more interesting patients, or those suffering from a disturbance which the consultant psychiatrist was particularly interested in, were offered places in the therapeutic communities.

This progressive movement within mental healthcare had been made possible less out of a sudden concern for those patients – although mental health workers cared very much for their patients – but rather because money had been made available to increase staff, brighten wards, stimulate patients, open therapeutic units, support halfway houses. It had arrived like a light breeze on a sultry summer's day.

The situation wasn't to last. When the cuts in healthcare financing started to take effect, mental healthcare was in the front line, despite a DHSS policy document stating that it should be given a high priority. Mental patients, like their equally poor relations in geriatric care, lacked political muscle. Staffing ratios were cut, fewer nurses recruited, units closed, no new ones opened, notwithstanding a recommendation that special secure units should be established at general hospitals in all Regions to deal with the violently disturbed, or the special funding that had been made available; the unions, nursing staff and local community alike opposed such units, fearing the patients, while the money for them was used elsewhere. The progressive units that managed to stay open did so precariously; money was withdrawn for halfway houses, some of which closed with patients who weren't ready to survive unsupported being returned to the bins. Because of staff shortages wards were locked, it being easier to supervise contained patients with few staff. These regressive moves, like the earlier progressive moves, happened quietly without people noticing, apart from those working and living in the loony bins.

Coldbrook was a mental hospital set in twenty-seven acres of once disciplined landscape gardens; the most striking change due to cuts was the gardens' appearance. Although no longer immaculate, well-stocked or colourful now that the staff gardeners had gone, leaving a firm of contractor gardeners to trim the grass and hedges every two months, the gardens were easier to live with for not being a reflection of someone so evidently avoiding inner chaos. The old and rambling buildings were austere, uninviting, three-storeyed, connected by wire-meshed-in walkways open to the weather; the windows were locked and would open only a few inches. Coldbrook was built in the nineteenth century at a safe distance from the city, but had subsequently been overtaken by urban sprawl. Like most of its kind Coldbrook, which was part of St Clair's District, was often a dumping ground for the chronic mentally ill and patients too disturbed to hold any interest for psychiatrists with specialized units.

A hangover from more progressive times were the work programmes. Patients capable of industrial therapy could go to the workshops within the hospital and pack plastic washers or light plug fuses for cigarettes and sweet money; it was boring, repetitive work that kept their hands occupied, but did nothing for their minds; the more stimulating work programmes which were supervisor-intensive had been scrapped.

Within the hospital was an enclave of resistance to traditional psychiatric care in the form of a therapeutic community, which was run by Dr Clive Hendrix. However, because of its independent nature this unit was under threat from most quarters of hospital management, who saw the prevailing attitudes eroding their power base. The current administration preferred the more easily managed locked wards; as these patients had little freedom and few rights, they were clothed, cleaned, fed, medicated. Concern was expressed about the lack of stimulation, but none of the psychiatrists and certainly none of the patients themselves came banging on the administrator's door, unlike those involved in the therapeutic community whenever cuts affected them.

It was for one of the old locked wards that Henry Staples was destined when he arrived at reception by ambulance. He was the only patient, the other two people in the vehicle were the two nurses who had brought him from St Clair's.

The escort was hardly necessary as Henry Staples offered no resistance, in fact he seemed barely aware of his surroundings. He shuffled like the old man he now was, having lost the spring in his step. He had kept going on his own for three months after his wife's death. Initially he had become depressed and agitated, then followed a steady intellectual and personality deterioration; he was failing to keep himself clean, and had become urinary incontinent, something which was expected to get worse.

'Mr Staples?' Staffnurse Bridget Carr arrived from the ward to collect him. 'Mr Staples?' she repeated, believing he hadn't heard her. 'Would you like to come over to the ward for supper?' She gave him a pleasant smile, but no choice. 'Take my arm, dear. Come on, we'll get supper.'

Without protest Henry Staples allowed himself to be led away.

Food was an occasion on the disturbed ward where Henry Staples was taken. Patients with any awareness of time and place looked forward to it not for the culinary expertise of the hospital cooks, but to relieve the monotony, and eating was one of the few sensual pleasures left to most patients. Some didn't even have that; the senile dementia patients had to be fed by the nursing staff.

On Allen Ward there were both male and female patients, their age from seventeen years old, which Bernice Attwood was, to Henry Staples, who on rising eighty-one was the oldest; their troubles ranged from paranoid schizophrenia to subnormality with violent behaviour. Allen was two separate wards, male and female, which for convenience were supervised together. It ran the length of the huge block, with divisions to give some semblance of privacy, though not much; then a lot of the patients were often so doped that absence of privacy wasn't an issue. Heavy medication was a necessary supervisory aid as there were forty-eight patients and only four nurses.

Medication came directly after meals. The drugs trolley was chained to a pillar in the centre of the room, the only key held by the charge nurse on duty. This evening Ali Baig was supervising the whole ward, although his official responsibility was for the male section. Most of the patients were eating the wholly unappetizing supper in the communal dining area which separated the male and female sections, along with bathrooms and communal day rooms. They chomped away, unconcerned what it was they were eating. Those who finished ahead of the others either smoked cigarettes or tried to cadge cigarettes from those who were smoking. The haze of tobacco smoke became thickest after meals.

Among the patients at one of the tables was Bernice Attwood, who had lost her early teenage plumpness, and was now an attractive young woman. There were one or two patients not much older than Bernice, but none as bright. She disliked meal-times, both for the low standard of food and seeing these patients eat, especially when nurses forced them – this happened at almost every meal with Jeannie Jinman, who was at the next table. Also she didn't like the drugs associated with meals, but couldn't avoid them as the nurses waited until the medication was swallowed.

'Will you open your mouth, Jeannie?' Nurse Carr said, having difficulty getting her to eat. She had a tolerant smile that could disappear in an instant, leaving a sharp frost. 'Will you, open for me, Jeannie? Will you?' When she didn't: 'Open it!' Gentle coercion flashed to menace as patience evaporated; it often did nowadays. She had been on this locked ward sixteen months, which was too long a stint for anyone. 'Open it, you stupid woman!'

Revolting as she found this, Bernice's attention was riveted on Nurse Carr.

So too was that of 2nd-year Student Nurse Jackie Peek, who was new to psychiatric nursing, which was a part of her general training. She stopped feeding Henry Staples and watched Nurse Carr, who tried to force food into the patient's mouth.

Charge Nurse Baig called her away. 'Jackie. You help with medications?' He accepted the limitations of the system and pretended such things didn't happen.

He unchained the drugs trolley as Nurse Peek joined him. 'It not always difficult – but often is,' he said.

'Eat!' Nurse Carr crashed the spoon against the patient's teeth.

'Mrs Adamson. 50mg Largactil. 50mg of Surmontil,' Charge Nurse Baig said running his thick finger across the register. He measured out the syrup, and put the green and white capsule into a small cup. Nurse Peek checked it, then took it to the patient.

Ronnie Bhad was the fourth nurse on duty, and as he helped clear plates on to the dinner trolley, a very fat girl approached in a panic.

'Nurse Bhad! More, nurse, more,' she said.

'There is not more, Junie,' the Asian nurse told her pleasantly.

'More, more. I want more.' She scrabbled through the dinner trolley looking for more food, grabbing at scraps.

The next patient for medication was Brenda Andrews, who was twenty-one and overweight. She was reluctant to take her tablets, but appeared to after a little encouragement.

'Have you swallowed them?' Nurse Peek asked. Brenda nodded.

When Nurse Peek turned back to the trolley Brenda pushed them out of her mouth and laughed.

Bernice smiled. She was too scared to do that herself, for when she had acted up over her medication she had been put in the pad, which was what they called the padded cell.

The nurse brought her two yellow 25mg tablets of Neulactil.

'Oh, do I have to?' Bernice said, choosing this moment to show her reluctance.

'I think you should,' Nurse Peek wasn't very firm.

'Bernice,' Nurse Carr said from the next table. 'Be a dear, take your medication.'

'I feel fine.' Bernice's resolve was ebbing.

‘You don’t want your trouble flaring up, do you?’ Nurse Carr stopped what she was doing.

‘Please. It won’t.’ It was said in a small voice.

‘Bernice. Be a good girl.’ She took the tablet from Nurse Peek and extended it to Bernice, who reluctantly swallowed it.

Everyone took their medicine for Nurse Carr.

There was no stimulation at all for patients in the evening; drugged towards a peaceful night, they grouped in front of the colour TV to watch a quiz show.

Patients not watching TV were sitting in chairs, or standing against radiators, staring into space. There was no conversation apart from noises of patients trying to cadge cigarettes, or those with cigarettes trying to get lighted. Any movement, such as the porter arriving to collect the food trolley, was an immediate focus of attention for some.

Charlie Williams let himself through the door then locked it. The ward had a one key system for every door.

‘Hello, pretty.’ He greeted Bernice, who emerged from the bathroom as he came along the ward.

She didn’t respond, and when he tried to take her arm, she wrenched it away.

‘What you doing tonight, girl? How’d you like to come dancing?’ Still there was no response, but he wasn’t put off. ‘Would you like me to come to your room. I’ll give you a pound.’ It was a serious offer. He never expected to pay more than one pound.

She slowly shook her head.

‘Go on, girl. Don’t be afraid of getting pregnant. They’ll put you on the pill.’ All the younger women were given contraceptive pills.

Brenda Andrews, who was slightly subnormal, or had been when she arrived here two years ago, grew excited at seeing Charlie Williams. She got out of her chair and shuffled off to meet him, her movements imitative of senile dementia patients. Brenda was a lady who was suffering more the effects of being here than what had brought her here.

'Charlie, you come to see me,' she said. 'You come see me.'

'I come for the dinner trolley, my pretty,' he said, unplugging it.

'You come to my room, Charlie,' Brenda wailed.

The secret was out. Then Brenda had never kept the relationship a secret, she was too simple-minded.

Instinctively Bernice withdrew, while Brenda who enjoyed sex more than anything, became upset at the rebuff. Bernice watched in alarm, turning the anger she felt at her friend's distress towards herself. She ground her teeth and dug her fingers into her palms. Sometimes when her nails weren't chewed she drew blood.

'I can't, my pretty, I gotta get back.'

Charlie Williams was but one of the staff who had sex with patients. He wasn't totally blatant in this, but had no regard for the law concerning sexual intercourse with mental defectives. He was vaguely aware that it was unlawful, but had never heard of anyone being prosecuted.

'No! No!' She seized hold of the dinner trolley to prevent him leaving.

Her holding the trolley made leaving impossible and he knew it, but still Charlie Williams tried.

Screaming, 'No! No!' Brenda shook the trolley. Other patients began to get excited, despite their drugs. The psychiatric nurses appeared almost at once. They rarely ran to a disturbance as that excited patients more, and if all the patients acted up at once there would be no way the four of them could cope.

'Brenda! Stop that,' Nurse Carr ordered, without considering the possible rightness of the young woman's protests.

'He come to room. He come to room,' she repeated over and over.

'Let go, Brenda. Let go,' Charge Nurse Baig said, trying to break her grip on the trolley. 'Be a good girl, Brenda.'

With no interest in being a good girl Brenda eventually turned the trolley over, sending dishes clattering. This caused other patients to jump about and cry out as if at some programmed entertainment.

Ali Baig became determined. 'She'd better go to the pad,' he said, knowing they would have to take her there by force.

'Leave her alone!'

Bernice suddenly launched herself off the wall. Although Nurse Carr was the object of her hostility, she pounded her balled up fists against the charge nurse. 'Leave her. Leave her.'

Surprise stopped them completely. The shock of this response stopped Bernice.

'You calm down, Bernice,' Nurse Carr told her, 'or you'll go to the pad as well.'

Bernice retreated to the wall as the nurses dragged Brenda away.

The padded cells were the size of the single rooms some patients had, only isolated on a corridor. Unlike patients' bedrooms, the one item of furniture was a rubber covered foam mattress on the floor, which with the walls was a thick vinyl pad. Around the edge was a trough for when patients relieved themselves, and for the water when the pad was subsequently hosed down. The sturdy door, which had a viewer, was covered in the same way. The door was unbolted and Brenda Andrews was brought in. When she was released she immediately tried to crash through the nurses to be with 'her Charlie'.

'You calm down, Brenda. If good we let you out,' Baig said, closing the inner door on her protests. He locked the outer door. 'It looks like being a busy night,' Baig observed.

Despite a DHA circular suggesting that patients should

only be in the pad for up to thirty minutes, Brenda would stay there until morning.

'She'll settle down, she usually does,' Nurse Carr said.

'I better get the doctor to give her something,' he said, anticipating an argument from Nurse Carr. 'Dr Hindmarch is on call. He want to see Bernice after her outburst.'

A lopsided face was the only response Nurse Carr made. She was in favour of calling on the medical staff to support the nursing staff, but resented the attention the registrar gave Bernice.

When she had arrived on Allen Ward ten months ago Bernice had shared a dormitory with eight other patients; being allowed a single room as she had been three months ago was a privilege that could easily be withdrawn, as Nurse Carr frequently reminded her. Bernice wondered if she would be moved back into the dormitory, as she lay on the bed in her untidy room refusing to look at Robin Hindmarch, the psychiatric registrar. Although this doctor controlled her treatment, she decided not to mention her anxiety over losing the room, for even when he ordered something done, Nurse Carr wouldn't necessarily do it, for she controlled Bernice's life. Her mentioning anything to the doctor would get her into the nurse's bad books.

'Why do you think you had that outburst, Bernice?' the doctor asked after a long silence. He was short, stocky, intense, about thirty-four, with close-cropped hair, and looked as if he was in the front line.

'I don't know.' It was the alternative to blankness.

'I think it's good that you start turning your anger outwards,' Dr Hindmarch said, 'instead of at yourself.' He saw that as a positive move.

Bernice hesitated, then said, 'They pick on Brenda. Some of the patients and staff make her have sex.'

'That concerns you, does it?' He wasn't unaware that it went on. 'Doesn't she want that? Wasn't that why she got into a state?'

'I don't know.' She waited. 'She's my friend.'

'Sometimes we feel better for an outburst,' Dr Hindmarch told her. 'It often releases the feelings of frustration we have, and can't put into words. Is that how you felt?'

There was silence from Bernice.

'Would you like to try and sort that through, Bernice?'

After a long silence, during which she stared at the posters of pop and TV stars on the walls, she said, 'I got angry about what they were doing to Brenda.' She paused, not certain where she was going, and uneasy about what she was saying. It wasn't that she didn't trust this doctor, but knew he would be leaving the hospital before she did.

Robin Hindmarch waited, unconcerned about long silences, believing them more productive than pushing patients along prescribed paths.

'She shouldn't be on this ward,' Bernice paused again, believing she had said something she shouldn't. 'I've heard the nurses say she shouldn't, not this long.'

'What would you do with Brenda?'

'She wants to go home to her Mum and Dad,' Bernice said. That seemed a simple solution, though wasn't one she saw for herself.

'What if they don't want her?' the doctor ventured. That was an accurate appraisal; Brenda had been placed here for the sake of her family.

'It's not fair,' Bernice said, 'she's been here for over two years. Why can't she go to sheltered accommodation?'

'There aren't enough places for subnormal patients basically.' He smiled at her. The only real answer for the Brendas of the world was to have someone truly care for them, then they could function outside of the hospital society. But Dr Hindmarch knew there was no way to make people care. 'Are you okay now, or do you need something?'

The girl shrugged. 'I don't like taking pills. They make me feel funny.'

'How's that?' he asked.

'I don't know. It's like I'm here and seeing myself over there at the same time.'

'Do you think it's the drugs?' he asked. 'Perhaps it's more to do with you.'

'I think it is the drugs,' Bernice said.

'I'll look into that. You'd prefer not to take anything?' He rose off the chair and considered her. He had an idea about moving her out of this environment and on to the therapeutic community, and wondered if he would meet with objections from his boss. Schizophrenics didn't usually respond in therapeutic community, but he thought Bernice might. 'How would you feel about getting off this ward?'

She looked at him with a feeling of unease. The thought that this was a trick initiated by Nurse Carr crossed her mind, even though she didn't associate her with Dr Hindmarch. 'Not sleeping here?' she said. When she understood that was what he meant, she added, 'I'd do anything not to be here. It's sending me mad.'

'How are you getting on in the workshop?'

She shrugged.

'It's not very stimulating, packing washers,' he said. 'Especially not for someone with your intelligence. I'll have a word with Dr Hendrix, see if you can come over to Brechin Ward.' He was sure it could be arranged if he was prepared to accept the responsibility for her.

'Could I really?' she asked with childlike disbelief.

'I think you'd get a lot from that sort of community.'

The prospect gave Bernice a sudden lift, and momentarily she forgot all the doubts that crowded in and confused her. She experienced pleasure of anticipation, something she had not known in a long while, and uncertain how to express it, she began to masturbate unselfconsciously, rocking to and fro on the bed.

47

Brechin Ward was a single-storeyed, triple-winged building serving several functions. One wing comprised the therapeutic community, which had fourteen patients, and was run by the consultant psychiatrist, Dr Clive Hendrix. Another wing was the admissions ward, where the consultant shared the beds with Dr Peter Grant – each of the eleven firms in the hospital had their own admissions ward. The third wing, which ran at a right angle to the rest housed a psychiatric day hospital, with occupational therapy rooms where patients could paint, make pottery or have music therapy. Each of the units was separate but patients from any of the sections could use the therapy rooms.

In the therapeutic community's common room twenty-five people sat in a large circle on a variety of chairs, these being both patients and staff. Group therapy was the main activity of the community and three mornings a week all the staff sat in, giving a patient–staff ratio of almost one to one. No one sat in any particular order, and with no one wearing a uniform or a white coat it wasn't immediately apparent to Bernice Attwood, as a newcomer, who was who, with the exception of Dr Hindmarch, and Rose Sutton, a psychologist who had seen her on Allen Ward. She didn't remember Dr Marvill who had seen her two years ago when she was doing her gynae rotation. Nor did Jessie Marvill remember Bernice, and it was only after reading in her file about the case where she had given evidence about Bernice suffocating the baby she had delivered herself that a familiar chord had been struck. On recalling the details she had taken an interest in Bernice and had spoken to Robin Hindmarch about her. The result was

Bernice visiting for the day to see whether she fitted in, and whether the other patients would be willing to take her; however, if they said no the staff wouldn't say otherwise. Although confused about roles, Bernice soon realized that the three Asians, a woman and two men, were staff; the patients were all white and under thirty. Rose Sutton who was the oldest at sixty, was also distinguished by her two-piece suit; everyone else, apart from Dr Hendrix, wore jeans of some sort. Although the patients here were all young, ambulant and receiving no medication, they were generally lethargic, even apathetic, but none the less awe-inspiring to Bernice for the freedom of choice they seemed to have, and the way they exercised it.

Peter Parker, who was tall, good looking and in his twenties, was chairing the meeting with the large, battered minutes book open on his lap. Unable to come to terms with his homosexual tendencies, he had several times tried to kill himself. 'Eh, we have a newcomer here today,' he was saying, using the book as a prop, rather than to extract details for this meeting that had been noted the previous day. He prefaced and punctuated his speech with a nervous 'eh'. A patient hurried in and found a seat, distracting Parker, who had only recently taken the chair, which passed to a different patient each month. 'She's eh, Bernice Attwood . . .' He looked up as another late-comer arrived, the OT. 'Is, eh, Doris not joining us?' he asked, realizing the psychology student was missing.

'She's got a dental appointment,' Marion Spinks informed the group. She was the senior ward nurse, a Malaysian, who like the other nurses wore denim.

'Eh, she didn't say,' Parker commented.

'She did,' Marion Spinks told him. 'You wrote it up.'

'Did I?' He refused to look for the reference. 'So, eh, back to our visitor. She's, eh, Bernice, she comes from Allen Ward,' Peter Parker said. He faltered and studied the repressed scrawl in the book as if having difficulty. 'Do you want to tell us about yourself, Bernice? Eh, how you came to be here. Eh, why you want to. Stuff like that.'

Bernice squirmed uncomfortably. Had she known this was required she might have said no to coming. She detested speaking publicly, had hated it whenever her parents had thrust her forward for praise for her work. At school she had dreaded morning assemblies in case her name had been called. She felt physically sick and looked round at Dr Hindmarch, who waited like everyone else.

'Well, my name is Bernice Attwood, I'm seventeen years old, sixteen and ten months, I've been on Allen Ward for ten months . . .' she said quickly and in a low voice. Then pulled herself up, believing she had made a mistake. 'No, yes, ten months. I've been doing a workshop for the last three months, packing washers. That's all, I think.' While speaking she avoided looking at anyone, but dug at her palms, and finally made her hands bleed.

A long silence followed. This was a frequent feature of group therapy.

'How did you come to be here?' Anne Drinkwater asked. She was a patient.

Bernice remained silent, unable to answer the question.

'What happens here, Bernice,' Marion Spinks said, 'I don't know if it was explained. We talk things through. Anything you can't cope with here you talk about in your small group. Then every week someone presents his or her progress report to the group.' That had been explained to Bernice, but it was worth repeating as few patients from the locked wards readily grasped the democratic process. 'Do you feel you can answer Anne's question?'

'Question?' Bernice said.

'How you're here.'

'Here? Well, Dr Hindmarch said I should try it,' she replied. Her hands weren't still for a moment. No one told her to stop that as they would have on Allen Ward.

'How did you come to this hospital?' Anne Drinkwater

wanted to know.

'This hospital?' Repeating the last part of the question gave her time to think. 'I was sent here.'

'Eh, the sort of thing we'd like to know, Bernice,' Peter Parker interrupted, 'is why you were. Eh, it might be something you can only talk about in the small group.'

They waited while Bernice tidied her bleeding palms with a piece of crumpled tissue.

'It's nearer to where I live,' she said, like that was reasonable.

'Where's that?'

'That? I lived with . . .' she hesitated. 'My parents.'

Identifying a block here, Dr Hendrix asked, 'Do you see your parents, Bernice?'

'See them? They visit me some weekends.'

'How do you feel about that?' Dr Hendrix said. Knowing what their relationship was, he looked for her to express the hostility she felt.

Bernice resumed attacking her hands.

'What hospital were you at?' Anne Drinkwater asked. One of the more vocal members of the community, she was about twenty-six, but looked older, and had the least dress sense. Having tried several times to kill herself she bore scars on her arms and wrists, and one on her throat. When not in group session, where cigarettes weren't allowed, she chainsmoked.

'Hospital?' Bernice hesitated, feeling stigmatized even here. 'I was in Broadmoor.'

There was no significance to the pause that followed.

'What do you hope to get from this community?' Rose Sutton asked.

'Get?' Bernice searched for an answer, mistakenly believing that questions from the staff were more important. Finally she shrugged.

'Why should we let you come here?' James Watson, another patient, asked.

'Oh, Dr Hindmarch said it would help me,' Bernice said.

'How will it help us?' Watson asked.

Bernice wasn't ready for that.

'What James is asking,' Rose Sutton said, 'd'you think you will be able to contribute to this community?'

'Contribute? I could take an interest in what you're doing,' Bernice said.

'Would you be prepared to stay for at least six months?' asked Anne Drinkwater.

This apparent option confused Bernice. She raised her eyes towards Dr Hindmarch.

'I'm not sure that question has much relevance,' Dr Hindmarch explained. 'Bernice has to be somewhere.' He didn't explain here that the court had sent Bernice to Broadmoor, nor would he even if the fire alarm had not sounded in the corridor.

There was no stampede for the exits. 'Oh not again,' was the collective reaction. Such false alarms were frequent.

'I'm beginning to suspect someone is doing this purposely,' Dr Clive Hendrix said. It was meant lightly, but there were other threats to this community.

'Eh, is that paranoia, Clive?' Peter Parker joked.

'Probably,' Dr Hendrix responded coolly. He didn't enjoy such observations from patients, any more than he would tolerate inquiries from them about his personal life.

Michael Gallagher, a withdrawn twenty-year-old, got up and strode out. The exit of this former skinhead with his much scarred body from self-inflicted wounds was a way of drawing attention to himself. This time no one rushed out to coax him back as often happened.

'Eh, what'll we do, close the meeting?' Peter Parker tried.

'I think we should work through,' Marion Spinks said. 'We had a short meeting on Tuesday.'

'Can't we shut it off?' Anne Drinkwater said. She knew the answer.

'I tried before,' Dr Hendrix said. 'It got us into trouble

with the union. Not to mention the Fire Officer!' For some reason, that no one in administration could explain to the consultant's satisfaction, it took hours to convey the fact that it was a false alarm, and shut the bell off. He dreaded the day there was a real fire.

'Perhaps we could muffle it.'

'Or tear it off the wall,' James Watson suggested, getting out of his chair. He went into the adjoining bedroom area behind a steel partition wall and reappeared with a blanket.

'So,' Peter Parker said. 'Eh, we're not going to close the meeting?' He shrugged resignedly, and went back to the minute book for the next item.

The group meetings with the entire staff in attendance usually lasted about an hour. Afterwards the staff met in the spare room, and the patients had some free time. After most large group therapies they went off to their small groups, but with none of the staff available to sit in there was little point; these patients weren't self-starters.

The alarm bell, although muffled, continued to ring throughout the staff meeting. A minor irritation, but one that served to make the eleven staff members brief in their observations. Not everyone spoke, while the psychiatric liaison officer's only comment was that the alarm might have been the result of all the cigarette smoke in the room. He got up and threw open a window. Having recently given up smoking he was a bit obsessive.

'I accept that Bernice needs a chance to relearn how to relate to people,' Dr Hendrix was saying. 'What I'm questioning, Robin, is whether Brechin is the right environment. Her placement here would be fairly controversial.' He was thinking of her position *vis-à-vis* the court.

'I think she's worth the risk. During her stay at Broadmoor she got a lot of stimulation,' Dr Hindmarch said. 'She made good progress. Clearly Broadmoor wasn't the right environment for her any more than the disturbed wards here are. They are lucky to have two qualified nurses coping with forty-eight patients. The last OT to visit the ward stayed only an hour.'

'We are very understaffed,' Olga Richardson, the occupational therapist, said defensively.

'I understand that. My point is, even with so little stimulation and help during her ten months on Allen Ward she's still managed to make a more realistic appraisal of herself and the mess she's in. She is often angry now instead of sullen and inward-looking.'

'But what about this patient regarding the courts?' Hendrix wanted to know. He had enough battles currently with the administrators without placing a patient within what for her was a proscribed environment.

'I can't deny there is a problem. But Roger knows more about that.' Hindmarch referred the question to the lean, forty-five-year-old social worker, Roger Brentwood.

'Simply she's not free to leave when she's fit to be discharged.' He had a habit of sucking his teeth and lips. 'She was sent to Broadmoor by the court. It's more accident than design that she was transferred here instead of to a secure unit.'

Secure provision had been designated for St Clair's, but the unions objected to having violent patients there, and the money to run the unit was subsequently spent elsewhere.

'That's not much of a future,' Dr Hendrix observed. 'But I question the high input Brechin would provide. Schizophrenics don't normally do well in therapeutic communities.'

'I'm not sure that what she did warranted such attention from the court,' Dr Marvill said. She was doing a six month psychiatry job following a long period out of work after she had finally turned down the offer of becoming a geriatric registrar. Jobs seemed harder to come by each time she went looking. This one job would be accredited for her GP vocational training scheme, but she was no less reluctant about going in that direction.

'I think Jessie's right,' Robin Hindmarch said. 'An unfortunate set of circumstances led her through the courts rather than to hospital. She burned down her parents' house and was supposed to have told the police that she tried to kill them. I think there's some doubt, though at the time she was clearly psychotic.' He resisted going into her history, as it would have meant listing a catalogue of deeds which he sensed his colleagues might judge her for.

'How do you see her future?' Dr Hendrix asked.

'I think she would certainly benefit from the stimulation she would get here. We might even think in terms of her going on to a group home, perhaps Ebury Road. Or maybe having extended weekends at home.'

'Isn't that ambitious?' Rose Sutton, the psychologist, asked. 'I saw her on Allen. I didn't think her ability to cope with life situations that good.'

'A month ago I would have agreed, Rose.'

'She doesn't seem to have any worthwhile relationship with her parents,' Rose Sutton said.

'All the effort comes from them. They very much want her back home,' Roger Brentwood informed them.

'I won't resist her coming here if you see that much potential,' Dr Hendrix said. 'I think we might have problems. Anyone have any objections?'

'Does she need to be warded?' Ray Bheemul, one of the male nurses asked. Patients likely to run away were warded, which meant their clothes being removed, leaving them with pyjamas.

'I don't think so,' Dr Hindmarch said. 'She may go through a disruptive stage. What I believe we should do is ignore where she's been, or whether she came to Coldbrook by accident.'

'Let's see what the community thinks of her. If they're agreeable, offer her a place.' Dr Hendrix believed that the community itself would reject the girl.

48

Mental institutions for many patients were often safe environments which they were reluctant to leave, and the longer they stayed the more difficult it was to leave; the familiar and known, however oppressive, frequently gave comfort and shelter from the harsh realities of the world outside. Some simply couldn't cope with those realities; some had stayed too long ever to leave and pick up threads of former lives, others had no recollection of former existence and no one to help them through the transition. A number of patients at Coldbrook had been there all their adult lives, mostly women, incarcerated by their families, with the aid of their GPs, for being thought morally rather than mentally defective. One such patient had been in residence forty-nine years, her problem had been masturbation; she not only still had it, she was now as mad as anyone. That happened to a lot of patients who came into hospitals like this. It was widely acknowledged among the medical establishment that the public would be very alarmed if patients who went into a general hospital deteriorated like patients in mental hospitals, to a point where they couldn't come out.

With lip service still being paid to the notion of closing the bins, an effort was made to rehabilitate some long-stay patients back into society. One such was Samuel Irons, a burnt out schizophrenic in his early fifties. He had been at Coldbrook for twenty years and had become institutionalized to a considerable degree. He still didn't understand the decision to send him out, despite Dr Hindmarch carefully explaining that he was well enough to leave, and that if he didn't go now he never would.

In the six-bedded dormitory on Allen Ward he was slowly packing his suitcase. He had few possessions, but had been at this task a long while, as though believing that if he didn't get packed he wouldn't have to leave.

The ward door was unlocked and Charge Nurse Baig appeared.

'Ah, Samuel,' he said. The old and the deranged were quickly stripped of any formal address. 'It soon won't be worth you leaving us, you take so long.'

A glimmer of hope rose in Samuel Irons and sped across his long, thin face. 'Is the doctor coming?' He didn't immediately see Dr Hindmarch behind the large Asian nurse.

'Your big day, Samuel?' Dr Hindmarch told him.

'I'm having a bit of the old trouble again, doctor,' Samuel Irons said with breathless anxiety. 'If I could hang on for a day or two, give my chest chance to clear up. Give it a chance to clear.'

'Not to worry. We've given you some tablets for that. The social worker's fixed up your digs,' the doctor said. 'I hear it's a nice room.'

'Yes, it's a nice room,' he said. 'I met the landlady. She knows I'm from here. They got a nice telly room.'

'And you've a job,' Dr Hindmarch said. He wondered how long this man would survive on his own. Ideally he should have been going to sheltered accommodation, which a lonely room, even with a sympathetic landlady, fell short of, but there were no places available. However Dr Hindmarch was of the opinion that it was better for him to have tried and failed, and if he didn't do it now he never would.

Samuel nodded. 'It's a good job, stacking shelves in Tesco's.' His first choice was a job in a bakery, and at the thought of hot cakes he would smack his hands together in excitement. But he had abandoned that prospect as being too ambitious.

'If I could hang on for a few days.' He coughed and wheezed.

'I think we'd best keep to our schedule.' The psychiatrist gave him an encouraging nod. 'You've enough medication for a week. We'll give you another prescription when you come to outpatients.'

No one on the main ward said goodbye or wished him luck, and Samuel Irons avoided saying goodbye to anyone and by so doing avoided acknowledging his departure. Someone leaving the ward with the hospital-supplied cardboard suitcase was unusual enough for most patients to be aware of, but it prompted no discussion. When he was gone he was instantly forgotten, and the patients' attention fell into the middle distance once more.

'I've only managed to get myself pregnant again,' Mary, a toothless, round-shouldered young woman, said with dismay to no one in particular. Mary often got herself pregnant, and in order to support that fantasy she would even retain urine until she started to swell up. The last time her 'baby' was delivered she peed the bed and had become violent when the nurses tried to change the sheet.

Bernice gave her no more than a glance. She was sitting with Brenda, who was cradling a rag doll and not taking in what was being told her about Brechin Unit. When Bernice left this ward Brenda would get upset and start attacking the staff.

Other patients were sitting around after lunch, some watching the television while awaiting their medication.

Nurse Carr who was handing out the drugs with Ronnie Bhad, brought both Brenda's and Bernice's to them in time to hear Bernice say, '. . . It's not a bit like this ward. Everyone's really friendly. You can come and go as you please and do what you like. It's really great. I can't wait to go there . . .'

'I'm not sure you'll be going anywhere, Bernice,' Nurse Carr told her, 'not if you keep spreading wicked lies.'

Panic loomed in Bernice. She wanted to smash this woman, but instead found herself attacking her own palms.

'I know you told Dr Hindmarch staff are having sex with patients on my ward.' She managed this with a calm, even tone. 'Why do you try to get us into trouble? After we've been so nice.'

Struggling to articulate some protest, Bernice experienced difficulty and frustration; her palms bled as her nails bit deeper. Suddenly she let out a cry. 'I'm not! I didn't! I didn't!' Words burst out of her with a flood of anger, she swiped the medicine from Nurse Carr's hands.

Her explosion stopped everything in the ward. The nurses were down on her before she could press home an attack; that wasn't Bernice's intention, but they had no means of knowing.

Kicking and screaming she was taken to the padded cell.

This was another transient point of interest in the patients' day.

'You can jolly well stay there until you calm down,' Nurse Carr informed her with a suggestion of satisfaction. She didn't like Bernice Attwood, and hadn't from very early on. The reason for this was her objection to the special attention she received from Dr Hindmarch. There was no one special here unless she chose to make them special. She also resented the way he allowed Bernice direct access to himself as a higher authority, but it was less productive being cross with doctors.

'I don't want to stay here. I want to go to my room,' Bernice said, suddenly confused about why she was here.

'Now you just stay there.'

'I want to go to my room,' Bernice said with childlike insistence.

'You are a silly girl, Bernice,' Nurse Carr told her reasonably. 'You've spoiled your chances. I don't think you're ready to go to Brechin Ward. You're too disturbed.'

With that Bernice hurled herself futilely at the barrier formed by Nurses Baig and Bhad. And after they left Bernice threw herself at the door, even though she knew from experience it wouldn't yield. She hated more than anything being put in the padded cell. It was small, windowless and oppressive, and had a sickly smell of urine, vomit and disinfectant. Feelings of desperation and desolation at not being allowed to go to Brechin Ward drove her against the door. She screamed and cried to be let out, but no one heard, no one came, and eventually when hoarse from exhaustion, she slid down the plastic wall to the damp plastic floor, which was unpleasant to touch. She drew her knees in front of her chest, and her arms across her face to shut out everything.

It was a long time before anyone came to her.

The three nurses on the disturbed ward frequently played cards in the office during quiet periods, and didn't stop when Dr Marvill came along the ward and appeared at the door, other than to let her in.

'You wanted me to have a look at Bernice Attwood,' she said. She was having her evening meal when she received the call, and had willingly abandoned dinner.

'She's quietened down now, doctor,' Nurse Carr said, coming around the desk and getting Bernice's file. 'She can probably come out of the pad. She got over-excited about going to Brechin Ward. What a shame it's making her like this. She was settling down nicely.'

'Do you have Droperidol on the ward?' Dr Marvill asked, checking the patient's medication record. Like most doctors she tended to prescribe what she could most easily spell. 'I'll give her 20mg. That'll see her through the evening. I'll just have a word.'

Bernice was still against the wall with her knees drawn into herself when the doctor unlocked the cell door and didn't react.

'Hello, Bernice,' Dr Marvill said. 'How are you feeling?

You had a little flare up. Feeling a bit calmer now . . . ? Would you like me to give you something to calm you down? What was the problem . . . ? Would you care to tell me about it?'

Finally Bernice shrugged.

Dr Marvill felt even that was an achievement. 'Was it just excitement about going to the Brechin Unit?' she asked.

Hope pierced the dullness of her eyes. 'Can I still go?' she whispered hoarsely, unfolding her arms.

'You wouldn't be prevented from going as punishment, Bernice,' the doctor said.

'Did Dr Hindmarch say I could?' – responding more.

'I'm not sure they'll want you, Bernice,' Nurse Carr informed her as she came into the room with the medication. 'They have enough problems without you getting out of control.'

When the nurse arrived Dr Marvill noticed how the patient retreated like a tortoise into its shell. She wondered about saying something as Nurse Carr proffered the yellow tablets. Sometimes it was better to defer to the nursing staff as they were with the patients day and night; but sensing the agitation the nurse's presence caused Bernice she decided to stay and talk with her after the nurse had left, and reassure her about being allowed to go to Brechin still.

The following morning she made a point of speaking to Dr Hindmarch about Bernice. The only opportunity was on the way to an outpatients clinic. She had seven patients of her own to see. It wasn't the ideal moment as Dr Hindmarch was late.

'How violent was her outburst?' It wasn't something he was alarmed about.

'I'm not entirely sure. She was calm and quite lucid when I saw her.'

'Had she heard any "voices" prior to her outburst?' – this was of more concern.

'The nursing staff seemed to think so when I spoke to

them afterwards. But Bernice said that she hadn't,' Dr Marvill said. 'I didn't challenge her on that.'

'She seems to have that side pretty much in control,' Dr Hindmarch said. 'I'm not sure there would be any point in letting her come to Brechin otherwise. What do you make of her?'

'She's a very intelligent girl. And I think she's very sensitive to her environment. As I recall when I saw her at St Clair's I thought if the parents had had some sort of therapy it might have saved Bernice a lot of pain.'

'You don't think her schizophrenia is real?' Dr Hindmarch said.

'Possibly it could have been less crippling. From what I've seen on Allen Ward I think possibly she's intimidated by the staff. Certainly she's inhibited by them. Possibly she sees Nurse Carr as a parental figure who she's distressed about disappointing.' Images of herself as a girl younger than Bernice sped across her inner eye, and she knew how crippling it was to have little value to one's parents in other than what one achieved. Jessie made a mental note to explore this area with her own therapist at her next session.

'She was under a lot of pressure at home,' Dr Hindmarch said. 'I think she was worried about the possibility of failing. I'm really interested in what you made of the parents. Bernice was a bit unusual in that her "voices" didn't tell her to do things. Instead they told her to take responsibility. I think she's going to make out all right on Brechin,' he said enthusiastically. 'Incidentally, Jessie, be careful about what you put in this patient's notes, remembering her relation with the court,' he advised, glancing about as he said it. 'In fact it's probably not a bad idea generally to be careful about what you put in patients' notes. Especially if they tell you anything incriminating.'

Dr Marvill was puzzled. Inadequate note-taking in psychiatric medicine perhaps more than any other specialty made for inadequate treatment. 'I've been trying to make comprehensive notes. I can't say I always succeed.' Like most other doctors she got tired or disinterested, let things go and then couldn't catch up.

'I'm aware of the consequences. But with the trend towards computerization it means all kinds of people could tap into our records. Especially the police.' Dr Hindmarch made an apologetic face.

The situation was a serious worry and he didn't have an answer. The consequence of such actions was that in six months he would move on to another job and his successor would find relatively no patient notes worth having. But he decided that that was preferable to losing confidential information through computer technology. He studiously avoided such technology by holding no credit cards, filling out computer information sheets incorrectly. If inconvenient at times, it did mean he wasn't a cypher in some data bank. He smiled to himself as he went into the outpatients clinic, wondering what he might have made of patients had he learned this about them. He didn't explain his smile to Jessie Marvill.

In the world outside that safe environment Samuel Irons had so recently and reluctantly left he wasn't getting on very well. His job was proving too much for him; it wasn't like packing washers in the hospital workshop. The money was better, not that he would know what to do with sixty-four pounds a week. The problem wasn't in stacking the shelves, but the fact that the shelves were in a shop busy with customers, any number of whom approached him wanting to know where certain items were. The pressures built up until they were more than Samuel Irons could reasonably cope with. The result was him sitting in the office while the pink-shirted, cigarette-smoking manager from behind the desk, dealt with six things at once. He signalled a cashier to come in as she appeared at the door. 'Be with you in a minute, June,' he said. Then into the phone, 'Six gross of eggs short. Yes, they weren't delivered.' He pulled an impatient face at the cashier as the party down the phone went to check. He turned back to Samuel Irons. 'Shelf stacking's not quite right for you, sunshine,' he said condescendingly. 'You want something better than that. But I don't know what. I've no alternative but to let you go I'm afraid. You will get a week's money in lieu of notice.'

'Thank you, doctor . . . I mean . . .' At once Samuel was confused and embarrassed. He rose as the cashier giggled.

'We've got your address. If I think of something to suit you,' he said hustling him out, 'I'll be in touch.'

'You'll be in touch?' Samuel Irons said, attaching hope to these words as if an offer of friendship.

'We'll write to you, 'we find the right pigeon-hole for you,' the manager said, his thoughts engaging the next problem.

Samuel Irons shuffled away, believing this was a temporary setback, and that the store manager would find him some job where he didn't have to meet people.

The letter from the store manager offering him another job didn't arrive, and Samuel Irons didn't quite grasp the fact that it never would. Each morning he waited on the stairs landing in his not very attractive digs as the mail dropped through the door. He didn't attempt to go down and collect it as it wasn't his place to. Almost before the letters reached the mat the landlady was out of her room scooping them up. She quickly identified the names on the three letters that arrived and glanced up at Samuel Irons.

'Nothing for you, Mr Irons.' She went back into her room. She lived frugally in a tiny part of the house and let out the rest.

Samuel was crestfallen. Eventually he would receive a registered envelope with his wages which would only endorse his faith in the store manager's sincerity. He shuffled back into his room.

He sat on the bed and stared at the faded wallpaper in his

dingy room, with its ill-fitting curtains. His suitcase hadn't been unpacked; the notion he clung to was that somehow he would soon be going back to Coldbrook where all his friends were. He was lonely, depressed, had no one to talk to, and was nervous about going down to the television room in case the landlady disapproved of him. Bedsitter-land was the worst possible world for Samuel Irons, but he had no alternative.

Having no less difficulty coping with the real world, though for different reasons, was Brenda Taylor. The problems that had beleaguered her soon after her husband's death two and a half years ago she knew were physical and real, despite being told that she was simply suffering from depression, but she had been unable to convince anyone, not her daughters, nor her doctor, and had become both desperate and depressed trying to. She had had numerous tests, which all proved negative, and the fact that in desperation she had taken an overdose of the tablets she had been prescribed only confirmed to people that her problem was mental rather than physical. Her doctor had called shortly after her youngest daughter's visit – she knew her daughter had rung him – he suggested she went into hospital as a psychiatric patient.

Mrs Taylor was perched on the edge of an armchair in her sitting-room, waiting for the doctor to return from the phone. She was in fact in poor health both physically and mentally, having lost weight, and taken on a vacant, distracted look; she had been too ground down by everyone's insistence that she was depressed to protest any longer, and only lassitude prevented her walking out of the house and under a bus. Having reached the point where she no longer had the energy to protest, she held to a vague notion that if she went into hospital, even on a psychiatric ward, they would discover what was really wrong with her.

In the hallway, in little better health himself, Dr Percy

Thurson was talking on the phone, trying to get Mrs Taylor admitted to Coldbrook. '. . . Don't tell me you can't cope, doctor,' he was saying, like someone hanging on only by his fingernails, 'I can't cope. This patient can't cope. What am I to do, leave her here where she might do herself an injury?'

'I think, doctor, that an admission here would be difficult,' the doctor on call said calmly. Admissions from GPs at night were resisted, the belief being that GPs tried to off-load patients at night but would be happier to cope with them during the day.

'Then what I'm to do?' Dr Thurson said, suddenly very quietly. 'Someone please tell me . . .' He was close to the point where he couldn't go on himself.

'I don't know,' the psychiatric SHO said. 'I think you'd better send her along to outpatients with a letter in the morning.'

'Thank you, Dr . . .' Dr Thurson put the phone down, not really aware of what he was doing. He paused to collect his thoughts before returning to the sitting-room.

'It seems there isn't a hospital bed available to you this evening, Mrs Taylor. Someone can see you at St Clair's in the morning. It's the best we can do.'

'Will they admit her, doctor,' Judith Taylor, the daughter asked.

'Not there, Judith,' the doctor said.

'I'm not disturbed, doctor,' Mrs Taylor said obsessively. 'There is something physically wrong. I know there is.'

'Yes, Mrs Taylor,' he said, too beaten to argue the point any more. 'Do you think you could stay with your mother tonight, Judith?'

The daughter seemed reluctant to commit herself. 'Yes, I suppose I could,' she said after a moment. 'If you think it necessary.'

'There's nothing wrong with my mind,' Mrs Taylor insisted in an enervated whisper as she sat in the waiting area of the outpatients clinic at St Clair's. Not having an appointment as such they had a long wait.

Judith Taylor seemed as though she didn't want to be associated with this woman. 'Mum,' she censured.

They had little else to say to each other. Judith surreptitiously eyed some of the more obviously disturbed people who came and went. Her mother mostly stared at her hands. It was late morning before Dr Hindmarch got to see them.

'I'm sorry you've had to wait,' he said as he brought them into the huge examination room, which had been part of a ward. 'What seems to be the problem?' The GP's note told him she had suffered from acute depression for about two years, and that she had made two attempts on her own life.

'My mother's been depressed,' Judith Taylor said. 'Ever since my father died of cancer.'

Dr Hindmarch looked at Mrs Taylor. 'Do you feel that's the picture, Mrs Taylor?'

'I'm not disturbed, doctor,' she said quietly. 'There is something physically wrong with me.'

'Mum, you've had tests and everything.'

'Could you let her answer,' the doctor said tactfully. 'You can fill in any details you think she's missed. What d'you think's wrong, Mrs Taylor?'

At that she burst into tears. It was the first time anyone had seriously asked her that question. 'I'm sorry,' she said. 'I'm sorry.'

'That's all right. Crying might help.' He waited for her to recover herself. 'What is it you feel is wrong with you?'

After a moment Mrs Taylor said, 'I think I have cancer, doctor.'

'Mum! For Godsake,' Judith said.

'I'm sure the tests were wrong, Judith.'

'Where do you think the cancer is, Mrs Taylor?'

'I'm not sure, sort of here,' she said, spreading her bony

hands across her chest.

'You think it's breast cancer? Perhaps I'd better start with a physical examination.'

During the examination he asked the daughter to wait outside; relatives often pressured patients and some doctors felt threatened by their presence. There was no indication of breast cancer that Dr Hindmarch could find, though he noted that the patient was rather thin.

'How long after your father's death did your mother start believing she had cancer?' Dr Hindmarch asked the daughter while Mrs Taylor was dressing.

'I don't know. Perhaps a year. She got depressed very soon afterwards.'

'It's not uncommon,' the doctor told her.

'She's always been a bit of a hypochondriac, even when my Dad was alive.'

'Do you think she might agree to come in for a while?'

'I don't know,' the daughter said, suddenly shying away from the possibility of madness.

'How do you feel in yourself generally, Mrs Taylor?' the doctor asked when he returned to the examination room. He didn't invite the daughter.

'I don't know. A bit low,' she replied quietly. 'I tend to look on the bleak side. I can't get enthusiastic about anything knowing I have this other thing.'

'Cancer? Why do you think the tests showed nothing?'

'It seems silly, but they keep it from me.'

'Why would anyone do that, Mrs Taylor?'

'I don't know, but they do.'

'Are you anxious about anything, apart from your health?'

She shook her head.

'Have you noticed yourself getting anxious at any particular time of the day?'

She shook her head again, but he waited as she seemed on the point of saying something.

'I'm to blame. I let Raymond down,' she said. 'That's why I have this other thing myself.'

'It's a sort of punishment, is it?'

'I suppose it must be.'

'Is that why you took an overdose of drugs?' He waited, but she didn't respond. 'Do you remember taking anything?'

'I feel I've let my children down. I wake at night worrying about that.'

'What would you say to coming into hospital for a while?' he asked. 'Would you like to?'

She shook her head. 'There's nothing wrong with me mentally, doctor.'

'We can do some tests.'

'I don't want to,' she said, getting agitated.

'I think you should.'

'I'm not mad, doctor.'

'I'm not suggesting you are. But I just think we might be able to help you out of your depression.'

He didn't push her now as she became more agitated, and certainly didn't want to Section her, but felt she would be better off in Coldbrook where they could do a full assessment. He thought she was suffering from endogenous depression triggered by her husband's death, and although hypochondria was symptomatic of that he didn't entirely rule out the possibility of her being physically ill as well.

49

Brechin Unit community in its attempt to run on democratic lines – but with the staff having the final say if necessary – could veto anyone joining them. The theory was that if someone coming in was too far out of line with the community then the majority would be harmed. An *ad hoc* committee of patients, with two staff members sitting in interviewed Bernice Attwood. They met in a small, not very well furnished room. But only two patients showed up, Peter Parker and Anne Drinkwater. The interview was quite informal, but still Bernice was tense and nervous. She tried to control her fears by sitting on her hands and so avoid digging her nails into her palms.

'Eh, what you have to do if you come here is sign a contract,' Peter Parker explained. 'It's, eh, an agreement about your therapy. You agree to stay, eh, not have booze here or drugs or anything. Eh, you have to be part of the community. Everyone signs it.'

Bernice was nodding, but taking little of this in.

'It's a formality,' Marion Spinks, the nurse said. 'But you shouldn't treat it lightly.'

'Eh, if you don't keep it, eh, your side of the bargain, you can be warded,' Peter Parker continued. He explained what that would mean. Finally he looked at the doctor. 'Eh, that's it.'

There was a long silence. Bernice wasn't sure what happened next.

'When d'you want to move in?' Anne Drinkwater asked.

At first bemused, then almost speechless with delight, Bernice at last managed, 'Eh, you really mean I can? I don't have to go back to Allen?'

'That's what she said,' Dr Hindmarch told her. 'Perhaps you should collect your stuff.'

That suddenly alarmed Bernice. 'They might try and keep me there,' she said, not meaning to reveal her fears like this. She tried to retrieve the situation. 'I mean, I . . .' she moved her mouth but the words wouldn't emerge as she dug her nails into the palms of her hands. She said, 'I don't want anything. I don't need anything, I don't.'

There was an awkward silence as they watched her.

'Why do you think they might try to keep you, Bernice?' Dr Hindmarch asked.

Without thinking Bernice said, 'They don't want me to leave.'

'What do you mean by that?" the doctor asked. 'Why won't they want you to leave?'

'I don't know. I don't think they want me to be better,' Bernice explained.

'How might they stop you, Bernice?'

'Lock me up, or give me some more drugs?'

'But I've changed your treatment,' Dr Hindmarch explained. 'You won't have any more medication.'

'Oh, I see,' Bernice said, her mood suddenly changing.

'I'll go with you,' Anne Drinkwater offered, partly understanding her fears.

'I won't have to take any more drugs?' Bernice asked again.

'I've stopped them all,' Dr Hindmarch told her again. 'We don't use drug therapy here. We might give you something if you get into difficulty, but we try not to.' Dr Hindmarch looked at his watch, it was a frequent habit. 'Good. I'm sure you'll get on very well here.'

'I'll show you the ward, Bernice,' Anne Drinkwater said, opening the door for her.

Stepping out on to the corridor with Marion Spinks, Dr Hindmarch said, 'Anne's really beginning to sort herself out.'

‘She’s doing very well,’ Marion Spinks said. ‘She’s making a lot of contact with her family.’

Two patients appeared, one with bleeding arms, having used a razor on himself. It was Michael Gallagher. James Worth was helping him.

Neither the doctor nor nurse responded as Worth explained what had happened, while Gallagher continued along the corridor to seek help.

‘Eh, Michael’s having a hard time,’ Peter Parker said as he approached from behind. ‘Mostly to do with money. He didn’t get his giro this morning.’

They watched them go. The student nurse would clean him up and bandage his arms.

‘Did the group consider my suggestion about trying to contract work from the administration?’ Dr Hindmarch was a great believer in self-help, and a number of these patients were sufficiently in control now to cope with some occupation for which they would be paid and responsible, rather than controlled therapy.

‘Eh, there’s not much interest,’ Parker explained. He was embarrassed by the lack of interest. ‘It is on the agenda this afternoon.’

‘It would be constructive and might even provide some money.’ Dr Hindmarch didn’t really think it would prevent Michael Gallagher going at his arms.

The work programme proposal got a hostile reception at the afternoon group meeting, which all the patients, including Bernice attended, but only three nursing staff and Olga Richardson, the OT. For some of them work outside the unit was associated with life outside, and was a threat; some were reluctant to do the work in the unit, but most could cope with that.

‘Contracting jobs from the hospital management,’ James Worth said forcefully, ‘sounds like a lot of hard work to me. I mean gardening’s one thing. I don’t mind planting some lettuces and radish. But who wants to do painting and cleaning?’

‘Who would do all this work?’ Anne Drinkwater wanted to know. ‘Assuming they ever let us, which they won’t.’

‘Eh, well, there are enough of us.’ Peter Parker quite liked the idea, but tended to be swayed by the majority. ‘We have, eh, a cooking rota. We could organize other work in the same way.’

‘It’s an excellent idea,’ Olga Richardson said. ‘One of your main complaints is boredom. What to do with yourselves between therapy.’

‘Anyway, eh, think of the money we could make. That was why Michael did his arms this morning,’ Peter Parker said. ‘Right, Mike?’ He gave him a deferential smile. He admired Gallagher for his hardness, but avoided acknowledging any sexual attraction.

Michael Gallagher resented not having money, but knew what problems there would be if he had to work with someone looking over his shoulder, and disapproving. He’d get angry and start smashing things.

‘They wouldn’t gi’ us money,’ Alan MacIntosh said. ‘Not money.’

‘How much would we earn?’ Anne Drinkwater said, feeling it was pointless. ‘We can’t go on painting this place indefinitely.’

‘I don’t know. Eh, Brechin’s a sort of hospital within the hospital. It could become independent,’ Peter Parker suggested, ‘if, eh, we could persuade management to let us run it. Eh, I mean, the cleaning, window-cleaning, even buying our food.’

‘Yeah, well they do no’ like that. Is that no’ so, Marion?’ MacIntosh said. ‘Do they no’ resent our independence?’

‘You know as much as I do,’ Marion Spinks said. Although her commitment to this unit had set her apart from the general psychiatric nursing staff, curiously she felt a certain loyalty to management, despite knowing that they disapproved of the exclusiveness of the unit. ‘They’re trying to reduce staffing ratios here. But then so they are everywhere.’

'It would be great not having to eat that rubbish from the canteen,' James Worth put in.

'They wouldn't let us – they have contract cleaners,' Anne Drinkwater tended to be pessimistic even when things were going well.

'You could undercut them,' the OT suggested. 'The administration is always trying to save money.'

'That'll put people out of work,' said a patient who had so far remained silent.

'Eh, what about us?' Parker was momentarily enjoying the only voice in favour of the proposal.

'Food's probably bought in bulk,' Anne Drinkwater pointed out. 'They wouldn't let us buy our own.'

'What if we run out of money?' Alan MacIntosh said. 'What would we do for food?'

'You don't know what will happen unless you try,' Marion Spinks said, attempting to stir them up. 'Use this as therapy. Even if you only start a dialogue with management at least that's progress.'

'Eh, what do you say, Bernice?' Peter Parker suddenly asked the newcomer.

'Say? Oh, I don't know.' Until now she had been in a dream, hardly believing the reality of choice: the option to say no was a luxury. Throughout her stay in Broadmoor and on Allen Ward she had been given no option, nor when she lived with her parents. 'I think they'll try and stop it.'

'Oh,' Marion Spinks said, picking up on that, 'why do you think so, Bernice?'

Panic clawed at the young woman's vocal chords, and for a moment she believed this openness within the group was simply to trick her into saying something she shouldn't. She could only manage to shake her head agitatedly.

The meeting moved on, hardly missing a beat.

'Eh, Mike?' Peter Parker said, trying to bring his hero into the fold.

Gallagher shrugged.

'Be great to have some decent food,' James Worth said. He was tall, heavy-framed and needed lots of food to keep him going. Adding to his problem was the fact that he had been thoroughly spoiled by his mother and sister, and he generally expected such treatment as of right.

For a reason that she hadn't managed to identify, Chloë Shallcross found that the burden of fulfilling such needs had fallen to her in the six months she had been on the unit.

'You try cooking,' she said angrily. It was bad enough that she had to do the work, worse that it wasn't appreciated. 'You avoid your turn every time, James.'

'I don't want to poison anyone.'

'Eh, all we have to do is decide, is, eh, anyone going to talk to admin,' Parker said. He needed some names for the minutes book. But there were no volunteers, and he wasn't sufficiently self-assured to select anyone.

Although the prospect of such a thing was exciting, Bernice dreaded being asked to join a committee to approach the hospital administrator in case he realized who she was and sent her back to Allen Ward, as if the doctors had had no authority to place her on Brechin. The discussion she had had yesterday with Dr Hindmarch when he had said that if she continued to maintain her progress he foresaw the possibility of her going on to sheltered accommodation, might not have taken place. No time limit had been given her for this future move, but she wanted nothing to jeopardize her chances.

'You might think about this problem, and decide how to resolve it,' Marion Spinks said at the end of the meeting, knowing how much Dr Hindmarch wanted them to attempt this. 'Put it in the minutes book for the meeting tomorrow morning.'

Peter Parker did so and everyone sighed with relief at this being put off for another day.

* * *

The sheltered accommodation Dr Hindmarch had in mind for Bernice was more ambitious than the cottages within the hospital grounds, or those immediately outside the perimeter. It was a house that the local council were negotiating for. Ebury Road was, in residential terms, a desirable street of substantial detached houses, most of which had been converted into flats. Number 35 hadn't, and that fact made it ideal for a hostel where adjusted psychiatric patients could adjust further to the impact of life and its pressures. From the driveway of the house, which had been empty for a number of years, yet had avoided being vandalized, girls could be seen playing hockey on the field of the private school opposite. Therein lay the main problem for Dr Hendrix and those who supported him in his plans for this house.

Two men and a woman were waiting on the short drive as Dr Hendrix's middle-range Datsun drew up. Stephen Morwell, the District Administrator responsible for Coldbrook, Marjorie Forks, who chaired the Community Health Council, and Bill Williamson, a local councillor, were all in favour of this property becoming a psychiatric halfway hostel, but as the scheme wasn't without its opponents, the purpose of their meeting this morning was to determine how hard they should fight for it.

'Am I late?' Dr Hendrix said. He knew he was. 'Morning. Good morning.'

'Morning, Clive,' Stephen Morwell said. 'You know Mrs Forks, from the CHC?'

'We've met, and rowed,' Dr Hendrix said.

The memory of that previous meeting caused Mrs Forks to chuckle now.

'And Councillor Bill Williamson.'

They shook hands.

'That might be a distraction for some,' Dr Hendrix joked, motioning towards the hockey game.

'That could prove a serious impediment,' Councillor Williamson informed him. 'The school doesn't welcome the notion of this becoming psychiatric accommodation.'

'Not very charitable,' Dr Hendrix observed.

'Were charity and private education ever bedfellows?' he said sourly.

Knowing this councillor's socialist views, Dr Hendrix decided he could live with them in order to secure the hostel. 'Can we really afford this?' he said. He appreciated that the money which was being found jointly by the local council and the health authority hadn't yet been allocated.

'Not even the rates,' Stephen Morwell said. 'If it finally goes ahead.'

'There's no reason why it shouldn't, Stephen. Provided it suits the desired purpose. The council has no serious objections,' Bill Williamson said.

'The house is ideal,' Dr Hendrix said, unlocking the door to admit them.

The guided tour was valuable PR and could make the proposal a reality, Dr Hendrix decided, even though it took time he should have been spending elsewhere. Arriving late and arranging to be in two places at once was an indication of his belief in his own importance. To him all people were like patients, who would wait because what he had to give them was worth waiting for.

The group therapy in the common room on Brechin was almost over by the time Clive Hendrix arrived, but he slid into a seat without interrupting.

'Approaching the hospital management will be a complete waste of time,' Anne Drinkwater was saying. 'They won't take any notice.'

They hadn't, it seemed, progressed very far with the practical aspects of Dr Hindmarch's proposal, the consultant noted.

'How do you know until you try?' Dr Hindmarch asked.

'They'll not let us sub-contract work, not sub-contracted work. They won't even let you do it on a voluntary basis.' Anne Drinkwater knew this because she knew people who had volunteered in order to get access to drugs, only to be told there was no mechanism for making use of such volunteers.

'Eh, I don't know,' Peter Parker said. 'I'll eh, go if someone goes with me. Eh, anyone interested?'

After a moment Chloë Shallcross raised her hand, so too did Ruth Martin, who like Chloë got landed with more than her share of the chores. 'I'll go as well.'

'Did you, eh, have some sort of problem this morning?' Parker asked, as if only now registering Dr Hendrix's late appearance.

'The meeting at Ebury Road went on longer than expected. The group home project is finally underway,' Dr Hendrix announced. 'Barring hiccups.'

'What sort of hiccups?' James Worth had his hand down his jeans and was fondling his genitals.

'Some local residents are calling for a public inquiry over the scheme,' Dr Hendrix informed them, and glanced around the group during the silence that followed. This was a worthwhile exercise, as any of these patients might go on to the hostel. 'The council has received some objections from the school opposite over the proposed change of use of the house.'

'But patients will be living there,' James Worth pointed out, adopting an exaggerated frown, as if thinking hard about the problem.

'That is residential,' Dr Hendrix conceded. 'You know the real problem.' He waited. 'Those good Christians don't want my unit for neighbours. Maybe they're concerned about property values.'

That provoked agitation, but no verbal response.

'What are your feelings about this?'

Still there was silence.

'Well, put yourself in their place,' Dr Hendrix continued. 'Here you are, a good Christian neighbour keeping your end up. Would you want a psychiatric unit in your street? Maybe next door?'

'It's gotta fucking well go somewhere,' a young patient called Greg Wilson stated angrily.

'Why?' Dr Hendrix knew they would have a discussion now. He saw Dr Hindmarch look at his watch.

'Why shouldn't we become part of what's going on outside?' twenty-seven-year-old Katherine Trelford said, equally angrily. She was the most articulate of the patients when she chose to be.

'A good point, Katherine. Consider this, maybe these good neighbours are afraid of people who are suffering emotional or mental disturbance,' the psychiatrist said.

'Most of them aren't coping any better than the people in here,' she argued. 'They only give the appearance of doing so because they're all on Valium or booze. How will we ever adjust and become an integral part of society if people won't accept us?'

'Are you saying that society rather than you has the problem?'

'No, but I am suggesting that they helped with most of the problems we have.'

'Do they think we'll attack their children or something?' James Worth said, bringing the discussion down to action rather than ideas.

'What do you mean, James?'

'I mean you said the school was worried. You said it.'

'Sometimes things do happen to children,' Ruth Martin said.

'Are you talking about me?' Greg Wilson said, springing up and throwing his chair back. His relationship with a young boy was central to his being here, the guilt he was made to feel overwhelmed him. 'I'm not taking this.' No one tried to stop him as he slammed out of the room.

In the silence that followed Bernice heard a voice inside her quietly saying 'A lot of sane people do much worse to people, and to animals.' She decided not to tell them what had happened to people in Broadmoor, but instead told about the stray cats that were killed around this hospital. The people who ran the hospital put strychnine down for the cats even though some of the patients loved them more than anything. Bernice assumed that was why they were killed. Panic enveloped Bernice after her statement, and she feared retribution for making this known.

'What do you think causes this attitude towards the mentally ill?' Dr Hendrix asked, not picking up on Bernice's revelation.

'The newspapers stigmatize them,' Chloë Shallcross said, 'especially if a psychiatric patient commits a crime. No one says anything when a cancer patient commits a crime.'

'They sometimes do crazy things,' Ruth Martin said. 'Mentally ill patients.'

'No one knows what happens in mental hospitals.' Bernice felt a pressing need to tell her secret, even though she feared the consequences. 'Apart from patients.'

'Maybe you should enlighten the public. In the form of PR.'

'Eh, we could invite some of the objectors here,' Peter Parker suggested, and looked round, seeking praise for his idea.

'That'd be the end of the project,' James Worth said.

'Could we go to this meeting?' Anne Drinkwater wanted to know.

'I imagine it's going to be public.' Dr Hendrix turned to Michael Gallagher, who had made least progress and who he was considering moving off the unit. 'What do you think, Michael?'

He shrugged 'I don't want daytrippers looking at me. I'm not a monkey in a cage.'

Some of the others laughed.

Coming to his defence, Peter Parker said, 'On the old part of the hospital they have open grating to the cellars. Eh, people used to, eh, pay a penny to come and look at the lunatics.'

'Did they, Clive?' Katherine Trelford asked.

'That's part of this hospital's history. In those days they believed that the lunar rays affected people,' Hendrix said. 'That was the good Christian neighbours' Sunday afternoon entertainment.'

There was a long silence. This was the way the meetings usually closed.

50

Art was a subject Bernice had never taken seriously at school, principally because it was an unstructured subject that wouldn't have given her the academic kudos her parents sought for her, while pottery was a therapy for subnormals, something that was borne out by the existence of a pottery room within Brechin's occupational therapy complex.

Subconsciously Bernice chose pottery as a therapy rather than music or movement because her parents would disapprove, which said nothing for the talent she discovered, the empathy she had with clay, which the pottery OT, Jane Mitchell, actively encouraged. Bernice quickly learned the technique of structuring clay and achieving the correct proportions in her sculptures; the fine degree of expressiveness and sensitivity that she would go on to convey through her work were there in those very early pieces.

Whatever spare time she had away from therapy sessions Bernice spent in the pottery room, which was adjacent to the art room. One or two day-patients were usually to be found there, but none of them took pottery seriously and their presence didn't bother her. In fact she hardly noticed them. Not even the withdrawn chainsmoker who was at the end of the large bench where she was sculpting a head. He was making a floral bowl by rolling out snakes, lopping them into short lengths with a heavy knife, then setting them around a mould with a flower stamp. He glared at Peter Parker, who approached Bernice, feeling very possessive about this pretty girl who shared his bench. The fact that he had never spoken to her made him feel more possessive; she was flawless and he would kill anyone who said otherwise.

He would eventually kill himself without ever speaking to Bernice.

'How's it going?' Peter Parker said, clutching his clipboard as if for protection.

'How's it going?' She shrugged. 'It won't come right.'

'Eh, who's it meant to be?'

She shrugged again. 'I don't know. That, I suppose,' – indicating the book open before her. ''S not very good. I know it's not very good.'

The man at the end of the bench wanted to tell her that her sculpture was wonderful. At one point he thought it was himself.

'It's, eh, all right,' Peter Parker said.

'All right. It's only all right.' Bernice was disappointed. She prodded the head with a modelling knife.

Peter Parker wondered if he shouldn't have been more tactful. 'Eh, we saw the hospital manager. Eh, some of us did. Eh, he said it isn't up to him – eh, contracting painting or cleaning.'

'Oh,' Bernice wasn't especially interested.

'Eh, he's not against it. Eh, he said he wasn't. He said, eh he'd discuss it with the District Administrator. Robin Hindmarch said we should talk to the District Administrator. Eh, so, we're going to, so could I put you down to, eh, go with us?' he asked.

'With you? Oh, why me?' Bernice was immediately confused. Although committed to the community she now felt pressured to get on with her sculpting and not put her current placement in jeopardy.

'Eh, Robin Hindmarch said we should all go. We'll, eh, be taken seriously then,' Peter Parker explained, expecting her to agree at once.

'My parents are coming,' she said, grabbing at an excuse as she became quickly agitated. Her inner state was reflected by what she was doing with the modelling knife.

'Well, eh, I don't even know when he'll give us an

appointment even. Eh, but it'd be good if you could go with us.'

There was no response from Bernice as she systematically destroyed the mouth of the clay head.

'Look, you piss off,' the floral bowl man managed to say, waggling the knife at Peter Parker.

When Peter Parker departed Bernice didn't even acknowledge her rescuer at the end of the table. She was left thinking about her parents' impending visit. They came once a fortnight and each time Bernice felt a crushing sense of panic, it was as if they sucked up all the air around her so that she could no longer breathe. In their presence someone else took her over completely and Bernice became an entirely different person.

She tried to explain this during a therapy session with Dr Hindmarch and Jessie Marvill in a small side ward that was littered with used coffee cups which no one ever seemed to remove. Bernice had withdrawn as if for protection from even talking about her parents' visit. In her hands she constantly shredded a Kleenex, which Dr Hindmarch saw as an advance on tearing open her palms.

'How do you feel your relationship with your parents has progressed over the last month?' he asked.

There was silence from Bernice. Crumbs of tissue paper spilled over her lap, and she refused to look at either doctor.

Finally Bernice said, 'I don't know. I disappoint them,' the words barely audible.

'Why do you feel that matters?' Dr Hindmarch asked.

The girl didn't reply.

'You're very accomplished. Do you feel you could have an existence outside your parents' opinion of you?' Dr Hindmarch tried to get everything from the patient rather than offer his opinions.

'They were very disappointed with me doing pottery.'

'Did you discuss your work? What it means to you?'

She shook her head.

'Why do you think you have these feelings about being crushed when they visit you?'

Bernice didn't answer. She resisted the urge to scream, but wanted to shut out all thoughts of her parents, and go instead to the pottery room, take the damp wrappings off her sculpture and do some more work.

'If their visits are so upsetting why do you agree to them?'

'I don't want to disappoint them,' Bernice found herself saying, knowing it wasn't her saying it.

'Why does that matter to you, Bernice?' When she didn't reply, he asked, 'Do you resent your parents?'

'Of course not,' she insisted. 'They've always wanted what's best for me.'

'How would you feel if you never saw them again?'

Bernice almost laughed, but stopped herself in time. She wasn't going to fall for that. She knew the consequences of telling what she truly felt.

After a long silence Dr Hindmarch glanced at his watch.

'That'll be fine for today, Bernice.'

Bernice went without saying anything. She knew what she had to do, it was the only answer.

'What did you think?' he asked Dr Marvill as he made a cryptic note on the file about Bernice's reaction to her parents. Later his successor would misinterpret this.

'She's very torn about her parents. She still has a lot of hostility for them,' Jessie Marvill observed.

'That side of things is much more under control now.'

'Is she getting any benefit from continuing to see her parents?'

'I think there might be more to gain from letting it go on at this stage, especially in this freer atmosphere. If the visits cause a real crisis we'll look at the situation again,' Dr Hindmarch said. 'My feeling is that she'll not only come to terms with the visits, but learn to dominate them.' He looked at his watch, then got up, putting his pen away. He had a game of squash with a Chinese obstetrician.

The squash courts at Coldbrook, which had been built as part of the doctors' recreational facilities, were the best for miles and there was never any difficulty finding someone to play. Jessie Marvill had recently taken up the game, but wasn't fanatical. Winning or losing was equally good exercise. She enjoyed playing squash with Robin Hindmarch more than she did working with him, feeling he was more mixed up in himself than any other doctor she had worked with, and that he was using medicine to mask his own problems. Like her boss, Clive Hendrix, he was both dogmatic and authoritarian, she felt, while affecting a mask of liberalism. She knew she might have felt better disposed to either or both had they involved her more in the psychotherapy side of the firm rather than the psychotropic element which took her mostly to long-stay wards. She felt her involvement in the large and small group therapy was tokenism, even though there were inherent dangers in forming relationships with the psychologically and emotionally disturbed when one's contract only ran for six months. No matter what her involvement she soon realized that psychiatry wasn't a field where she would want to invest her future. This was confirmed by Robin Hindmarch's reaction when she had told him that she was going to therapy herself, the idea being to try and sort out her own confusions while trying to help others with theirs. He had responded rather as if she were a patient. Whether it was approved of or not, Jessie Marvill decided it was the best thing she had done. As a result she had even managed to stop sleeping with Roger Trentham on the occasions they now met two years after their relationship had ended.

Bernice wasn't around when her parents arrived. Unchallenged she had walked down the long drive and out of the hospital past the gatekeeper. Such freedom was a dreamed of luxury, and tasting it had caused her to tremble with apprehension. She had had her story ready in case, but without any impediment she turned along the street and was swamped by the roar of traffic. Suddenly finding freedom she hadn't known what to do with it, there being nowhere she had wanted to go, and nothing she had wanted to do. It was enough just to have it.

Frederick and Mary Attwood, both of whom were teachers in their early fifties, waited in the office on Brechin Ward while Marion Spinks went to try and locate their daughter. Mr Attwood was tense and sighed impatiently at his daughter not being there; his wife picked up his tension. Each sat stiffly on their chairs and were distinctly uneasy amid the madness on display: Chloë Shallcross was getting upset with her husband on the telephone, telling him he shouldn't listen to what another patient from her small group told him she had said. 'James is a fucking pathological liar,' she was shouting. The psychology student and the student nurse attached to the unit, were discussing the level of sexual activity on the ward. Eileen Topolski who was thirty and large and wearing a towelling robe, was haranguing Ray Bheemul for her clothes. She spoke of the injustice as well as the indignity. He countered that being warded was the result of wandering off, and that she should discuss it with Dr Hendrix; he stayed calm in the face of her agitation. The Attwoods avoided raising their eyes in case anyone noticed them.

'We're still trying to find her,' Marion Spinks said, returning and bringing them white coffee. 'She seems to have disappeared.'

'You mean she's allowed to walk out?' Frederick Attwood was alarmed. This had never happened in any of the secure units.

'She did know we were coming to see her?' Mrs Attwood chose to ignore her daughter's problem.

'I doubt she's gone far,' Marion Spinks said, with an untroubled smile. She gave them the coffee. 'I'm afraid the milk's gone a bit sour.'

Mrs Attwood sipped her coffee for fear of giving offence, but had difficulty swallowing it. Her husband was equally afraid of giving offence, but more afraid to drink the coffee in case there was something worse than sour milk in it.

Impatience increased, along with tension, for Frederick Attwood had some sense of his own importance, he wouldn't wait around this madhouse, not even to see his daughter, who was very dear to him. If she didn't arrive soon then she would have to wait till their next visit. But he thought it a poor show that the hospital couldn't contain her long enough for their visit.

Just as she had intended, Bernice avoided her parents. Walking out was a short-term solution, but short-term was all she thought of anything these days.

In fact she hadn't gone far, to a nearby general hospital, where she found herself on the paediatric ward. She had seen young women, some with children and looking no older than her, go into the ward, and no one had challenged her when she approached a cot which held a small baby. Before she could retreat a nurse was saying she could pick baby up, and asked if she would like to feed it. Bernice quickly realized that the nurse had mistaken her for the mother, so she didn't disillusion her. In fact she enjoyed the mistake. The baby was eleven months old, Bernice read from the cot card, and called Joseph; he responded well when fed from a bottle. A mother who had arrived at the adjacent cot, bringing another child, accepted Bernice without question, which fuelled her fantasy. Bernice never thought about her own baby which she had delivered herself when she was fourteen and had then suffocated; that might have happened in another life or to someone else.

'You watch,' the mother at the next cot said when she was getting ready to leave. 'She'll scream the place down the moment I go, she always does.' She was in her late twenties, and worn out. Besides the two here she had two children at school.

'That's all right,' Bernice told her. 'I'll sit with Loraine.'

'Oh, that's really nice of you, Bernice,' she said, seeing her way out without too much fuss. 'I bet you won't feel like that when you've got another two or three of your own.'

'I want a large family,' Bernice smiled, feeling great about being treated like an ordinary person. 'I was an only child. It was a real bore.'

'I was one of six, that's a drag too,' she said like she meant it. 'Okay, I've gotta go. 'Bye, Loraine, 'bye darling, see you tomorrow.' She gave her a kiss and a hug. 'Just shove the bottle in her mouth, 'she starts,' she advised Bernice.

'Oh she'll be all right,' Bernice said confidently, going to the other woman's baby, while managing her own on her arm.

The mother left with the older child, stopping briefly for a word with the sister, who just then appeared. Bernice felt a tug of panic as they both looked in her direction. It didn't subside when the young mother finally departed, for without turning Bernice was aware that the sister was watching her.

The ward sister stared across the bay, trying to make out who Bernice was. Finally she went across to her.

'Hello, how are you managing?' the sister asked. She knew this wasn't Joseph's mother now she saw her close to.

'Fine, he's great,' Bernice said enthusiastically, trying to disguise her nervousness. Her eyes flicked towards the exit, as she prepared to run. They wouldn't let her out of the hospital again if she was caught here, she realized.

'I haven't seen you before. Are you one of our Mums?' the sister asked, giving her the benefit of the doubt.

Anxiety prevented Bernice answering. She wanted to say she was a friend of the lady who had just left, but couldn't form the words. Confusion and panic appeared on her face. Bernice dropped the baby back on the cot and tried to run. The sister caught her by the sleeve.

'Just a moment,' she said. 'Who are you? Where do you come from?'

Bernice froze. Obviously she wasn't as ordinary as she imagined herself in this situation. Other mothers were staring now and Bernice wanted to die.

'It's not fair!' Bernice later declared angrily to the six people in her small group. 'No one objected to me being on the children's ward. I was helping out. The babies liked me. Joseph didn't cry at all when I fed him. But when I told the sister I was a patient here I had to leave. It's not fair.'

'Are you sure you were being victimized, Bernice?' Dr Marvill asked. 'Possibly they were concerned about you.'

'That's just hospital staff sticking together,' Bernice said. 'You all stick together.'

'She's right,' Anne Drinkwater said. 'People are quick to give you a bad name if you're a psychiatric patient.'

'Perhaps Bernice could arrange through the occupational therapist to help on the children's ward,' Marion Spinks suggested.

'I'm not going to. Mothers snatch their babies away from me. I'd sooner be back on the locked ward,' she said without thinking. 'At least you know what you are there.'

'Would you prefer to be back on Allen Ward?' Marion Spinks asked. If patients chose to go along a certain path her way was to let them.

That wasn't Dr Marvill's way. When Bernice didn't respond, she said, 'Let's return to your reason for going out of the hospital.'

There was a long silence while they waited for Bernice. She wasn't forthcoming.

During each small group session the whole time was often spent on one person's particular problems rather than dealing briefly with everyone. Talking in the small group and gradually building up trust and confidence in them as a whole helped patients to externalize their problems and deal with the feelings of alienation which had resulted.

'What were you feeling about your parents coming, Bernice?'

After a moment Bernice said, 'I don't know.' She checked the tension that was spreading through her. She kept her hands apart, which someone in the group had suggested she try, but they now worked as hard plucking and rubbing at her jeans.

'Do you like your Mum and Dad?' one of the patients asked.

'Of course I do,' Bernice said as though any other answer would lose her points. Deep inside something was saying that she hated them, and she was terrified in case those words emerged.

'Why do you like them, Bernice?' asked Marion Spinks.

'How do you mean?' Bernice said, as if not understanding the question. 'They're my parents.'

'Is that necessarily a reason for liking them?' the nurse asked, surprising Bernice.

She looked at her for a long while, then said, 'You're supposed to like your parents.'

Through her own personal therapy Jessie Marvill discovered she had some problems that complemented such an assumption. Within herself there was a lot of the child who was still attached to her parents through unresolved emotions that hadn't allowed the adult in her to develop in all forms. She recognized in her parents the same resistance to that development as she had seen in Bernice's parents, despite both wanting their child to achieve. This was reflected in her parents' attitude when she had spoken of her disenchantment with orthodox medicine, they had both agreed on the foolhardiness of any alternative course – it was the only thing they had agreed on in years.

'Tell me, Bernice,' Dr Marvill said, 'if they weren't your parents, would you choose them for your friends?'

'No,' Bernice said without thinking. Inside alarms were going off, and she knew she should be more cautious.

'Why wouldn't you?' Dr Marvill asked.

'Well . . .' She was becoming breathless with anxiety. Her hands came together under a will of their own and her nails bit into the tender flesh of her palms. 'They're my parents,' she said finally, and side-stepped the question.

'Assuming you met them in a park for the first time,' the doctor ventured, 'but knew everything about them in an instant. What is it about those two people you don't like?'

Bernice grappled with this proposition, then said, 'They make me behave in a strange way. In a way that doesn't seem like me. I say things I don't want to say to please them. I do things so they won't be disappointed. I just hate them for making me like this. I just hate them. I hate them . . .'

This was a point of departure for Bernice, one that she expanded on in subsequent small group sessions, always following the same tack, that her parents turned her into someone she didn't want to be and wasn't happy with. This acknowledgement of her feelings towards her parents was a large step forward, but one that left Bernice a long way short of where she needed to be, actually tackling her parents in relation to this knowledge.

The fact that she wasn't able to face her parents on their next visit wasn't something Dr Hindmarch saw as negative response; however her walking out of the hospital again wasn't something that Dr Hendrix was as sanguine about.

'It's going to get very tedious if she makes a habit of running off every time her parents visit her,' he said, coming along the corridor on Brechin with Marion Spinks. 'Have the police been notified?'

'An hour ago – they were mostly concerned to know if she was dangerous,' the ward sister said. 'I didn't give them her background.'

'I don't suppose she'll come to much harm,' he said, checking his irritation. 'Was she very upset?'

'Dr Marvill said she was mostly anxious about Dr

Hindmarch going on leave next week. Jane Mitchell, her pottery OT, is away also.'

'Oh, is she,' was the consultant's only comment about that.

They went into the general office, where several members of staff were, including Dr Hindmarch and Dr Peter Grant, the consultant psychiatrist who shared the admissions unit on Brechin Ward.

'I think she'd better be warded when she returns. At least while you're away, Robin,' Dr Hendrix said. 'The Attwood girl.'

'It's inconvenient her skipping off,' Dr Hindmarch said. 'But I think it's consistent with her progress. She's no longer prepared to be suppressed by her parents.'

'I'd be happier if she expressed it in some other way.'

'In time I'm sure she will,' Dr Hindmarch said, undeterred by his boss's worry over the responsibility of such patients. The worry was compounded by the fact that another patient had gone missing from the assessment unit.

'What about Mrs Taylor?' Dr Hendrix asked.

'She was brought back a short while ago,' Dr Hindmarch told him. 'I think the trip out exaggerated her depression. The moment she was left she tried to suffocate herself.'

'Perhaps she'd better have a course of ECT, Robin. It will certainly alleviate her depression. Assuming we ever get another anaesthetist,' Dr Hendrix added.

'There's a chap coming along this afternoon, Clive,' Dr Peter Grant informed him, looking up from his search through a patient's records. Peter Grant hadn't adequately learned how to delegate, and justified himself in such menial tasks by saying he understood his own notes best. 'Not exactly ideal, but I suppose he'll do.'

'I thought they'd be forming a not too orderly queue,' Hendrix said, without acknowledging the problem they had had with their last anaesthetist, who had managed to put three patients in coma, one of them permanently. He turned to his secretary, who held his appointments book, 'When are we seeing him?'

'Right after your ward round.'

'Oh dear. In that case could you see a presenile at St Clair's, Robin?'

'Be a bit difficult,' Dr Hindmarch said. 'Possibly after my outpatients there – if it doesn't go on too long. I have a game of squash booked.'

'I don't think I really want him here. See how urgently he needs a psychiatric bed. He's Dr Mathias's patient.'

Dr Hindmarch welcomed the opportunity of speaking to someone on Mathias's firm to ask them to see Mrs Taylor. He had been putting off sending her to St Clair's mostly due to his laziness rather than being entirely convinced that she was a reactive depressive and not physically ill. Now nearing the end of her assessment and having tried to kill herself, the matter needed his urgent attention, unless she was simply treated for the depression that she was undoubtedly suffering, and placed on one of the wards.

He found and had examined the presenile patient in the modern single-bedded room on the medical ward. The test was comprised mainly of a series of standardized questions relating to time, place and memory, and the response indicated widespread degeneration of the cells of the cerebral cortex. Just as he was about to leave Dr Crick, who was the medical registrar, came into the room.

'I'm sorry,' he said, 'I've only just been given the message you were here.'

'Oh, that's all right,' Dr Hindmarch said. 'I was about to leave as I'm a bit pushed for time.' He looked at his watch. 'Is there any history of mental illness here?'

'Difficult to arrive at. It seems so. His father had "them funny turns",' Dr Crick said, mimicking the patient's wife. 'He's gone rapidly downhill within about four months.'

'It looks like Alzheimer's disease. The spatial and temporal disorders are well pronounced. There's loss of short-term memory and marked aphasia. All in all he's pretty knocked off.'

Dr Crick nodded abstractedly, thinking about how he might persuade the psychiatrist to take this patient on board at Coldbrook. 'There's not much more we can do for him here,' he said.

'Or anywhere else,' Hindmarch pointed out. He would simply be nursed while he continued to degenerate. Death usually occurred within five years of the onset of the illness.

Crick considered the patient, and avoided looking at his colleague. 'Could you find him a bed?'

Hindmarch was expecting the question. 'I can't see that my boss will want him. He's not particularly interesting or unusual.'

'My boss certainly doesn't want him taking up a bed for the rest of his days. Couldn't you squeeze him in somewhere?'

Dr Hindmarch met the physician's embarrassed look briefly. He knew eventually that they would get this patient. 'Could you see a patient we have at Coldbrook? A Mrs Taylor. She's been diagnosed as a reactive, but insists there's something physically wrong. I'm not totally convinced she's hypochondriacal.'

'What's her background?' Dr Crick asked.

'Lost her husband with cancer just over two years ago. Her GP's been treating her for depression,' Hindmarch explained. 'She walked out on us yesterday. When she was returned this morning I asked where she had been going. She said to the sea to wash all the disease out of her. It does sound like a depressive delusion.' He didn't mention the conversation he had had with Jessie Marvill about that or her saying how she knew a healer who recommended to patients that image of a tide washing away the disease. He had wondered if Dr Marvill wasn't perhaps a little disturbed herself. 'I don't know if Mrs Taylor's previous tests were particularly thorough, or if there was a failure to follow them up. I feel we should start over again with her.'

'It seems like horsetrading,' Dr Crick said. 'Send her up in the morning. I'll find her a temporary bed so tests can start right away.'

'I'm equally embarrassed, but I will stress the needs of our friend to my boss,' he offered in return as they left the bedside.

The patient was oblivious to all this, and forever would be.

51

Although psychiatrists were little different from other consultants in their need to form themselves into committees for mutual advance, the format tended to prove less effective than for other specialties; not because they were less effective in committee, more that at the end of the day they had less muscle, the reason being that psychiatry wasn't considered an acute specialty that achieved turnover.

The consultant psychiatrists made up a subcommittee of the District medical committee and met on an *ad hoc* basis in the old-fashioned boardroom at Coldbrook. Dr Rahan Singh was in the chair, and the fact that he had managed to get no less than seven other consultants there indicated their anger over the failure by District to provide much promised psycho-geriatric provision. This was why the District Administrator had been invited.

'. . . reluctant as I am to admit this,' Dr Grant was saying, 'locked wards are once again becoming a prominent feature of psychiatric medicine. The main reason, of course, is lack of staff.' If conservative in both his appearance and attitude, few were more vociferous than Peter Grant over what he believed was the equitable entitlement of his specialty; unlike his closest colleague he wouldn't consider speaking to the press about poor conditions at his hospital.

'I'm not sure we can expect direct action by the District, Peter,' Dr Singh said. 'This is surely the knock-on effect of government policy.'

'Well, District certainly can influence the number of senile dementias we keep on locked wards, which is what we're here to discuss. I have twenty-seven. They're there through lack of alternative accommodation. Is the promised psycho-geriatric unit at St Clair's ever to open?'

'I am aware of the problem,' Stephen Morwell said defensively. 'It's something the DMT wants to see open, but I must be frank, I can't say when. At present there's barely enough money available to keep open the present level of beds. What I will keep to is the earlier promise I made that when there is money spare the psycho-geriatric unit will get first call.'

Both to further convince the administrator of their need, and because they had heard such earnest promises before, Dr Hendrix said, 'A lot of these patients are taking acute psychiatric beds, and acute geriatric beds, even acute medical beds. That's putting unnecessary strain on those specialties, with no lasting benefit. The fact is that the aged population's not only increasing, it's becoming more unbalanced. It's utter nonsense to shovel most of the resources in at the sharp end to extend life when locked wards in Coldbrook is where they so often end up.' It was a familiar theme, and something that frustrated him more and more, especially when he knew money was being squandered in 'glamorous' specialties such as heart and cancer surgery where it rarely improved the quality of life.

'I can only repeat that we hoped to include a psycho-geriatric unit in the next building programme at St Clair's,' Stephen Morwell said, refusing to be drawn.

'As I recall,' Dr Grant said, bending and straightening one of a series of paperclips, 'we were consulted on the basis of some temporary psycho-geriatric provision in Nightingale Block within this financial year.'

'I know,' Morwell conceded. 'The money ran out.'

'What are the long-term prospects of that block eventually being turned into a psycho-geriatric unit?'

'Well of course, that would mean a big saving,' Morwell replied like the politician he was. 'And the block was thought suitable.'

'That was the purpose of the subsequent closure procedures consultations,' Dr Grant reminded him.

'The point is we can't begin these procedures on a day-to-day basis. By the time the consultation was completed the finance was no longer available,' Stephen Morwell said.

'What is the future for that block, Stephen?' one of the other consultants asked. 'I'd be unhappy about it being put to any other use.'

'I don't think there is any question of that. It will at some stage become a psycho-geriatric unit.'

'Does this absence of finance explain the cut in nursing staff proposed for the therapeutic community on Brechin Ward?' Dr Hendrix asked, suspecting that wasn't the sole reason.

'District has to find a five per cent cut across the board. It's felt that the nursing ratios on Brechin could comfortably be reduced.' He looked at Alan Ryder, the hospital manager for further explanation.

'We thought trimming a bit there wouldn't hurt, in view of the sacrifices we're all making,' Alan Ryder said.

'I suggest management tries nursing patients in practice rather than theory,' Dr Hendrix said crossly.

'I think the cuts have to be apportioned, Clive,' Stephen Morwell suggested.

'How might they affect Ebury Road?' Hendrix wanted to know. He saw the half-way hostel under threat. Anything out of the mainstream was vulnerable, especially when money was scarce.

'Most of that money is coming from the local authority. Residents' objections are more likely to jeopardize that project, Clive,' Morwell told him. 'There've been more calls for a public inquiry.'

'That could mean months of delay.'

'This isn't something we have control over, I'm afraid.' Morwell simply resigned himself to the possibility.

Almost without exception these meetings failed to arrive at any conclusion resulting in direct action. Rather they served to formulate policy, which if subsequently veered away from, did help keep the pressure on the administration. Stephen Morwell could do without such pressure, but it was something he was finding harder and harder to ignore, even though he couldn't give the consultants what they wanted.

Coming along a seemingly endless corridor at Coldbrook, Stephen Morwell quickened his stride on seeing Dr Hendrix. This was a long way for him to come personally for a subcommittee meeting, but he didn't mind on account of the hospital's squash facilities. He had fixed up a game with Dr Rahan Singh, who played well, but who he would beat.

'Clive,' he said in a friendly manner. 'Would you be prepared to address a public meeting about Ebury Road?'

'If it'll help our cause. When is this?'

'I'll let you know. It'll be a question and answer format. It might allay local residents' more obvious fears,' Morwell said. 'Incidentally, some of your patients are seeking a meeting to discuss their taking on cleaning and painting around Brechin Ward.'

'Yes, it's Robin Hindmarch's project. If these patients could organize themselves in that way they wouldn't be here,' Dr Hendrix said, effectively sinking the scheme. Although he didn't wish to discourage initiative, he did see this as an added threat to his therapeutic community. Its independence was generally resented, and this scheme, if airborne, would appear to make it more independent of management.

'I don't somehow think it's on. But I'll hear what they have to say.'

Without the sanction from Dr Hendrix, Stephen Morwell would have dismissed both the psychiatric patients and their scheme out of hand. Now he would be seen to listen even though he wouldn't take up the idea.

Better than any of his contemporaries Mr Philip Montagu,

the consultant gynaecologist, knew where the equivalent of the jugular vein was when it came to exerting pressure on the medical establishment. What was more he had no compunction about going for it when the need arose, as it did over the drawn out fate of Nightingale Block. Plans for his private gynae-obstetrics clinic had reached a point where he needed an answer to his company's offer for the block, but the District Management Team which was responsible initially for its disposal was vacillating.

'What infuriates me, Graham, is the waste of time. Time is a very expensive commodity.' He was with the Minister of Health in Locketts restaurant, which was within the Division bell. Other familiar parliamentarians were being entertained to expensive lunch by lobbyists of various kinds. 'Nightingale Block has been empty for almost a year while the DMT procrastinates.'

'Plans for your hospital were approved six months ago,' Graham Peacock responded, pushing apple pie with thick cream into his tiny mouth. He was a less than well-polished ex-grammar-schoolboy who didn't particularly like Philip Montagu, but admired his enterprise, and often thought that someone of his calibre was needed to run the NHS as a going concern.

'If the decision to sell isn't going to be made soon, we must make alternative arrangements.' He delivered this as an ultimatum, knowing the government's policy on disposing of NHS property.

'As you know from my statement to the House, Philip, we see hospitals like the one you're proposing as the means of relieving pressure on the NHS. We want to see healthcare standing on its own feet.' He hesitated, realizing that his unconcrete declaration wasn't enough. 'How do you see my department helping?'

'A recommendation from you to the Chairman of the Regional Health Authority would get some decision.'

'Ah but would it be the right one, Philip?' Graham

Peacock asked with a smile, as if his own man. Montagu remained unimpressed. 'All concerned have been consulted on the closure procedure? Any objections?'

'Those one would expect – principally the CHC and unions,' Philip Montagu said sourly. He had no time for either.

'It sounds like there's a case for my Department to make a recommendation to Region. John Murry-Parke is the Chairman. Amenable sort – I appointed him myself.'

The Division bell sounded for prayers in the House; this galvanized half the restaurant into finger waggling and plastic flapping for their bills, ready to rush back for Question Time which followed immediately.

'I must go,' the Minister said swallowing the last of his pie, 'I'm fielding the health questions. We have several on anaesthetic disasters. Leave it with me, Philip. I'll see if I can't get things moving.' He smiled accommodatingly before rushing away.

Although the Regional Health Authority – where the Minister of State for Health had most direct influence – funded all levels of administration below, it wasn't their business to instruct Districts how to conduct their affairs; however suggestions were made, and pressure sometimes exerted by financial means. District Administrators with various Capital Schemes to set before Region usually heeded suggestions or requests.

Unfortunately for the long-term prospects of his District, but not those of Mr Montagu's clinic, Stephen Morwell was one such administrator.

Impressed as he had been by the potential enterprise of the psychiatric patients from Coldbrook in looking to contract work from the hospital, Stephen Morwell was more impressed that this delegation of six patients could get themselves all the way to his office by public transport without harm befalling them. Peter Parker, Ruth Martin,

Bernice Attwood, Alan MacIntosh, Anne Drinkwater, James Worth sat in a half circle in front of the desk with tea and biscuits and the District Administrator sat behind his desk and listened, almost without interruption, while Peter Parker outlined the scheme. But he had already made up his mind. Despite pursuing the Ebury Road half-way house for patients such as these, his notion of clients from a psychiatric hospital was synonymous with locked wards.

'. . . Your scheme to start a vegetable garden sounds first-rate,' Stephen Morwell said, appearing to give encouragement. 'It seems an excellent way of supplementing food from the canteen. However I will have to speak to the District catering officer about the feasibility of your holding the budget to buy your own food. This may not be possible on account of our contract.'

There were uncertain looks from the delegation.

'We buy food on a contract for a given period,' he explained. 'It's more economic. The supplier maintains the price at a guaranteed volume.'

'Eh, what about the, eh, cleaning and painting?' Peter Parker asked.

'It's an excellent idea to clean the windows and keep the ward looking nice, very therapeutic,' Morwell told them condescendingly. 'But whether we could separate it from the main contract? I did discuss this with the hospital administrator. Although Mr Ryder doesn't particularly like the idea of Brechin becoming too independent, he agrees that it shows great initiative.'

His secretary knocked and opened the door. 'Excuse me, Mr Morwell. The chairman of the Regional Health Authority is on the telephone,' she said with a sense of significance. 'Sir John Murry-Parke.'

'Ah,' he responded, at once surprised. There wasn't ordinarily direct contact between them; he talked to George Christian at Region often. 'I'd better take it out there. Excuse me.' He went out, leaving his secretary to close the door, and the patients to talk among themselves.

Picking up the phone, almost gingerly, 'Stephen Morwell,' he said. His confidence hadn't disappeared, but his attitude was different to that when talking to psychiatric patients.

'Stephen. John Murry-Parke here,' the chairman said as though they were old friends, which they weren't. 'What's the current position with Nightingale Block?'

'It's rather stagnant at present. The consensus is a psycho-geriatric unit.'

'I saw the proposals, thought them excellent. It's in line with DHSS's policy document, and much needed, I dare-say,' he commented. 'Do you have the necessary finance available at District?'

'God, no! We're preparing a Capital Scheme to put up,' Morwell explained. 'Hopefully for inclusion in the next financial year.'

'There's little immediate prospect, Stephen. Public sector borrowing's unlikely to be increased.' He hesitated and dropped his voice as if entering into some conspiracy. 'Between ourselves, the Department is indicating further reductions on next year's expenditure. Somewhere in the order of five per cent again. I can't see much hope of your scheme getting off the ground.'

'I see,' Morwell said circumspectly, knowing this man wasn't idly passing the time of day.

'That leaves the question of Nightingale Block. Perhaps it's time to sit down with Philip Montagu,' Murry-Parke advised. 'He has a pile of Arab money. His scheme for that old block appears very attractive.'

'I'm sure. What I'm not sure about is the consultant psychiatrists agreeing. Or the geriatricians, come to that.'

'They must be realistic like everyone else,' Sir John Murry-Parke said. 'Set the ball rolling, Stephen,' he went on as if that leap had been made by the District Administrator. 'Make the recommendations for the disposal of the block. I'll put our people together with the District Valuer to see how it should be disposed of and for what price.' The District Valuer was an Inland Revenue chartered surveyor who assessed the value and advised on the disposal of government property. 'Keep me posted about progress, there's a good fellow.'

Morwell found himself quietly agreeing as the phone went down. In theory he could have said no, but to have done so would have benefited no one in the long run, as there would never have been any money available for doing anything with the block at District.

If he had resisted the suggestion by the Regional Chairman and not proposed disposing of Nightingale Block, then what happened subsequently, their losing local authority finance for Ebury Road, might have made him subscribe to the conspiracy theory. But when he learned the council was withdrawing its support as a direct result of the government cutting the rate support grant, Morwell could only assume it was a coincidence. No argument put forward by the District Administrator could change that position, but he put the argument all the same, and proceeded to explore other means of finance. One possible source of funding was offered by Region, and made Stephen Morwell feel more optimistic when he approached Clive Hendrix in the doctors' dining-room at St Clair's where he was bolting his lunch.

'Do you mind if I join you a moment, Clive?' Stephen Morwell said. He was there to have lunch with Roy Needham.

'A moment's about all I have got,' Hendrix replied.

'I doubt if that will improve your digestion.'

'The faster one eats this the better it seems to taste.'

Morwell settled himself and took up the menu as a distraction. 'I'm afraid there's been a setback with the Ebury Road hostel.' He gave the details.

Although clearly disappointed, Clive Hendrix didn't stop

eating. 'What about alternatives. MIND? The Rowntree Trust?'

'We're exploring those, but I'm not hopeful,' Morwell told him.

'That really is too bad. The unit is much needed.'

'I know,' Morwell sympathized. 'One complicated but feasible possibility is to finance it ourselves . . . from selling Nightingale Block.' He suggested this with a degree of uncertainty, and as if this idea hadn't been mooted elsewhere.

After a long, silent look, the consultant said, 'If that building goes it would certainly mean no immediate hope for a psycho-geriatric unit.'

'That's true, Clive. But the DMT will continue to give psycho-geriatric provision priority,' Morwell assured him, a little too earnestly. 'But I honestly can't speculate about when such a unit might materialize.'

Dr Hendrix considered him. 'I don't like this sort of bartering, Stephen,' he said ironically, 'especially not over what amounts to patients' basic rights. But I'll settle for some small gain. How quickly could Ebury Road go forward?'

Feeling hugely relieved, Stephen Morwell said, 'Assuming Region's goodwill, finance could be allocated the moment the Council give the go-ahead.'

That might have dealt with funding the project, but other problems emanated from Ebury Road itself, or rather some of the ratepayers living there.

An *ad hoc* committee gathered in the flat of Walter Edwards to formulate a means of stopping the psychiatric hostel opening in their street. There were nine people grouped informally about the sitting-room. The host, who was wearing a three-piece suit, had assumed the chair, while his wife Sally, who had just admitted a late arrival, was seeing that everyone had coffee.

‘We’re all here now,’ Edwards said. He had a tight, strawberry-shaped mouth that was too small for his fleshy face.

‘Is Reverend Gillet not coming?’ the late arrival asked. He had only agreed to join because of the vicar’s involvement.

‘He phoned to say start without him,’ said Miss Raleigh, the headmistress of the girls’ school opposite. ‘He had a last minute hitch with the scouts’ do on Saturday.’

‘Then we’ll start,’ Edwards said. ‘We all know why we’re here.’ There was a burble of agreement, but Edwards was the sort of person who, for the sake of his own security, reiterated things. ‘It’s to organize opposition to 35 being turned into a halfway house for lunatics.’

‘The scheme is absolutely wicked,’ a woman said. ‘This is a nice neighbourhood.’

‘More than that, Marjorie,’ Edwards said. ‘It’s safe.’

There was vocal agreement. Edwards, having found a nerve, then sought to prod it. ‘I wonder how safe it would be if they open that hostel.’

‘It’s our children I’m worried about,’ Marjorie said.

‘Will anyone be able to walk the street without being molested?’ The fear was posed by the good neighbour who had arrived late.

‘Before we get too deeply embroiled, Mr Edwards,’ Miss Raleigh said, ’I think it might be advisable to elect a chairman, and ask someone to keep the minutes. That is the correct way to go about things.’

‘That’s a good idea.’

‘The authority will take us more seriously,’ Miss Raleigh added. ‘Might I propose Mr Edwards as chairman?’

‘I’ll second that.’

There was no dissent.

‘Well, that seems to have been carried,’ Edwards said with a chuckle of pleasure. He was the sort of person who would list this chairmanship in his ‘other interests’ on application forms. 'Would one of the ladies like to take the minutes?'

A hand was raised, this neighbour clearly recognizing her role.

'Good. Then we can get down to business.'

The sole object of their business was to stop the local authority opening a hostel for psychiatric patients in Ebury Road, the belief being that its residents would be both a threat to the good and law-abiding neighbours, as well as their property values. Nothing gave some people a greater sense of unity and purpose.

52

The staff this morning on the Brechin unit had an air of apprehension and bemusement due to the expected visit by some administrators and a local councillor, who was also a member of the DHA. No one knew quite why they were coming, and although the visit wouldn't be unique, the fact that it was happening now led Dr Hendrix to suspect that it might have some connection with either Ebury Road or the future viability of Brechin unit itself.

In the office, where the staff gathered before the morning session, the proposed visit wasn't occupying them, rather the prospect of having their nursing ratios cut. No one but Dr Hendrix yet saw the connection.

'Does anyone else want coffee?' Rose Sutton said as she made some for herself. 'We are definitely losing one of our nurses then?'

'Half a nurse,' Dr Hendrix told her. 'Management has somehow decided that we can do without a nurse on duty at night.'

'That's silly,' Marion Spinks said angrily. 'Just because these patients are ambulant doesn't mean they don't have problems at night.'

'Is this in any way connected with our visitors this morning?' Dr Marvill asked, as she collected her coffee from the psychologist.

'That's not impossible,' the consultant confessed, and added sourly, 'but I suspect they're coming to make sure patients aren't smearing the bedroom walls with excrement, and to see that the floors are properly polished. An exercise in management self-justification.'

'Could you have a word with Bernice?' the student nurse

said to Dr Hindmarch when she came in for her coffee. 'She's on her bed protesting about being in nightclothes.'

'It must be catching,' he said. 'Eileen Topolski was protesting about that earlier.' He finished his coffee before going to sort her out.

'She was threatening all sorts of mayhem unless she got her clothes back,' Marion Spinks said.

'Bernice was?' Dr Hindmarch said.

'Mrs Topolski,' the ward sister said.

'I'm not sure how much longer we should put up with Eileen Topolski,' Dr Hendrix said. 'She was an experiment that hasn't really worked out.'

Dr Hindmarch said nothing, but arched his eyebrows as if to suggest they couldn't always back winners. Eileen Topolski had been one of the consultant's experiments.

In protest against being warded as a result of walking off again before her parents' visit Bernice was naked on her bed in the empty dormitory. She didn't move when Dr Hindmarch came in. He wondered briefly if this wasn't a sex game for his benefit as he sat on the edge of the bed and watched her make patterns with her hands on the cover. Here each bed had its own standard contract Formica wardrobe and dressing table unit which separated one bed from the next, suggesting privacy without achieving it.

After a long silence, during which Bernice darted glances at the doctor to measure his reaction, she said, 'I'm not going to wear bedclothes and look stupid. I'd sooner go about like this.'

'Is that how you plan to go to group therapy?' he asked.

She shook her head. 'I'll stay in bed.'

'I'd be showing favouritism if I allowed you your clothes back,' he told her.

'But I am your favourite,' she declared, like the child she inescapably was at times.

'I don't have favourites, Bernice. It would cause complications. But I do care what happens to you.' He laughed to hide his guilt, finding difficulty in denying what he felt about her. He didn't know whether her statement was perception or guess-work, but at that moment he felt sexually attracted.

'Why can't I have my clothes back?' she wanted to know. 'I won't go off again. I can face my parents now.'

'Do you feel that's realistic?' he asked.

'Yes, I'm beginning to understand how I feel about them.'

'Good. That's good, Bernice.' He considered her a moment. 'You help make the rules you live by here. Why not join the group and change them?'

She foundered on this line of logic, then put a tangential argument. 'You're not even taking my small group.'

'You'd twist me around your little finger if I did,' he told her unwisely. 'Both Marion and Dr Marvill are capable therapists, and you seem to be getting on well with them. If you invest all your trust in one person, what will happen when he's not around?' he cautioned.

'You're not leaving?' A note of alarm entered her voice. 'You're not!'

'My contract with the hospital's only for a year. When it runs out I have to find another job.'

She didn't answer, and he assumed she blocked against the prospect. There was no denying that the constant turnover of medical staff on short contracts was detrimental to patients in therapy when they formed relationships.

'Come on, put your pants and dressing gown on,' he encouraged her. 'Join in with the group. When Angela next goes to Ebury Road to see about modifications I'll ask her to take you along.'

She looked at him, not understanding what he was suggesting. She knew why Angela Plane the occupational therapist went, but the reason for her going along was too big a jump. 'Take me? What, can I go there? To live?'

'If you continue to progress like you have over the past four months,' he told her. 'I discussed this with Dr Hendrix. He feels it would be useful if you had a goal to work towards.'

'Oh great!' Joy bubbled through her initial disbelief. Throwing herself forward, she locked her arms around his neck and kissed him.

The gesture was a spontaneous expression of her feelings of joy – love hadn't yet surfaced – but one that was readily misinterpreted by the visitors who were brought into the dormitory by Tony O'Roake, the senior nursing officer. They stopped at the end of Bernice's bedspace and stared at them, the SNO's commentary ceasing abruptly. In the party were George Christian, the Regional Administrator, Betty Morrish, a local councillor and DHA member, Dr Alan O'Brien, the district medical officer, and Alan Ryder the hospital administrator.

The SNO said, 'Ah, Dr Hindmarch', and quickly moved the party out of the room.

Dr Hindmarch felt inclined to rush after them and explain himself, even though there was nothing that he need justify; however if they chose to believe otherwise his justification would make matters worse. Because of his own insecurity Dr Hindmarch would find himself explaining his position to the senior nursing officer away from Brechin.

'There goes my job,' he joked to Bernice. 'Come on, or the group will start without you.'

There was a lot of activity in the corridor as patients went to the common room, some anything but orderly. The fact that visitors were attending this session had been noted in the minutes book, but if any of the patients remembered, they didn't respond as if they believed these five people waiting near the office could in any way affect their future, or that of the unit itself.

'Ah, hello,' Dr Hendrix said as he emerged from the office and saw Alan Ryder. 'Seen everything, have you?'

'I think so.' He glanced at Dr Hindmarch, who passed along the corridor.

'You are sitting in on the therapy session?' Dr Hendrix confirmed.

'For ten minutes or so, if that's all right. Just to get some idea of what you're up to,' Ryder said. 'This is Mr Christian, the Regional Administrator. And Councillor Morrish.'

'I think we've met. The patients are expecting visitors,' Hendrix explained, steering them towards the common room. 'No one joins these sessions without the reason being given. Just find seats anywhere.'

'Can I have my clothes back, doctor?' Eileen Topolski asked as she approached, wearing a dressing gown.

'I think you should stay as you are for a while, Eileen,' Hendrix told her reasonably. 'Certainly until you settle down.'

'I won't run away again. I won't bring alcohol on to the ward. I won't, I promise.' There was an urgent appeal in her voice.

'You promised that before. We expect you to honour your agreement. I think the group had better decide when your privileges can be restored.' He smiled. 'Are you coming to the meeting?'

'You fuck your meeting,' she blurted out angrily.

'We do try to keep it informal,' he said pleasantly.

As he turned towards the common room Eileen sprang on his back, seizing him around the throat. Other patients in the corridor stopped and watched, but showed none of the alarm that registered on the faces of the visitors. Some of the staff prised Eileen off. She was screaming, and threatening mayhem, and it took four of the staff to hold her.

'I think she'd better go back to the disturbed ward,' the consultant told Dr Marvill, as he recovered himself. 'Give her 50mg of Largactil for now. That'll quieten her down.'

Without any resistance at all Dr Marvill knew she would do as her boss told her, but this was a part of the job she least liked. It made her feel more like a custodian than a doctor.

'All right everybody,' Marion Spinks said, 'the drama's over.'

The group therapy session got started, while Eileen Topolski got put to bed.

The five visitors, who huddled together as if for protection in the group therapy circle, seemed no more impressed by what went on here than what they had seen elsewhere in the unit; any notions they had had that psychiatric patients should be contained tended to be reinforced.

Anne Drinkwater was chairing the meeting and making an impressive job of it, until she had shouted at a fellow patient to, 'Shut the fuck up,' when he interrupted Bernice. She inevitably tended to favour female patients.

'The thing is,' Bernice was saying quietly, 'I can't continue in my small group unless Malcolm has a serious change of attitude.'

'Look, she keeps saying this,' a tall, lean youth called Malcolm Beedle said. Like James Worth he lived with his hand in the front of his trousers, and at times seemed to be masturbating. 'I don't know what I'm supposed to have done.'

'He won't participate,' Bernice continued, refusing to acknowledge his presence. She was wearing a towelling robe. 'He's not prepared to become part of the group.'

'Ballocks, I go to every session,' protested Beedle, who was a relative newcomer. 'Except when I've got something important to do.'

'What could be more important,' Chloë Shallcross asked. 'Than trying to sort out your life?'

'That's what I have to attend to.' Malcolm Beedle suffered mild delusions about important meetings with solicitors about some property of his mother's. 'I'm there most times.'

'He sets himself apart, and criticizes the whole time,' Bernice said, not speaking directly to him. 'What's worse, Malcolm told my parents something I had talked about in my small group. I have enough problems, especially with Marion going on leave. There's no point going to my small group if I can't trust people in it. I'll have to stop going to my small group.'

'So you're saying Malcolm should change his attitude or leave the community?' Anne Drinkwater summarized.

'That's not fair,' Malcolm Beedle argued. 'There's nothing wrong with my attitude.'

'Bernice is right,' Ruth Martin told him. 'Most of the time you don't participate. It's like it's all a game to you. All this going off on business you do.'

'I do have important business to deal with,' Malcolm Beedle said.

'If someone's attitude is making the exercise self-defeating,' Dr Hendrix suggested, 'then you should try to explore the reasons. Do you want to tell us about this important business, Malcolm?'

'I can't,' Malcolm Beedle responded, actively pulling at his genitals. 'It'd be a breach of confidence.'

After a few nods between them the visitors tried to slip away, causing as little disturbance as possible.

'Thank you, Dr Hendrix,' Alan Ryder said. They offered no opinions or conclusion.

'Any time,' Dr Hendrix said casually.

'Seen enough, dear?' Malcolm Beedle asked Councillor Morrish as she went pass him. His hand remained down the front of his trousers.

She gave him a polite smile. A buzz of relief followed their departure, rather like when a teacher stepped out of the classroom.

'Do you think they were impressed?' Peter Parker asked.

'Was that the object, do you think?' Dr Hendrix said, suggesting otherwise, 'to impress hospital management?'

No one ventured an opinion.

'Fortunately the management has no say in matters of clinical treatment,' Dr Hendrix told them. What he left unsaid was that there could be no treatment without management providing the facilities.

Resulting from this visit there was no immediate feedback about the management planning to pull the rug from under them. But that was something Dr Hendrix dwelt on silently, and meanwhile life continued, with progress for some patients, while others stood still or regressed. Bernice got her clothes back, Eileen Topolski went to the disturbed ward. She was there under Section 26 of the Mental Health Act, so had little choice - unlike some of the patients on Brechin who weren't Sectioned - and none at all in the treatment she received. After the initial period of one year for which she would be detained the Section would be renewed; at this point she had the right to appeal to the Mental Health Review Tribunal against the decision to detain her. But no one would inform Eileen Topolski of that right, and it would be nine years before she would be discharged from Coldbrook.

53

Although the property in Ebury Road had lost the former splendour of a single family residence, it was still the most attractive house Bernice Attwood had seen. Set back from the road, with two huge horse chestnut trees at either end of a small crescent-shaped drive, the building was three storeys high on a cellar. The windows were grimy and had old nets at them; paint flaked from walls and woodwork, and weeds grew out of the front steps, but Bernice noticed none of that, seeing only a home where she might live with the choices she made. The whole business of viewing the house like a prospective tenant made her tingle with excitement, there was a perceptible buzzing inside her.

Angela Plane, who was forty, bone thin, with wild-looking hair, opened the front door of the house and stepped aside to let Bernice in. The younger woman hesitated on the threshold, and looked at the occupational therapist, who had a habit of pushing at her hair as if trying to get it into shape. She smiled. 'Go on, honey. See what you think.'

Energy suddenly spilled everywhere from Bernice, she rushed into one room, then out and into another. Rejecting this, she rushed on to a third. Leaping up the stairs to the first floor, she explored in the same way. 'Can this one be my room,' she said. 'Can it?'

Before Angela Plane, who was climbing the stairs, could answer her, Bernice rushed out into a room across the hallway.

'No, this one! This one!' Bernice said.

Catching her up, Angela Plane lit another cigarette from her butt, which she then ground out on the floor. 'I thought you'd want a room of your own, honey?'

'Oh I do, I do, more than anything!' Bernice said.

'Well, we have to fit in eleven others, and two staff. We'll have to turn the bigger rooms into sort of dormitories. You can think about one of the smaller rooms on the next floor. Or you could share a big room.'

Angela Plane smiled as Bernice hurried on up to the next floor.

The first room Bernice entered there was the one she wanted for her own. It was small but had lots of sunlight streaming into it, despite the dirty windows. Being situated in the front of the house, the room had a view across the school fields opposite. Bernice felt at once a sense of tranquillity and security here, as if this had always been her room.

'Can I have this room as my own?' she asked quietly when the OT found her.

'I don't see why not, if everything goes to plan.'

A feeling of joy spread through Bernice. That was all she wanted to hear, she didn't consider any possibility of snags.

Meanwhile Samuel Irons who had come out of Coldbrook to re-enter the world after twenty years would have liked nothing more than to be out of his own little room and back on the ward at Coldbrook.

His room was as small and stark as Bernice's, only his was cheerless too, with its narrow, sagging bed, plywood wardrobe and gas fire.

Loneliness and isolation had reached into Samuel Irons and had stirred up feelings that everyone had long since thought dead. He yearned for the community he had known at Coldbrook, even though there was often little communication; he missed having someone caring whether or not he dressed, had his dinner or had taken his medicine. Here no one cared and as a result he sometimes didn't bother to dress or get himself food, and simply forgot to take his medicine. Generally he lost his enthusiasm for living, everything became an effort, even making a cup of tea or going out to cash his Social Security giro.

Kneeling by the grate to put on the gas fire, Samuel Irons heard voices and turned in their direction with a sense of yearning. These weren't a recurrence of those deluded voices which had burnt out with his schizophrenia, but daytime television heard through the thin partition wall as it drowned someone else's loneliness. Samuel hugged himself, trying to shut out his feeling of isolation. He stared down at the broken mantle of the fire, from which gas was steadily hissing. The noise seemed to be speaking to him, it was the only voice that had spoken directly to him for days, and he enjoyed what it seemed to be saying.

After a moment he would light the gas, but there would be other times when he would be totally mesmerized by the sound. One of these occasions would help him get back to Coldbrook.

'Would you like me to pour you some?' Student Nurse Sally Guenin said to a patient, who was hugging a plastic bottle of orange squash to herself. Being new to psychiatric nursing – this sojourn on the disturbed ward being part of her general training – she didn't understand what importance some patients attached to often the most meagre of possessions. It was a vestige of property rights that were given up on entering this world.

The patient had taken the juice which she had brought from her locker on Allen Ward with, what she recognized and the nurse failed to, great risk of having it stolen. The disturbed wards were marked by the absence of juices, fruit, and flowers that were on general wards.

'I'll dilute it for you,' Nurse Guenin said, managing to take the bottle.

The moment it was in her hand other patients clamoured for it, just as they did for other patients' cigarettes.

‘Orange, orange. Give me some. Me, me!’

‘Let me have some orange, let me have some . . .’

‘Let’s ’ave some orange . . .’

‘I wanna drink. I’ve not got any orange.’

Feeling pressurized, the lady whose squash it was snatched it from the startled nurse, and hurried away. ‘You know I’m not well,’ she said. ‘Why don’t you leave me alone. Leave me alone.’

No one was going to have her orange squash.

‘Eileen,’ Nurse Carr said to Mrs Topolski, as she came along the ward. Eileen Topolski was one of the patients not interested in the squash. ‘Time to go across for your treatment.’

Nurse Carr was collecting patients who were having ECT on an adjacent ward. Eileen Topolski was reluctant to go.

‘Oh, do I have to?’ she said. Despite her medication she appeared reasonably alert and was able to function rationally. ‘I don’t want to.’

‘I think you should, dear.’ Nurse Carr was reassuring and slightly condescending. ‘You know how much better it’s made you. Come on, you’ve only two more sessions.’

‘I won’t get upset. I promise I won’t,’ she said, growing agitated.

‘Don’t be silly, Eileen, it’s for your own good.’ Nurse Carr was becoming firmer. ‘You know how you were before you started ECT. You don’t want to go in the pad again, do you? You don’t want that.’

‘Please!’ the woman screamed, going instantly out of control as she tried to repress her aggression. ‘Please!’

‘All right,’ Nurse Carr said. ‘I’ll get you something.’ She turned and went back along the ward, puzzling Nurse Guenin.

‘What happens when a patient refuses treatment?’ Nurse Guenin asked.

‘Sometimes if it’s Dr Hindmarch’s patient he doesn’t push it. But there’s no question of this patient refusing,’

Nurse Carr told her. 'We'll give her something to calm her before taking her over.'

Curiously Eileen Topolski didn't resist the sedative that calmed her enough to go for ECT. She offered no resistance when Nurse Guenin led her on to the ward which was used for the treatment.

The regular patients on this ward could come and go at will, and mornings of the ECT treatment they were all turned out so that their beds could be used.

The empty beds on one side in a line were brought down for patients in turn to where the anaesthetist was with Dr Marvill. The next patient, Eileen Topolski was put on top of the bed, which would afterwards be wheeled to the other side of the ward, where patients were left to recover behind drawn screens.

Having been given 20mg of Valium, Eileen Topolski should have stayed calm until given her anaesthetic. But through the fog of sedation she still managed to protest at the notion of ECT as an Asian staffnurse sat her on the bed and removed her slippers, which she popped under the pillow.

'Oh no, please. Do I have to?' Eileen said thickly, trying to thrash her way out of the fog.

'You won't feel a thing,' the Indian anaesthetist said, preparing the two hypodermic syringes. One was a muscle relaxant to stop the spasm and breaking bones from the jolt when the electric current was put through her brain, the smaller injection was a short-acting anaesthetic.

'No! I don't want it. I don't,' Eileen protested.

Finding a pocket of manic energy she struggled forcefully against the treatment, throwing herself up from the bed and thrusting the staffnurse away. The other nurse came from across the ward to help restrain her, and without thinking Jessie Marvill helped too. It wasn't till after that she would realize what she had done and hate herself for being an unquestioning part of it.

'Just a small prick now. That's all,' the anaesthetist told her, smiling and showing his tombstone teeth.

Eileen Topolski went under quickly. The oxygen mask was placed over her mouth and nose, and the anaesthetist squeezed the bag a couple of times. Meanwhile Dr Marvill took a piece of cottonwool and wet the woman's temples for a good contact. When the anaesthetist indicated that the patient was fully under, she removed the electrodes from the same antiseptic solution, and clamped them on to Eileen Topolski's forehead. The 30 joules that passed through her brain from the small, brown electrical impulse box caused the patient to convulse. It lasted a half second, indicated by the red light on the box going off. Dr Marvill had completely repressed her feelings about administering this treatment, rather than being persuaded by Dr Hindmarch's argument that it was beneficial. She suspected there was an element of punishment used in the treatment, but didn't acknowledge it.

When she left the ward that day Jessie Marvill would feel physically sick. It would signal the start of a major crisis in her career about where she would go from here: whether to continue practising scientific medicine, which would call on her to repress more and more her feelings until they ceased to be, find a viable alternative, or get out altogether.

Eileen Topolski's bed was wheeled across the ward and placed behind the curtains next to Mrs Taylor, who had preceded her. The eight other patients here were mostly awake now, and ready to go back to their wards. The slightly dead-behind-the-eyes look would wear off, along with immediate memory impairment.

'Is she all right?' the staffnurse said, seeing that Mrs Taylor was still unconscious. She slapped her face gently to rouse her.

'I think he gave her too much anaesthetic,' the second nurse whispered.

'Mrs Taylor!' The staffnurse patted her face again. 'It

affects some people differently,' she assured her colleague. 'Mrs Taylor?'

The woman on the bed started to come to.

'She's all right,' the staffnurse announced, and returned across the room. 'I think Mrs Topolski was the last, doctor.'

'Oh excellent,' the anaesthetist said, looking at his watch, ready to hurry away. 'Thank you.' He glanced at Dr Marvill, as if daring her to delay him. He went out almost at a run.

'They can go back to their wards as soon as they've recovered, Staff,' Dr Marvill told her, packing up the ECT equipment on the small glass topped trolley.

Still a little vague with the effects of ECT some two hours later, Eileen Topolski wandered aimlessly through the disturbed ward, not knowing where she was going, and having no idea how she had got here. In fact she had made her own way back. Other patients were moving along to the dining area for their lunch. Nurse Guenin was rounding up those who were going astray.

'Going to have some lunch, Mrs Topolski?' she invited. 'That's it, you go and have your food while it's hot. There's a good girl.' Although she was not yet twenty, and nursing little over a year, she had picked up the habit of treating patients condescendingly and speaking to them like children. It wouldn't be long before she started reducing patients' dignity with the casual use of given names.

'Come on, Mr Staples,' she said, turning to the old man who hadn't moved from his chair. 'Lunch time.' She helped him up and going in the right direction. Remembering the problem with Henry Staples's incontinence, she went to discuss it with Nurse Carr, who was at the drugs trolley checking through the medications charts.

'What about Mr Staples's bed, Staff?'

'What about it?' She was puzzled.

'He messed in it last night. I wondered if I should change

it.' Despite being new, Nurse Guenin was aware of what was going on, that this patient was being punished, otherwise the night staff would have changed the bed linen. This sort of practice upset her. She knew the patient could no more help doing that than he could help being here; the question was her way of registering concern without openly protesting.

'It might teach him a lesson if he has to sleep in it again tonight,' Nurse Carr said constructively.

'But that's awful!'

'Don't argue with me.' Nurse Carr flared up and rounded on her. 'He's a dirty old man and has to be punished.'

This reaction caused Nurse Guenin to freeze like a petrified rabbit. But she was completely confused when in the next moment Nurse Carr was calm and charming.

'After we get the lunches started, I'd like you to give me a hand with medications, Sally,' she said. 'Then you can go for your break.'

There might have been no mention of Henry Staples's incontinence.

Most of the patients were in the final stages of lunch when the drugs trolley was brought in. Some had eaten hardly anything, while others had eaten two or three lunches. At the slightest suggestion of anyone leaving food Fat June scooped it up like a gannet, barely letting it touch the sides of her mouth. One of those who hadn't eaten any food was Brenda, who had long since forgotten about Bernice's departure, upset as she had been at the time. What was distressing her now and causing her not to eat was the missing cats that she had become attached to around the grounds. She had been allowed a cat on the ward soon after her friend's departure, and she took food out to it and others. There was an estimated population of one hundred cats throughout the hospital before management started its blitz. Now cats were rarely to be seen anywhere. Brenda knew why. Although patients like her were unaware of most of what went on around them, some things they picked up on very quickly. Nothing else would take Brenda's interest, and when after frustrated protests she was offered another cat, her violent outburst had got her sent to the pad. Now she sat without interest in anything. Food was put in front of her and pounced upon by Fat June, who would not only oblige patients by eating their food, but also their drugs if given the chance.

Patients watched Fat June roll about, slurping up the remnants of food, or watched Nurse Guenin, who eventually got to them with their medication. Along with their liberty, rights and a voice in the running of their affairs, these patients had lost any say about their appearance too, along with most of their personal clothes. Due both to cuts and the District linen budget being overspent, the clothes they were given tended to be ill-assorted, but no one noticed or complained. Nurse Guenin noticed when she first arrived and helped dress a patient, thinking she had picked up the wrong clothes. But very soon she would accept the normality of this.

'Mrs Taylor.' Staffnurse Carr dropped the patient's pink and green Amitriptyline capsule into a plastic cup.

'I don't think she came back from ECT this morning,' Nurse Guenin informed her.

'Hasn't she had lunch?' Nurse Carr asked.

'I haven't seen her.'

'Could you check that she's still on Blair Ward when you go for your break, Sally?' She set the cup aside and went on to the next patient. Doctors didn't usually keep disturbed patients over if they had a bad reaction to ECT, but it wasn't unheard of.

Leaving Brechin Ward on his way to the canteen, Dr Hindmarch was called back by the psychology student, who put her head out of the office door.

'Robin! Dr Crick is on the phone from St Clair's.'

Dr Hindmarch hesitated. He looked at his watch, then flapped his hand, indicating that he wasn't available.

Being the only other doctor around, Jessie Marvill took the call.

'We've just had the results of the tests on Mrs Taylor,' Dr Crick said down the line after prelusive niceties. He was in the corner of the doctors' sitting-room at St Clair's with the patient's file open on his knees. 'Your patient really is very sick. The last of the tests suggest leukaemia. Certainly being on a psychiatric ward isn't doing her much good.'

Dr Marvill felt rather depressed, not at the thought of Mrs Taylor's future, but the fact that they had been treating her for the wrong complaint, despite her protests. 'At worst we thought she was suffering Valium withdrawal.' That was getting to be a common problem.

'If you can get her sent up here, I'll arrange a bed.'

Putting the phone down, Jessie Marvill thought about Mrs Taylor, and what she had unnecessarily been put through. There was nothing she could do about it, apart from getting her to St Clair's as soon as possible and started on the right treatment.

After stopping to phone Dr Hendrix, then making arrangements to transfer Mrs Taylor, she was late for her game of squash and didn't feel much like playing anyway, so didn't go, but went to lunch instead. There was little left that was appetizing in the canteen servery. Dr Marvill decided she could live without limp salad, and certainly without dried-up stew and cold chips. Instead she had coffee and two chocolate biscuits.

Neither the canteen's decoration nor arrangement improved her mood. The tables were bare of flowers, condiments and cloths, some of them left uncleared through lack of efficient staff. The food was no different from that which patients ate, and no more attention was paid to its presentation. Odd bits of conversation she heard at the next table didn't help lift her.

'Making that poor old man sleep in his own mess,' Nurse Guenin said to her colleague, 'it can't be right, Jo, can it? It can't be.' She fell silent and her gaze vacantly found a burnt out schizophrenic, who long ago had become institutionalized, at the canteen servery trying to cadge food. Patients weren't permitted to eat here, but he went away with a styrofoam cup of chips. 'I think it ought to be reported.'

'Who would you report it to?' Nurse Slaney wanted to know. Experience made her more realistic.

'I don't know. The nursing officer, I suppose.'

'Nothing'll get done,' Nurse Slaney counselled. 'On the geriatric ward on my last week they put a patient in an unheated side ward with the windows open so he got pneumonia,' she said illogically, as if believing that was how people got pneumonia. 'It doesn't do any good complaining. You make trouble for yourself.' She casually accepted the situation. Being a year longer in training, but still not fully trained, she was unaffected by what she saw. No longer did she become upset at the things that went on.

'It's not right though.' Nurse Guenin couldn't accept such things. 'They took out a patient's penis the other day and put it on the table. The charge nurse hit it with a ruler.'

'What had he wet himself?' Nurse Slaney said. 'I've seen that for wetting. And their noses rubbed in mess. When I first came here I thought double incontinence was a symptom of senile dementia. Sometimes you can't get them to the toilet in time. You have to leave them in their mess like little babies or you'd be changing them all day long.'

'They shouldn't be punished, Jo,' Nurse Guenin argued, feeling frustrated, but not explosive.

'Some of them do it purposely. They're really sneaky. You got to watch them like anything.'

'I'm thinking of complaining to the union,' Nurse Guenin ventured. 'When I go back to St Clair's.'

Nurse Slaney said nothing, but knew her colleague would be wasting her time.

'Would you come with me, Jo?'

Reluctant to be pinned down, Jo Slaney shrugged, but saw

from her friend's look that it wouldn't do. 'It won't do any good. I mean, you get so frustrated when they won't do what they're told, you have to take it out on someone, Sal.'

That thought depressed Jessie Marvill further. She told herself it wasn't the norm, but if it was those nurses shouldn't have been doing the job nor the doctors who tolerated the situation; also, if it was normal practice, it meant there was no hope for the patients. She determined to do something but said nothing as the nurses rose and went out.

'Did you find Mrs Taylor?' Staffnurse Carr asked when Sally Guenin arrived back on Allen Ward.

'No. She wasn't on Blair Ward,' Nurse Guenin informed her. 'They said she came back here after her ECT.'

'You took her. You should have made sure she returned,' Nurse Carr said, angrily slamming the filing cabinet drawer on some nursing notes. 'They want her at St Clair's. Must I do everything myself?'

She bustled out of the office to get a search organized. Nurse Guenin knew it wasn't her fault that a patient was missing but in this hierarchical structure she had no means of not taking the blame.

Searching the ward, which included both male and female sections, involved all the staff, but revealed no sign of Mrs Taylor.

'You're certain she wasn't on Blair?' Nurse Carr said to the student nurse when they met up in the middle of the ward.

'They looked everywhere for her,' the young woman said earnestly, as if to redeem herself for the mistake she hadn't made.

'There's no sign of her down there,' the ancillary said, joining them.

The two male nurses on duty brought the same message.

'I'll have to report her missing,' Nurse Carr said reluctantly. 'The nursing officer will have to organize a search of the hospital.'

At this point Henry Staples snatched the bunch of keys from Nurse Carr as he passed and quickly shuffled away with them.

The agility which this old man mustered startled Nurse Carr. 'You! Come back here with those!'

The order stopped Henry Staples, and he turned. The staffnurse pursued him.

'My keys! Give them back.' She extended her hand, but the keys were firmly planted in the old man's jacket pocket, which he held on to. 'Give them back. Give them to me.'

Still Henry Staples didn't budge.

Finally in a fit of pique Nurse Carr wrenched his hand clear and thrust hers into the pocket. She withdrew it with a cry of disgust, recognizing immediately that she had put her hand into human excrement.

'You vile animal!'

Whether this was intentional Nurse Carr wouldn't know as frequently dementia patients did such unsociable things. As she went to wash her hands Henry Staples, whose expression had remained blank until now, smiled, enjoying this single gem of awareness.

Searching the hospital grounds was a big undertaking and done reluctantly. But for the fact that Brenda Taylor was urgently wanted for treatment at St Clair's, it would possibly have been left a while to see if she turned up of her own accord. Most psychiatric patients who walked out did return. But not Mrs Taylor.

Tony O'Roake, the senior nursing officer, who had organized the search, brought the news that Mrs Taylor wasn't found to the hospital administrator. Both men were in their early fifties.

'What about informing the police, Tony?' Alan Ryder said.

'Ah, we don't need to involve them at this stage,' the senior nursing officer said, as if to do so would reflect badly on him. 'The only danger she is is to herself.'

'That's what I'm afraid of.' He thought about the situation. 'I suppose there's no possibility she's still somewhere in the hospital? Could she have been missed somehow.'

'Pretty remote,' O'Roake told him. 'But we'll keep looking. If she was anywhere in this hospital we'd have found her.'

'Give her till nightfall. If she hasn't shown up by then, I'll make it official,' Alan Ryder said. He was a man who got anxious about straying too far from the rules. 'I might have a word with Inspector Leigh, to cover ourselves, just in case she's not in the grounds.'

The search would continue; the police would eventually be informed; Mrs Taylor's daughters would make a fuss about their mother being allowed to walk out, and complain more as their guilt increased on learning what was wrong with her.

But Brenda Taylor wouldn't be found.

54

Lately things had happened so fast around Bernice Attwood that she could scarcely believe it was her they were happening to. She won a prize for sculpture in a local arts society show that her OT had entered her for; found she could actively function in both her large and small groups, and had chaired the large group and been told by Robin Hindmarch – who she now realized she was in love with – that she was the most effective chairwoman so far. She was coping with her parents' visits, and had been out with them. Dr Hendrix had confirmed that she could move into the hostel in Ebury Road; that truly denoted significant progress for her. But what made her feel especially good was her application to art school, which she had made with the help of Jane Mitchell, her pottery OT, even though the appointment for an interview had caused her an anxious sleepless week.

Reluctantly Bernice had caught the bus to the art college, and on several occasions had almost got off. Now as she sat in the principal's office while he went through her slim portfolio, she wished she had got off the bus. He hated her stuff, she could tell. She wanted to run out, but was too scared to move from the edge of her chair.

'It's not a very large portfolio,' he observed, without looking at her, 'but there's some terrific stuff here. Really smashing.' He was a huge, enthusiastic man in a denim jacket, and had a bushy beard and penetrating eyes.

Anxiety and fear of rejection gnawed at Bernice, making her feel that she was about to come unglued. Her thumbs were pressed hard into her palms to stop herself screaming, and she registered almost nothing about this interview, not what was said, nor the profusion of artwork and posters about the room. All she had in mind was that possibility of rejection.

The man behind the cluttered table was intuitively aware of the state Bernice was in, but allowed that to have no bearing on what he said. 'Your sculpture's well structured. It's got a good sense of balance, without being too technical. You've managed to capture a lot of emotion. That's terrific. Jane Mitchell's the only formal tuition you've had in art and sculpture, is she?'

Bernice managed a nod.

'She's a terrific teacher – she was a student of mine.' That way he accepted some of the credit for this. He smiled, then picked up another photo out of the portfolio. 'Did she take the photographs, or did you?'

'Robin . . . One of the doctors.' The words were difficult to get out.

'There won't be a problem offering you a place here . . . Your academic record's good – you got some of your O-levels. Yes, why don't you come and join us.'

A small voice inside told Bernice that she wasn't hearing this, but she ignored it, as she tried to separate the reality from unreality. 'You mean I can come here? I can?'

'I think that'll be smashing, Bernice,' he told her sincerely.

Her portfolio gripped in her hand, and glowing with pleasure, Bernice walked for the bus as if she was on air. Acceptance to the art school had given her a surge of confidence about functioning in the world outside the hospital. She stopped to look in a shoe shop, thinking she might buy some canvas shoes similar to those she had seen students wearing when she had been shown around. Before she could decide she became caught up with the pavement crowd who broke step to stare at a mad lady, for whom no place had been found in somewhere like Coldbrook. She was in as much of a state as any on the locked ward, Bernice noticed, and was loaded with newspapers. On her legs was dried blood, which had also stained her skirt. She was rattling on about losing her baby, and was trying to interest passers-by in a newspaper story. People lingered only for as long as this lady's attention didn't find them, when it did they quickly moved on.

As she paused to watch, Bernice came to realize that there was no noticeable difference between herself and the crowd. No one would single her out like they had this mad lady. Pity welled up in Bernice, but when the woman noticed her, she responded like everyone else, just in case she was somehow identifiable after all.

It wasn't chance that led so many doctors to play squash. The game ideally suited their lifestyle, it was fast, very physical, and required mental alertness, and, best of all, it was over in forty minutes. It could be fitted in at short notice and odd times between sessions, and needed no organizing, apart from booking the court.

Even though Vernon Davis had been on an assessment ward for the best part of two weeks and Jessie Marvill had been sympathetic towards the surgeon to the last, she hadn't seen much of him at Coldbrook, and felt guilty about that, which was why she had fixed up the game of squash they were playing. He was the better player, despite not having played for a long while. He could handle that now, only tomorrow when his limbs were stiff he would regret it. Jessie Marvill ran forward and took Davis's volley return and slammed it against the left hand sideway, it cut across to the forewall and came right back to Vernon Davis. He showed no mercy as he volleyed the ball again with force on to the floor close to the forewall, bringing it up at a sharp angle to the ceiling, then hitting the backwall and diving to the floor. Jessie Marvill couldn't pull herself back from her last stroke in order to reach the ball before it hit the floor a second time, giving Davis the match and game.

'Oh well,' she said. She was hot and sweaty, and had been

feeling generally dejected before playing. She would like to have won, but was pleased to see how the game had given Vernon Davis a lift.

'I must try this more often,' he said. 'It makes one feel almost human.'

Jessie Marvill smiled. 'I might feel like that after a shower.'

Having showered and changed they got some tea from the canteen and took it out into the spring morning sunshine. There were few other people in the garden.

Vernon Davis was silent and simply stared into the middle distance. His mood had gone flat since the game. On the occasions she had seen him here Dr Marvill had noticed how inconsistent his mood states were. That was a great shame, she felt, as he was one of the few doctors who cared more about people than he had his career. The story was that he had been sent here after threatening to kill an anaesthetist, whose supposed miscalculations sent one of his patients into coma, but Dr Marvill hadn't checked with the firm who Vernon Davis was under. He wouldn't be here much longer than his assessment, for if needed, he would be offered a place in a private nursing home.

'This is the last stint of your GP training scheme, Jessie, isn't it?' Vernon Davis asked. They had had a conversation about her job last week.

'I'm not sure. I might need to do another job, if I can get one,' she told him. 'I don't know if my surgical job was accredited. It'll be a bit of a bore if it wasn't.'

Without commenting he went back to watching people shuffling along the paths beyond the garden.

'To be quite honest I'm getting to the point where I don't really care very much,' Jessie Marvill said. 'More and more I seem to be doing all the right things for the wrong reasons. Or is it the wrong thing for the right reasons. I can no longer tell most of the time.' She paused, hopeful of some response, but got none. 'Did you hear that Laurence James was suspended? For giving a patient healing. It was considered unethical,' she said, and paused again. Vernon Davis didn't seem to appreciate the irony, yet it was part of that same self-interested bureaucracy which had helped him to his nervous breakdown. He had found his struggle against chauvinist and medical dogma too uphill. Jessie Marvill sympathized, knowing how he must have felt when he tried to throw the medical money-changers out of the temple of healing. His nervous breakdown confirmed what the hospital hierarchy had known all along, that Mr Vernon Davis was quite mad and shouldn't be let loose on patients; however they would accept no part of the responsibility. 'I think more and more about leaving medicine. But I don't know if I have the nerve.'

'That would be a loss, Jessie,' Vernon Davis told her quietly, surprising her for she had thought she wasn't getting through to him. 'I always thought you managed to communicate your concern. Perhaps that's a mistake.'

'I'm not sure I can face another job in institutionalized medicine. Not even one as a GP if it takes me along that same path. I'm not sure things would necessarily be any better there.' She hesitated, uncertain about where this was leading. As she progressed further with her personal therapy she realized more and more that she had been using medicine as a way of dealing with her own insecurity. The acceptance of her position within the medical institution, its power as a source of self-esteem, enhanced the feeling of insecurity, because they were transient possessions which could readily be lost. That was why so many of her colleagues were seeking more and more qualifications to raise their status without attempting to resolve their emotional problems. 'It might be nice to get back to dealing with people somewhere. I'm not sure how.'

Vernon Davis looked at her, then said, 'If you go on like that, someone will think you're mad.'

Doubt sped across her face. Jessie Marvill appreciated the irony, and had been about to smile, only wasn't sure that he was being ironical. She held his look, realizing she had been talking about her own problems, when she was there to maybe talk about his. There were times when she felt that her future was even less clear than his, and if she didn't make a decision about her life she knew her career was likely to overtake her and she might end up similarly to Vernon Davis, or possibly become a dope fiend or booze head like so many of her contemporaries.

'How about you, Vernon?' she asked, bringing the subject back to him. 'Are you sorting anything through being here like this?'

'There are times when I feel I'm beginning to see the problems as clearly as could be,' he said. 'Other times, Jessie, there is complete fog, and I know I'm as crazy as anything. But it's some form of shelter here.' He paused, then added quietly, 'It's shelter.'

That was what each of them needed at times, she thought, rather than the belief that as doctors they were neither vulnerable to ill-health nor subject to human needs.

'Could I come to your room, Jessie?' he said quietly.

Jessie Marvill wasn't sure whether her response was as a doctor or a potential patient, and if she would be offered a pound, which she knew was the going rate for sex on the locked wards. But at that moment she was equally in need of shelter.

As they started across the grass to the doctors' block a brightly polished two-year-old Austin Metro turned carefully off the hospital drive on to the nearby visitors' carpark. Although Dr Marvill knew Mr and Mrs Attwood from their visits – she didn't remember them from their meeting a couple of years ago – she didn't acknowledge them now as she went away with Vernon Davis. It was as though she was ashamed of him and what she was doing, she would later discover in therapy, in the same way that she had been apprehensive about taking boyfriends home in case they didn't match up to her parents', and especially her father's expectations for her.

Having stopped the car precisely within the white-lined parking space, Frederick Attwood stared after the doctor, feeling slightly uneasy at her not greeting him. He told himself she couldn't have seen him, but he didn't like the attitudes of these doctors on Bernice's ward one bit. Having locked the car door, he went around to the other door and carefully checked that it was locked, then the boot. Finally he came back to the driver's door, unlocked and re-locked it. It was the sort of obsessive behaviour that wasn't at all out of place at Coldbrook, only he wasn't a patient.

Satisfied at last, he started toward Brechin with his wife, taking a backwards glance at his car, which still had the clear plastic covering on the seats from when it was delivered.

'Doctor!' Frederick Attwood called after Dr Hindmarch, who passed through the reception area going towards the office. When Dr Hindmarch turned back, the visitor rose, and waited, expecting his reason for being there to be acknowledged.

'We've come to take Bernice out,' he explained.

'Oh yes,' Dr Hindmarch responded. 'She talked about your visit yesterday. You have a busy day planned.'

'We'll do our best,' Attwood said, misunderstanding the implied criticism. 'We're going to the House of Commons, and Westminster Abbey. We planned some shopping after lunch. Then *Richard the Third* at the Barbican this evening.'

'That sounds a very full day,' Dr Hindmarch said.

'Should be diverting enough,' Attwood said as if it was a virtue.

Dr Hindmarch looked at him, wondering whether he could take these people on also. That was necessary if they were to help Bernice. 'I wouldn't have thought she needs diverting.'

'She seems completely settled, doctor,' Mrs Attwood commented politely.

'She's making excellent progress, Mrs Attwood. It was

useful giving her some objective to grow towards.' He thought of explaining further to these parents, but let the opportunity go. 'Did someone tell her you're here?'

'One of those male nurses did, eleven minutes ago,' Attwood said, checking his watch.

'I'll see if I can find her.' Dr Hindmarch looked at his watch.

If not in her therapy group Bernice was invariably in the pottery room, which was where Robin Hindmarch found her.

'Tell them I can't go,' Bernice said, and continued pushing clay on to the head she was sculpting. 'I'm too busy.'

'D'you think that's fair?' Dr Hindmarch asked.

'Well, they bloody well insist on coming.' She told herself she was angry at having to stop work.

'Perhaps you should see them,' he suggested, 'and tell them how you feel about their visits. It might help you.'

'Why should you care?' Bernice demanded. 'Why should anyone around here care? You're all leaving. Dr Marvill's going this month. You're leaving at the end of next month.' She viewed those changes with much unease, but had managed to talk about it in her small group.

Lack of continuity within psychiatric care concerned Dr Hindmarch, the upheaval the departure of staff caused was potentially damaging, but there was little he could do other than attempt to help patients come to terms with it. His contract as a psychiatric registrar took no account of the relationships he might have formed in this type of unit; he was leaving to take up a post at the Maudsley which was necessary to further his career. 'It's a familiar life situation,' he explained. 'You'll have to cope with similar things whether I'm around or not.'

Tension swiftly built up in Bernice and was translated to the modelling tool, which she finally stabbed into the clay head before marching out through the adjacent art room.

Dr Hindmarch watched her go, feeling it was a minor

victory that she went towards where her parents were, regardless of what he said to her.

He was joined by Jane Mitchell, the pottery instructor, who inspected the damaged sculpture.

'What a pity,' she said. 'That's a month's work.' This was how she related to Bernice, rather than as a disturbed young woman.

'Sorry, I had forgot you were coming,' Bernice told her parents, as each in turn offered a cheek to be kissed. At one time Frederick Attwood had placed his finger on his cheek to signal his expectation.

'Forgotten,' Attwood corrected.

'Yes,' she responded, coping with this.

'We've been so looking forward to taking you out,' her mother said, sensing the tension creeping in. She had always been conciliatory, and brushed over the cracks that her husband mostly ignored.

'Hey, Rufus, how you doing, man?' Bernice said to a black patient who wandered past.

'Hi, Bernice. D'you see that notice about the public meeting tonight?' he responded expansively.

'Yes, I did.' Usually she didn't get involved with patients on the assessment ward, but did so now because her parents would disapprove. As Rufus went away Bernice glanced at her parents; they believed themselves as liberal as the next person.

'He's one of Dr Grant's patients. He stabbed his wife forty-six times,' she explained, delighting in shocking them. In fact he had only attempted to kill her.

'They let him wander around?' Mrs Attwood said.

'Oh, it was only his wife he felt hostile towards,' Bernice said, enjoying her joke.

An awkward silence followed.

'We understand there are arrangements for you to continue your education,' her father said.

'Yes,' Bernice said apprehensively. She had asked that her

parents not be told initially. 'I'm doing a foundation course at art school. I expect to take sculpture.'

'Oh, I see.' Attwood's tone was disapproving. 'Art? I see. Something more structured, something in the sciences might have been more suitable.'

That caused an awkward moment. Bernice grew tense, and fought hard against simply running away from them now.

'I expect you'll meet a lot of interesting people there, Bernice,' Mrs Attwood commented, watching Rufus along the corridor, disturbed about being so close to him. She didn't think about her daughter being this close to such a person the whole time.

Attwood looked at his watch, feeling impatient to get started. 'We've a jolly interesting programme planned.'

'Look, would you mind if we, well, just had lunch,' Bernice suggested nervously, clamping her hands together.

'Oh, I see . . .'

'It's just that, well, we have the public meeting this evening about the group home,' she managed.

'Perhaps we could come?'

'We have theatre tickets booked,' Attwood reminded his wife.

'I was going to put you off, but, well, I didn't want to disappoint you.' Bernice's nervousness was increasing.

'You don't disappoint us, Bernice.' Her mother couldn't hide her obvious disappointment.

'I'm sorry, well, about the theatre,' Bernice said.

'You keep using well as a conjunctive adverb, Bernice. There's no need for it.'

'I'm sorry, Daddy.' She was suddenly squashed.

'Daddy's only teasing, darling,' Mrs Attwood said, trying to defuse the tension.

Bernice was driven back emotionally.

'I'll . . . I'll get my . . .' she couldn't complete the sentence.

She edged away, then suddenly turned and ran.

It was a long while before Bernice was calm enough to face her parents again, and then only with a lot of support from Marion Spinks. The day was as difficult and as disastrous as Bernice knew it would be. All that sustained her was the certain belief that she would soon be free to live her own life, going to art school, living in the hostel in Ebury Road. Those thoughts made her parents sufferable.

However, there were clouds rolling across the horizon, and although Bernice was aware of them, she chose to ignore the possibility that they could make any difference to her progress.

In a local church hall, where the public meeting about the proposed psychiatric hostel in Ebury Road was being held there wasn't a spare seat to be had, and a lot of people had to stand along the side and at the back. Credit for this turnout was due to Mr Walter Edwards, the local action committee chairman, who had worked hard at mustering opposition. However not everyone present was hostile to the half-way house. There were familiar faces of both patients and staff from Brechin Ward.

Sitting at the table at the top of the hall was a panel of six speakers chaired by Mrs Forks of the CHC. These included both Drs Hendrix and Grant, Stephen Morwell, a senior psychiatric social worker, and Councillor Bill Williamson.

Standing in the body of the hall, wearing a three-piece suit and clutching a sheaf of papers, Walter Edwards was saying, 'I would like it on record that we have nothing personal against these patients. It's nothing personal. Not personal. We're not against the people using this hostel, not as individuals. In fact, I have the greatest sympathy for them. What I'm saying is this, Ebury Road isn't the right place for that hostel. It's not.' There was murmured agreement and head-nodding from around him. 'Apart from anything else it's a very busy road. It's a main bus route. There are bound to be accidents.'

'Are you suggesting,' Dr Hendrix wanted to know, 'that

the people living in this hostel would be incapable of crossing the road?'

'I don't know if that is the case,' Edwards retorted, sensing the doctor's mockery. 'But what should be considered is how unfair it is to burden this neighbourhood with yet another establishment of this sort. It's not fair, it's not. Within a radius of a mile, eh, one mile, there are four such places. There's a mentally-handicapped home; and a hostel for subnormal children.' He referred to his notes. 'In addition to all this the Health Authority is planning on opening a special secure unit for violent patients at St Mary's. Why can't they put these places somewhere else? It's not fair that it's always around here.'

'Thank you, Mr Edwards,' Mrs Forks said, shutting him off. 'Mr Morwell, would you like to come in on that?'

'Well, St Mary's is not my District,' he said. 'But my understanding of the situation is that as a result of local resident objections, that secure unit won't now be opened. As for this community being asked to bear any special burden, that's not the case. The hostel in Ebury Road will be self-contained, and at some point in the future almost entirely self-supporting.' He was avoiding the questioner's meaning.

'But will we be safe?' The voice from the hall brought a rattle of concern. 'It's all very well to talk about how it's financed. That's not the point. We know what some of these people get up to, why they've been put away. You're planning to set up this hostel immediately opposite a girls' school. That's asking for trouble.'

Immediately Mrs Forks referred the question to Dr Hendrix.

'There's a general misconception here,' Dr Hendrix said. 'These patients haven't been put anywhere. Most of them are at Coldbrook voluntarily. Their reasons vary, but it's mostly because they're unable to cope with the stresses confronting them at a particularly vulnerable time. They are not being contained because they wish to molest school children, or anyone else. I can reassure you of that. The patients using this hostel are those who are ready to rejoin the community but who would benefit from continuing support.'

'But mistakes do happen, doctor, as our newspapers will attest to,' Miss Raleigh said. 'I'm the headmistress of the school in question. I would like to know what guarantees you can give that my girls won't be in danger. I suspect the answer is that you cannot.'

'Of course there are no guarantees, any more than there are that any one of us won't break down and need the shelter of a therapeutic community,' Dr Hendrix told her. 'Statistically one in four suffer stress-related problems and need help. That includes one in four of this audience, but we don't restrict them in where they live.'

'Will they be free to come and go as they please?' a man asked, unable to disguise his incredulity.

'I don't see why not,' the senior social worker said. 'How else will they get employment and re-establish themselves within society?'

Mrs Forks indicated she would take a question from a woman with her hand up.

'How far have plans for this hostel got?'

It was referred to Councillor Williamson.

'The council is considering the draft proposals,' he said. 'This means once approved the hostel could be open as soon as it could be made ready. Perhaps three months.' There was silence from the hall. 'I must say,' Bill Williamson went on, 'that there are a number of council members, myself included, who are very much in favour of this type of project. We would like to see many more community-based hostels. These are the acceptable alternative to the ugly institutions like Coldbrook, which continue to exist to our shame as a compassionate society.'

That caused a buzz of anger around the hall.

'Most of the local residents will oppose this scheme all the way, I guarantee that,' Mr Edwards declared, embracing the entire hall. 'Even if it means forming a human barricade across number 35. We won't allow our families to be put in jeopardy or have our neighbourhood overrun in this way.'

The strength of feeling around the hall against the hostel opening depressed Bernice to a point of making her feel physically sick. Having always been in closed mental institutions where she had had no option and no contact with the outside world, she had never experienced this raw fear people had of the mentally ill, or the hostility at the prospect of having them as neighbours. She assumed most people on the outside would be the same, and understood the reluctance of some patients to leave the therapeutic community. The meeting didn't reach any conclusion or pass any resolution. Rather its purpose was to enlighten and allay unease of local residents, which it clearly didn't do, and report their feelings to the local council to help them arrive at making their final decision.

On leaving the hall, even as part of the crowd, Bernice felt completely isolated and totally rejected. It was as though her would-be neighbours had identified her and were making a point of shunning her. This evening had brought her down rapidly from the high she had been existing on for the past month or so, and she had a premonition that things would start going wrong for her now. Panic almost overcame her as she felt like doing something violent to these horrible people. With a lot of effort she held those feelings in and turned the violence against herself.

She was startled and let out a cry of distress as Dr Hindmarch joined her and put his arm around her shoulder to comfort her.

'Don't feel too badly, Bernice,' he told her. He was angry himself, but more in control. 'Mental eunuchs like these are rarely sensitive to the needs of others. You have to try to focus on what you believe.'

He squeezed her shoulder, drawing her close to himself

with more affection than he ought to have been displaying.

She smiled, enjoying this contact. But it was fleeting and she couldn't free herself from that uneasy feeling she had for her own future.

55

Being both enthusiastic and successful in his drives to recruit more members to his union, time to attend to details often evaporated leaving Chris Hogan, the NUPE branch secretary, high on the rock of good intentions. Grievances from members were always listened to, and where possible dealt with. But having no professional help some were dealt with more satisfactorily than others; some complaints got lost in his 'put it on the desk' filing system at St Clair's.

Hogan wasn't unsympathetic about the complaint Nurse Guenin had brought him over the mistreatment of patients at Coldbrook. He was sorting through the mess of papers on his desk, preparing himself for this evening's Branch meeting and giving only part of his attention to Nurse Guenin who, he thought, should have made her complaint while at Coldbrook. He told her so.

'I would have done,' she said crossly. 'But I joined NUPE, not COHSE. Maybe I joined the wrong union.'

That remark finally got to him. 'All right, point taken. I do understand the problem. But the thing is, love, before I can take action, what's needed is someone to corroborate what you say's happening to the patients down there. That's what's needed.'

'Only to some of them,' Sally Guenin said.

'Oh, I thought you said they was all getting stick,' Hogan said, making good this small advantage. 'You got someone to back you up, have you?'

She shook her head. 'The nurse I asked thought it was a waste of time,' she said glumly.

'I don't know what we can do on our own, love.' He paused. 'You find someone who'll say the same as you –

preferably a qualified nurse. Then we can have a go at them.'

Nurse Guenin rose despondently.

Hogan watched her, sharing nothing of her disappointment. 'I'm sorry, love. You gotta back up that sort of complaint. Sorry. Eh, you coming to the meeting tonight?' he added cheekily.

'I think it'll be a waste of time,' she told him.

'I tell you, you won't have a hospital left to complain about soon, 'they have their way.'

He failed to convince her. The branch meetings were attended by no more than two dozen or so stalwarts; and even when there was an immediately contentious issue like the sale of Nightingale Block to the private sector the attendance no more than doubled. The trouble was that Nightingale Block had been on the agenda so often that most members probably believed it was there from habit, and that from habit the block would go on being emptied and then re-occupied. Chris Hogan knew this time it was for real, the block would be lost altogether unless they did something.

That much he managed to convey to the forty-six members who attended the branch meeting; the upshot was a delegation to see the District Administrator to convince him that the sale would have serious consequences for the smooth running of the hospital.

Believing he would be taken more seriously if he was dressed up Chris Hogan put on his best suit, a clean shirt and a dark tie for the meeting with the District Administrator. The two shop stewards who went with him nodded at the same notion. They were early for their appointment, but were kept waiting while Stephen Morwell signed letters at his desk, then telephoned the Regional Administrator to find out what the most up-to-date position was about the sale of the block.

'Would you show them in, Sandra,' Morwell said through the intercom to his secretary. He didn't rise as the two men and a woman came in, but indicated chairs for them. 'I know what you're going to say, Mr Hogan. But there is nothing more I can do to save Nightingale Block.'

'Well that's what we came about, Mr Morwell,' Hogan said as if he didn't believe him. 'To stop the sale.'

'That's something I'd like. I always saw it as a viable part of St Clair's,' Morwell explained. 'But it's no longer within my control. If you want to discuss it further you'll have to take your argument to Mr Christian at Region.' Stephen Morwell was sympathetic to the cause but knew it to be lost and had resigned himself to the fact, even though the contracts hadn't yet been exchanged.

'Our union is a hundred per cent against that block being sold,' Hogan told him pointlessly. 'We'll oppose it all the way.' There were nods of agreement from the two shop stewards.

'My position is the same as it always was,' Morwell said. 'I thought the block could most usefully be turned into a psycho-geriatric unit. But unlike you I have to be totally practical. There isn't the money available. The only way to change that situation is via the ballot box.' He paused. 'You're welcome to take your argument to Region, but I think it's rather late in the day.'

It was late in the day for the rearguard action Chris Hogan was taking, but that had more to do with lack of information than energy. Receiving no satisfaction at District, he continued with the grievance procedure, going on up the hierarchical structure.

Getting to see the Regional Administrator took time, and ironically Hogan was given an appointment on the day that contracts for the sale of Nightingale were due to be exchanged. That was another piece of information that wasn't made available to the NUPE branch secretary.

Although the sale or leasing of NHS property to private sector medicine was happening more and more, the exchange of contracts for Nightingale Block was made into an occasion by the invitation to the parties concerned to attend from Sir John Murry-Parkes the Regional chairman. The transaction was concluded in his comfortable office. Present were George Christian, Sir Randolph Spence – Mr Philip Montagu couldn't attend because he was in theatre – their solicitor, and the Regional solicitor. The Regional chairman and Sir Randolph Spence each signed the agreement relating to use of building access, easements and ancillary rights, wearing rather serious expressions until their signatures were on the papers. Then they were smiling.

'I trust you have a large bag of dinars for us, Randolph,' Murry-Parkes joked. He knew they were partly backed by Arab money.

'Almost,' Sir Randolph chuckled. 'I think this calls for a small celebration. After all, one doesn't buy a hospital everyday.'

The very least everyone present expected was a decent lunch. They would get nothing less. Sir Randolph would undertake such an expenditure on behalf of Nightingale Hospital Medical Services International Ltd, which was formed to buy the block. He telephoned his partner, Philip Montagu to get him to the lunch also.

When the call came from Sir Randolph the consultant gynaecologist was removing an ovarian cyst from a private patient. It was his last operation of the morning, but nowhere near complete.

'Could you tell him I'm scrubbed?' Montagu said to the OTA, who brought the telephone message.

'He did say it was important, sir.'

Mr Montagu nodded, indicating he would come. Completing a blood vessel tie, he asked his registrar to take over. 'Be especially careful, Sam,' he said lightly. 'She's one of my wealthier patients.'

Not being given to jokes, much less about private patients, the remark today reflected his mood at the expectation of the deal he knew would be satisfactorily concluded. Although this caution was addressed to his registrar, Mr Montagu might have been wiser to have directed the anaesthetist to recheck his equipment. Had he done so it could have prevented the patient getting too much of the halothane and nitrous oxide mixture, the cause of which would later be described as a breathing circuit disconnection. By some unaccountable error the anaesthetist would switch off the oxygen supply – the most frequent of mistakes – causing irreversible brain damage. The patient wouldn't wake from the anaesthetic and would remain in coma before dying. Even paying for private medical treatment was no guarantee against human error; what it did guarantee was that the excuses for it happening would be more elaborately explained. Publicly Mr Philip Montagu would support his anaesthetist; while privately making efforts to see he didn't work again.

Dragging off his mask and gloves as he entered the office, Mr Montagu picked up the phone. 'Randolph.'

'Well, the contracts are exchanged,' Spence said buoyantly. 'We've bought our hospital, Philip.'

'Excellent!' Mr Montagu felt a deep sense of pleasure.

'As an act of faith I've invited Murry-Parkes and Christian to lunch at Leiths,' Spence informed him. 'Can you join us for one o'clock.'

Montagu glanced at the clock on the office wall. 'Goodness. I can be with you by 1.30.' It would mean his registrar closing.

Slightly pissed from the wine over a long lunch, George Christian considered going home and might have but for his meeting with the NUPE branch secretary; he wasn't exactly witless when confronting Chris Hogan and his colleagues across the linen covered table in the senior management dining-room at Regional headquarters. This venue was chosen as neutral ground, but it also meant Christian could get an endless supply of black tea. The RHA treasurer was with them.

'I don't understand this line you're taking,' George Christian said, not believing his own rhetoric. 'My understanding of the situation is that the unions were not only consulted but had agreed the closure.'

'The fact is, Mr Christian,' Hogan said fractiously to the smiling face, 'we were consulted on the basis of Nightingale Block becoming a psycho-geriatric unit. We were told it was being upgraded and brought back into service, that was why we agreed to it closing.'

'I'm not sure that truly reflects the situation,' Christian said. He caught the eye of the supervisor who was moving around in the kitchen. 'Could we get some more tea, Mrs Belsted?' He smiled his thanks, then turned back to Hogan. 'Psycho-geriatric provision was only one alternative in the consultative document.'

'Selling it to private medicine wasn't even put as an alternative,' Hogan countered.

'The prevailing economic climate dictates rather,' said Rex Dundobbin. 'Regrettably finance wasn't available for that or any other units.' It seemed he had been over this a hundred times before.

'Well, I think this is going to bring a lot of grief,' Hogan warned. He felt cheated, not only on behalf of his members but the patients who needed beds in their catchment area. 'My members are abso-bloody-lutely livid.'

'This is not very realistic,' George Christian suggested. Regrettable as it was to close beds, he couldn't understand such fuss.

'You're threatening the livelihood of my members.' Hogan ran his argument into a cul-de-sac.

'Has one single health service job been lost as a result of this closure?' Christian asked. 'If that's so I'd like to know about it.'

'It'll eventually mean people leaving the service,' Hogan insisted, deflecting the question. 'Patients not being able to get beds – that's gonna affect my members in the long run.'

'You must appreciate, Mr Hogan,' Rex Dundobbin said, 'the Health Service can't keep expanding and continuing to spend money the country isn't earning, whatever the needs of those people who use it.'

The implication of the treasurer's words was that the nation's health should be based on book-balancing that bore no relation necessarily to public need. The logical extension was for all decisions about who received treatment to become value judgements, with people who were determined vital economic factors taking preference. Although Chris Hogan instinctively realized this, he didn't articulate it.

'I can't see it myself,' he said, as if punching at wind.

'It was a difficult choice, on the one hand, leaving this block empty, possibly having it deteriorate to a point where it was worthless to anyone,' Dundobbin explained. 'Or disposing of it, and putting the money back into the service.'

Seizing on that, Hogan said, 'Is St Clair's going to get the money? Is the quarter of a million pounds going to go back there?'

'Indeed.' Rex Dundobbin glanced at his colleague, then pushed his spectacles up on the bridge of his nose with his little finger. It was a habit. 'And the price involved is considerably more than the sum mentioned. Double in fact.'

Hogan remained unimpressed. 'That's still no bargain for the health service.'

'The price was arrived at by the Chief Valuer's office at the Inland Revenue,' Dundobbin informed them as if to stress its independence. 'In view of the block being directly adjacent to the existing St Clair's, the limitations placed on it by the DHSS make it considerably less valuable than one might imagine. Certainly less than if it had been available for general development.'

'But what sort of sense is that,' Hogan countered, 'when

all them wards on Nightingale were upgraded for £270,000 each. In the last two years more than three times as much has been spent on that block than you sold it for.'

The two union representatives with Hogan nodded. The facts he had spelled out spoke for themselves, and made this administration look stupid and incompetent.

'I see no profit in further discussion of old policies that neither of us can do anything about.' Having identified how shaky their case was Christian wanted to close this avenue.

'That's all very well, Mr Christian,' Hogan said querulously, enjoying his advantage. 'But while that sort of money was being squandered the porters have had no regular overtime.'

'Well let's talk about the overtime position,' Christian offered, seeing the means of manoeuvring the Authority out of an embarrassing corner. 'Let's see if we can find some mutually acceptable ground.'

'All we'd be interested in is having the regular overtime restored,' Hogan told him. Knowing that they couldn't win over the sale of Nightingale Block, that all they could do was embarrass the Authority, and at the end of the day still be on square one, he decided to exploit the situation to give them something they could take away.

Mrs Belsted brought them all fresh tea, while they sat and traded. By the end of the meeting both sides had settled for what they could live with.

Coming down the steps of the RHA building with his two silent delegates, Hogan felt uneasy. He was unsure whether they believed he had let them down. It was important to him that he wasn't seen to fail in his job as he had proved impotent elsewhere in life. 'Well, it wasn't exactly what we went for,' he said, testing the water.

'No it wasn't,' the female delegate said solemnly. 'But they gave us more than they expected to.'

Hogan looked at Roland Morly, the shop steward from the laundry. He nodded in the same solemn fashion. But as soon as he was outside the building, which was slightly inhibiting, he smiled. 'We got a right result, Chris, getting our regular overtime restored. That was a real victory, man.'

'Yes, it sure was,' Hogan said, suddenly enjoying his victory. 'A strike wouldn't have benefited the membership. We got a result all right.'

They had of course. And Nightingale Block was not only lost, but now a forgotten issue.

56

Sunday lunch with her parents wasn't something Jessie Marvill actively sought at the best of times, as they were tense, awkward occasions at which they failed to communicate other than as doctors. Her father would talk about surgical procedures or the registrar whose work he had to re-do; her mother would speak about patients' medical problems, psychological problems, even their emotional problems, but never her own, or those they had as a family; that might have been strictly forbidden. It never ceased to amaze Jessie how doctors set themselves up to help others, mostly content in the presumption that they didn't need help themselves; she didn't believe them incapable of helping others while themselves in a state of need, but the right thing to do was to try and get one's own problems sorted through at the same time. She believed her mother was an excellent and caring GP, her father a skilful surgeon, but each invested everything in their work in order to avoid the real issue, it seemed. Worse was the fact that she had recognized that she was doing exactly the same. Despite what her therapist suggested, that to recognize the problem was to begin to deal with it, Jessie wasn't sure that was enough, which was why she had telephoned her mother and invited herself to lunch.

The atmosphere was more edgy than usual because she had asked for a vegetarian lunch. Jessie had said she wouldn't sit at the table with them eating a dead animal. The housekeeper had managed a quiche, which Jessie had almost refused as she knew it would have been made with battery hen eggs, but her father's objection to this sort of meal rather than a traditional roast was enough to have to cope with. The more she learned about herself, the less she liked her father for repressing her as he had, and her mother for acquiescing in that, yet paradoxically the more she understood them.

'I'm not surprised you're looking exhausted as you are, Jess,' David Marvill, her father, said, noting that she had left most of the quiche and had only eaten some of the cooked vegetables. 'You certainly don't get the right essential amino acids in that sort of food.'

'If you combine the right vegetables, you do,' Jessie Marvill said.

'Eating at the hospital must present problems,' Brigid Marvill, her mother, added ironically.

'I take vitamins.'

'You need complete protein,' David Marvill said. 'You work too hard to do without. You should eat meat. It's the most readily available complete protein.'

Jessie Marvill knew that arguing on a moral platform would shut them up, but took the wrong tack. She said, 'Cooking destroys most of the vitamins in meat. The amino acid methionine breaks down into the very toxic homocysteine.'

'Only in the absence of B6,' Brigid Marvill said. She had quite a number of patients who were faddish about their diets.

'I saw the paper on arteriosclerosis that supposed low levels of B6 were the cause. It's not proven,' David Marvill said.

'That's the trouble with this profession,' Jessie said angrily. 'Nothing is ever taken on faith, despite what your instincts tell you. That's why I'm thinking of leaving medicine.'

The reason for her coming to lunch was out and a thoughtful silence followed.

'You're not serious, Jessie?' Brigid Marvill said finally.

Her father stared across the table at her a moment

longer. 'If that's your decision, I think it ill considered, Jess,' he said in a reasonable voice. 'All the time, energy and expense that went into training you. It's a great waste.'

'Yes, I agree, David, it is,' Jessie Marvill said, taking his argument to what she saw as its logical conclusion. 'The man or woman in the street can heal themselves and others without all the science and mythology we've walled ourselves in with.'

'That's rather insulting, Jessie,' David Marvill said, on the same even tone. 'Certainly the will has a strong influence, as do the powers of suggestion. But if anyone was foolish enough to do any serious research in that area, you would see how little the crank-element contributes. Either you've been too long with your mental patients and need a decent holiday, or you should perhaps give up medicine.' He rose from the table. 'I've some papers to read in my study. I'll have tea with you later.'

Another awkward silence was left in his wake.

'I think you've rather upset your father,' Brigid Marvill said.

Jessie didn't move or say anything, but felt suddenly a little girl again, disapproved of and in need of Daddy's forgiveness. She might have gone after her father and said she was sorry, let him put his arms around her and tell her he loved her, only now she realized he had never done that. It was why she had gone out picking up men as she had. She had been looking for that comfort.

'There's a young woman at the hospital called Bernice,' Jessie said, 'who's really extremely bright and creative and talented. She's seventeen and she's just come to realize that she doesn't exist solely as an object of achievement for her parents, that she has a value as a person in her own right, regardless of her parents. I'm twenty-seven, Brigid, and it's taken me this long.'

'I think that rather unfair, Jess,' Brigid Marvill said. 'You were given every opportunity to decide for yourself what you did with your life. It was your choice.'

'But it was your approval that was the perimeter,' Jessie said. 'All I've done at this point is recognize the problem. I don't know if I can do anything about it. I still feel the need to go in there to David and seek his approval. Show him what good marks I've got, how pretty my new dress is.'

'I would think very hard about quitting medicine, Jess,' Brigid said.

'D'you know this is the first thing I can remember you and David agreeing on in years,' Jessie said, as if that added weight to her argument.

'Why don't you take a year off, and maybe travel. I'll lend you the money. See how you feel when you come back.' She had the habit of making suggestions and presuming they would be taken up. She rose and came around the table to her daughter and put her hand on the side of her head. 'How have you been sleeping? Do you need anything to help you sleep. Perhaps a man? Is there anyone special?'

Jessie almost laughed, but didn't answer as she leaned against Brigid and felt the ground slipping away. She was looking for a mother, but only ever found a doctor.

She wouldn't take time out from medicine but would backslide and casually pick up men again only to sleep with them just once. That was a habit therapy would eventually help her overcome.

57

The news Stephen Morwell received this morning about the hostel in Ebury Road was as much a surprise to him as he knew it would be to Dr Hendrix. But that wasn't the worst of what he had to tell the consultant psychiatrist. This was a telephone call he would rather not be making at all, but preferred not to delegate the task. Hendrix was reasonable, he agreed to himself, and would appreciate that there was little he could do in the face of economic expediency. He drew pictures of huge, ill-proportioned aircraft on his blotter as he waited for his call to the consultant psychiatrist. Idly he wondered how much might be trimmed from the District budget if they stopped issuing blotters for people to draw on in felt-tip. He didn't know anyone who used ink any more.

'Ah, Clive . . . Stephen Morwell,' he said into the phone. 'Caught you at a bad moment?' He had, but was told not to worry. 'Do you have a few moments to spare this morning?'

'Not without difficulty,' the consultant said, glancing at the clock in his office at Coldbrook. 'I've a meeting in about ten minutes. Then outpatients directly after lunch. Was it urgent?' He suspected it was for the administrator to be phoning and began to fear the worst.

'The council has turned down the hostel for Ebury Road,' Morwell informed him. 'Bureaucratic hoop-jumping of course.'

'I'm not entirely surprised,' Dr Hendrix said evenly, despite what he felt. 'The patients will be disappointed.'

'Yes.' Morwell hesitated. 'Look, there is something else. Perhaps it would be best if we met.'

'Now you're beginning to alarm me, Stephen.'

'I'd rather not discuss it on the telephone.' He waited.

'Could we meet at St Clair's immediately after lunch?' Dr Hendrix suggested. 'If it'll keep till then.'

'I've a lunch. I'm not sure how long it will go on.'

'I intend having lunch at St Clair's,' Dr Hendrix said. 'So perhaps I could see you there just before.'

After his meeting with the District Administrator Dr Hendrix didn't go on to lunch. He was too angry to sit and eat food, but drove back to Coldbrook, by which time he was calmer. He looked for Dr Hindmarch, and was told by a nurse on Brechin that he was in the garden.

The garden that had been allocated to the patients from Brechin was so overgrown that it might always have been that way and the tools they had been loaned looked as if they had been left by Adam.

Six patients were breaking sod, one of them, Malcolm Beedle, was participating under protest.

'This is a big con,' he said to Dr Hindmarch, who was watching. 'We'll put in all this work and won't get any benefit. We'll be gone by the time this garden's producing good veggies.'

'That's what a community is supposed to be about, Malcolm,' Dr Hindmarch told him. 'It's an emotional and physical continuum. You don't put in on the basis of what you get out.'

'That's what life's about,' James Worth said.

'That's what it's come to mean,' the psychiatrist informed him. 'Isn't that why so many have problems coping?'

Seeing the consultant approaching, Dr Hindmarch started along the path to meet him, knowing his boss wouldn't come out here without good reason.

'That looks like it might have been productive,' Dr Hendrix said, referring to the digging. His colleague said nothing. 'Can you take my outpatients this afternoon?'

'With some adjustment to my schedule,' Dr Hindmarch told him. 'It shouldn't be a problem.'

'The Brechin residents' scheme to contract work has finally been turned down officially. It's not practical, it seems. They don't want self-help,' he added bitterly, conveniently forgetting his own earlier dismissive attitude. 'This incompetent administration would sooner cut programmes.' He hesitated. 'Ebury Road has gone down.'

Dr Hindmarch nodded. 'That really is a shame,' was all he said, knowing expressions of regret or anger would achieve nothing.

'Worse is to come, Robin,' Dr Hindmarch said. 'There are plans to close the unit.'

That slap in the face left Dr Hindmarch reeling. Personally he would be affected not at all, as he was going to the Maudsley. But he felt a sense of outrage for the patients, and for psychiatric medicine. Closing down such a progressive unit would be a definite setback for both. 'Is this why they were snipping at our staffing levels?'

'Possibly it's the result of the unit being too independent,' Dr Hendrix said, 'too controversial. Perhaps we simply don't achieve turnover. District's saying that the proposal comes from Region. The Regional Administrator has an entirely different story. I'm calling a meeting of the community for fifteen minutes. I want to talk to everyone here before I go to Region later this afternoon.'

'I'll miss that if I'm to do your outpatients,' Dr Hindmarch said.

'I thought you wouldn't mind as you're moving on.'

Gathering the therapeutic community and staff together at such short notice wasn't a problem but as word went around about the purpose the atmosphere in the common room became very depressed.

When he started outlining why he had called them together Dr Hendrix found the going as heavy as wading through mud. There was no relief, nor would there be until he was through with what he had to say and everyone had dealt with it. That was an over-optimistic expectation, he realized. The news would totally disturb some of the patients, who had no defence for dealing with such an onslaught, other than to retreat and punish themselves.

'The only reason I was able to get from the council for not finally approving the hostel was the volume and the nature of the objections,' he told them. 'They wouldn't go into details. They never do of course. But it seems our expectations can be dashed at will. We can appeal to the Secretary of State, but I must say on reflection I think you're better off without those sort of neighbours.' He hesitated.

'Does that mean there won't be a hostel at all?' Anne Drinkwater asked. 'I mean, not anywhere? Not just in Ebury Road.'

'That's likely to prove the case, Anne,' the consultant told her quietly, as if to let her down gently. 'I don't believe the reason was entirely for that stated. I think its funding is an issue. As you probably know the occupants of the hostel were going to largely be drawn from this unit. With a few from other wards. It's not difficult to understand why they wouldn't want to proceed when I tell you the next piece of bad news.' He paused briefly. 'I'm afraid for reasons best known to itself the administration is looking at the feasibility of closing this unit.'

That sent a shock wave through the community. While not expecting the news to be good, no one had any idea it would be so bad.

'One assumes their reason for such a shortsighted move is to save money,' Dr Hendrix added. 'Though I'm not entirely convinced; then perhaps I'm being paranoid. Savings such as this on psychiatric services are not in line with current DHSS policy, so I will certainly take it as high as the Secretary of State.'

'What will happen to us?' Chloë Shallcross asked. Although she had successfully been back to live with her husband and baby for short periods she wasn't ready for that as a single alternative.

'Nothing, except in the event of the unit closing,' Dr Hendrix said. 'At this stage we shouldn't accept closure as inevitable. It's only a possibility. The reason I mention it is because my policy has been to keep you informed about everything. I'd rather you heard this from me than rumours.'

'Some of us have no other home,' Ruth Martin said. She was speaking for herself, but had hit on a general truth. A number of patients here had nowhere to go, other than another ward.

'If this unit does close, then it will almost certainly be run down over a long period,' Dr Hendrix tried to reassure them. He was less concerned about these patients than those who might follow. There was less point to this sort of psychiatric work without continuity. 'During that time a lot of you will have rejoined the threads of your lives. Sheltered accommodation, or a similar therapeutic community would hopefully be found for others. Meanwhile each of you should continue to work for your own personal objectives. What we will do is fight any closure, in every way we can. I'm sure the health employees' unions will give some support. What we must do is see what positive elements can be got from this.'

First the news of the hostel not opening, then the threat of the therapeutic community closing sent Bernice into shock, and she heard nothing else throughout the meeting. She felt as though she had been struck in the face with a brick, her skin smarted and her head throbbed. She wanted to kill herself, she wanted to kill the entire hospital administration and everyone in this meeting. They had done this to her on purpose; they had tricked her into believing she could live in the hostel and go to art school and become like an ordinary human being. It had all been a trick and she wanted to get even with them for that.

'Are you all right, Bernice?' Rose Sutton the psychologist

asked after the meeting had broken.

Bernice nodded, keeping in check the turmoil she was feeling. 'I'm going to the pottery room,' she said in a reasonably controlled manner.

'I shouldn't worry. It might not happen.'

Had Dr Hindmarch been around he might have got some inkling of what was going on inside this girl, seen the likely effect of her suddenly being faced with dim prospects for her future. Or had Dr Marvill been there instead of at an interview for yet another six month job in order to complete her vocational training scheme, she could have talked Bernice through her turmoil, exlained that there was no reason she should let slip the gains she had made; that because of her progress she could keep her place at art school, be found another hostel or therapeutic community. But these two doctors weren't around, and everyone else in the community was too caught up in how this move to close the unit would affect them personally to notice Bernice.

In the deserted pottery room Bernice resumed working intensely on a head and shoulders sculpture of herself, which wasn't quite right. Jane Mitchell, the OT, had suggested she do the sculpture of herself as she saw herself. The present representation was a long way from her original slightly grotesque conception. But as Bernice achieved worldly success so she came to like the person she was more and as a result her appearance in clay had changed. Now as she worked on it Bernice realized it was totally wrong, that this girl who was going to live in the hostel and go to art school and cope with life didn't exist. Without thinking about this she started systematically destroying the model by slicing damp clay off the face until finally it had no sort of identity. Each of her actions became more angry than the last, until she was making wild slashing gestures at the clay. Finally all that remained was to smash the sculpture to the floor and destroy the last identifiable vestiges of that girl.

Not knowing where she was going, but hurting and wanting to hurt back, Bernice raged through the room sweeping pottery and sculpture to the floor with her arm. When she reached the equally deserted art room she wreaked havoc there, as jars of brushes and tubs of paint and turps flew from shelves. The top burst off a plastic container of turps.

The gurgling motion as it spilled out over the floor galvanized Bernice for a moment. Then she calmly reached some matches off the bench by the gas ring and set a fire going with rags and paper and turps.

She stood and watched with satisfaction as smoke and flames billowed and ran across the linoleum floor to the cupboard where art paper was stacked, along with canvas and raffia for weaving. Soon it was all ablaze, and not long afterwards the old familiar fire alarm started, but no one responded to the bell other than with a groan – as if they hadn't enough to contend with at present. It was a while before anyone realized there was a fire or discovered Bernice. By which time it was too late to do anything about the art rooms – also a lot of Brechin Ward was burned.

A huge sense of excitement swelled through Samuel Irons as he was led into the cream and green painted reception at Coldbrook by the ambulance driver who had brought him there.

When he was handed over and the receptionist satisfied herself that this was where he should be, she said pleasantly, 'Have a seat over there, love,' pointing out the bench along the wall. 'You'll be just in time for lunch,' – as if a special treat.

Samuel Irons clapped his hands with pleasure at the prospect of having food on the ward with all his friends. His pleasure increased when a man in ill-fitting day-clothes shuffled through reception. He rushed over to him, causing the patient to cower, as if believing this was an attack.

'You're George Tremlett,' Samuel announced. 'You're George Tremlett.' It might have been his long-lost brother. It was that exciting to Samuel Irons who, apart from the doctor at the outpatients clinic, had seen no one he knew since leaving the hospital.

'Silly old bugger tried to kill himself, didn't he,' the ambulance driver explained. 'No one had told him North Sea gas wasn't poisonous. You got one to go to Queen's for a brain scan? Henry Staples.'

'I'll phone the ward, see if he's ready,' she said, checking her sheet. 'You staying for lunch?'

'If he's ready I'd like to get straight off,' the driver told her. 'I'll just have a little wee-wee first.'

'Those ones here are still out of order. You'll have to go across to records,' she informed him as he went out.

Approaching the lavatories with a 'Not in Use' sign up, the ambulance driver glanced about him then slipped in there to save time.

The inner door scraped along the floor and he forced it. The smell was almost overpowering.

'Phaw, stroll on!' he said in disgust, at first believing it was a smell from the broken lavatories. Then immediately realized what it was, having smelt decomposing bodies before. Fighting an inclination to vomit he tried to open the door of the second WC, but finally clambered on to the seat of the toilet next door and looked over the partition.

'Oh my God,' he said on an intake of breath.

The almost unrecognizable body of a woman was crumpled in the corner by the WC pan with two plastic bags over her head and tied.

Although the ambulance driver didn't connect this woman with the missing patient of two weeks ago, it wouldn't be long before someone would realize it was Mrs Taylor.

Jessie Marvill took the death of Mrs Taylor as badly as the relapse Bernice Attwood had suffered. One following so soon after the other brought her to a point where she couldn't function for several days. Her therapist was of some help when she saw her over that period, helping her to realize that this sense of failure resulted out of her bruised ego and self-esteem; Jessie Marvill read that as arrogance, her belief, despite what she told herself intellectually, that she could help the likes of these patients.

'Guilt won't get you one bit nearer to heaven, Jessie,' Vernon Davis said when she talked to him in the doctors' small sitting-room after a game of squash.

She had told him that she had decided not to take the job she had been offered at Queen Mary's. 'Why shouldn't I feel guilty?' she argued. 'After all I didn't manage to help either of them very much.'

'You did what you could,' Vernon Davis said, 'and you gave more than most. What you did more than anyone else was care, Jessie.'

Thinking about that in relation to this man, Jessie Marvill wondered if there was any point to that and whether one could care and survive without the same thing happening. She didn't point out the obvious, but Vernon Davis clearly knew what she was thinking. 'I suppose we're not really the heroic figures we've allowed ourselves to be described as. Even if we're prepared to take on all the problems of our patients, most of us find we're not up to it. The only alternative is to shut down our emotions or leave the profession.' After a lot of indecision Jessie would change her mind about the job of Medical SHO she had been offered. She would learn not to get involved with patients, and go on to a partnership in a firm of general practitioners, where her feelings would stop at concern, even then she would be sought by patients as the caring doctor in the group practice.

An inquest would subsequently find that Brenda Taylor had taken her life while suffering a severe depression associated with leukaemia. The coroner would attach no blame to the tragedy, other than to comment that as she had been in a mental hospital at the time the supervisory procedures of that establishment should perhaps be looked at.

The inquiry into the circumstances of Mrs Taylor's suicide at Coldbrook wouldn't attach blame either. It would conclude that inadequate supervision resulted from insufficient staffing levels, most especially on the locked wards. However, because that was likely to cause more problems than could be solved, the report was quietly buried.

The staff on Allen Ward where Mrs Taylor had been would be changed, and increased by one nurse each shift. But that would be the only change.

None of the routines or rules on Allen Ward changed, but they were carried out more efficiently. Denis Murphy, the new charge nurse, was very efficient. Having come to Coldbrook from Rampton Hospital, he brought considerable experience of dealing with disturbed patients. He wasn't unsympathetic, but wouldn't put up with any nonsense.

During the medication procedure after meals everyone took their medicine, no patient missed it, spat it out or passed tablets on to other patients. Denis Murphy handed a plastic cup containing two capsules to the student nurse who was helping to dish out the drugs.

'That's the last – to the old grunter there,' he said with a boyish smile, indicating a patient, 'Mrs Zackery.'

The student nurse made quite certain that the woman suffering from senile dementia swallowed them. Charge Nurse Murphy collected three medications prepared in turn for patients in the padded cells, then locked the trolley and padlocked it to a pillar. He went off towards the pads, which were used quite a lot nowadays.

Unlocking the first pad, he removed the key before

opening the inner door.

Bernice was crouched in the corner. She was already subdued from the drugs she had swishing around in her bloodstream. But Charge Nurse Murphy proffered the next dose.

With just enough awareness to recognize this routine, Bernice was able to slowly shake her head.

'Take them, Bernice, there's a good girl,' Murphy said in a helpful manner. 'You know what happens to you if you don't have them.'

'I don't . . . no . . .' was all she managed to say.

'Please . . . I don't . . . I don't . . . Please . . .' Her plea remained on one level and was barely audible.

'Ah c'mon,' he coaxed, using all of his charm. 'They're for your own good, m' darling.'

'Please . . .' she repeated, managing to cling to a single thought, which was to resist.

'Bernice.' His tone was firmer. 'You wouldn't be wanting me to get Dr Patel to give it you by injection.'

Facing this alternative she took her tablets.

The charge nurse smiled reassuringly. 'That's a good girl,' he said and waited for her to put them in her mouth and take some water. 'Did you swallow them?'

She put out her tongue to show that she had.

'Good girl,' he said encouragingly. He was unsure how much she understood nowadays, but added, 'You know we wouldn't give you anything that'd harm you, don't you.'

Bernice heard the words but didn't know what they meant so didn't respond. Deep inside she was angry and desperate and boiling and wanting to explode, but each day that passed there seemed a new layer of deadness added to her, and each day that passed made it more difficult for her to surface and protest. Somehow she understood that this was the way life would be for her for all her days now. And she was helpless to do anything about it.